Praise for Nikola Scott's unforgettable novels:

'A well-written, intriguing read full of family secrets . . . Brilliant' *Fabulous*

'An emotional and involving story' *Woman & Home*

'An intriguing, twisting story with a lush opening and beautifully descriptive writing throughout. I loved it' Dinah Jefferies, author of *The Sapphire Widow*

'The perfect summer read' Liz Trenow, author of *In L and War*

'Thoughtful, sad and beautifully written' *Daily Mail*

'Compelling and satisfying. It was beautifully written' Judith Lennox, author of *Hidden Lives*

'A delightful debut about family and secrets' *Prima*

'A compelling family story . . . beautifully written and evokes vivid pictures of an English summer in the 1950s' Sheila O'Flanagan, author of *What Happened That Night*

'Gripping, poignant and heart-warming' Beth, Bibliobeth

'A profoundly moving debut that trembles with family secrets . . . I adored it' Victoria Fox, author of *The Silent Fountain*

'A beautifully written novel . . . absolutely captivating' Jo, Jo's Book Blog

'A gripping family mystery told in lush, evocative prose' Erin Kelly, author of *He Said, She Said*

'Absolutely blew me away! It had me gripped from the start and is loaded with scenes that pull at the heart strings! I cannot recommend this novel enough' Abby, Anne Bonny Book Reviews

'Delightful family mystery ... beautifully written and hugely enjoyable' *The People*

'A charming and beautifully written story . . . hugely pleasurable to read and a little bit heartbreaking. I'll definitely be looking out for Nikola Scott's next book' Nicola, Short Book and Scribes

'An intriguing book of family drama, with a little bit of mystery between the pages . . . a perfect read' Karen, My Reading Corner

'A compelling and intriguing story of the lives of different generations of women and their families that is impossible to put down! Highly recommended!' *Hot Brands Cool Places*

'A beautiful, heartwarming and at times a gut-wrenching story . . . would highly recommend' Melisa, Broadbean's Books

'An emotional rollercoaster . . . I wanted to keep reading and reading' Trish, Between My Lines

'A truly gripping and beautifully written story . . . I would highly recommend' Kirsty, Curious Ginger Cat

'Full of intrigue, suspense and self-discovery' Lilac, Lilac Mills

'An emotional story about unearthing well-buried family secrets' Michelle, The Book Magnet

Born in Germany, Nikola Scott studied English and American literature before moving abroad to work as a fiction editor in New York and London. After over a decade in book publishing, she decided to take the leap into becoming a full-time writer herself.

Nikola's debut novel *My Mother's Shadow* has been translated into more than ten languages. She lives in Frankfurt with her husband and two sons.

By Nikola Scott

My Mother's Shadow

Summer of Secrets

Summer of Secrets

NIKOLA SCOTT

First published in Great Britain in 2018 by
HEADLINE REVIEW
An imprint of HEADLINE PUBLISHING GROUP

1

Cataloguing in Publication Data is available from the British Library

ISBN 978 1 4722 4118 4

Typeset in Garamond MT Std by Jouve (UK), Milton Keynes

Printed and bound in Great Britain by CPI Group (UK) Ltd, Croydon, CR0 4YY

HEADLINE PUBLISHING GROUP
An Hachette UK Company
Carmelite House
50 Victoria Embankment
London EC4Y 0DZ

www.headline.co.uk
www.hachette.co.uk

For my parents

One

Maddy

I could find Summerhill anywhere on a map. Blindfolded, without pause or hesitation, I could draw it from memory. It looked like a heart, its flank lining up with the edge of the river, the sharp end pointing out to sea. In reality, of course, the estate was more sprawling, a tumble of greens and browns tugged at by the tide, the house clinging onto the side where the river widened into the bay. But my mind had carved it out of the land exactly like that, a heart-shaped map of my childhood where I was safe and where nothing could touch me.

Even now that Chamberlain had grudgingly decided it was time for action and my Aunt Marjorie was either glued to the wireless or watching the horizon for signs of a German invasion, it seemed impossible that life here would change.

My father would have disagreed. *War is like love*, he used to say when I was six or seven. *It always finds a way, Maddy. We forget, but before we know it, there it is again.* He had always thought we needed to know, my sister Georgiana and I, about all the terrible things humans were capable of doing. I never wanted to listen, but Georgiana did, would beg him for stories about the Great War, about surviving the horrors of Ypres and the Western Front. Leaving them to it, I would run down to the kitchen for one of Cookie's rock cakes, whistle for the dogs and disappear outside with my sketchbook. Through the woods and down to the river, lying face-down on the jetty to draw the tadpoles in the mudflats and wade through rock pools at low tide. To the little islet where swimming was best and where the sun sank into the water at the end of yet another glorious Summerhill day, flooding the bay with fiery reds and oranges that defied the entire contents of my colour palette.

And today, with the wireless forever spitting out new and alarming updates from Germany, the village crowded with uniformed men from the nearby army base and Hobson despairing over ever producing blackout curtains big enough for the enormous stained-glass windows in the entrance hall, I did exactly what I always had. I left Aunt Marjorie poring over Herr Hitler's advance on Danzig in the newspaper, fetched my sketchbook and a shovel – the wall up in Fairings Corner had collapsed yet again – and disappeared into the grounds.

Surveying the small avalanche of stones washed out by the heavy rains of last week's storm, my heart sank slightly. I started picking up rocks and stuffing dirt into holes as best as I could. That wall really should be looked at properly one of these days. The fence up by Pixie's Wood needed patching up too, and the well at the bottom of the garden was leaking. Without Papa's quelling eye, the garden had been allowed to explode in the last six years, so overgrown now that Georgiana often said we would wake up one day to discover it had swallowed us whole.

At the thought of my sister, I shoved the last rock into the wall and hurried up the hill. From the top you could watch the road coming up from the village, and I wanted to be the first one to see my sister arrive. Georgie had left for Europe six months ago despite all the dire news from Germany. Having invited herself to stay with any and all distant relatives across the Continent, she'd driven Papa's old car up to London and then on to Amsterdam and France, sending ecstatic postcards that made it very clear she was not remotely ready to cut her trip short. Eventually Cousin Xenia had called from Nantes, entreating dear Marjorie to rein in that hell-raising niece of hers and pointing out that all sensible English folk were fleeing the Continent. Georgiana had

had no choice but to return and I was glad. I'd never been without my sister for a single day, and the last six months were the longest I could remember.

Sternly ordering the dogs not to dig anywhere in the vicinity of the wall, I pulled myself up into the ancient oak tree that towered over the hillside and settled back against the trunk to keep an eye on the road. Georgiana always drove fast. She had taught herself when she was seventeen, despite Aunt Marjorie standing in the courtyard and muttering disgruntled things about needlework and French lessons. Having pestered Frank into helping her get my father's old Morris back up and running, she'd practised in the courtyard using hay bales as road markers, and later roared through the lanes with me glued to the passenger seat because I knew she'd kill herself and the least I could do was to be with her when that happened.

The lane lay as still and sleepy as ever, though, and with a small sigh of contentment, I pulled out my sketchbook. The green, linen-covered brick of paper was almost full, because with Georgie gone I'd been drawing more than usual. Aunt Marjorie, who was a great one for lecturing on a variety of subjects, had been on at me about conserving paper, and I had tried, squeezing sketches close together and using all available space, because it seemed quite likely that if I didn't start conserving paper soon, the world would actually run out. I was always drawing. The house. The kitchen. My favourite fox cub, persecuting the hedgehog living behind the rotten tree in Pixie's Wood. The way the light came through the trees in the little copse where the wild strawberries grew. People, too: Cookie making plum cobbler; Hobson sneaking a smoke behind the stables; Susan running up and down the stairs with a bucket. Georgiana, who couldn't draw a straight line if you held a gun to her head, loved writing, and together we'd come up with countless stories over the years. All summer I'd been working on finishing a funny series featuring the fox cub and his best friend, a worried little squirrel we'd called Stu. I flicked slowly through to where I'd left Foxy trying to survive a fall into the rain barrel, and started colouring his fur with tiny red strokes.

The late summer's warmth was lingering, and up high the sky was the colour of bluebells, effervescent with the kind of brightness that made you believe you simply had to push off and you'd be flying. Little gusts rustled through the leaves, and it was so quiet I could hear my pencil moving across the page, the dogs digging surreptitiously at a rabbit hole by the wall, and swallows singing above. Georgiana was finally coming home, and it wasn't at all hard to forget that it was late August 1939 and war was brewing in the world.

Without warning, a roar split the morning air, and seemingly out of nowhere the bluebell sky above the oak tree was filled with dark shapes. Planes. In formation, like the geese that left the coast in November to head south across the Channel, they roared past me, shadows flitting over fields and pastures. I let out a breath I hadn't realised I was holding and sagged back against the tree. Get a grip, Maddy, for heaven's sake. They're ours, *our* planes. From the airfield up north, out on a training exercise. Aunt Marjorie had talked about them excitedly only this morning: wasn't it splendid how the nation's boys were rising to the occasion and standing up to Herr Hitler in the way that only the British could? I tracked the shapes getting smaller along the horizon, waiting for the noise to fade. But it didn't. Far out, they turned in a wide arc and came back, flying straight at me, it seemed, almost as if they'd seen me hiding among the branches, honing in like an arrow on my Summerhill heart. Now they were above me, so close I thought I could make out the little wheels underneath them, hear the engines turning and smell the fumes.

The dogs cowered below me, ears flattened against furry heads, yipping anxiously, and together we watched the planes manoeuvring above us, their ear-splitting noise filling the canopy of the ancient oak tree. It seemed to go on for ever – figures and turns – but just as I didn't think I could possibly bear it any longer, they finally started heading inland one by one.

Even after they were gone, though, engine noise filled the air, and when I turned towards the sea, I realised that one of them had stayed behind, still practising its turns. The dogs and I watched it for a few moments before I noticed that something didn't look quite right. The plane was flying in an odd pattern, and even though it was partly obscured by the headland cliffs, you could see that it . . . yes, it seemed to be dropping. The branches above me were too fragile for my sixteen-year-old weight, but I started climbing nonetheless, my hands and feet scrabbling for footholds amid the slender, swaying greenery. There it was again now, level with the cliffs at – my mind proffered the two words before I could stop it – Hangman's Bluff. Shivers were running up and down my spine, and the skin at the back of my neck started tightening, squeezing inward, making me fight for breath, because I, of all people, knew how steep those cliffs were, how dangerous, how deadly . . .

Pushing another breath through my closed-up throat, I wanted to look away, wanted to slide back down and hide behind my sketchbook, draw Foxy loping across the little meadow behind Pixie's Wood at dawn. Instead, I kept watching, my eyes wide as the plane dropped above the cliffs, more quickly now, as if its occupant had already given up hope. And then it disappeared from sight altogether, and was lost.

War is like love, Maddy, it always finds a way.

My sweaty hands slipped on the bark of the tree; my eyes, still trained on the thin sliver of horizon, watered in the brightness of the sun. What if I'd been the only one to see it? What if no one would come to help? I could get to there from here, skirt the Muttonhole field, run along the little grassy path at the edge of the cliffs that my father and I had taken on a morning much like this six years ago. Frank said they let sheep graze right up to it these days because people were afraid to walk there any more.

But I hadn't been back to Hangman's Bluff, not since they retrieved my father's body from the cove below the cliffs, the one that was always submerged at high tide, with waves pounding against the rocks at the bottom. I hadn't left Summerhill much at all, and the most I'd seen of the sea was the blue-grey horizon from the top of the oak tree, where a few puffs of white cloud were now drifting along, unaware of the terrible thing that had happened.

Another noise cut through the air: a car horn from the village lane. I scrabbled for purchase on my branch, my eyes blinded for a moment from the sheer effort of looking into the distance, and when my vision cleared again, I saw a familiar battered car and an arm extending from the window, waving cheerfully in my direction, because my sister, who knew me better than anyone else in the world, knew that I'd be up in the oak tree waiting for her.

I dropped down from the tree, hardly noticing when a branch caught and ripped my trouser leg, and then I ran without stopping, without looking back, all the way down to the kitchen garden and the pear orchard, past our old tree house and the small pond with the massive carp that Georgiana hated, tumbling out into the courtyard and straight into my sister's arms.

Two

Chloe

'There's absolutely no doubt, Mrs MacAllister. None whatsoever.'

Chloe took in the man across from her, hands folded against the edge of his standard-issue NHS desk. Had fate ever sent a more unlikely harbinger than this balding, tetchy man sitting there frowning at her, tapping his fingers impatiently on her notes?

She saw the doctor's eyes flick briefly to the clock on the wall and tried to pull herself together. The NHS tried to keep consultations to ten minutes or less; Aidan had told her countless stories of patients who were too slow, dragging everyone else down and upsetting the system. She'd already overstayed her welcome by five minutes, four of which she'd wasted with white-faced silence and useless denial of the fact that there was no doubt whatsoever. None.

'I'll send the paperwork home with you,' the doctor said briskly, making little flapping motions with his hands as if to propel her into getting up from his yellow plastic chair. 'Now what you'll need to do in the next few weeks is—'

It was the word 'home' that did it, that finally unglued Chloe's tongue from the roof of her mouth and dimmed down the white noise whooshing in her ears just enough for her to say, 'I'm sorry, but please, would you mind checking just one more time? To be absolutely sure, I mean. There could be a mix-up, maybe?' She took a deep breath, dropping her hands into her lap. 'Mistakes are made all the time, aren't they?' She tried to add the last bit casually, as if to imply they were made by anyone but him.

'We've checked twice already, Mrs MacAllister,' Dr Webb said impatiently, 'and only because you were so insistent, but in reality, it's a waste. The test is accurate. I can't see what the issue is – your situation is perfect, your age is near-perfect. Do you work?'

She shook her head and he nodded approvingly. 'There you go. You don't drink, you don't smoke, you have a lovely home in,' he consulted her notes, 'the nicest part of Plymouth. Hartley. My godmother lives there.'

He waited a fraction of a second for Chloe to chime in, either with news of her connection with this undoubtedly eminent lady or else with something that would herald her imminent departure.

'From a medical point of view, you're ideal,' he continued. 'Couldn't be better really. Now, Margie will give you all the necessary information at the front desk.'

His voice washed over her, her ears picking out the odd word, like *lovely* and *blood* and *clinic*. And *perfect*. Yes, it was just all-round perfect. Her husband would be thrilled. He'd been waiting for this kind of news for months.

Dr Webb was by the door now, so she had no choice but to get up from her chair too, more slowly, trying to summon the wherewithal to ask a final crucial question.

'Could you . . . I mean, would it be possible not to let him know about this? My husband, that is?'

Dr Webb fumbled for his glasses, then squinted at her myopically.

'Why would I tell him?' Dr Webb didn't seem to worship Aidan in quite the same way everyone else did, which was partly why Chloe had chosen him as her GP, even though it did mean that she got the tetchy treatment on any of her infrequent visits. Still, the Plymouth medical world was a small one and chances were high that Dr Webb's path would cross that of Aidan MacAllister at some point soon, and Chloe would prefer that the ensuing conversation didn't include her.

'I'd just like to tell him myself. Pick the right moment.'

Dr Webb snorted in dismissal and flung open the door. 'Of course. Wouldn't dream of it. Confidentiality and all that. I heard that they're expanding the surgery. He must be busy. Anyhow, mum's the word,' he said heartily.

He made as if to close the door, but she held him back one last time. 'And Danny, you know, my brother – do you think it might be . . . a problem. For this?'

He considered for a second.

'I'd have to do some in-depth testing,' he said. 'Know more about your parents. You should make another appointment. And if your parents have had any recent blood tests, bring the results. We'll talk.'

Before she could add anything else, such as the pertinent fact that there were no parents and no blood tests, he had shooed her out of the door and closed it behind her.

Three minutes later, Chloe was standing outside the surgery. She hadn't asked any more questions of the nurses at the front desk, who always enquired after 'the lovely Dr MacAllister', wondering laughingly why on earth she bothered coming all the way out here when she had someone to cure her ailments at home. 'I know *I* wouldn't,' a pretty red-headed nurse had giggled under her breath to the other one as Chloe stuffed the leaflets they'd handed her into her bag with a little more force than necessary.

She stood for a long time watching buses taking people to work and school and the supermarket for milk. 14. 44. 62. The numbers fluttered by as if trying to convey some sort of secret code, telling her how to make the conversation with Dr Webb become a part of her, rather than just an abstract test result. She might buy some sparkling grape juice. She'd heard somewhere that grape juice was the drink of choice in these situations.

The 5. Then the 62 again. It was warm and humid and clouds were building up towards the east after weeks of strangely restless, unsettled weather. Whooshes of diesel-scented slipstream sent her hair fluttering and tugged on her skirt and reminded her that Aidan didn't like her taking public transport. *It's a staph infection waiting to happen, Chloe.* And the people. *Anyone could be on that bus. The next Suffolk Strangler.* Lucky Chloe, who didn't need to go out too often. And when she did, he could always leave her the car, couldn't he?

He hadn't left her the car this morning, because he didn't know that she had somewhere to go. But buses used to be her only mode of getting about, and she quite liked them, the way they neatly traversed the country. A closely knitted grid of connection that would take you anywhere you wanted, right across England if that was what you were after. And she liked the anonymity of it all, how no one cared one iota what she did, what she wore, what she thought. *Penny for your thoughts*, Aidan was fond of saying, his eyes resting on her closely, as if he needed to try just a little bit harder, look just a little bit longer, and he might be able to squeeze right into her mind. People on buses looked straight through you and you could sit with your thoughts and not always have to share.

She needed to take the 14 and she needed to take it quickly if she didn't want to be late. On Mondays, Aidan was due home straight after his last surgery, and then he wanted her there to sit on their roof terrace and have a civilised drink, talk about the day. Who he'd operated on and what'd they do at the weekend. The new doctor they were looking to take on at the surgery. Where they might go on holiday. And tonight, they'd talk about the fact – unignorable, undeniable and all round without any doubt whatsoever – that she, Chloe MacAllister, was going to have a baby. That she was twenty-eight years old, perfectly healthy and living the perfect life, which would now be perfectly complete. A family.

A taxi pulled up at the bus stop, depositing a gaggle of girls bound for the cinema in the shopping centre, and Chloe stuck her head in the window and asked the cabbie to take her home.

Three

She pushed open the front door and stood on the threshold for a moment. She could smell the washing drying in the utility room, and the lasagne she'd made earlier because she knew she'd be cutting it close after her appointment. The sweet, heady scent of the calla lilies Aidan had brought back the evening before, a complicated arrangement from his go-to florist. *Anything to make you feel special, Chloe.* He'd been so busy with his surgery expansion lately that he'd been a little curt with her at times. Had wanted to make up for it.

Her hands twitched across her stomach in a small, convulsive gesture and for one mad moment she fought the urge to turn round and walk back out the door, but then she shook herself. Don't be stupid, Chloe. Time to go and start dinner, and cut out the stamens from the blooms as Aidan had asked her to this morning, before they showered his expensive countertop with yellow goo.

She was about to hang up her jacket when the sound of a key behind her made her stop in her tracks.

'Hellooo!' Aidan had clearly assumed her to be where she always was at this time – in the kitchen at the back of the house – and he started when he saw her behind the door.

'Chloe, darling. I didn't see you there.' He came in, set down his briefcase and shrugged off his suit jacket, then bent to give her a kiss. 'Where've you been?' He frowned at her jacket, swinging slightly on the hook.

Now was the time to tell him. This exact moment was the time to say, *Aidan, I've got such brilliant news.*

'Just popped out to the shops,' she said quickly.

'Getting what?' He handed her his jacket. 'No, not on the hook, darling, on the hanger.'

'Just . . . something for dinner,' she said hastily before realising the absence of a shopping bag. 'But they didn't have what I wanted,' she improvised, disappearing into the kitchen to preclude further questions.

'I can always bring back stuff,' he called. 'You know there's that deli right next to the surgery.'

'Of course.' Chloe flicked the oven on. Now. She had to do it now. When he came back down, changed and showered and ready to chat. It would be good, actually, to get it out there, the hard nugget of good news that had been stuck deep inside her belly for hours now. It could start becoming part of her future; *their* future together. She took a deep breath to ease the nugget upwards, but when she exhaled, a horrible sort of sob suddenly escaped, rasping across the tiled kitchen.

'Oh for heaven's sake, just pull yourself together,' she hissed, wrenching open the oven door and shoving the lasagne inside. A waft of Parmesan rose on the warm air, and she pressed her lips together, feeling a twinge of nausea, the same kind she'd been ignoring for days now and which finally made sense. *Expectant parents often don't tell family and friends about Baby coming until twelve weeks*, the nurse had said earlier today when she'd caught Chloe reading the brochures in the waiting room. *It's nothing to dwell on, but until twelve weeks, anything can happen. Afterwards too, of course. But most miscarriages occur in the first three months.*

So anything could happen. Chloe closed the oven door and thought about that for a moment. Anything. Maybe . . . She inhaled sharply and straightened as she heard Aidan come in through the glass door, quickly fixing a smile to her face.

'I got a call today,' he said from behind her.

'A call?' A twinge of dread went through her. Surely Dr Webb's office wouldn't have . . .

'It was from a publishing house. In London.'

He turned to hand her a gin and tonic and she masked her exhale of relief by taking a sip, then remembered that she wasn't actually allowed. She raised the glass again and surreptitiously let the mouthful slide back. She didn't particularly care for gin to begin with, but according to Aidan there was nothing better than a cold G&T after a hard day's work. Not that she knew much about that these days. *No wife of mine will ever have to work*, Aidan was fond of saying, sounding faintly biblical, as if gathering a whole slew of wives around him, none of them engaged in any meaningful profession whatsoever.

'Who do you know in publishing?' she said, cutting a tomato into perfect, even pieces because, after all, *Food is a feast for the eyes too, Chloe, darling.*

'Aidan?' She looked up when he didn't answer immediately.

'He wanted to speak to you.' Aidan had become quite still, which Chloe knew meant that all his attention was fixed on her. 'Said he had a job for you. A portrait.'

She stared at him. 'But . . . I haven't worked in ages,' she said. Two years, to be precise, not since the lovely sunny day in June when she and Aidan had sneaked off to the Plymouth registry office to get married. His mother had been deeply disapproving when she'd found out that her only son had shacked up with a poor photographer with no family to speak of. It made Aidan laugh, but Chloe did feel sorry that his mum had been cheated out of a big wedding. He'd shrugged it off. *I'm your family now*, he'd said. *You and I belong together.*

Giving up her photography hadn't been an easy trade-off at first. But moving across to Plymouth from Torquay, settling into their new home, all that took time, and when the moment had come for her to pick up her Nikon again, start advertising for new clients, there'd always been one reason or another to delay it. *No wife of mine will ever have to work*, Aidan would say, and Chloe, who had taken it as a joke at first, soon realised that he actually meant it. And eventually, she'd come to see the sense of it too, even felt relieved not to have to rely on the unpredictable work flow, the constant worrying over money.

She'd trained with a photographer called Liz Tallis, a brilliantly talented diva who'd been a pain and an inspiration in equal measure and whose many demands had had Chloe constantly on the verge of being fired from all her real jobs – one behind the till at the cash and carry, the other manning the front desk at a small private hospital at night. Liz had been incredulous at first, then furious when Chloe handed in her resignation, even going so far as to acknowledge that she had 'some promise', the highest praise in her book. She didn't give up easily either: she'd send Chloe flyers for exhibitions and showcases, invite her to openings in London, New York, Edinburgh, none of which she ever attended. There'd be Christmas cards bearing Liz's hasty, impatient scrawl: *Merry everything. Happy Happy.* And occasionally a more elaborate if vaguely threatening *Are you working? Call me.*

But it was important to Aidan for Chloe to be at home, and Chloe had been surprised how easy it was to slip away from it all and simply enjoy the fact that the pressure of providing for herself and Danny had eased.

'He seemed to know *you*, anyway,' Aidan said slowly, intent on her face. Chloe had the very delicate, very pale skin that often came with copper hair: *So fine I can look right through it, darling*, Aidan often said. He narrowed his eyes a little now, as if it might help him do just that – look into Chloe's mind to discover the connection between his wife and this mystery man. 'He had your mobile number. A Matt Cooper. Said he couldn't reach you on it. Did you give it to him?'

'Give him what?'

'Did you. Give him. Your mobile number?' Aidan repeated, enunciating every word.

'No!' she said. 'I don't know him.'

Aidan looked at her. 'I told him you were busy, of course,' he then said.

He pushed her drink towards her, but she shook her head, setting the plates into the warming drawer. A portrait. She'd been good at portraits, she thought with a sudden, fierce pang of longing.

'Chloe? Are we going to eat any time soon?'

'Ten minutes,' she said mechanically.

He hovered next to her. The sweetish smell of the antiseptic he used at the surgery dropped straight down to the bottom of her stomach, where small waves of nausea were churning around the baby secret. Why on earth would they call it morning sickness when it was really an all-day kind of thing? she wondered. She must have made a small movement of withdrawal, because Aidan's arms came around her to keep her where she was, cradling her into his chest. When she felt his hands on her sides, moving towards her belly, she jerked backwards, her arm colliding with his chest.

'What the hell, Chloe?' He surveyed his sleeve, which was covered in a fine red spray of tomato juice, then looked back up at her, frowning at her red face, the knife in her hand.

'I'm so sorry,' she said. 'Here, give it to me now. If I put some stain remover on, it'll come out.'

He made a face, started unbuttoning his cuffs.

'You're very distracted today,' he said accusingly.

'You know,' Chloe spoke quickly, before she could change her mind, 'it would have been nice to talk to this Matt Cooper – in person, I mean. It might have been a job I could have done, without taking too much time away from here.'

'Oh, Chloe.' Aidan laughed easily. 'Why would you want to go and take some old woman's picture? It's bound to be hideously depressing.'

'An old woman?' she repeated doggedly. 'Who?'

'Hamilton, I think,' he said carelessly. 'She writes children's books. *Wrote* them, I guess, since it sounded like she had one foot in the grave, what with her never leaving her house, and—'

'Hamilton?' Chloe cut in. 'Georgiana and Madeleine Hamilton?'

Aidan stopped midway through shrugging off his shirt. 'Could have been,' he said cautiously. 'Why?'

'*The Grand Adventures of Foxy the Great.* Whizzy Witch. Pipper the Dog,' Chloe reeled off. 'Danny and I adored them; they're brilliant and so funny. Which one was it, Georgiana or Madeleine?'

'Never heard of either.' Aidan draped his shirt across the countertop, scraping at a fleck of tomato juice, clearly regretting having mentioned the name. 'But it doesn't matter. You have me and the house; you love making things pretty.'

'The house is already pretty.' She didn't know why she was pushing it. It had to be something to do with the secret lodged in her belly. So she did it again. 'And being here, it only fills so many hours. I could easily take on a small job, Aidan. It wouldn't distract me from anything.'

'But darling, he made it sound as if it was a big deal. Important. A rush, too. You couldn't possibly do it.'

He folded his shirt in an exact rectangle, stacked his tie and jacket on top, the same exact rectangle, and ended the conversation by disappearing through the glass doors with his drink, leaving Chloe to poke at the tomato salad.

The Hamilton sisters. Their creations Whizzy Witch and Pipper the Dog had become a staple in every bookshop and classroom, but not many people these days remembered their very first book, about a little fox who got up to no good. Foxy had never returned with a series like Whizzy and Pipper did; he'd slunk quietly out of the public eye before he could become part of the popular canon. But he'd been so much a part of Chloe's childhood that she couldn't think of him without remembering reading with her father in their cramped, shabby council flat.

She'd pad into the lounge in her too-big pyjamas and thick socks – their heating was perpetually giving out – carefully carrying the book, which was so old that her father used to read it with his mum when he was little. Climbing up onto her dad's knee, she'd feel his arms go round her to hold the book open on her lap, the weight of the spine digging into her thighs as she settled herself more comfortably. She recalled his voice, the smell of Old Spice soap, the feel of his shirt, which was soft and worn and familiar, the creak of the chair as they settled into the half-hour that belonged just to her. Away from bills and illness and her father's long day at the garage; away from Chloe's mum, who'd left them when her brother Danny was a baby; away from Danny, who was a restless, squirmy child and needed every other minute of her time.

Chloe didn't think much about those early days, when her father was still alive and Danny was still, well, Danny. That was one of the things about time moving forward: it pushed memories so far behind you that you only ever saw what came after. The worry and the responsibility and the growing up fast. Sometimes, she thought, it would be nice if she could remember Danny or her father without any of that; remember them the way they used to be during those long-ago moments that had been exactly like Foxy: safe and warm.

Foxy. Just the word made her close her eyes and pause, reaching for the memory of a little reddish-brown fox peeping out irreverently from behind a woodpile, slinking around a tumbledown wall, hiding inside a bucket, always where you least expected him. *Spot the fox, lovey? Let's hope he doesn't get caught.*

Dimly she felt movement behind her, and a moment later, music came crooning out of the enormous speakers standing on either side of the sofa. 'My Blue Heaven', one of the old records that Aidan collected. A soft, throaty burr of a voice overlaid with piano twinkles, scratchy and irregular beneath the needle of the old record player. The evening was velvety soft and sweet-smelling and the music threaded itself through the breeze. Without warning, Aidan put his arms around her again, turned her towards him and started dancing with her, right in front of the oven.

'You know I love you, darling,' he murmured into her ear. 'You're the most important, precious thing. I just want you to be happy here at home with me, not out with some stranger. Just you and me, together for ever.' He gathered her closer still, wrapping his arms tightly around her, his whispers all she heard, words dripping with love like honey, until she found herself pushing her lips up into a smile and releasing her shoulders as she relaxed into his embrace, held on tight. All would be well. She'd tell him, soon. They would be happy.

'Of course,' she whispered back. 'Always.'

She kept her eyes closed, willing the memory of her father and the little brown fox to stay with her, but already it was slipping away, dissolving in tendrils and shimmering fibres until it was just Chloe and her husband and their secret unborn child, all three swaying to the music in their perfect, perfect home.

Four

Maddy

'A plane's gone down! A plane's gone down . . .'

My arms were wrapped around my sister's neck and I held on tight, like I had when I was nine and she was fifteen and I'd crawled into her bed after a nightmare. Dimly I noticed that she smelled strange: of perfume and other big-city smells rather than dogs and grass and the violet-scented soap Aunt Marjorie gave us for birthdays to combat the disgraceful state of our hands. But when she ran her palms across my shoulders and down my back as if checking me over, her touch was exactly the way it always had been: comforting and warm.

'Foxy, what on earth are you talking about?' she laughed into my ear. 'The roads have been hell, I almost didn't make it. All of England is on the move, you know.'

Abruptly I pulled away. 'We must send someone right away. They were flying, Georgie, I didn't think anything of it at first, and then . . . I was afraid to go and look. So stupid, I'm so sorry . . . One fell behind, and then it fell altogether . . .' I broke off and stared at her, dimly noticing that she'd cut her hair, a short glossy cap that swung into her face as she leaned forward, all laughter gone now.

'Are you sure, Maddy?' she said urgently, then, without waiting for my answer, 'Where exactly, close to the bay or further towards the harbour?'

'By Hangman's Bluff,' I said desperately, and she closed her eyes. I could see her throat move as she swallowed. 'Oh Georgie, I should have gone to make sure, to help.'

'Hush, lovey, it'll be all right.' For the briefest moment she cupped my face with her hands, laid her forehead against mine, her thumbs tracing the curve of my jawbone. 'It'll be fine. I'm here now.'

And then she was running, took the front steps with a big jump, and I was right behind her, my hands making little flapping motions to make us go faster.

'Aunt!' Georgiana shouted. 'Hobson!'

'Georgiana, finally!' Aunt Marjorie's grey corkscrew curls bounced around her face as she emerged from her little sitting room, where she'd been waiting for news by the wireless. 'Whatever has kept you so long on the Continent I simply cannot imagine, and what with Herr Hitler and Stalin now being bedfellows, of all the outrageous things—'

'There's been a plane accident, out on the bay,' Georgiana said without preamble.

Aunt Marjorie stopped in mid flow, her open mouth an O of horror. Then she found her voice and surged forward in a flurry of shawls and skirts. 'Oh, this godforsaken war,' she exclaimed. 'Didn't I tell you? Didn't I? Untold tragedies already!' She sounded vaguely triumphant that the horrors she'd been predicting for over a year now had finally come to pass. 'Oh, what *can* we do, what can we possibly *do*?'

'Ring the airfield on the telephone, Aunt,' Georgiana said impatiently. 'And someone needs to get out there, look for . . .' she threw me a quick glance, 'survivors,' she finished firmly. 'Hobson!'

'All right, all right.' A gruff voice came from somewhere inside the house. 'Hold your horses, Miss Georgie, just a-coming now. Glad to know they haven't managed to slow you down one bit on the Continent.'

'Never,' she called back, giving me a pained half-grin just as Hobson emerged, holding a vase in one hand and a heap of black velvet in the other. His eyes lit up when he saw her.

'Miss Georgie, I'll say, you're as pretty as a day—'

'Hobson, terrible news,' Georgiana interjected quickly, just as Cookie and Susan came hurrying up the stairs, Susan holding another armful of black fabric and Cookie surging ahead, beaming because her beloved Georgiana, who'd been marooned on the Continent for far too long, was finally home and she'd made a Victoria sponge.

Both of them stopped in their tracks when they caught Georgiana's last words.

'It's never the Germans already?' Hobson got the words out with some difficulty, and I suddenly remembered that he had fought in 1918 alongside my father, who had brought him back to Summerhill half blind from gas and terror and never entirely fit for the world at large again. After Papa had died and Aunt Marjorie moved in, grimly stoical at being forced to live in this godforsaken place that had claimed both her sister and her brother-in-law, it had been Hobson who had kept things going with quiet, efficient order, while Frank had roped me into his daily battle with gardens and grounds to keep us sane and fed, and Cookie had brought Susan to work at Summerhill and supplied us with tea and cake, believing that it would make even the grimmest day a little bit better.

'Worse!' Aunt Marjorie shrieked from her sitting room, where she was hovering over the telephone. It had arrived to great fanfare a year before my father died, and Aunt Marjorie regarded it as the second greatest gift after the wireless because it meant she could call her sister, my Aunt Hilly, in Yorkshire. 'Futile death and destruction already and no one's even near Herr Hitler yet. Yes? Mrs Claxton, be a dear and put me through to the commander of the Royal Air Force.'

Cookie clapped a hand over her mouth in horror. With great presence of mind, Susan shut the door on Aunt Marjorie's mutterings about cold watery graves and useless death, and I put my arm around Cookie's broad back and steered everyone towards the library and the sherry bottle my father had always kept on top of the glass cabinet for emergencies.

'Get Frank and take a boat out there,' Georgiana said to Hobson. 'The roads are so crowded, any army personnel will take ages to get down to the coast.'

'Can't go via the river, though, not against the tide coming in.' Hobson was untying his green apron with flying hands. 'The jetty on the other side of Hangman's Cove, I think. There're always a few skiffs moored. Where in heaven's name is Frank?'

'Weeding the marrow bed,' Cookie said in a faint voice, downing the rest of her sherry in one go.

'Hobson, wait.' I snatched a woollen cape from the hallway cupboard. It had belonged to my father and had escaped Hobson's search for additional blackout material. 'For when you find the pilot.' I held it out to him. 'He must be cold.'

'Oh, I don't know that we'll need it by the time . . .' Hobson caught himself, reached to pat my arm and took the cape. He rolled it up carefully and slung it over his shoulder. 'Of course, Miss Maddy. You're right. When we find him.'

A moment of silence fell in the wake of Hobson's departure. Cookie stood close to us, one arm around Susan, the other resting on my shoulder. She'd just opened her mouth to greet Georgiana properly when another sound came through the open front door. The rumbling purr of a motor, and tyres crunching on the shell-covered courtyard.

'Goodness, what now?' Susan said anxiously.

'Oh, they're here already! Driving way too fast, as usual.' Georgiana jumped up. 'Maddy, come quick. I want to introduce you.'

Five

She was through the door in a flash, her new high heels making an unfamiliar clacking sound on the flagstones, her arms moving wildly to direct two cars that had pulled into the courtyard. A young man perched on the side of one of them gave her an exuberant wave that almost sent him flying. The driver, a rather portly young man wearing large sunglasses, his hair so shiny that the sun bounced off it, tooted the horn several times, causing a flock of birds in a nearby sycamore tree to depart, chattering furiously. Random bits were tied to the roof of a second car. I could make out suitcases, tennis rackets and what looked like fishing rods.

'Georgiana!' I ran after her and managed to catch her arm, held her back. 'Who on earth are all these people?'

'Now don't be alarmed.' Georgiana turned to me. 'They're my new friends. It was a bit spur-of-the-moment, but they were simply dying to come and I couldn't deter them, not when Laney was nice enough to put me up in her flat in Paris when my money ran out.' She gripped my elbow. 'Say you don't mind, please? I know the timing's horrid, but there's someone I wanted you to meet especially. I did ring Aunt last week and she seemed all right with it.'

I'd been avoiding Aunt Marjorie, who rarely left her seat next to the wireless, clutching her gas mask and thinking about one thing only: how not to be murdered in her bed by the Germans.

'I don't think she's passed on the message,' I said faintly. 'Nothing's ready, food, bedrooms . . .'

'Ah, that's easily done. They prefer drinks over food anyway, and they're not fussy about where they sleep. Half the time they kip on someone's sofa when they come in late from the clubs. Quick, we can send the boys down to the cliffs after Hobson. All hands on deck now.'

There were six of them – although it seemed like sixteen at first, the way they exploded upon the courtyard. Three men and three women. The young man sitting on the side of the car – Jonathan, Georgie had greeted him – half slid, half fell from his perch in a fit of helpless laughter. The portly man, Gregory, I thought she'd said, was improbably dressed in hunting tweeds. His hair glistened in the sun as he stood with his arms stretched open, apparently in wordless rapture. The young women, one of them holding a cage containing a parrot, were studying the rows of Frank's precious cabbages, which he'd planted all round the house because they were the only vegetable hardy enough to withstand enemy onslaught.

'My gosh, Miss Maddy, what a to-do!' Susan deposited her armful of fabric into a wheelbarrow and came to stand next to me. She was about my age, a slip of a girl, her white-blond hair pulled back tightly, and so fine that wisps of it escaped everywhere, giving her a halo of brightness. Her bulky dress, which she insisted on as a sort of maid's uniform, always seemed too big around her middle and shoulders, no matter how much it was taken in. 'Quite a fancy bunch, aren't they?' She swatted at her apron, which was covered in fine black fuzz.

'And if those are their travelling clothes,' I said, 'what on earth will they be wearing for normal?' I smoothed down my blouse, supremely conscious of my tattered trousers and the rip in one leg.

Susan gave me a sideways look, her eyes creasing at the corners with sudden merriment, giving her the look of a skinny, cheerful monkey. 'I think we're fighting a losing battle here, Miss Maddy. I'll help get them settled then, shall I?'

When I turned back to Georgiana, she had gone, walking

quickly towards the second car, where a blond man had emerged and was leaning against the car, smoking as he surveyed the mayhem in the courtyard. As soon as the man saw her, he straightened and tossed his cigarette into the rhododendron bush before – I blinked and swallowed, because nothing made much sense on this mad day, but this least of all – drawing her close. I felt a pang of something, that arm around my sister's waist as foreign as her newly short hair, but I shook my head, tried to focus on his face, which dipped down to Georgiana's for a kiss.

Just for a moment, her body melted against his, her shoulders trembling slightly, before she drew away, talking urgently, motioning back to the house and me. He nodded, turned to rummage in the car. Dashing a quick hand under her eyes, Georgiana came running back to me.

'Maddy—'

'Georgiana, who is *that*?' I cut in.

She hesitated for a moment, then said, very quickly, 'That's my new beau!' She leaned close and whispered, 'Dumpy little me, can you believe it? His name is Victor Deverill. Isn't he the most handsome creature you've ever seen?'

She lifted her arms in an expansive gesture, jiggling her eyebrows comically. She looked so different, I suddenly noticed. It wasn't only her short hair, but her face, which had always been bare of make-up and was now perfectly even with a coat of powder around dramatically made-up eyes.

'You're not dumpy, Georgiana Hamilton,' I said, incensed. 'Anyone would be glad to have you. So, a *beau*?' I lingered on the foreign-sounding word to buy myself a little time and master my . . . not dismay, never dismay when Georgiana was pink-cheeked with pride, lovely with happiness . . . my *surprise*. 'That's great, Georgie. You never said, in any of your letters.'

'I wanted to tell you properly. It's all been fantastically exciting.' Georgiana threaded my arm through hers and started pulling me towards the car. 'I really wanted you to meet him, and the way things are going with bloody Germany, he might have to leave soon, so I *had* to bring him. You understand, don't you, Foxy?' She scanned my face anxiously.

'Of course,' I said carefully.

She beamed at me. 'I know you'll love him. Everyone does. He's something important at Wilson's, that big fancy department store in London. His family think it's a bit beneath him, he says, but he likes working. He'll be so good in a crisis like this. He's terribly clever, you know, can turn his hand to anything. And so lovely, too . . .'

We'd almost reached the car. Georgiana was still burbling happily next to me, and I could feel her body quivering a little as the man straightened up slowly. His suit jacket was now folded neatly on a trunk sitting in the back, and he was turning up the sleeves of his shirt, a smile lighting his features when he saw us.

'Victor Deverill, meet my sister, the great and very wonderful Madeleine Hamilton,' Georgiana said happily. She flung out her hands, then added in a stage whisper, 'And she's so grown up now, I almost didn't recognise her. When I left, she was still a gawky teenager, and now look at you, Foxy. You're ready to be a woman.'

'For heaven's sake, Georgie, will you *stop*?' I hissed, my face on fire, but she laughed again and thrust me towards the man as if presenting me on a dish.

'It's wonderful to finally meet you, Madeleine. Gigi has told me so much about you.'

My hand, still covered with traces of mud from the stone wall, disappeared in Victor's large palm and the sound of my name lingered between us for a moment. His diction was smooth and even, nothing like the homely West Country burr I heard around me from Frank and Cookie and Susan all day. I sounded different in that voice, more grown up, and when I finally looked up and into his face, I saw his eyes on me, a beautiful deep green lit up by amusement.

'Maddy is fine,' I said awkwardly.

'Victor, darling, let's get going; Maddy, maybe you can help Susan sort out the bedrooms.'

Victor extracted another cigarette from his pack as we followed Georgiana, tapped it on the back of his hand, lit it and took a deep drag, then another. I'd never seen anyone smoke like that, in hard pulls that sucked in his cheeks and made the end of the cigarette light up brightly. He gave me a sideways smile.

'Gigi talks about you all the time. I wish we'd met in less awful times, but I'm glad to be here. I hope you and I will be great friends. Coming, Gi,' he called ahead to where Jonathan and Gregory were bouncing in Georgie's wake like excited puppies. 'I'll see you later, Madeleine.'

'Yes,' I said to his retreating back, not entirely sure what had just happened. 'I'm sure you will.'

Six

'You can see boats out on the water now, and the tide's in properly. And loads of people all the way across on the harbour looking back at Hangman's Cove.'

The three ladies had been settled in their rooms, Aunt Marjorie was keeping vigil by the telephone, and Susan had just come into the kitchen, where I was seated at the long, scrubbed servants' table, peeling potatoes and waiting for news.

'Could you see the plane?' Cookie asked anxiously, bustling to the table with a bowl of flour.

Susan slipped onto the bench across from me. She looked tired and there was a streak of dust above one eyebrow. 'Not from the Widow's Watch, but that's probably because the cliffs are in the way.'

The Widow's Watch was a small platform on the roof dating back to the 1800s, where wives would wait for their seafaring husbands' boats to come back home after a storm. My father had mounted a telescope on the original cast-iron pillar, from which you could see much of the coastline: stretches of steep cliffs dipping down towards harbours and villages, coves and sandy beaches.

Summerhill's grounds extended all the way out to the cliffs, but the house itself was set back about a mile inland. Perched on the side of the hill, it overlooked the wide mouth of the tidal estuary, that peculiar kind of coastal river that ebbed and flowed with the tide as it funnelled the Atlantic deep into the Cornish countryside. Just north of Summerhill, the estuary narrowed down to the river and eventually petered out in a myriad of smaller streams and inlets further inland.

I pushed the big brown teapot in Susan's direction and she downed two cups of tea seemingly in one gulp. 'That pretty lady with the blond hair brought sixteen dresses and she didn't help a bit with hanging them up,' she said darkly. 'Can't she see that things are difficult today?'

'I wonder what they all think is going to be happening here.' Picturing the tweeds and fishing poles, I doodled a little googly-eyed angler fish on the open page of my sketchbook, using a streak of potato dust to colour it an ugly sludgy brown.

'They're only staying for a few days, the lady said. Here, Miss Maddy, let me help with those potatoes.' Susan picked up a knife.

'Oh, I do hope Hobson and Frank will be back soon.' Cookie peered out of the back door for the third time. 'It makes me anxious, and the house full now, too. Not that I don't think a spot of proper cooking will be a nice change from your dear aunt's supper tray, Miss Maddy,' she added firmly, in case her comment could be taken as a criticism of Georgiana. 'But it doesn't quite seem right to be jolly. Well, dinner isn't going to make itself.' She shook herself and started gathering the nubby heap of peeled potatoes, handing me a wet rag for my dirty hands. 'Let's set the table early, Sue. Hobson'll be tired. We can use the good dishes, the ones with the silver rim.' She tapped her chin thoughtfully. 'And Frank brought back those beautiful sea basses early this morning, which . . . Ah, there you are!'

Georgiana closed the kitchen door and sat down heavily, rubbing her eyes. 'The boys are walking westwards, along that stretch of coast between the cliffs and the village harbour; there's a couple of beaches there where someone might be able to crawl onshore if they were swept away by the current. Hobson is out on the water, and by the time we got down there, other boats were already arriving. I think the plane has sunk, from what I could see anyhow. Surf's high now; you could hear it pounding.'

She shivered and scooted closer to me. Cookie put a cup of tea and a plate of cake in front of her, pausing to pat our backs for a moment. I laid my head on Georgiana's shoulder and she turned to drop a kiss on my hair.

'That we'd see the day again, Maddy,' she said quietly. 'So much sadness.'

She drank her tea in silence. The sun fell sideways along her shoulder, picking out the delicate curve of her cheek, the downward sweep of her jaw. In the rush of the last few hours, her skin had lost the mask-like sheen of powder from before, was pale and delicate, her hair tousled. Almost automatically, my hand started moving across the paper. Quick, light pencil strokes at first, meant to dispel the nameless anxiety that had settled in me since I'd seen the plane go down in the place where our father had died six years ago, gradually slowing to more exact, even ones to capture the sheer relief of having my sister home.

'Goodness, Maddy.' She broke the silence. 'It's like time has sped up while I was gone. Your face has changed so much; even your cheekbones have grown up, I think.'

'Georgie, please!' I shook my head and bent back over my drawing, reaching for my watercolours, using a few drops from the damp rag for moisture. 'And do stop going around telling everyone. It's quite mortifying, especially when I'm still exactly the way I used to be.' I held up my hands which were vivid with red and green, gestured to my torn trousers and dusty blouse, which I hadn't had time to change out of between getting rooms ready and lugging trunks and bags up the stairs.

'Yes,' she sighed, but her half-smile faded. 'Still, there's no denying that things are changing. At some point, we'll have to sit down and think seriously, about us and about Summerhill.'

My pencil stopped in mid movement and I stared at her. 'Whatever is there to think about?'

'You being stuck here for six years,' she said. 'You suddenly growing up. The estate falling apart. War. Take your pick.'

I shook my head. 'Summerhill is more than enough for me, Georgie, it always will be. And Papa would want us to look after it, especially now.'

Georgiana leaned close to look at my drawing. 'Papa isn't here any more, though, is he? He—'

'So it's all a bit rough around the edges these days,' I said quickly. 'But Frank says people will need farming land and crops more than ever now, so things are bound to improve soon.'

'Oh Maddy, be reasonable.' Georgiana lifted her shoulders in a helpless shrug. Her breath was warm on my cheek, and when I closed my eyes, I felt the delicate flutter of her lashes against the side of my temple. Her voice, when it came, was barely a whisper in my ear. 'Maybe the plane crash . . . maybe it's a sign. That we need to make a change. That war is coming and Summerhill needs a plan.'

Without opening my eyes, I felt for her hands, intertwined my fingers in hers.

'But not today,' I said. 'Today I just want to sit here, with you, in peace.'

'Peace won't be with us much longer,' she said quietly.

Suddenly I caught a small rustling noise and the faintest hint of cigarette smoke, and when I opened my eyes, I found myself staring straight at Victor Deverill, hand poised to knock on the kitchen door.

'I didn't mean to startle you,' he said apologetically. Georgiana's head snapped up and she hurriedly disentangled her hands from mine.

'It's just, we were wondering where you'd got to,' he said. 'We're back and could murder a drink.'

'Of course.' Georgiana jumped up. 'Thank you so much, darling, for pitching in. What news from the cliffs?'

'One man has been saved; they picked him up from a buoy, your . . . er, butler was saying. He's very badly shaken, swallowed water, being taken to hospital. They weren't quite sure yet if he was going to make it. But the second man – it was a training plane, takes two or three – is still missing.'

Victor pushed his hand through his hair tiredly, and I could see the bones in his jaw grinding slightly. Cookie braced herself on the table next to me.

'Oh, those poor, poor boys,' she murmured. 'Not even at war yet and already . . . Go on up, girls. I'll wait for Hobson and Frank.'

Victor looked at her, then at Susan, who'd clambered up from the bench and dropped a tired sort of half-curtsey in his direction. As he took in my bare feet propped up on the bench, the heap of potato peel and the wet rag next to my sketchbook, watercolour reds and blues bleeding into the mud, he smiled in a polite but nonplussed sort of way, and when I saw Georgie's slightly embarrassed expression, it occurred to me that where he came from, and where Georgie had just been for the last six months, people probably didn't sit down in the kitchen drinking tea with the servants.

I gave a mental shrug – because really, who cared about any of that? – then got up from the bench, sweeping the potato peelings together for the slop bucket. When I straightened up, I saw that Victor had picked up my sketchbook.

'Gigi did tell me you're quite an artist,' he said.

'Oh, well, I don't think . . .' Out of the corner of my eye I could see Cookie throwing an alarmed look at Susan, because everyone knew my sketchbook was private. Victor, however, was turning the pages curiously, peering at a drawing of the house, and then at another, a ladybird sitting on a rose and waving a tiny petal as a family of cross-looking ants marched up the stem.

'Might I have it back?' I held out my hand, mustering my most polite smile.

'Of course,' Victor said, but he kept looking. 'The detail is quite astonishing. And this one – it's beautiful, Madeleine.'

Ignoring my stretched-out hand, he held up the book to show us all the drawing of Georgiana I had just finished. I'd sketched myself in it, too, the way we'd sat closely, arms intertwined; had started filling in slashes of auburn for her hair, my own curls a darker chestnut, our faces pale cream hearts above the scrubbed oak of the kitchen table.

'You look lovely.' He smiled at my sister, giving her a gallant little bow. His eyes went back to the drawing. 'You wouldn't consider giving it to me?' he asked suddenly. 'The two beautiful Summerhill sisters? It would be such a wonderful reminder of my stay here.'

'Oh, I'm . . .' I was absurdly flattered. And yet that drawing was meant for Georgiana, really, it was personal.

'What a charming idea,' Georgiana beamed proudly. 'It would be a lovely gift.'

'It's not really finished,' I hedged.

'Looks perfect to me.' Victor's gaze lingered on the picture. 'Although I don't think you've used quite the right colour for your eyes, Madeleine. They're more of a gold. And brown, like mahogany. But they're changing all the time, so it's hard to say.'

It was so unexpected a comment that I didn't even have the wherewithal to flush. I just stared at him, and I didn't come to until Georgiana laughed and shook her head, taking the sketchbook from him and saying something about men not understanding these things at all and how about he make himself useful by mixing up a batch of drinks. He smiled and shrugged and allowed himself to be towed away by my sister, who gave Cookie a quick one-armed hug as she passed. 'Thanks for making me a cake, Cookie.'

'Anything for you, pet,' Cookie said, and just like that, everyone dispersed, leaving me standing with my sketchbook and a handful of potato peel.

Seven

The restless, moody summer's day had melted into a warm, heavy kind of night, but if I'd expected the earlier events to cast a pall over the evening, I would soon learn that nothing short of a volcanic eruption could deter Georgiana's friends from having a good time.

Eschewing the drawing room as far too stuffy – Aunt Marjorie had been lecturing us about the blackout for weeks now, with the result that most of Summerhill was swathed in black fabric days ahead of the rest of the nation – they had pushed out through the wide glass doors onto the terrace. Hugging two sides of the house in the shape of a long L and overlooking the steep downward slope of the hill, the terrace wasn't used much any more. The ornate stone balustrade was lichen-covered and crumbling in places, the enormous white flagstones underfoot pitted with holes.

To me, too, the house had begun to feel claustrophobic under the strain of the missing airman and the endless stream of news issuing from the wireless – Germany threatening Poland, British children being evacuated, the navy mobilised – and I was relieved to follow the group outside, where I sat out of the way on a stone ledge, my fingers twitching in my lap, eager to capture this strange new world that Georgiana had brought to Summerhill. The men resplendent in perfectly fitting evening suits like I'd never seen before. Her girlfriends: Laney in a skirt that looked like a cloud and Rana, with her startling eye make-up and lashes so long they touched her eyebrows. Clementine, who was trying to tempt the parrot to dip its beak into a gin cocktail and falling about laughing when it cackled hysterically and fluffed up its plumage.

And then Georgiana. She'd been visibly shaken after talking to Hobson but refused to tell me anything more about it, then tried in vain to persuade Aunt Marjorie to leave her post by the wireless and come and eat dinner with us. Even now, in a gold dress that shimmered across her body, her hair like a flame above her beautifully made-up face, she still looked edgy, although she made a valiant effort to smile and chat, finally coming to perch next to me on my ledge.

'So I thought we could show them the maze tomorrow, Maddy, maybe have a picnic there. That'd be easy for Cookie. And I *had* written to the Melrose twins and Molly Teague, inviting them over for Saturday night. And the Penberthy boys. I haven't seen them all in so long. But now, with the plane and all, I suppose . . .' She lapsed into a brooding silence. 'Oh, I know I should cancel,' she sighed eventually. 'All this bloody war horror, it's just too much. And Aunt Marjorie – honestly, Maddy, you should have heard her. Going on and on about Jonathan not having enlisted yet, fawning all over Victor when he said he was in the reserves. She'd have made a good press-gang officer in the Napoleonic Wars. Has she been like this since I left?'

'I haven't really seen her much,' I said, slightly guiltily, because I'd gone to a lot of trouble to stay away from my aunt's gloomy predictions of death and destruction. 'She's turned that sitting room into a kind of war room. All those maps and newspapers and endless letters and calls to Aunt Hilly.'

'She thinks Yorkshire is much safer than here. I hope she's not losing her mind.' Georgiana took a long sip of her drink and eyed me moodily. 'Lecturing me about having friends round this weekend, which, all right, maybe wasn't the best idea in the world . . .'

'She's just worried, and rightly so.' Victor materialised next to her with a tray of drinks. 'I asked your maid for some fruit cordial for you, Madeleine; I thought you might prefer it.'

It was an unexpectedly perceptive gesture, when I'd just been thinking about a glass of something cool and sweet, and I only managed a surprised 'Thanks.'

'Do *you* think I should cancel people on Saturday, Vic?' Georgie asked him mulishly. 'I was just going to have a few drinks, a little music. Dancing. Ask Mrs Claxton round to help – she's Cookie's sister, lives in the village. But should I send you all home instead? Not you, darling, of course, but the rest?'

'Ah, I don't think it'll do any harm, Gigi,' Victor said soothingly. 'It'll take people's minds off things. Now stop fretting, will you?'

Gigi, that was what they called her. At first, I hadn't been able to imagine a person less like a Gigi than Georgiana, my Georgiana, tapping away at her typewriter, frowning in furious concentration behind the wheel of Father's old car. But as the evening wore on, I could almost see her taking shape in front of me, a beautiful stranger in gold amidst beautiful, grown-up people, drinking brandy and blowing cigarette smoke in intricate clouds out into the night air.

Oddly, they seemed to like me, her friends, although they clearly thought I was a sort of alien specimen they'd happened upon in a foreign land. Laney touched my dress in wonder – pressed for time, I'd pulled out the first thing I could find: a sensible navy dress with a lot of fabric and a round collar – and offered to make me a turban out of her silk scarf 'to brighten things up a bit'. The men gallantly protested her critique of my dress and complimented me with ridiculous extravagance as they toasted my arrival in their club. *All hail, glorious sister of Gigi the Great.* Clementine had taken a particular shine to me, pressing seeds into my hand to get her parrot to land on my arm, and trying for several minutes to describe the dance floor of a particular London nightclub. She stayed close to me – too close, I secretly thought, as the slick skin of her arm slid along mine yet again and the heavy musk of her perfume flattened the night breeze. I held my breath and took a step back, and then another, but she followed me, holding out the parrot like an offering, its sharp button eyes squinting at me malevolently.

'Oh Clem, do leave her alone, she doesn't want your silly bird.' Victor materialised next to me, snapping his fingers sharply, and with an indignant squawk, the parrot took flight. 'Run along and find someone your own age to play with. Or man the gramophone, will you?' He inserted himself neatly between us and, laughing, Clementine left to coax her parrot down from the eaves.

'She doesn't mean any harm,' he explained to me as I took a few grateful breaths of clean air, unsure why Clementine would want to harm me in any way but glad she was gone all the same. I settled back against the wall, waiting for Victor to leave, but he didn't, instead perching himself next to me and lighting a cigarette.

'You'll soon realise that their one and only skill in life is to turn everything into a party,' he remarked conversationally, nodding towards Georgiana, who was trying to teach Jonathan an old country dance. Jonathan was loudly professing himself too stupid to manage it, while Laney executed the steps perfectly, graceful as a ballet dancer, almost ethereal, like a sprite in her airy white dress.

'They're just beautiful.' I shook my head in wonder. 'How they have the energy to be so . . .'

'Wild?'

'Excited. They think country life is the most curious thing in the world. And Jonathan, he's—'

I broke off, not quite sure how to describe Jonathan's expansiveness, his over-the-top smile, in a polite way. Even at dinner tonight, telling us about the search for the missing airman, he had been dramatic, using big hand gestures meant to convey empathy but which came across as overblown and almost mocking.

'He thought eggs magically appeared scrambled or fried until he came across the chickens on his way back from the coast,' I said instead.

Victor laughed. 'He's actually quite clever, you know, he just gets bored easily. He wants to be an actor, that's why he's being so silly at the moment. They're engaged, Jonathan and Laney, but you wouldn't know to look at them. Her family is broke and he's quite rich. And utterly in love with her. Love and money, a perfect match, don't you think?' He laughed and lit another cigarette.

I considered the question. 'I can't imagine it would be,' I finally replied as Jonathan twirled Laney around and around, every time almost letting her go, until she begged him to stop.

Victor stopped laughing and regarded me with a quizzical look. 'You know, Gi's talked about you endlessly, but you're not at all how I thought you'd be.'

As if on cue, Georgiana came tripping over to us, slightly flushed but laughing.

'Jonathan's so hopeless, isn't he? I can't believe it, but I'm actually having fun now. Hard to stay sad when it's so lovely out.' She plucked Victor's glass out of his hand and took a deep swallow. 'Is Victor taking good care of you, Foxy? I really want you two to get along, you know.' She wagged her finger in mock-admonishment.

At that moment Laney came and asked for more records because, she claimed, the music was positively ancient, and she and Georgiana disappeared into the house. I threw Victor a quick sideways look, but he seemed in no rush to follow Georgiana's order to get along with me, so we sat in comfortable silence for a few minutes.

'You didn't like me looking at your book today, did you?'

I turned my head, surprised, but Victor was watching Gregory dancing a slow, earnest waltz with a rather haughty-looking Rana.

'Not really,' I said, then thought that might have sounded rude, so followed it up with a quick 'But it's all right.'

'I'm sorry,' he said. 'I didn't mean to intrude.'

Gregory did a ponderous turn and waltzed Rana past us again.

'Why does Georgiana call you Foxy? Quite a stretch from Madeleine, isn't it?' Victor broke the silence again.

'Why do you call her Gigi?' I said back.

He chuckled, lifted his glass in a salute. 'Madeleine it is.'

He stubbed out his cigarette and lit another, studying me through the smoke. I pushed away the sudden recollection of his strange comment in the kitchen earlier, although among all these wild, carefree people, it suddenly didn't seem quite so strange any more, and neither did the way he said my name, 'Madeleine', which made me sound like a melody, light and airy and beautiful, instead of thin and brown Maddy in her old-fashioned dress.

Zingy scents of lemon and herbs drifted across as he breathed out. People didn't drink at Summerhill really: Hobson might have a beer in the evening, and Cookie occasionally poured a round of sherry for everyone at the end of a particularly trying day, but this smelled different and fresh.

'Could I try?' I asked, pointing at his glass.

'Go on, then.' He held it out, amusement lurking in the corners of his eyes.

The drink was bitter, and not terribly lemony, but it slid down my throat with obliging ease, so much so that I took a second, bigger sip, and then a third.

'Hey, leave some for me.' Victor took the glass out of my hand.

'It's actually quite good,' I said. 'Thank you.'

'It's called a Red Lion. Gregory's obsessed with them, brought all the fixings down with him in a little portable suitcase. You open it up and you have a whole miniature bar in there, fold-up glasses and tongs and leather-covered flasks of liquor. Quite astonishing, actually. Must be an American thing.' He rolled his eyes comically at the extravagance. 'My aunt was always partial to a good gin cocktail, too: two knuckles of gin mixed in one knuckle of tonic.' He nudged me. 'She used a Waterford vase, of course. Died of a heart attack at sixty-eight, and I bet if we exhumed her now, she'd be perfectly preserved, pickled in gin.'

He laughed and I laughed back at him as the Red Lion fizzed its way towards my head, making me feel light and slightly woozy. He slid off the bench and beckoned to me.

'Come, I'll show you something.'

Eight

Over by the drinks trolley, he picked up a couple of lemons. 'Gregory brought down a whole crate of these,' he said. He threw one in the air, then the other, juggling the bright, nubby shapes so fast they became a yellow blur. Frank had grown lemons in the greenhouse at one time, but they'd been spotty and misshapen, while these were perfect, even and almost unblemished. Victor caught them in his hands, fished for a small knife and, keeping it angled, started turning one of them.

I wasn't sure if it was the gin or the candlelight or both, but the peel wavered in front of my eyes, a hard yellow against the white pith underneath, the citrus smell joining the bitter taste of the cocktail at the back of my throat as the night narrowed down to long-fingered hands and a yellow spiral slowly curling on the table. I blinked and squinted to bring it into focus, but already Victor had picked up a toothpick and, holding it at the ready, was winding the peel carefully round and round, securing it with the pick to make – a rose. I held out my hand, delighted because it was so pretty, but he shook his head.

'Not yet!' He poured two more drinks and gently floated the rose in one before presenting it to me with a flourish.

'Now! A pretty rose for a pretty lady,' he said gallantly, and bowed.

'Oh, it's so perfect,' I breathed, turning my glass to make the lemon rose drift in tiny circles. 'How did you do that? I'd have broken the peel at the first try.'

He looked pleased with himself. 'A little trick I picked up. Completely useless and impractical, but there you go.'

I gazed up at him as he leaned back and lit a cigarette, his face liquid gold in the candlelight, and suddenly, out of nowhere, I found myself wondering what life would be like if you were friends with someone like this, someone who made you laugh and brought you cold cordial and fashioned you a lemon rose out of nowhere, just because. As quickly as it had come I pushed the thought away and took a step backwards, scanning the group for a sign of Georgiana.

'I think I'll just go and see if I can help Georgie . . .'

But Victor held me back. 'Look! Didn't I tell you that he gets bored easily?'

Across the terrace from us, Jonathan had jumped up onto the stone balustrade and was balancing along it. He was surprisingly nimble as he skipped back and forth, executing the dance steps Georgiana had shown him perfectly – Victor had been right, it had all been an act – and pretending to fence with an invisible opponent. He tore off his shirt in a dramatic gesture, his chest shining whitely in the moonlight, a faint sheen of sweat on his collarbone. He was so thin that his stomach was a hollow below his ribcage, giving him the faint look of a skeletal ghost, a disconcerting image I had to blink away because it was so real. The others watched him, laughing, as he held out his hand for Laney. She was swaying and humming to herself and her eyes were half closed, but she didn't need much encouragement before jumping up on the balustrade too. Jonathan threw away his pretend rapier and took her hands, and they danced lightly back and forth, a little further each time.

'Someone should tell him to get down,' I said, keeping my eyes on the white figures. 'It's steep there.'

'He'll be fine. He's like a cat, he's got nine lives.' Victor lit another cigarette and settled himself back on the wall.

Jonathan skipped backwards, now singing loudly, and Laney followed him, accompanying him in a surprisingly sweet soprano. Their voices soared into the night, high-pitched and oddly unearthly, two sprites tiptoe-dancing. I couldn't look away from them. The ground fell away steeply from the edge of the terrace here, at least twelve feet in parts. Where on earth was Georgiana?

I took a step forward. 'Really, Victor, it's not safe . . .'

And that was when it happened. Jonathan slipped on some loose gravel atop the wall but recovered quickly and shouted a laugh to indicate how *hilarious* it'd been. Laney, looking slightly alarmed but shaking with helpless laughter, snatched her hand out of his and moved backwards. Jonathan leaned out and teetered above the abyss in an exaggerated show of losing his balance, berating her for her shameful cowardice. *Live a little, Laney.*

Maybe he would have been fine. But when he teetered again, this time involuntarily, and I saw something shift in his face – a split second when fear slid into horror – I didn't stop to think. Head spinning and gin sloshing round my stomach, I ran towards him, swept my arm sideways and by pure luck managed to hook my hand around his elbow.

I pulled him on top of me, all slick, cold skin and sinewy limbs, and he knocked the wind right out of me, leaving me choking on my back, my skirt billowing around both of us. Arms flailing, he extricated himself and stood, breathing heavily. Already his mouth was opening and his throat working to form a witty comment, but from down on the ground I could also see his eyes, wide and terrified, and the hand he now held out to me was shaking. It seemed churlish not to take it, but the touch of his clammy skin on mine was repulsive, and I dropped his hand the moment I stood, forcing down the sickly swirl of acidy gin in my stomach.

'Are you all right, Maddy? Good God, Jonathan, how stupid are you?' Georgiana had finally reappeared and rushed over. Taking my arm, she glowered at Jonathan. 'You could have broken your neck.'

'I'm fine, honestly. What are you, afraid?' Jonathan raised his arms above his head in the mock-victory salute of a sportsman, and made a few elaborate bows in the direction of the others, who were slowly advancing.

'*You* should have been,' she snapped, putting her arm round my shoulder. But Jonathan was back on form and the others fell in line with his show of bravado, pronouncing me the heroine of the evening, *and in your gown, too*, Laney said, slightly awed, fingering the material again as if it now had magical properties.

They swarmed around me, a cloud of perfume and wine and cigarette smells, before turning their minds back to the party. I stood on the sidelines, the faces blurring around me as I tried hard to forget that split second right before he would have fallen. The expression on his face, the dawning of horror, the realisation of what was to come; exactly the same expression I had seen once before.

Nine

'I don't think I've ever seen anyone move so fast. Here, sit, you do look a bit green.' Victor gestured to the stone bench. 'I'm sorry I was so flip. He really *would* have—'

'Don't,' I cut in roughly, my skin starting to prickle uncomfortably at the bottom of my skull. I felt raw and vulnerable, fraying around the edges, and the drink had made me dizzy. 'Please.'

I turned and walked the length of the terrace towards the corner. Here, I stood and leaned back against the wall of the house, breathing deeply. But the breeze brought scents of salt and tangy wetness that sent more goosebumps down my back, making the skin around my neck tighten, like a hand squeezing hard.

'You all right?' Victor was suddenly next to me, and I started.

'Yeah, sure,' I said. 'Great.'

'Your father?' he said tentatively. 'Gigi told me about the accident. He fell on the cliffs, didn't he?'

'I'd rather not talk about it,' I said curtly.

I had never told anyone about it. Not when they had asked about it back then, in turn agog for drama or solicitous for my well-being, not when the constable had questioned me until Georgiana made him stop, not when the vicar had called round to comfort the Summerhill orphans. *The spirit returns to God who gave it.* 'What a load of rubbish,' I remember Georgiana saying when Aunt Marjorie summoned us to tea. Throughout, she refused to say a word, sitting next to me and fixing the vicar with a quelling stare whenever he tried to address me. No, I never talked about it, not even to Georgiana; especially not to Georgiana. I couldn't bear for her to go through that morning with me, to feel what I felt. Instead, I had worked hard to push it right outside of me, far away into that blank space outside my Summerhill heart. It wasn't always easy to keep it there. Memories would come without warning, dreams from which I woke with my heart hammering. And today, when the plane crash had infused every conversation, every moment with a looming sense of déjà vu and dread, that split second of Jonathan arching backwards on the balustrade had arrowed straight into the darkest recesses of my mind and I found I couldn't stop thinking at all.

'Maddy love.' Georgiana's violet scent washed over me. 'Why don't you come back to the party? We're playing "My Blue Heaven". Your favourite.'

'Oh, leave her alone for a moment, Georgiana,' Victor said impatiently. 'You can see she's a bit shaken. We're just talking and—'

'I was trying to take her mind off things, darling,' Georgiana said, but Victor shook his head.

'Just have her go to bed. It's probably my fault,' he said. 'All that gin, what was I thinking?'

'Will you both stop?' I couldn't stand it any longer. 'I'm fine. Of course I'll stay. "My Blue Heaven". Wonderful.'

I threw myself into the party with all my might; would gladly have spent the night on the terrace if it meant not going back to the darkness of my own room, where there was nothing to do but think. I was good at dancing, actually. Georgie, who loved playing my parents' old records, had made Miss Keane, our governess, teach us and Susan on winter evenings, even roping in a very reluctant Hobson when she could.

So I danced with Georgie, a lot, and with Victor, and sometimes with both of them, a whirl of green eyes and gold and the navy blue of my sensible dress. Gregory taught me some complicated American twirling thing, and the girls giggled over an old-fashioned country dance Georgiana and I performed for everyone; Georgie threw back her head and collapsed in helpless laughter when we made each other fall. I could hear myself laughing too, loudly and giddily, adding to the fun. Because it *was* fun, yes. Such fun.

But even my most determined efforts to enjoy myself couldn't keep the evening from winding down eventually. The music turned into something softer. Gregory went to sleep on my stone bench, his jacket folded up under his head. Laney disappeared with Jonathan, and Georgie was dancing with Victor, a slow swaying, his hand splayed across the small of her back to guide her and hold her close. With no one to talk to and nothing more to say myself, I stood for a moment, my arms hanging down at my sides, watching them. Georgie had her eyes closed, but his were open, and when he turned, he found mine. He smiled. *Come*, he mouthed. Gently disentangling one arm from Georgiana, he held it out to me, gestured for me to join them.

I shook my head and quickly looked down at Gregory, who was snoring gently. But the warmth of Victor's smile lingered, and I suddenly thought about what it would feel like to bring it out into the open, that day at Hangman's Bluff. To hand it to someone else. How my father and I had gone out to the fields close to Tremarron, checking on the newly laid pipes that he needed to discuss with Mr Pritchard, our long-time estate manager. How we'd taken a shortcut along Hangman's Bluff on the way back to make it in time for Cookie's breakfast. How the rain had washed away some of the narrow path, a treacherous overhang above the cliffs, just waiting for someone to fall.

It was a beautiful walk, that coast path. Lined with gorse and shrubs, interspersed with the occasional cluster of low, twisted pine trees. Parts of it were sheltered and warm and fragrant, a little like pictures of Italy that Miss Keane had shown us, but on the stretches facing the sea it was wilder, and you could hear the water churning below as waves pounded the cliffs. There was a bench right up high, where Father had proposed to our mother in 1913. The memory of her wind-blown hair and smiling eyes as she replied, *yes, please, with all my love* had got him through the muddy trenches in France, through gas, and shell splinters lodged in his thigh, and whatever other dreams of terror we could sometimes hear from his room in the middle of the night. He'd survived all that and come back, only to lose her a few years later during a difficult birth that left him with a five-year-old daughter and an infant and the memory of his wife smiling at him on top of the world.

He must have hit an invisible fault line in the ground, a place where rain and wind had eroded the soil beneath, because a whole piece of the edge came away when he stepped on it. A scream cut the morning air as, for a split second, he swayed back and forth. For one breathtaking instant of hope, he managed to throw himself forward, scrabbling for a hold on the small rock outcroppings, digging his fingers desperately into the loose soil. I lunged to reach for his hands, but even though I was a skinny little thing at ten years old, the edge crumbled threateningly under my weight and my father shouted for me to get back, kept shouting as he tried to get his leg up over the edge, and I kept reaching, pressing myself flat on the ground for a better hold.

And then he fell.

He slid down the side of the cliff, through gorse and patches of scrubby grass, none of which were strong enough to hold the weight of a grown man. Crouching above, I watched him fall. I *felt* him fall; deep in my belly, I felt that pull of gravity, long grasses sliding through fingers, thorns slashing cheeks and hands. And when he dropped the last bit, where the cliff walls had curved inwards under the force of the surf at high tide, I felt that too, his bones and flesh, soul and heart in a moment of free fall, the wind swallowing his screams, and then the sound of a body hitting the rocks below.

For far too long, I lay still, before I finally started running.

Around the other side of the cove, small, roughly hewn steps took you down to the beach at low tide. You had to be careful, because the way the cove was shaped, the tide could trap you there and refuse to let you back up. I felt my way down more than seeing where I was going, blind with panic. The steps were slippery and my knees shook so hard I slid part of the way into the wet sand at the bottom. There were rivulets and pools of water everywhere and the sand gave under my feet with every step, making progress slow and syrupy, that nameless terror of nightmare running that never gets you where you so desperately need to go. And then I had to climb the big boulders at the bottom of the cliff where he'd landed, my hands slipping on the wet surface of the rocks, my toes fighting for foothold.

When I finally reached him, he was still alive. His leg was bent backwards in a strange way – I'd never seen a leg look like that before – and his body was oddly contorted. For a long, heart-stopping moment I had no idea what I should do. Details jumped at me, hitting my senses with devastating clarity: the sharp edges of the rocks, the barnacles covering them, the screech of seagulls overhead, the smell of salt water. But the rational part of my mind was blank and helpless.

What I should have done was to fetch help right then and there. He told me to, his voice coming in a hiss through clenched teeth. *Back up the stairs, Maddy. Fast as you can. The tide is coming in.* And indeed, while I'd been making my interminable way across the sand, water had started filling the cove, and when I looked back, I saw that waves were already pushing up the stone steps. It hadn't yet reached us up here, but I had lived on the coast and with the coast all my life; I knew well enough the creep of the tide. Each wavelet would come closer to the shore, little splashing advances that seemed friendly enough at first, like a playful tease, but would become more insistent as time progressed. The cove would fill; water would run almost casually into the tidal pools and slide between the rocks. More would arrive and still more, until the pressure was too much and the lapping wavelets would transform into waves as the estuary swelled with the insistent surge of the incoming tide.

Ten

Chloe

The MacAllisters' attic was very clean and very organised, in the way that everything Aidan touched immediately fell into place: square-edged and clean, right-angled and neat, labelled in big block letters. He had a thing for right angles, Aidan did: the way he folded his clothes, arranged his books, sliced his lemons. Chloe walked slowly past CHRISTMAS DECORATIONS, WINTER COATS and DUVETS; small pieces of furniture, spare china, a set of silver given to them by Aidan's parents that was too fussy for Aidan, who preferred the square cutlery he'd picked out instead. There was a whole slew of boxes filled with old medical books, and there, in the very back corner, a stack labelled CHLOE.

They hadn't lived together before they got married. Things had happened too quickly for them to ease into life together like other couples. A fresh start for both of them, Aidan had said delightedly, arriving at her flat with a set of crisp new boxes, unlike the ragtag collection of bags and crates from the cash and carry that Chloe quickly hid when he came into the lounge. Aidan, too, was crisp, the contours of his face sharp and confident, everything about him clearly defined. He was graceful, too, and tall among the small, shabby rooms that had been perfectly adequate for Danny, Chloe and Owen Archer.

The Archers had been moved through a variety of council flats and had got into the habit of not keeping a lot of stuff. And Aidan was a demon at packing, as Chloe quickly discovered, so the whole moving-out process took less than an afternoon. Aidan didn't linger over things. He didn't exclaim at Chloe's photography portfolio or smile at pictures of her as a little girl, her small face solemn as she held Danny on her lap for a Christmas picture, or clutched his hand at West Wittering beach on a weekend trip they'd won in a raffle. He didn't bat an eye when, with an embarrassed laugh, she produced her father's good suit, which she hadn't been able to throw away because she so clearly remembered the times when it had made an appearance: greeting baby Danny at the hospital; taking them for a meal at their favourite café to celebrate Danny's first day of school; watching Chloe's memorable nativity performance as the chief angel. He just folded everything neatly into those crisp new boxes and carried them up to the attic.

That was where they'd been ever since, and during those heady early years with Aidan, Chloe hadn't felt the need to come back to them once. Instead, she'd surrendered to their fast and furious relationship, the marriage that had come out of the blue for everyone who knew them, and which seemed to bring one new thrill after another, her glorious discovery of what it was like to be in love, and the prospect that she would spend the rest of her life feeling exactly like that, like nothing else she'd ever experienced.

But all through dinner last night, and later, going to bed, Foxy had refused to leave her; had instead needled her with small snatches of memories. The day she'd become *too big* to read with her father and *big enough* to watch Danny when Owen was doing a double shift at work. Looking back, it sometimes seemed that the moment they'd stopped reading Foxy together, her dad had slowly faded from her childhood, the feel of his shirt and the smell of Old Spice replaced by little boy smells, spaghetti hoops heating on the hob and wet clothes drying over the bath. Taking Danny to Oxfam for school shoes. Helping him with his reading. She'd been the one to measure him against the kitchen door, the one who marvelled over trousers that seemed to perpetually shrink as he grew. She'd organised play dates and taken him to football in the park. And eventually, she'd been the one to notice the strange way his eyelid sometimes drooped. How he had trouble with certain words and got tired more easily than other children.

Just a quick look, she told herself now, lifting down the first carton. She put her mobile down next to her – Aidan had lectured her again on her phone usage, although he was obviously torn: while he didn't want her to take any job calls from mysterious men, he expected her to answer his own calls promptly – and opened the lid. A couple of old books; an art project that had won her first prize at primary school; wrapped in newspaper, a shard from her dad's favourite mug, which had broken after he died. It had said something about life handing you lemons, and on the fragment you could still read the words 'make lemonade'. She didn't much like the cheesy optimism, but it reminded her of her dad drinking from it at the tiny fold-down table in their kitchen. There were a couple of letters and one of the three postcards her mum had sent after she left.

At the very bottom, she found *The Grand Adventures of Foxy the Great* by Madeleine and Georgiana Hamilton. The dust jacket had long been lost, but she remembered the thick, creamy paper with a picture of Foxy slinking through the woods, dragging a dead chicken, with a faintly apologetic expression. She flicked past the scrawled inscription on the first page – *For Owen, 1956* – past the half-ripped-off second page that had taken one of Foxy's paws with it, and came to the first story.

There lived, once upon a time, at the very end of the lane, where the world was done, a small brown fox with his best friend.

Tears suddenly blurred the drawing of a tiny bushy-tailed creature pulling Foxy's tail to keep him away from the pie on the windowsill. Stu, the silver squirrel, had been Foxy's sensible shadow. *You're just like Stu*, Danny would say at this point, the two of them sitting on Chloe's bed, her blanket wrapped around them because she couldn't reach the knob at the top of the boiler, which you had to bang when the heating went out. *Always helping people. Keeping them out of trouble.* Well, she hadn't been very good at keeping Danny out of trouble, had she?

She turned her face to the ceiling and blinked, then shut the book quickly, her fingernails scratching across the worn cardboard cover. This was stupid. She should never have come up here. She had other things to focus on, such as the future. Having a baby – Aidan's baby. She'd go out and buy the sparkling grape juice today. She'd tell him tonight. He'd be thrilled. He was an only child; he wanted children, had been talking about getting the two of them checked out, starting to think about it in earnest. *We don't want to run out of time. Because we won't just have one, Chloe, but at least two. One of each, like you and Danny . . .*

She swallowed, touched the cover of the book again, more gently now, stroking the small engraved outline of the squirrel leaning against Foxy's flank, a paw looped around his neck. They were looking up at a smattering of tiny squiggly stars, and their faces, animated in every other drawing, were unusually still, although Foxy's cheeky smile hinted at more mischief to come. How much Danny had loved Foxy. It was the first book he'd read by himself, the book he'd brought Chloe when he was so tired he couldn't hold it on his own any more, the familiar sentences sending him to sleep when he was anxious.

For the first time since she'd stepped out of Dr Webb's office the previous afternoon, Chloe touched her stomach. Tentatively at first, then more boldly, kneading the flat stretch of skin to probe for a sign of life beneath, the way Dr Webb had. What would it be like to read to the baby, sitting on the bed, a blanket around the two of them? *Spot the fox, lovey.* She wouldn't be alone with it, the way she'd been with her brother. She had Aidan now. Aidan, who'd play with the baby and cradle it and wrap it tightly with his love, watching over it, always watching, like he did with

Chloe when they were out at a restaurant, on holiday, running errands together, his eyes fixed on her see-through face. She tried to imagine her husband's expression when the nurse handed the baby to him, the look of joy. But all she could see were his hands. Long-fingered and smooth-skinned, they would be reaching for the tiny body, taking it from the nurse, bringing its face close to his.

With a sudden convulsive movement, Chloe's fingernails dug into her skin and she gasped out loud as her finger hooked painfully behind her pubic bone. The book clattered to the floor and she hunched over, her cheeks wet with tears. When the sound of the phone shrilled through the tidy space she jerked upright.

Eleven

She breathed in, a deep, juddery breath so Aidan wouldn't think anything amiss, then snatched up the phone.

'Chloe MacAllister speaking.'

She made her voice as calm and confident as she could. Even when it was only him calling, Aidan liked her to say her name properly, not like any old hoyden, rushed off her feet.

'I'm very glad I caught you, Mrs MacAllister. You're not an easy person to get hold of.'

'Er, excuse me?' Chloe cleared her throat.

'Matt Cooper. Wonderly Books.' His voice was brusque. 'I'd like to ask you to reconsider taking on the Hamilton project.'

'I can't,' Chloe said, wiping her cheeks with her cardigan and slowly taking her hand away from her belly, smoothing down her shirt. 'I'm very sorry.'

'Upper body, soft contours, bookshelves, that sort of thing,' Matt Cooper said, as if she hadn't spoken. 'Nothing fancy, very simple. Looking stark, artistic. You'll know what to do.'

'Mr Cooper,' Chloe said a little louder. 'I'm sorry, I can't. And how did you get my number anyway?'

'Liz Tallis, of course,' he said, as if it was ludicrous she hadn't known. 'Old school mate of mine.'

'But isn't Liz in America?' Chloe asked, trying to remember the exact wording of last Christmas's card, which had mentioned setting up atrium displays for a bank chain across the East Coast. *Bankers! Probably the only art they'll come across in their lifetime.*

'Yep. Told me to call you, and in no uncertain terms, might I add. Always was a bully, that woman.'

Chloe suppressed an incredulous laugh, because, even two minutes into the conversation, it was hard to imagine two people more suited than snappy Liz Tallis and this rather tetchy-sounding man.

'Wasn't sure she'd given me the right number to begin with,' he said accusingly. 'You really should have your phone looked at; makes all sorts of funny noises. But thankfully it wasn't hard to find your husband. And I'm glad, because we're in a bit of a bind, actually, and Liz said you'd definitely be available.'

Chloe, who had found herself nodding, swept along by the man's energy, forced herself to focus. 'I'm sorry, I can't,' she said again, regretfully.

'Why?'

The fact that he was finally paying attention caught her off guard, and she paused for a second.

'Because . . . well, for one, I haven't worked in two years, and for another, I live all the way down in Plymouth. Surely there must be other, more suitable people you can ask?'

She stood up and put the shoebox back into the carton, carefully lining it up with the rest of the stack.

'It's close to you, somewhere along the south coast.'

'The south coast is hundreds of miles long,' Chloe pointed out.

Matt Cooper exhaled impatiently. 'Goodness, Liz didn't mention how difficult you are. Somewhere around Truro. Silliest address, too. Summerhill. The End of the Lane. Can you believe it?'

For the first time that morning, Chloe felt something inside her lighten. 'That's Foxy's address.'

'It is?' Matt Cooper sounded sceptical.

'Yes. *At the very end of the lane, where the world was done.* First page. You should know that, shouldn't you?'

'Aha!' To her great surprise, Matt Cooper gave a laugh. 'Good on you, girl. And funny. You're right, of course. They made her add a proper postcode sometime in the sixties, you know. It's all in the files. In any case,' he was back to barking, 'I told your husband all of this yesterday. The only photo we have of her—'

'So just one of them?' Chloe frowned into the phone. 'I wasn't sure yesterday, when my husband— is it Georgiana or Madeleine?'

'Has anyone ever told you that interrupting people is one of the cardinal sins? Georgiana Hamilton passed away years ago; the only shot we have of Madeleine by herself she's wearing some hideous seventies garb, and even then you can't see her face properly. She doesn't like having her picture taken, doesn't go out and about much at all. Who doesn't like having their picture taken?'

'Take it from me, loads of people,' Chloe said, surprising herself by laughing out loud.

'Silliest thing,' Matt Cooper said disapprovingly. 'Making it difficult for everyone else. She's amazingly good at working that recluse angle, I'll give her that. It's nigh on impossible to get hold of her. So we're desperate for something a tad, shall we say, more up to date so we can announce her new book, start whipping up excitement—'

'A new book?' Chloe said, her hand closing around the spine of *Foxy the Great*, which she'd been about to slide back into the top of the box. 'Whizzy or Pipper?'

'O-ho!' Matt Cooper's voice had taken on a distinctly thrilled timbre. 'You *are* a fan. Well, well, just think, wouldn't it be something to meet the author in person, sit down for a chat about her new book, take her out in the gardens, click click, and you're done. And don't feed me any nonsense about your lack of talent. I've seen your pictures.'

'You have?' Chloe frowned again. 'I didn't think anyone'd ever seen my pictures.'

'Tsk tsk, self-pity, the scourge of the artist. Best rid yourself of it now while you're still young. I'm talking about that award, the old people's home in Exeter, the faces.'

'That was a little local exhibition in aid of an Alzheimer's charity,' she said guardedly. 'It just so happened that the woman in charge put me up for the West's Best Newcomer award.'

'And well deserved, too: they were brilliant. A little less tortured with this one, please, and more fine-boned creativity, and *voilà*, you're done. Listen.' Matt Cooper must have leaned into the phone, because his voice came closer. 'I deal with artistic egos every day. Too many of them, to be honest; you'd think the whole world's gone soft, needs everything dipped in fairy sugar.'

'I'm sure *you* have never dipped anything in fairy sugar,' Chloe said acidly. 'And I certainly don't need things dipped in it.'

'Well, fabulous, then shall we speak plainly?'

'Because we haven't been so far.' Chloe rolled her eyes.

'Exactly. And no more nonsense about not being able to do it. I want you. And I'm used to getting what I want.' He barked a short laugh. 'Just so you know, Liz sounded positively jealous that she wasn't able to take it on . . .' He let the words hang there for a moment, then continued. 'Just get down there and give it a try. All I'm asking. We'll pay you well, you get up close and personal with your Foxy, we get our picture. Happiness all round.'

Chloe didn't say anything, and, astonishingly, Matt Cooper didn't either. She could hear him breathing at the other end of the line, the occasional *brrring* of a phone in his offices. Studying the five boxes that encapsulated her old life, she thought about the equipment nestling somewhere inside: her tripod, her one precious long lens that she'd had to work nights at the cash and carry to pay for, the camera bag she'd fashioned out of her father's old leather lunch bag, padding it with soft foam until it cradled her Nikon exactly the way she wanted it to. Maybe it would—

'Chloe? Darling!'

She frowned at the phone and was about to chide Matt Cooper for taking unwarranted liberties when she realised that the voice was coming from below her.

'Chloe? Are you here?' Aidan was closer now. Any moment now he'd be at the top of the stairs, see the ladder.

Perhaps Matt Cooper had heard him too, because he said, not impatiently at all, but quite gently, 'Come, Mrs MacAllister, you'll be wonderful.'

'Darling! Where on earth *are* you?'

Aidan was so close now. He was always close. Sometimes it was hard to see where he stopped and she began.

'I'll do it,' she said suddenly.

'Excellent,' Matt Cooper said approvingly. 'I'll call—'

'No, *I* will call *you*,' she said ferociously, and hung up before he could say anything else. She closed the box on Foxy's face and slid the phone into her back pocket just as Aidan's hand appeared, long-fingered and smooth-skinned, groping for traction at the top of the ladder.

Twelve

Chloe didn't say anything to Aidan, telling herself that it would be exactly as Matt Cooper had said: pop by, click click, leave, done. It would be over before it had even really started and it wasn't something she needed to worry Aidan with. He did worry about her, he said it all the time. And she didn't need to be out there any more, wasn't that the brilliance of it all, wasn't that why he was working so hard, so that she could just stay at home? Worrying him would be entirely disproportionate to what this was, a quick dash along the coast that she'd agreed to for some ungodly reason and which would take less than a day. Less than half a day.

Then followed the patchwork of small but necessary lies: an unarguable and long-overdue errand so that Aidan agreed to leave the Vauxhall for her on Monday, which she'd picked because it was his full day at the hospital, from which he rarely returned before seven. Complaining about the patchy reception on her mobile so he wouldn't think anything amiss when he tried to call her and she didn't answer. She might take it into the O2 shop, didn't he think?

Only two things kept her going: the prospect of meeting Madeleine Hamilton, and Liz Tallis. The knowledge that Liz had talked about her, praised her to the extent that Matt Cooper wanted her despite her reluctance and obvious inexperience – that fact was like a small, warm presence at the back of her mind, a tiny tether to the old Chloe, the one that had been packed away with the boxes two years ago.

Still, by the time she'd retrieved everything she needed from the attic, along with her copy of *Foxy the Great*, just for luck, and was lugging her equipment out to the garage, nausea was chasing her mounting anxiety furiously round her stomach. And then came the dawning realisation that although she'd driven in Plymouth before, she hadn't really ventured out into the countryside. What with Aidan's aversion to public transport, Chloe had had driving lessons after they got married, but he preferred to drive himself when they were out and about. And he would never let her touch their second car, a vintage Porsche, in which he loved whizzing Chloe around at the weekends.

Eyeing the Vauxhall warily, she loaded up her gear, then stood, her forehead braced against the frame, willing her stomach to calm down. Dimly she felt her phone buzz in her back pocket and fumbled for it, hitching a smile onto her face for her husband's call.

'Wanted to wish you good luck,' said a gravelly voice at the other end. 'Call me and let me know how it goes.'

'Oh, it's you.' Chloe cleared her throat hard, swallowing down a surge of acid. 'So . . .' she said tentatively.

'No,' he said.

'No what?'

'No, you're not going to tell me you won't do it,' he said cheerfully.

'I can if I want to, you know,' she said mulishly. 'But—'

'But thank God, you're a professional and you'll be brilliant.'

'Of course,' Chloe said through gritted teeth.

'And if you see any evidence of the new book,' Matt Cooper said, 'take a sneaky picture for us.' He paused, then added, more quickly now – and, Chloe was pleased to notice, slightly less in command of the situation – 'To be honest, we're waiting for Mrs Hamilton to deliver, well, anything really in the way of material.'

'What do you mean?' Chloe frowned.

'Let's just say the book's been scheduled but details have been scant so far. Ah, heck, we're in it together now, so I might as well come clean. It's supposed to be finished already, but we haven't seen a single scrap of it. So . . .' He paused meaningfully. 'Should you see a heap of drawings lying around, make up some excuse to take a picture of them. Or maybe get her to talk about the new book. You sound as if you're pretty good with old ladies. Sort of softly spoken. Unintimidating.'

'In other words, a wimp?' she said incredulously. 'And you're asking me to *spy* for you? What do you want me to do, send her out of the room so I can start taking pictures of her sketch-book? We're talking about Madeleine Hamilton here, I'm not going to—'

'Don't be stroppy now,' he said soothingly. 'It was Liz who mentioned that old ladies were your speciality. And no one said anything about spying. Just walk through the house with your eyes open. Say you're scouting locations and such. And anything you see, you simply let me know. Good luck.'

She mouthed wordlessly, but he'd hung up before she could say anything else. Still fuming, she ripped open the door of the Vauxhall, plopped herself down into the driver's seat and jammed the keys into the ignition, daring the world outside Plymouth's city limits to defy her.

The narrow lane cut through a densely wooded tunnel, where the air seemed to stand still beneath branches touching above, and moss, tall grasses and ferns grew as high as her car windows. Chloe's heart was still pounding from a terrifying drive along the busy dual carriageways, most of which she spent chanting her driving instructor's advice, and she was glad to slow down now, gripping the steering wheel hard as she squinted through the green half-light for the enormous rusty gates that Matt Cooper had said would be open for her. Beyond them, the trees thinned out. She emerged onto a courtyard and came to a bumpy stop that would have had her driving instructor fainting in the passenger seat.

Taking a deep breath, she closed the car door behind her. So this was famous Madeleine Hamilton's home. Woods and gardens grew right up to it, only reluctantly sparing the house, which looked as if it had become tired of fending off nature and had taken a few steps backwards. It was a bit shabby, with slates missing on the roof, a broken window in the top floor on the left, and some of the shutters seemingly hanging on by a single screw. But it was compact and sturdy, too, and cheerful somehow, with its sandy-coloured stone and tall windows sparkling with reflections of sky and clouds and sun. Cradling her camera, Chloe looked around her.

There was something about the house, actually, something oddly familiar. She'd never been here before, and yet it tugged at the edges of her mind, this strange something. The low trellised garden gate with the tangle of honeysuckle above. The pattern scratched into the heavy wood of the front door. Her mind supplied other images that were only in her memory: bottle-green wellies next to the kitchen range, the funny little outhouse with the heart in the door, washing flapping on a line. She felt a small lump in her throat. Of course. This was Foxy's world. A watercolour world of greens and browns and sandy gold that had once belonged to her and Danny. She closed her eyes and breathed deeply to smell the breeze, fresh and earthy, a hint of salt. The trees behind her whispered and rustled, swaying in the wind—

'Are you going to stand there all day?'

Chloe started so violently that she collided with the sharp edge of the still-open car door. Clutching her side, she tried to locate the source of the voice.

'The door is open.' The voice spoke again, and this time Chloe realised that it had come from behind one of the tall windows. With the sun beaming straight on them, the inside was obscured, but when she squinted, she thought she saw someone sitting there. She tensed slightly when she realised that the person had been watching her, presumably since the moment she'd arrived.

'Of course.' She retrieved the small case that held her gear from the passenger seat and quickly crossed the last few paces to the front door, half expecting it to open with a grinding gothic squeak. But it swung easily on its hinges, and before she knew it, Chloe was standing in the front hall, blessedly cool and shadowy after the brightness outside, and turning towards the room where Madeleine Hamilton, famous creator of Whizzy Witch and Pipper the Dog, sat in a high-backed armchair.

Thirteen

After the staccato commands through the window, Chloe expected a testy sort of welcome, but Madeleine Hamilton remained silent as her visitor made her way past an enormous desk and through a phalanx of low armchairs and sofas, coming to a stop in front of her. Even then, she didn't say anything as Chloe towered awkwardly above her.

'I'm Chloe MacAllister.' Chloe finally thrust out her hand, involuntarily dropping her case on the ground with a loud clang.

Madeleine nodded. 'Welcome to Summerhill.' She cleared her throat and raised her left hand, and Chloe had already taken it when she noticed the woman's other hand, the wrist bent at a slight but distinctly odd angle, the hand curled around itself on the arm of the chair. She would have done anything to take back her audible gasp when she saw the expression on Madeleine's face.

'An accident. When I was a girl,' the old woman said abruptly.

'But how can you . . . work like that?' Chloe forced her eyes away from the clawed hand. 'Draw, I mean?'

'I'm left-handed,' Madeleine said evenly. 'Luckily for me.' *Not that it's any of your business* hung heavy in the air, and Chloe blushed crimson.

'I am, too,' she said inconsequentially.

Madeleine allowed the silence to grow until even the house seemed to momentarily hold its breath. Chloe forced herself to look away, starting when she caught sight of her own face in one of the long-mirrored panels opposite: bright flashes of copper and auburn framing a pale, thin face with anxious eyes. She looked about fifteen years old and not remotely in command of this job.

'So, about this photo,' Madeleine Hamilton suddenly said, as if she'd read Chloe's mind. 'I don't see why it's necessary at all. However, the publisher said there is some urgency, so I suppose we should get on with it.'

'Yes, of course, I'm sorry.' Chloe stepped away and fumbled for her camera, suddenly embarrassed by her dad's leather lunch bag, which grew even shabbier under Madeleine Hamilton's inscrutable gaze. Her precious lens started to slide out, and she caught it at the last moment, half dropping to her knees in the process.

'Now, where best to place you?' she said, her voice high with clumsiness as she started wrestling with the tripod. Madeleine didn't offer a suggestion. She clearly didn't want anyone here, let alone doing something as intrusive as taking a picture. Resisting with difficulty the urge to kick the tripod legs into obedience, Chloe ended up leaving it there like a gigantic three-legged spider, and started pacing the room, ostensibly to look for a location but really to try and pull herself together.

They were in what had to be the library, because the walls were lined with shelves of books and ledgers. There wasn't much in the way of drawing equipment, except for a sketchpad on a long, low sideboard by the window, brand-new-looking, and a handful of pencils so firmly wedged inside an elastic band that they clearly hadn't been used in a while. Maybe Madeleine worked elsewhere, Chloe thought as she turned towards a pair of wide sliding doors opening into an enormous second room that disappeared towards the back of the house. The walls were dark, the wallpaper faded and torn in places, the cornicing crumbling or missing. She could make out a half-open wardrobe, and further back, the curve of a heavy wooden bed frame.

'Get them in a familiar environment,' Liz Tallis had always said. 'Fade away and make it about *them*. And then just go with it.'

So, just bloody go with it, you idiot, Chloe told herself. *Do something. Anything at all.*

'The best spot will be here.' She came to a stop next to one of the windows. 'If we hurry, we can use the light from that window there. And a chair, but not . . .' She glanced at the purple armchair, which made Madeleine look like an embroidered cushion, then pointed decisively at the desk chair. 'That one.'

It felt good to make decisions, and the chair was beautiful: old and masculine, with a simple curve to the armrests that would support Madeleine's arms and hide her hand. Without waiting for her answer, Chloe dragged it across the floor, then busied herself with her camera to give the old lady time to swap seats, lower herself onto the chair. She still didn't say anything and Chloe didn't waste her breath. Portraits were hard, because nothing else distracted from the main focus of the image. You only had a few bones, a pair of eyes, temples, cheeks, a mouth, and all had to be set at just the right position, the perfect angle of the light.

Chloe scanned the face across from her through the viewfinder. Madeleine Hamilton had clearly been beautiful once, her features framing a pair of eyes a startling sherry gold, like liquid amber. She was still striking, although her face was now covered in a web of lines and her body curved a little awkwardly to the right, clearly accustomed to working around the useless wrist. But if you looked only at her eyes, the colour changing in the light, she could be any age at all. They needed to be the centre, really; if she got those right, then everything else would fall into place around them.

'Mrs MacAllister?' Madeleine Hamilton said.

Chloe started at the sound of the name and resisted looking over her shoulder. The errands-and-patchy-reception story would hold Aidan off for a little while longer but he would have tried to call. Quickly, she bent down to the camera again.

Her heart moved steadily up into her throat as she started clicking the shutter. The older woman sat in her chair, still and unsmiling.

'Lift your head,' Chloe said, trying to sound authoritative and wincing at her own presumption at the same time. 'And look over there?'

It was probably only thirty minutes, forty-five at the most, but to Chloe it felt as if time seeped across a morass of syrup. Madeleine Hamilton moved her shoulders three millimetres to the left, dropped her chin and lifted her chin, looked left and right and straight at the camera, mouth open, mouth closed. Chloe adjusted the angles and heights, sweaty hands fiddling unseeingly with settings, straining to remember Liz Tallis's imperious voice issuing commands, and forgetting everything she'd ever known about photography altogether.

'I'm sorry,' she said desperately as she moved towards the woman again, motioning at her hands. 'Could you . . .'

Madeleine set her right hand on the armrest, then put her other one on top of it, perhaps wishing to hide it.

'No,' Chloe said. 'Not like that . . .' But neither did she know how exactly it should be. She stood back and looked down at her Nikon, which had once been so much part of her and now seemed to have deserted her altogether, and horribly, awfully, she felt tears springing into her eyes. She bit down hard on the inside of her cheek, almost glad when the pain distracted her. Aidan had been right. She was useless at this, she should never have—

'Mrs MacAllister?'

'Please,' she said roughly without looking up, 'please, will you just call me Chloe?'

It came out a lot more abruptly than she'd meant it to, and Madeleine blinked.

'Yes,' she said after a moment. 'Yes. Of course.'

'I'm sorry.' Chloe looked around for her camera bag, squeezing her eyes shut because she'd rather die than cry now. 'It's just, my husband, he's waiting for me . . . I don't have a whole lot of time and—'

'Chloe.' Madeleine Hamilton's voice was surprisingly gentle. 'Why don't we try a prop of some kind? A book, maybe? Or pen and paper? It might help. With the hand, I mean.'

'It's not your hand, it's me, I don't think I'm right for this . . .' Chloe choked out, untying the bag.

'Nonsense,' Madeleine Hamilton said firmly, and her good hand came up to tug the empty camera bag out of Chloe's grip. 'The light'll be here for another hour or so. I should know, I sit here all day long. Get a book and we'll try again.'

'All right,' Chloe said after a small pause. 'One of those?' She pointed to the shelves next to her.

'Whatever you like.' Madeleine nodded encouragingly.

'*Understanding Architectural Defects*?' Chloe read out loud. '*Construction and Surveying*?'

'Gracious. Perhaps not quite.' Madeleine gave a soft chuckle and Chloe smiled, her breath coming more easily, the push of tears receding.

'*Reinforced Structural Design*?' she continued, and Madeleine laughed.

'Those were my father's books. He was a great one for tinkering. Laid a lot of the electricity to the house. Made sure we had proper lavatories, too, ahead of all the other old piles in the county. Most of them worked as well, I'll have you know. Half the time anyway,' she added with another small laugh.

Chloe had to walk all the way along the shelves, dismissing the heavy leather spines and metal-plated tomes, before she spied something smaller, less intimidating. A notebook bound in faded green linen. She pulled it out and it obligingly fell open at one of the inner hinges. She gasped.

'More scintillating engineering marvels?' Madeleine said from the window. 'I always meant to have a clear-out, but obviously these days . . .'

'No,' Chloe said, staring down at the book disbelievingly, a huge smile breaking out across her face. The faint hint of Old Spice, the hum of her father's voice. Danny's little-boy laugh, bright and chirpy inside a blanket cocoon. 'It's Foxy.'

Fourteen

It was Foxy indeed. Sketches and studies of pointy ears and bushy whiskers, a long tail peeking out from behind a chicken coop. There were early spreads of the stories Chloe knew so well, pictures of Foxy being locked into the outhouse, one baleful eye peeking through the heart cut in the door. Stealing sausages, falling into the rainwater barrel, and befriending the young hedgehog at the bottom of the woods despite the fact that their families were at war. And other images, too. Faces and hands. Tree trunks in shadow and light, a wall of symmetrical shapes. Ants on a leaf, spidery with bright-green veins—

'What do you mean, Foxy?' The old lady's voice cut sharply into her rapture.

'Look!' Chloe was across the room in two paces. 'This should be in the photograph; it's where it all started after all.'

To her surprise, Madeleine didn't take the notebook from her.

'Where did you find that?' she said in a slightly strangled voice. 'I haven't seen that old thing in decades.'

'Right next to all your father's books.' Chloe was smiling at a trail of tiny feathers across two pages. 'My brother and I loved him best,' she said suddenly. 'Of all your books. I even— I brought the book with me today.' She flicked a glance at her suitcase, then back at Madeleine. 'Why didn't you . . . I mean, why didn't you write anything else about Foxy? We used to look sometimes for a second book, but it never came. He deserved it.'

Madeleine looked at the sketchbook in Chloe's hand for a long moment.

'Foxy was born before the war. He was part of Summerhill,

and when we published his stories – mostly because we were desperate for money, to be honest – I was surprised, actually, that people liked him so much. Maybe it was his innocence and exuberance, this small, idyllic place where nothing ever changed, where everything was still the way people remembered from before the war, before all the loss and pain and death.'

The light settled into the fine lines around her mouth, giving her a distant glow and hiding her eyes so that her voice sounded disembodied and strangely far away. For a moment it seemed as if she'd forgotten Chloe altogether.

'But he was part of a dying world; I had to face up to that. Whizzy was more adventurous, more modern, she could grow with the times. Pipper too, so they kept coming back. My husband was like you, though, he liked Foxy best. And I'm glad you remember him. Not many people do these days.'

Her smile faded into a half-grimace before she straightened and, with an obvious effort, pulled herself back into the moment. Deftly plucking the green sketchbook from Chloe's hands, she leaned over the armrest and set it on the sideboard, out of sight behind her sketchpad, as if to preclude any further requests for Foxy to return from the past.

'I'm sorry,' Chloe said. 'I didn't mean to pry. It's just . . . it's fascinating to see how it all started. Wait, something fell out.' She bent to pick up a piece of paper that had landed on the floor beside the chair. 'Oh, it's you.'

It was. And it wasn't. The features were clearly the same, as were the eyes, but the rest of it seemed from a different age entirely. Madeleine, no more than fifteen or sixteen, was sitting at a table with another young woman, who had her hand lifted, perhaps to emphasise a point, because she was smiling, her mouth open in mid-sentence. Teacups and a half-eaten cake sat before them, and if you looked very closely, you could see a tiny mouse delightedly making off with a large crumb in the bottom corner of the sketch.

‘This is your sister?’ The paper matched the notebook, but it must have been sliced out of it a long while ago, because the edges were curling up slightly.

Madeleine took a moment to straighten, but she didn’t take the piece of paper from Chloe’s outstretched hand. ‘Yes,’ she said finally. ‘That’s Georgiana.’

‘She’s beautiful.’ Chloe studied the picture closely.

‘She rarely sat still long enough for me to draw her. And she’d changed her hair, her clothes after coming back from Europe, literally three days before the war started.’ Madeleine nodded at the picture. ‘I was still getting used to it; she looked so different. The way her hair swung over her face, and that front part just wouldn’t stay.’

‘What was she like?’ Chloe touched the pencil strokes that had captured the woman’s nose with just a few perfect angles, the face with its slightly shortened upper lip that lent her smile a mischievous air.

‘A force of nature.’ Madeleine gave Chloe a half-smile. ‘Aunt Marjorie, my mother’s sister, had moved in after my father died to be in charge of us. She did so very reluctantly, I have to say, hated how remote it all was, my father’s strange inventions, the wet and wild winters on the coast. But she felt it was the proper thing to do. Summerhill orphans, that’s what they called us across the county. I didn’t care, because that’s what we were after all, and as long as everyone left us in peace, I was fine with it. But Georgiana didn’t like it one bit. Said it made us sound pathetic and helpless when we were getting on with things just fine.’ Madeleine made a brief sound that might have passed for laughter. ‘Oh listen to me, how maudlin I am.’

‘Not at all,’ Chloe set the picture on a low table behind the armchair, next to her case. ‘And I’m sorry about your parents.’

‘Don’t be. I had Georgiana, after all. From the time I was a baby, she was the only mother I ever knew.’

Her body was perfectly still, and yet Chloe could feel her pulling away, as if she regretted saying too much, until her face closed altogether, the earlier flash of humour gone, her eyes unreadable. Without thinking, Chloe bent forward and touched her hand, a real touch, not the awkward, hesitant prodding from before, one that was meant to bring her back from wherever she'd gone.

'My brother Danny and I, we were like that too,' she said, feeling the papery skin beneath her fingers, the thin bones on the back of Madeleine's hand. 'Torquay orphans, I guess you might say,' she grimaced, 'because my dad worked so much he was hardly ever around properly, until he had a heart attack. A year earlier and they'd have taken Danny away from me, put him into care, but luckily he was old enough to continue living with me.'

'I'm sorry—'

'Don't be,' Chloe cut in quickly, her voice an unconscious echo of Madeleine's, because she suddenly didn't want to talk about it either. Her fingertips twitched, but Madeleine turned her hand and clasped Chloe's.

'And Foxy?' she asked.

'We had a toy fox when we were little, actually.' Chloe smiled. 'In his honour. Danny christened him Cuppy.'

'Cuppy. I like that.' The old lady settled back in her chair, not letting go of Chloe's hand. 'What happened to him?'

Chloe strained to picture the saggy little fox, who'd been so worn at the end that you could hear the Styrofoam pearls rattle inside, bald patches across his back where his fur had been the softest.

'One of the girls from school came home with me one day,' Chloe said. 'He broke.'

It probably hadn't been Lou's fault. Cuppy had been cheap and he was soft with age, but Chloe rarely had anyone over and

Lou had initiated some kind of energetic game. She was older – a bold strap of a girl, her father had called her – and Cuppy had at some point simply capitulated, with a soft sigh of fabric, shedding Styrofoam pearls everywhere. Lou had stopped only briefly to exclaim about the mess, and then gone on with the game. Chloe hadn't dared cry in case Lou spread the news of her childishness at school, but at that moment she felt as if she herself had capitulated too, with a sigh and a spilling of her insides.

'It was nothing,' she added quickly when she realised that Madeleine was still waiting. 'Although Danny was devastated. He insisted we bury him properly, in one of the planters along the front window. We decorated a box and I made a little gravestone from papier mâché.'

She made a sound at the back of her throat, not unlike the one that Madeleine had made earlier, the laugh-that-wasn't-a-laugh kind of sound.

'It's rarely nothing,' the old lady said quietly.

Chloe nodded, but when she glanced at the clock, she started.

'Oh, look at the time. I have to go.' She pulled her hand from Madeleine's grasp, and this time the older woman let her go. But their touch lingered, echoing all the tiny points of contact that had sprung up between the two of them, like a children's dot-to-dot. Summerhill. Foxy. Georgiana. Danny. Madeleine, Chloe.

Chloe stowed the reflector, her light meter and spare batteries with quick, automatic movements, her eyes straying back to the drawing of the two girls. Maybe it was the house, she thought, this hidden, tucked-away place *where the world was done*, which funnelled them all into a strange sense of timelessness, of parallel lives where a little girl drew foxes and told stories with her sister, which, decades later, another other little girl would read to her brother as she tucked him into bed. Without pausing to think, without even questioning what she was about to do, she picked up the sketch and slid it carefully between the reflector and the copy of *Foxy the Great* in her bag, before straightening – a little guiltily, but it was too late to do anything about it now – to say goodbye.

The sun had moved past the window and Madeleine looked oddly small in the vast room, which in turn seemed more desolate than before, with its dusty curtains, the fireplace towering on the back wall. Chloe imagined the evening lying ahead, Madeleine sitting here until darkness had fallen, then laboriously getting up and making her way to bed. Imagined her own evening: going back to her minimalist white home to sit under the bright beam of Aidan's attention and field a conversation about her day. About the baby.

She suddenly had the strangest feeling that the house was pulling at her, trying to stop her from leaving and instead sit with Madeleine and talk.

'I'll come back,' she said hesitantly. 'Tomorrow, if I can; we'll try and take some more pictures. If you like, that is.'

Madeleine's smile flashed briefly through the gloom. 'Yes,' she said. 'Please do.'

Outside, Chloe sat for a moment in her car, looking back at the house. The sun came slanting across the treetops behind her. It was hot still, a heavy, felty heat that was only occasionally broken by the sea breeze playing through the overgrown gardens. Slowly she unzipped the case, slipped out *Foxy the Great* and the drawing. Orphans, Madeleine had said, and yet the two girls in the picture didn't look like they'd needed anyone else to make them complete, so close were they sitting, a tangle of limbs that made it almost impossible to see where one began and the other ended. Their shoulders were touching and Georgiana's hand was curled around Madeleine's arm, the now-lopsided wrist still straight and strong. Chloe felt a sudden sting at the sight of them, a sharp, take-your-breath-away pain at the closeness of their pose, the intimacy of their smiles, and when she cautiously probed into the nature of that sting, she realised it was envy. She swallowed hard and started the car, leaving the drawing on the passenger seat next to her.

It was only just gone four. She still had time for one more stop.

Fifteen

'Hello?' Chloe peeked around the door. The hunched figure in the chair turned his head with some difficulty, then, eyes brightening, slowly touched a series of buttons that swung the wheelchair around.

'Chloe!' It came out awkwardly – more like 'Shlowee' – but the joy in his voice was unmistakable.

'Hi, Danny.' Chloe's heart gave a fierce, hard squeeze, the way it always did when she saw the left hand lying immobile and useless along the arm of the wheelchair, the feet, socked and shod, arranged on the footboard, and she raked her eyes over him furtively to scan for any changes since the last time she'd seen him.

'Not 'specting you,' he said with his big lopsided grin. 'Lovely.'

'I had a spare moment and the car. I wanted to see you,' she said. She bent to hug him, suddenly desperate to feel him properly: not the lifeless arms and crooked shoulders he had now, but the way he used to be, stocky and hard-muscled from physical therapy and endless weight-training exercises that had been meant to keep all *this* at bay.

He couldn't lift his arms to hug her back, but he leaned his face against hers for a moment.

'Hey,' he said softly. 'Tsematter?'

She disentangled herself and dropped into the chair next to his bed, rubbing her cheeks and laughing slightly self-consciously.

'Someone giving you grief?' He spoke slowly, trying to enunciate the way the speech therapist had taught him all those years ago. ''F I wanted to, could still take 'em, y'know.' He lifted his fingers and wriggled them about on the armrest. She laughed obediently.

'No, of course not,' she said quickly, taking a deep breath. 'No grief at all. I'm completely fine. And you? I see they've cut your hair?'

'Yep. Good?'

'I love it,' she said, although she'd have left it a little bit longer than the hairdresser had chosen to do it. 'Dashing as always.'

They used to think Danny was clumsy. Or lazy maybe, because he was forever tripping over, and his legs were black and blue with bruises.

'Just try to pick up your feet a little higher, darling,' Chloe would say worriedly, sitting him on the bed and patching up his skinned shins yet again.

'But I have wobbly knees,' he'd say in a puzzled way, looking down at them stretched out across Chloe's lap. 'And then sometimes they're gone altogether. Maybe I'm just tired, Chlo, like Dad always is.'

They didn't think anything of it, nor that he didn't seem to like chewing hard food and that his handwriting was so abysmal his teacher sent a note home with him every other day for an entire year. Chloe had gone to talk to her about it, promising she'd practise with Danny, and she did. But the wobbly knees often seemed to extend to his hands, making the pencil slip, and sometimes his lips slowed down, causing him to slur. Chloe would anxiously describe all these things to their GP, but it would be another year or two before Danny was finally diagnosed with a severe progressive neurological disorder, and yet more time until his illness was specified as something called Friedreich's ataxia.

Their father hadn't known what to do about it at all, he who'd never been sick a single day and who now had a boy with mysteriously disobeying muscles and nerves to take care of. He'd shepherded Danny through the medical system as best he could, but working as a mechanic in a difficult economic climate meant that it was mostly Chloe who waited for tests to be done in doctors' offices, who sat by the phone for results to come in, who helped Danny up and down the stairs until the council moved them to a ground-floor flat. She read to him when he found it tiring to hold a book, chatted with him when he woke in the middle of the night in a panic that this was now how it was going to be, trying not to panic herself when she noticed his lips drooping and his feet turning inward.

The illness was different for everyone, but there was one common denominator: there was no cure and no reversal. The most you could hope for was treatment of symptoms and a slow progression, possibly over decades, but 'Don't get your hopes up, darling,' Aidan often said warningly. 'When the onset is as early as your brother's, it's usually fast. There's very little—'

—Hope, yes. She'd been told the same thing many times, by doctors, nurses, therapists. And part of her knew it, of course, the rational part that had followed the test results for seventeen years. But there was also another part, deep inside her, that had never once stopped hoping that things would change, that the old Danny would come back to her one day, bright-eyed and laughing, miraculously and unexpectedly well again.

'Guess what? I had a job today,' she now said with determined cheerfulness. 'Remember Foxy?'

'Cuppy.' He nodded with a lopsided grin.

'I took pictures of the author today. You'd really like her. I saw her drawings, too, so lovely . . .'

'Can I see?' Danny flicked his eyes to Chloe's camera, which she hadn't wanted to leave in the car.

'I'll show you next time. I hope they're good, or Matt Cooper, the publisher who hired me, will come down here and cause a ruckus. He practically bullied me into going.'

'Good!' Danny said emphatically. 'Like him already.'

'There's nothing to like,' Chloe said mulishly. 'He's unspeakable.'

'Picture will be beautiful. Always are.' Danny nodded at his wall, where Chloe had hung two photos: one of him aged seven, flying high on the swings at the park, and one that Liz Tallis had taken when Chloe had brought Danny along to a job at a gallery in Bristol because she thought he could do with an outing.

Liz had been charmed by Danny, unexpectedly so, because she worked hard at being difficult to charm, and had insisted on taking some photos of the Archer siblings before the opening of the exhibition. She'd taken her time, too, deliberated over how to pose Danny, not in his wheelchair, but sitting on one of the gallery benches, waiting patiently for him to pull himself straight whenever he started sliding, and making them dissolve in helpless laughter with her acerbic comments about the artistic feats hanging on the walls around them. Chloe hadn't been able to stop smiling when she saw the final shots, the two of them so lively, so bright that they almost seemed to leap off the paper. 'You're magic,' she had said to Liz, who'd smiled uncharacteristically kindly and patted her arm. And almost as if Liz had known it would happen, shortly after that photo, Danny's condition had started worsening, making him hunch over, and he hadn't wanted to have his picture taken again.

'Tell me,' he said now.

'What?'

'Chloe, c'mon.'

He had to concentrate, but her name came out almost perfectly and she smiled. He didn't smile back, though, just kept his eyes on her. Maybe it was because the rest of him was so still, so unmoving, or maybe because it was one of the few things he could still do, but Danny's eyes always looked at you properly, focusing with a clear gaze that didn't seem to miss a thing.

Involuntarily, her hands slid up from her thighs, her thumb touching the base of her stomach. She thought about telling him, *how amazing, Danny, you'll be an uncle, just think!* She even opened her mouth to do it, but then closed it again. It was early days still. She would wait, just until it was certain . . .

'Aidan?' Danny's voice cut into her thoughts so abruptly that she flinched. He narrowed his eyes but didn't say any more. Danny wasn't so keen on Aidan, Chloe knew that, but she had decided early on that if she wasn't going to let her relationship with Danny be changed by her marriage to Aidan, then she wouldn't let Danny comment on her husband either. It wouldn't be fair. There had been one occasion, right after she'd met Aidan, when she'd lost her temper, had shouted at her brother that she needed Aidan in her life, that she just wanted to be happy and what was so bloody wrong with that. It had come completely out of nowhere and she had apologised immediately, but Danny had never mentioned his feelings about Aidan ever again.

'Aidan is doing great.' She fixed a cheerful expression on her face. 'He's about to hire a new doctor. Says he wants to be home more. He wants us to spend more time together.'

''S'that so?' Danny frowned and pushed his fingertips so hard into the armrest of the wheelchair that she could see his knuckles turning white.

'It'll be great,' said Chloe, who'd been avoiding thinking about it altogether. 'It does get,' she cast around for something positive to say, 'quiet in the house sometimes.'

Another pause fell.

'Wish I could be there.' Danny's eyes had gone a flat blue, and he pushed out the next two words with some effort. 'I wish . . .'

'I wish that too,' Chloe said, 'so much. Maybe one day you will be.'

His eyes softened at that, shimmering strangely in the light from the lamp on the side table. He made a small movement with his head, and all of a sudden, blocking out everything around her – the chair, the care home – she could see the old Danny, the one who could still throw his head back and fizz with laughter.

Her eyes stung and her heart squeezed inside her chest so hard that, just for a moment, she didn't think she could bear it any more, none of it. Not the memories of her dad and Foxy, not telling Madeleine about Cuppy, not the way things were right now. The loneliness, the bleakness lurking just behind all that stupid hope in her heart that things would still change, that every new day could be the one to turn her life around. It was Foxy and his silly book, bringing back the old Danny, the one who still ran and jumped, and whose image in her head had, over time, slowly faded away to become that immobile person in the contraption opposite her.

She busied herself with straightening the edge of the little blanket across his thighs so he couldn't see any of that on her face, suddenly wishing that she could have left the old Danny up in the attic, where the memories of him didn't hurt quite so much. It was the same way she sometimes used to wonder, a fleeting, secret, horrible thought, why, if life had decided to take him from her, it hadn't taken him quickly, once and for all. The way it had separated them – was still separating them every day – agonisingly slowly, inch by inch, was almost more cruel than losing him in one go.

'Be all right, Chlo,' he said. 'You'll see.'

She sat up quickly and scanned his face, her heart pounding, for one ridiculous moment convinced she'd said it all out loud.

'Of course it will be. Of course . . .' She was groping for more words when the door opened behind her and a short, chubby woman stuck her head into the room.

'Oh goody, I thought I heard your voice,' she said in delight. 'Millicent, I was right, she *is* here today!'

'Hi, Dixie.' Chloe suppressed a small rush of relief at the interruption.

'Do c'm'in,' Danny said, rolling his eyes at her and shaking his head. 'Make y'self comfortable.'

Dixie, who'd already been in the process of lowering herself onto the chair next to the door, paused with a cursory 'May I?' before plopping all the way down. 'Wouldn't you know, I had no idea it was Tuesday,' she wheezed. 'And just when we're short of a fourth at cards. How fortunate.'

'It's Monday, and I can't, Dixie, I'm sorry. I was just about to leave.'

'Sugar cakes!' A woman with bright red hair appeared in the doorway. 'Didn't know you were here! Dix, get your stupid machine out of the corridor, you'll kill someone one of these days.'

Dixie and Milly had practically adopted Danny when he arrived at Oakwood, claiming they needed more young people to keep them alive. Knowing that they'd be around had made leaving him here a little bit easier, and over the last year they'd all become firm friends. Chloe didn't often mention them to Aidan, who would have insisted on meeting them properly. She wasn't entirely sure he would like Dixie, with her macabre sense of humour and the oxygen tank she pulled behind her on a trolley like a recalcitrant dog, or that he wouldn't start mocking Milly the moment they were out of earshot because she couldn't help but fawn over a handsome man.

'Your brother's been spoiled for company,' Dixie said. She jerked on the trolley and it jumped across the threshold with a loud clang. 'Oakwood agony aunt, that's what he is. Seeing as he's ever such a patient listener.' She grinned and poked Danny's immobile leg with her cane.

'Dixie!' Chloe said reprovingly, but Danny just chuckled.

'Am too,' he said, nodding resignedly. 'Not going anywhere, after all.'

'Penny!' Milly screeched out into the corridor. 'Chloe's here. Come and bring that book you promised her. Actually,' she turned back into the room, 'I think she's gone downstairs to get our card table. You staying, Chloe?'

'Maybe next time.' Chloe got up.

'Then bring that handsome husband of yours,' Milly said longingly. 'Haven't seen him in a while.'

'Yes, I will,' Chloe said quickly. Out of the corner of her eye she saw that Danny was tapping his fingers on the armrest again, looking down at his lap.

Sixteen

'Chloe! A word?' A thin nurse with a long, narrow face came out of the little cubicle behind the front desk.

'I'm sorry, Marie, I have to run.'

'Won't be a mo,' Marie said, motioning Chloe towards a white door opposite. 'It's just, storage in the cellar's getting a little thin with that burst pipe the other day, and we still have this old thing.' She started rummaging at the back of the room. 'You brought it in with your brother when he first came?' She gave a last pull and Danny's old wheelchair emerged.

Danny had always met each change to his body with a sort of furious, fiery resistance, and with every muscle fibre and nerve end fading, he had trained the still functioning ones all the harder, had done stretching and coordination training and used light weights for muscle strength. He'd swept Chloe up in it, too, had been so hell-bent on beating the gradual loss of mobility that she had started to believe that if anyone could do it, it would be her brother. Until he'd tripped and fallen and successive appointments had determined that it wouldn't be safe to continue on crutches.

'Get yourself used to a wheelchair, mate, sooner rather than later,' the physiotherapist had advised.

Danny, however, had stubbornly insisted on continuing to use his crutches, clenching his teeth through the effort of supporting himself, doing his exercises as often as he possibly could. Shortly after that, he fell on the threshold of their flat and almost broke Chloe's arm. When she came home from A&E later that afternoon, she'd heard him and Jerry, his carer at the time, talking about wheelchair options.

She would have given either of her arms not to have seen the fire and optimism drain out of her brother after that. His exercising things stayed under the sofa, where he sat pretending to read but really looking out into the street he was never going to walk on his own two feet again.

Now she took the handlebars from Marie, felt the green tape she'd wrapped around them, knobbly and slightly sticky around the edges, remembering the way Danny had hunched over in the seat the first time she'd wheeled him down the street in it, both of them determinedly refusing to meet the eye of any passing neighbour or acquaintance.

Eventually he'd come round to it, mainly because Jerry had simply refused to tolerate any 'wimpish goings-on'. He had flat-out refused to let them buy an 'old womanish' kind of chair, and then insisted on pimping it up properly. He'd taught Danny how to use it, too, helped him find ways of getting around the body parts that refused to cooperate, practised tricks and turns with him, until Danny and his battered wheelchair had become a bit of a neighbourhood menace.

Chloe shook her head, batting away the memories. The wheelchair looked the same as it always had: the various bits they'd added, such as a small motor and joystick, the power-assisted wheels, the cushion pushed into the crease of the seat as if it was simply waiting, ready for when . . . Her hands tightened around the handles.

'I'll take it with me,' she said quickly.

'But you won't need it any more.' Marie frowned. 'Let me donate it for you.'

'Oh . . . not quite yet,' Chloe said. The arrival of the wheelchair might have taken Danny's hope, but letting it go now would mean that there would never be any hope again. She snapped the chair around and wheeled it towards the exit before Marie could say anything else.

To her surprise, Dixie was waiting for her by the big glass doors.

'We lost our table to the ghastly Mrs Eldridge from number 8 and her crocheting circle. I blame Penny, she's such a push-over. Milly is giving her some mental training now.'

Chloe pushed the wheelchair through the door. 'Well, I have to run, Dixie.'

'I'll run with you.' Dixie shuffled slowly across the threshold.

'Is it me, or are your jokes getting more terrible every time I'm here?' Chloe sighed and slowed her steps. Dixie used to be a marathon runner until she was diagnosed with chronic lung disease.

'Got a step counter,' the older woman told her as they walked slowly down the path. 'Trying to do ten thousand a day.'

'Ten thousand? Are you sure that's good for you? That sounds like heaps more than I'd do.'

'Yep,' Dixie said, wheezing a little. 'Not surprised. You healthy people are too sedentary.'

They turned onto the path along the car park, the trolley squeaking resentfully behind them.

'Been meaning to tell you something,' Dixie said suddenly. 'I saw him here just recently, your husband.'

'Aidan was here?' Chloe stopped to look at her. 'I can't imagine why. He's been so busy and—'

'Yeah, yeah, never mind that,' Dixie said with unexpected vehemence. 'I know full well that he doesn't like coming here. Which is why I was even more surprised when I saw him popping into the office with that good-for-nothing Stella.'

Chloe digested this. 'He must have been doing some admin, stopped on his way home,' she said. 'Although his surgery isn't really that close.' And why hadn't he mentioned it?

'Well, wouldn't you know, I had to fix that dratted machine right by the office door,' Dixie continued cheerfully, miming a kick at the oxygen tank. 'I can't be a hundred per cent sure; he's not a loud talker, is he, your husband? At first, I thought maybe they were up to some jiggy-jiggy, you know what I mean – wouldn't put it past that Stella woman – but then I realised that they were looking at Danny's file. They were talking about whatever that thing is called when you're in charge of a cripple and get to make all their choices for them.'

'Dixie! You mean power of attorney?' Chloe frowned. 'Where someone gives you the authority to make their decisions with or for them? *I'm* Danny's, though, not Aidan.'

'Well, whatever it's called, I'm not lucky enough for anyone to be mine, but I'm pretty sure your husband wanted a piece of it.'

Seventeen

Maddy

Zingy lemon and fragments of laughter wove through the greenish foam of ocean surf; gauzy white fabric danced above a rock wall, a head thrown back in laughter. And then, the split second before a fall. I had drifted restlessly though the night, running for most of it, running from the incoming tide, running towards my father's body on the rocks ahead, my feet sinking deep into the wet sand as the distance between me and the cliffs widened with every step.

When I woke, I was wedged into a corner of the bed, my whole body rigid, the dream so vivid that I was convinced I was still back at Hangman's Cove, almost surprised I couldn't taste the salty air in my mouth. I kicked at the sheets twisted around my legs and tried to make my mind blank, tried to stop my head from spinning after a night of dancing and Red Lions. But memories were still hovering right beneath the surface, and however hard I tried, I couldn't push them away.

Breathing carefully, I rubbed my hands across my face, which felt dry and tight and sweaty at the same time. My mouth tasted like a small animal had gone to sleep there for the night. If this was how you felt after Red Lions and dancing, I didn't care to repeat the experience.

Georgiana, I thought. Sleeping along the landing. Her room was west-facing; it would be cool and dark at this hour, and she'd be spread across the bed, her arms flung out in all directions. We'd slept in the same room for years. Years when the last sound I heard was Georgiana's even breathing – she dropped into sleep quickly and heavily, like a rock into a dark pond – and the first thing I saw in the morning was her hand thrown over the edge of the bed as she sprawled starfish-like under the blankets. I was a troubled sleeper myself; I fidgeted and talked – *Honestly, Foxy, the way you carry on, it's like you're being murdered in your sleep* – and it was inevitable that at some point she would want the room to herself. I didn't think I slept much at all the first few weeks after we separated, without the knowledge that I could reach out and touch her hand if I wanted to, which I sometimes did, secretly and very lightly before finally drifting off into sleep.

I got up cautiously and dipped my face into the basin of water that Susan had thoughtfully set there the night before. Opening my eyes underwater, the silver inside of the pewter basin bright against my eyes, I decided to find Georgiana. It was early, not yet gone six, but maybe she'd come out with me – was even awake now, waiting for me – and we could walk the Summerhill grounds the way we always used to do on summer mornings.

A few minutes later, I was standing in front of her room, my hair curling moistly at the temples, my hand on the doorknob, when I heard a noise, not from the room itself but from the small bathroom my enterprising father had squeezed in between two bedrooms because Georgiana had wanted a loo close by.

I wasn't particularly keen on running into any of the visitors just now and was about to push open Georgiana's door to hide when my sister herself materialised, bare-legged and pale, her hair sticking out at strange angles. She started almost as violently as I did.

'What are you doing here?' she said hoarsely.

'Are you ill?' I eyed her swollen eyes, her mouth, which she quickly wiped on her sleeve.

'Too much to drink, I think.' She pushed past me towards the door.

'Can I come in for a moment?' I asked tentatively. 'I could fetch you some water or tea? We could . . .'

Chat, I'd been about to say, but she shook her head, then groaned and put her forehead on the jamb.

'Not right now, Maddy.' She groped blindly for the door and I pushed it open for her, was about to step back to let her through when I saw it. A bulky shape in her bed. The faint smell of cigarette smoke hung in the air, emanating perhaps from a jumble of clothes tossed across the back of a chair. Male clothes.

My mouth fell open as the sheet slipped, revealing a broad back, the sharp relief of shoulder blades, the taut swell of muscles along arms stretched out towards the empty space that had just held my sister.

I was too shocked to say anything at all. Georgiana made as if to move, but halfway through, her energy seemed to desert her, and instead she leaned her head back against the door jamb. She was wearing a thin nightshirt under her robe, and through the fabric I could see the small round outline of her navel against her belly, the dark shadow at the top of her legs. She pulled at the lapels of her robe, belted it tightly, and I looked away, hot and embarrassed.

'What on earth are you doing out here, girls?'

We both spun around; that is, I spun and Georgiana sort of half lumbered, hand pressed against her mouth again.

Aunt Marjorie, wearing an old dressing gown that reached her ankles in a vague, tent-like fashion, had appeared, her grey hair set in very small and very tight pin curls.

'Well?' she said in a loud whisper.

Over her hand, Georgiana threw me a pleading look.

'We were just about to . . . go out – you know how we always do. And I was, that is . . .' I pulled the door almost all the way closed behind me, obscuring the brown shoulder from sight. Georgiana gave a small, audible exhale of relief.

'And where is your gas mask, might I ask?' Aunt Marjorie

eyed me with displeasure. 'How many times do I have to tell you that these are dangerous times?'

'Er, I'm going to fetch it now, Aunt,' I said quickly, and stepped aside, forcing Aunt Marjorie to turn. Georgiana opened the door a sliver and squeezed herself through, throwing me one last grateful look before it closed with a small creak.

'Well, now that we're up, we might as well get dressed and wait for the news,' Aunt Marjorie said resignedly. 'Who knows what Herr Hitler's been up to during the night. You go and get your gas mask, Madeleine. I will see you downstairs. The morning news'll be on presently. We can chat in the interim.'

With this ominous pronouncement, she disappeared back into her room, leaving me standing in front of Georgiana's closed door. I touched the cool surface of the wood, imagined her not starfish-like across cool sheets, but warm and moving next to someone else's body, a brown arm reaching for her, drawing her close . . .

I turned abruptly and set off down the corridor, my footsteps swallowed by the faded carpet that we used to creep along at night when we wanted to watch the stars from the top of the stairs.

Eighteen

I could hear Cookie and Susan talking in the kitchen downstairs, but for the first time ever, I didn't want to join them. The thought of sitting on the bench at the long wooden table, my feet warmed by a dog, listening to Frank debating when to enlist, while Georgiana and Victor were whispering in the darkness above us, my sister's robe falling to the floor, a hand sliding down her naked back . . . I picked up my satchel from its place by the door and left the house.

The dogs followed me in a little pack, jostling down the small track through the orchard, past Frank's Louise Bonne of Jersey pears and through the small gate at the bottom of the garden, where the walls were overgrown with brambles and the copses became proper woods. Frank and I had certain rounds, but today I walked aimlessly, not really taking anything in, flushing every time I thought of standing in that corridor, wanting to take my sister on a walk – a *walk*! – while all along he'd been in there, so casually, so confidently, as if he belonged there. I had only the most shadowy ideas of what went on in a bedroom like that, but whatever it was, it didn't feel right. *I* didn't feel right. I flushed again when I remembered drinking from Victor's glass; my giddy laughter at the yellow shapes whizzing through the air; dancing endlessly and determinedly.

I veered left at a fork in the track, and when that path petered out, I pushed on into the woodland, walking on ground that was spongy and soft with leaves and needles, through small clearings, not really knowing where I was going and not caring until at last I stopped, slid down the trunk of a young beech tree and came to sit on the soft, mossy foliage.

The dogs had caught up with me and they came snuffling over to throw themselves onto the ground next to me. Leica, the oldest and most responsible of them, was sitting next to me, and I put my arms around her, feeling the warm, downy folds of her neck. For as long as I could remember, there'd been a Leica at Summerhill. She was my father's dog; well, her mother had been my father's dog, and *her* mother had been his as well. Leica would always be here, regardless of what else changed.

I leaned back against the tree and reached for my sketchbook, the pencil still wedged inside from the previous afternoon. Digging its tip hard into the paper, I started drawing the clearing. Big, bold strokes at first, leaving indentations across the page, but gradually my hand stopped trembling and the scent of pine needles slowly pushed everything else away until there was only the pencil in my hand and Summerhill all around me, a cool green borderland in the early-morning light, so dreamlike, so tucked away that you felt like you had reached the very edges of the world.

I would have stayed for ever, but something made Leica lift her head. She listened for a moment, her ears pricked, then turned her face the other way, black nose gleaming in the soft light of the undergrowth.

Looking around me, I realised only now how far I'd come and what a roundabout way I'd walked, and for a moment I wasn't completely sure where I was. The dogs were well trained and came running instantly when they heard my whistle, tongues hanging out and ready for breakfast, but Leica gave a sharp bark and then she was on her feet, loping across the clearing, her short, stubby tail disappearing between clumps of heather at the far end. Cursing slightly, I followed the sound of her rustling through the undergrowth, although I didn't think the house was that way at all, until I saw her waiting for me further on, her piebald face lifted.

My skin started prickling and my vision narrowed. I knew now exactly where I was, because even though I hadn't been back to the sea in six years, my body had stored the memory. The sound of waves and water, light bouncing off a glittering surface. We were right at the beginning of the headland that jutted out to sea, where a little cove marked the entrance of the bay. The woods were petering out around us, and just a little further on, the ground would start rising steeply towards the towering cliffs of Hangman's Bluff. And right in front of me was the old shed that used to house my father's boat.

I gave a low whistle for Leica, but she remained where she was, her eyes focused on the shed. It sat at the top of a slipway, which was partially submerged in water when the tide was high. In the old days, Summerhill tenants had kept their fishing boats here for easier access to the bay, but when the coast road had been built over on the other side of the cliffs, they began using the jetty there, leaving the shed free for the family. These days, though, the path down here had slowly been reclaimed by nature, while the shed had been abandoned and fallen into disrepair.

'Come, Leica,' I said quickly. 'Let's go home.'

The woodland, which had been a refuge only a moment ago, now felt isolated and empty, even more so when I suddenly heard a groan and then the shuffling sound of something moving inside the shed. My first instinct was to run, away from this part of Summerhill that was so redolent of death and horror. But then there was another groan, quieter now, and it sounded so pitiful that I took a deep breath and stepped towards the door.

'Hello? Is somebody there?'

Belatedly it occurred to me that approaching an isolated shed without knowing who was inside was possibly not the wisest thing to do, but the abrupt silence from inside made me gather the dogs around me and push open the door.

It took a moment for my eyes to adjust to the darkness before they finally found the source of the sounds. A figure in the shadows, slumped on the floor, one knee drawn up into his body, one arm cradled awkwardly with the other. A young man, judging by the smooth skin of his cheeks and the shock of dark hair falling over his face. The dogs crowded into the little shed, yipping softly and sniffing his legs, and he groaned again when one of them jostled his arm. Light caught on the water creeping underneath the wide wooden doors that used to let the boat out into the cove; it was sloshing and welling with the same slow, rhythmical movement I knew from another early morning on a beach not far from here. Little waves that would gradually come higher and higher, licking at the leg stretched out across the floor, until . . .

I pushed the dogs out of the way and crouched down next to the man, reached for his arm, panting with the necessity of getting him away from the water that was reaching for him, that would touch him soon. He pushed me away.

'The tide,' I said urgently, fumbling for a better grip. 'It's fast—'

'Stops there,' he rasped, pointing to the side of the shed. I squinted through the gloom, but when I saw the line of moss and damp wood around the slipway, I realised that of course he was right.

I sagged back against the wall and took a deep breath, which I regretted instantly. It smelled terrible inside the airless shed, rank with blood and algae and rotting wood.

'Who are you?' I said, resisting pressing my hands across my mouth.

He was shivering uncontrollably. There was a strange hum, too, and I looked around for its source until I realised that it was coming from him, a low keening that made the rank air close around both of us. I glanced past him to the battered remnants of a jacket, then gave a sharp exhale.

'You're the airman, the missing pilot,' I whispered. 'You went down with the plane. Oh, you poor thing!'

He didn't respond, and I sat back on my heels, tried to think.

'Listen,' I said finally, speaking very slowly and carefully. 'I will go and telephone them.' I bent closer so he could hear me better. 'They can come via the river, pick you up right here – look, by those doors.'

Yes, that was what I was going to do: leave this place that was filled with the sound of the creeping tide and fetch Frank or Georgiana or someone else who'd take over. I made as if to straighten, but his hand came out and grabbed my ankle. I staggered, gave a small yelp, and he dropped his hand immediately.

'Don't,' he said roughly. 'Please.'

Oddly, it was the 'please' that made me pause, because it was so incongruous: him remembering his manners like a good boy when he was shivering on the ground in an old shed.

'They'll be thrilled to know that you're all right. They're looking for you everywhere,' I said.

'I know.' The young man pushed himself up with an effort. 'I heard them on the river all yesterday. But I don't want them to find me.' He winced as the movement jostled his arm. 'You see, I'm not going back.'

Nineteen

It took me a second to understand what he meant.

'Not go back? You have to,' I said incredulously.

'But I won't.' He slumped down again, closing his eyes as if that settled the matter. 'Whatever happens, I'm not getting back in a plane. Ever.'

'But you'd be a deserter. They execute deserters, Frank told me; they shoot them, and it's no more than they deserve—'

I bit my lip hard. Frank's father had fallen in the first war. *Defending his country*, Frank would proudly tell my seven-year-old self trailing behind him through the cabbage beds. *That's what you do, Miss Maddy. You give it your all, you don't have a choice.* He'd supplemented his opinion with a lot of very graphic detail until I started waking up at night shaking with terror, and even my father, who wanted us to know about war, forbade Frank from talking to us about it any more. By then I had absorbed much of his romantic fervour, though, about duty and choices and doing your bit, my memory refreshed only recently because Frank was gearing up to enlist at the next opportunity and didn't let an hour go by without reminding us all.

'Well, what I mean to say is, you could die,' I finished quickly.

'Prison,' the young man said curtly. 'Or court-martialled. They don't shoot deserters any more. But I'm not a deserter. Well, technically, I suppose I am, but I'm in training . . .'

He lapsed into an irritated silence and looked pointedly away from me, but when Leica approached him, nudging his hand to sniff the bloodstains, I saw the edges of his mouth curl up and his fingers tighten around her ears.

'Are you hurt?' I broke the silence.

'I'm fine.' He stroked the soft underside of Leica's muzzle. 'And I won't be here long. Are you . . . I mean, is this yours? The shed?'

'Well, it belongs to the estate, if that's what you mean,' I said. 'But no one comes down here really.'

'The estate?' he repeated warily, and his eyes flicked across my old navy skirt, my knobbly brown cardigan. 'You live here, miss?'

'Yes, in the house up the hill.' I gave a small nod in the direction of the house. 'Where are you from, then?'

He hesitated, then said, 'Bristol. My father's a teacher there.'

His hand slid away from Leica's head and into his lap, but when she butted his arm reproachfully with her nose, he flinched and a loud groan escaped before he pressed his lips back together.

'You *are* hurt,' I said, eyeing him uneasily.

'I'm all right . . . well, my arm does feel a bit off,' he said through clenched teeth. 'I'm not sure what happened to it.' He hesitated, then said reluctantly, 'I can't see around it to check. Maybe . . .' sweat broke out across his forehead as he lifted his arm, 'maybe you could have a quick look. Just to tell me how bad it is.'

He proffered the bloodstained limb and I backed away, putting my hand in front of my mouth as, for the third time in twenty-four hours, images came that I hadn't allowed for years. A body sprawled across rocks, my father's twisted leg, his side split open, blood, raw flesh. I fumbled for the door behind me. 'I shouldn't, honestly, I don't know anything about doctoring.'

'I'm sorry. Of course. I didn't think.' He breathed hard for a moment. 'Might there be a place around here where I could find something to drink? I'm so thirsty, and with all this water, too. I can't think straight. Tried to collect dew or rainwater. They teach you that during training, how to survive when you're shot down over enemy territory. And other things, too. How to stay strong during torture. Rejoin your side.' He reeled it all off and I had the feeling that he was talking to stop himself thinking about everything else.

'Please, miss.' He suddenly sounded very young. I looked at his face and realised that actually he couldn't be much older than me. The bones in his face hadn't yet hardened and settled; the sweep of his lashes above his cheeks held a hint of boyishness.

'What's your name?' I asked, still hovering by the door.

He hesitated. 'William,' he said finally, 'William Davies.' I was touched and oddly proud that he had told me.

'I'm Maddy,' I said.

'Pleased to meet you, Miss Maddy.' His eyes glinted across the gloom inside the shed.

'Just Maddy.' I let go of the door.

'Just Maddy from the big house on the hill, huh? I'd be forgetting my manners, miss.' He smiled suddenly, a grin that rounded out his cheeks and gave him a cheeky, mischievous look very much at odds with the tattered clothes and bloodstains. 'But I'd very grateful if you'd have a look.'

Inch by inch I peeled away his shirt, forcing the inside of my head to be quiet and simply concentrating on the fibres of the fabric between my fingers. The shirt was ripped in places and I used a little knife from my satchel in others, until it fell away in shreds. The dogs were sitting on their haunches, watching me interestedly.

'Leica, come.' I made her sit down next to him, and the others came too, warm bodies crowding around his good side. Bit by bit William stopped trembling and relaxed into the heap of fur and shiny eyes.

I had to smile and felt the tension in my shoulders ease. 'It looks like there's a large cut just on the underside of the arm.' I squinted at it. 'It was all crusted against your shirt. And I think there's a piece of something lodged inside. A fairly sizeable piece.'

I studied the vicious gash along the arm and pursed my lips, then used a piece of his shirt to dab away blood and bits of dirt around the wound. The young airman followed me with his eyes, biting his lip hard so as not to make a sound. There was definitely something in there: I could see the distinct ridge of a long splinter or a metal shard of some kind. When I touched it, he made a strangled sound and moved his arm out of my reach.

'That hurts,' he said reproachfully.

'It'll have to come out.'

'Now?' He looked alarmed and shrank into the pile of dogs. After a moment's hesitation, he sat up and laid his arm carefully across my leg again.

'You'd need pliers or pincers or something, I think.' I resumed my dabbing, although I was careful not to touch the raised ridge again. 'So,' I didn't look up, 'what happened out there? The plane, I mean.'

He shook his head. 'I don't really know, miss.' He winced as I moved on to a cut by his wrist, curling his fingers briefly into mine, then unclenched his teeth. 'I was paired with Coleman in one of the training planes. I'm not sure, but I think an engine must have failed. There were all sorts of horrible grinding noises. Coleman panicked; he wanted to land it, anywhere, really, but I knew there wasn't enough space. We had to go into the water if we wanted to have a chance.' His fingers curled and uncurled against my palm again. 'We'd been through it so often on the ground. But when you're up there . . .' He paused.

'You don't have to tell me,' I focused on the edge of another cut, 'not if it's too hard.'

He looked at me properly for the first time since I'd walked into the shed, and smiled. 'It's all right, miss. I don't mind talking about it with you. It's just . . . I'm not quite sure . . .' He frowned. 'All I knew was to keep the plane straight. The nose is reinforced because it's a training plane, see, it's supposed to be more resistant to breaking that way. But even that can't help if you don't land it straight.' He started shivering again, his pale face sweaty underneath all the grime and the cuts and the blood. 'We were too close to use our bags, got thrown around an awful lot. Jumped at the last minute. I knew I had to pull us away from the plane as fast as I could – the suction is deadly, see. I had to help Coleman; he's a poor swimmer, no wonder he wasn't keen on a water landing. But then I lost sight of him in the waves. And then all I did was swim. I just kept swimming. Around the headland, crawled onto shore a little south of here. Found the shed.'

'But that's impossible,' I said faintly.

'Nothing is impossible if your life depends on it.' He looked at my hand dabbing at his arm. 'Something in me took over – sheer bloody willpower, I suppose . . .' He blushed. 'Begging your pardon, miss. I think I must have passed out for a while, and when I came to and heard them shouting out on the bay, saw the boats, I crawled in here and hid.'

There was a moment's silence.

'But why *hide*?' I finally asked.

His voice was faraway but steadier, as if that part was very clear in his mind. 'It's what I've been dreaming about for so long: a morning when I don't wake up dreading the day ahead, an evening without wishing I was a million miles away. I'm not cut out for flying, see? I enlisted voluntarily, was excited about it. And I liked the learning on the ground well enough, getting to know the planes, the theory. I'm quite good with machines.' He shrugged bashfully. 'But when we finally got on a plane and the hatch closed, I found that I couldn't breathe. My mind goes blank, my hands shake something fierce. And all I can think about from the moment we leave the ground until the moment we touch back down is getting out of that plane, as far away from it as I can. I don't think I'm brave enough for it, miss, see.' He hung his head.

'But when I was in the water, all that fell away, and there was only one thought in my mind. To swim. The relief of it, the release. It felt exactly like I'd escaped from prison. Until I realised . . .' he swallowed, and it took him a second to continue, 'that I'd left Coleman behind, and then all I felt was shame. I haven't been able to stop thinking about him. And the worst of it is that I know, without a shadow of a doubt, that I would do it again in a heartbeat.'

His eyes were so bleak under his matted hair that I reached involuntarily for his hand. He pulled it away.

'They picked him up, though, Coleman,' I said quickly.

'They did?' William looked up.

'He's . . . in hospital.' I tried to think back to Victor's exact words. 'They weren't sure if . . .' I couldn't bear to say the next bit, to put all that on this boy, who had let his head drop back down to his knees as if he'd confessed and was waiting for his penance. 'What will you do now?' I said instead.

'I don't know.' He rubbed his hand across his face, digging his knuckles into his bloodshot eyes. 'I feel so queer, so hollow. Can't really think straight.' He winced when he inadvertently moved his arm. 'I just . . . I need a little time. Would you let me stay here? Only for a day or two.'

I hesitated, wanted to say something about facing up to things and braving it out, but instead I looked at him out of the corner of my eye and tried to picture what I'd do in his place. I knew full well that war wasn't all about young men cheerfully marching towards the front line, a battle song on their lips, like Frank would have me believe. And I didn't have the first idea of what it would be like to set foot in a plane and fly. But my throat constricted and my cheeks coloured with the shameful realisation that, given the choice, I would most likely do exactly what this boy had done. I would run and hide.

I reached for the cloth and started dabbing at his cuts again. So maybe I was a coward, so what? Life didn't just need heroes;

it needed ordinary people, too, who were small and afraid. I frowned down at the wound, because I didn't quite like that either, that smallness of myself.

'I could come back,' I heard myself say. 'I've watched Frank treat the dogs. I could try to get the splinter out. If you like. Bring bandages, iodine. Proper food.'

He turned his head, studied me warily. 'You won't tell?'

I bristled a little. 'If I say I won't, I won't,' I snapped.

He gave me another of his unexpectedly sweet smiles, and I couldn't help but smile back, feeling a sudden odd twinge of pleasure at our secret complicity.

It's just for a day or two, I told myself a little later as I walked up through the orchards with the dogs, remembering how he'd tipped his head back to catch the last drops of the redcurrant juice I'd unearthed from my satchel.

'That's heaven,' he'd said fervently. 'And that's a lot of good crumbs you've just wasted,' he added disapprovingly when he saw me shake out the napkin that had held the dry rolls I'd found from the day before. He'd softened his mock-disapproval with a funny little whuff of laughter.

I motioned for the dogs to run ahead, wondering to myself whether boys were like that, their spirits restored with food and drink.

It would just be for a day or so.

Twenty

'Maddy! Over here!'

I was halfway up the orchard and had been about to cut across to the kitchen door when Georgiana caught up with me.

Sleek in pedal pushers and a blouse jauntily tied at the front, she was holding out a bulging bag. 'Elevenses. Cookie said you missed breakfast.' She smiled a little uncertainly. 'I thought we could steal away now. I'm sorry I wasn't up for it earlier. It's just . . .'

'Yes.' The awkwardness from earlier crowded back between us, now compounded by my own secret. I squirmed a bit as I imagined what Georgiana would say about my supposed bravery in hiding a runaway airman in the shed.

'Everyone's doing it,' she said quickly; almost a little angrily. It took me a moment to understand what she meant. 'Maybe not around here, but you needn't look quite so shocked. It's not a bad thing. It's rather lovely, actually,' she added with an attempt at a mischievous grin.

I couldn't think of anything to say to that, and she bristled.

'And who exactly made you the arbiter of good and evil?'

'I'm not the arbiter of good and evil,' I said, incensed. 'But you have to admit that it's a bit . . . I mean, how long have you known him, anyway?'

'Long enough not to care what people think,' she snapped. 'It's my life and my decision.'

'All right,' I said.

'And what's that supposed to mean? *All right.*' She mimicked my voice, slinging the bag of food over her shoulder with an annoyed flick of her arm.

'Just that, all right,' I said wearily, because I didn't know why we were fighting.

'Georgiana!' Victor's voice came from further up the path. 'Are you girls down there? There's someone here to see you.'

At the edge of the courtyard Georgiana set the picnic bag next to one of the enormous potted palm trees and Victor beckoned us forward to greet a thin man in uniform who was waiting by a military jeep carrying a sheaf of papers and looking worriedly important.

'Good morning, good morning. Sincere apologies for barging in.' The man sketched a crisp bow in our direction. 'Flight Lieutenant Hughes. I'm here about the plane.'

'What news?' Georgiana asked, her brisk, irritated tone matching his.

'One airman still missing and hope of retrieval quickly dwindling. The pull of the tide is strong right there, especially if you're injured and unable to fight it. Most likely he's been swept out into the bay and drowned there . . .'

I reached for Georgiana's hand, but it was Victor's voice that cut through Hughes's terse monologue.

'Flight Lieutenant, I beg of you.' He sounded uncharacteristically abrupt, sharp almost. 'No more detail needed.' He put a hand on my arm, and the solid bulk of his shoulder next to mine loosened the tight band around my throat, released the breath stuck there.

'It's fine.' I gave him a grateful smile.

'My sincere apologies. Ladies present, of course.' Hughes barely concealed his impatience. 'William Davies is a strong swimmer by all accounts. Junior champion in the Somerset County Swimming Club. Big lad, too, you know, might have managed to make it against the odds. I've had the headlands searched yesterday, and with your permission, I'd really like to send a search party through the upper grounds in case the river swept him all the way up towards the ferry.'

'Is that really necessary?' I said before I could stop myself. 'Surely he wouldn't be hiding anywhere . . .'

The moment I said it, I wished I hadn't, especially as they would be on the northern parts of the river and nowhere near the boat shed.

'Whatever in the world, miss!' Hughes's voice was sharp, and he shook his head. 'Hiding? Of course not. The lad's a hero.'

There was a moment's silence.

'A hero?' I said faintly. 'What . . .'

'Phil Coleman has finally come round, been able to shed some light on what happened. Apparently Davies pulled him away from the air bubble, otherwise he'd have been sucked under. Pushed him onto a buoy, which is where we picked him up. Saved his life, he did. Possibly paid for it with his own—'

'So Coleman made it?' I asked breathlessly, noticing the man's slightly protuberant eyes, the way his skin had tanned to a deep brown, like a leather hide.

'Mercifully he's out of immediate danger. Swallowed a lot of water, very weak. Can't swim, who'd have thought?' he added accusingly.

'Yes, well, it's obviously fine for you to search the upper grounds,' said Georgiana. 'Let us know if we can help in any way.'

'We're fine, thank you. But do alert us immediately if you spot anything, please.'

And without further ado, he jumped into the jeep, threw it into reverse and departed, gravel flying everywhere.

Over at the house, the front door opened and the girls poked their heads out.

'Is he gone?' Clementine called.

'Are we in trouble with the law?' Laney giggled behind her.

'I told him I didn't know anyone by the name of Elaine Fulton,' Victor called back, but he looked distracted and fumbled for a cigarette. 'Terrible business,' he said abruptly, flicking open his lighter. 'Are you sure you're all right, Madeleine?'

'It's fine,' I said again. 'But thank you.'

He looked down at me for a long moment, then nodded. 'They'll find him, don't you worry.' He patted my shoulder and went to join Jonathan, who'd emerged, yawning and tousle-haired, to see if it were too much to ask for a bit of peace and quiet this early in the morning, and since we were all up, could someone please fetch him a piece of toast and a drink.

'He's nice, isn't he?' Georgiana suddenly said next to me.

'Who, Victor? Yes, he's very nice.' I found myself drifting towards the edge of the driveway, restraining myself only with difficulty from slipping back down the hill to bring William the news about Coleman that would take away that horrible look in his eyes.

'Maddy?' Georgiana nudged me. 'Ah, never mind.' She gave me a quick hug. 'I'm sorry we were fighting about . . . you-know-what.'

'It's all right,' I said, and she laughed.

'You and your all right,' she said exasperatedly. 'Come on, let's go.'

The girls were calling for us to come inside – they were positively starving, and was it too early for a drink? – and Victor was reaching for Georgiana's arm as Aunt Marjorie belatedly took the stage, rushing out with her gas mask and exclaiming over the fate of the airman.

Heaving a small sigh, Georgiana started shepherding everyone inside, dispatching Victor to unearth something to drink. In the ensuing melee, I made my escape. Retrieving the bag Georgiana had meant for our breakfast, I detoured past the still room and the kitchen, collecting bandages, iodine, a bottle of gin and a rather terrifying-looking pair of long-nosed pliers that Frank had used to extract a chicken bone from one of the dogs' throats, then pulled down a dry shirt from the washing line and disappeared into the orchard before anyone could start asking questions.

Twenty-One

Chloe

He'd met Chloe at a wedding, Aidan was fond of telling friends and new acquaintances. It was a funny story, actually, how they'd run into each other – *quite literally*, he would chuckle at that point: *she barrelled into me, making me drop my ice cream all over the place* – and how it had been love at first sight. For both of them.

Chloe never did much more than smile in all the right places, because even though he'd left out some of the more pertinent details, the sentiment was right. She'd been twenty-six and had been swept off her feet by the young doctor who'd been crossing her path with his dessert bowl.

She hadn't been a guest at the wedding, though. Instead she'd been trailing behind Liz Tallis with armfuls of equipment, handing her cameras and lenses, while Josh, the silent assistant – there'd been a very strict division between assistant and apprentice, the menial work of one not to be confused with the upwardly mobile potential of the other – hid from the world behind the big reflector screen that always made Liz's subjects' faces glow with suffused pleasure. Normally Chloe had her eyes trained on Liz at all times, because those few photography hours she had carved out of the rest of her life were precious and costly. But earlier in the week, she'd started noticing that Danny seemed to have stopped using his left arm, and when she'd pressed him this morning, he'd inadvertently let slip that it did seem a little harder these days to manoeuvre the wheelchair.

Knowing she'd be out all afternoon, Chloe had run across to the neighbour, who'd been happy to pop in to help 'the poor dear boy', but just so Chloe knew, she'd be leaving promptly at eight for her Tae Bo class.

Usually Chloe loved weddings, the wonder of it all, the brightness and hope that was almost palpable among these care-free, sparkly people. Today, though, everything seemed a bit flat, people laughing and dancing and chattering away while her brother was losing the feeling in his left hand and might need a new wheelchair, one of those fancy ones that could be manoeu-vred with just his fingers and that would no doubt be difficult to wangle out of the NHS. They had a small emergency stash of valuables, but Chloe never broke into it unless she absolutely had to, although—

'Chloe,' Liz hissed when Chloe failed to produce a certain lens. Liz hadn't asked for it; she expected Chloe just to know, and Chloe usually did, except when she wasn't busy thinking about how to fit in another job and hoping that her neighbour wouldn't actually call Danny 'poor dear boy' to his face.

'Just coming.' She turned on her heel and rushed back into the main room for the lens, glancing at her watch as she did so. If Liz let her go in the next thirty minutes, she could catch the bus on the corner, which would let her out at the end of the road—

'Hey, watch out!' A sudden hard blow to her shoulder knocked her off course and she felt herself flying, landing on the floor in a tangle of arms and legs, her cheek pressed into something sticky and cold. She closed her eyes for a brief, panicked moment. Liz had a strict stance on not being seen or heard – even the camera shutter had to be silenced – and this certainly didn't qualify as being invisible.

'Are you all right?' a male voice asked, and before she could answer, a hand had pulled her upright, setting her back onto her feet.

'Of course,' Chloe whispered, cheeks burning. She pushed

her hair out of her face and winced at the sticky goo that was melting into her neck and the fancy black dress that Liz had insisted she wear to blend in. 'I'm so sorry.'

'Hey.' She felt a hand tip her chin, forcing her to look up. 'It's all right. You took a harder hit than I did, let me tell you. Here, I'll help you dust off.'

She met his eyes then, and noticed his smile, and whatever it was she saw there, it made her stomach flip, once, twice, and she let him fetch a cloth and dip it in iced water, not even feeling the shock on her neck as he dabbed at the ice cream. 'This won't hurt a bit,' he joked, winking at her. 'I should know, I'm a doctor.'

She laughed back giddily, then quickly made her escape to fetch Liz's lens, looking back once to see the man return to his table, catching her eye and winking again.

It was lucky, he said afterwards, that Liz Tallis was such a diva. She'd forgotten about her promise to let Chloe duck out early, and when Chloe finally ran down the drive, she saw the red tail lights of the bus turning the corner. 'I will cherish her for ever, because she gave me a chance to be your hero,' Aidan said afterwards, a funny, flowery thing to come up with after he'd screeched to a stop next to her and given her a lift home.

At first, she didn't quite know what Aidan MacAllister, who was easily the most charismatic, most confidently handsome man she'd ever met, could possibly want with her, Chloe Archer, who expended so much energy on simply coordinating her and Danny's schedules that she didn't really have anything left for the rest of life. When he called, she said no, almost automatically. She didn't really do relationships, not even when her stomach performed its strange somersault thing again when she picked up the phone. *Is this the lovely Miss Archer? I'd like to take you out. Name the day and I'm yours.*

But as she quickly discovered, there were not many people who successfully said no to Aidan MacAllister. And once she'd said yes for the first time, she discovered something else: there were many 'first times' where Aidan was concerned, a whole other life outside the walls of her little flat, in fact. Sitting in the window of the corner café talking for hours, until she rushed home, slightly guiltily, to help Danny get ready for bed. A meal Aidan cooked for her and Danny, so delicious and different from anything they'd ever eaten. Watching the stars at the planetarium over at Sidmouth. Swing dancing in a smoky cave-like bar. It was so easy to be with Aidan. He listened, he asked questions. He cared. And when she said no to a weekend away, he hired Jerry to stay overnight. Even then, she lingered by the door, holding her overnight case, reluctant to leave until her brother gently nudged her out. 'Chloe, we'll be fine.'

She and Aidan had walked on the beach in the fog and sat by the fire, before going through to the little bedroom, where Aidan had lit candles along the windowsill.

And *that* was a first too, the way her body responded to Aidan's touch. Maybe she'd never been touched like that before, or maybe Aidan was simply magic – it certainly seemed so that night by the beach – but Chloe had never before felt so alive, so completely in the moment. Afterwards, he'd kissed her flushed face and told her how much he loved her, that it was her and no one else he wanted to be with. 'Marry me, Chloe. Just you and me, together for ever.'

Looking back, she remembered the furious pace of those early months, the whirlwind of firsts spinning her too madly for her thoughts to keep up. House viewings and wedding plans flew by in a whirl of colours and decisions that were made with astonishing ease, and it wasn't until she realised that none of them seemed to include Danny that her feet hit the ground hard.

'Darling, be reasonable,' Aidan had said. 'The way he's deteriorating, he will *have* to go into a care home sooner or later. And won't it be so much nicer for him if he's taken care of in a facility that caters especially to his needs? People on hand who will take him to the loo and do the physio and the speech therapy and everything else right there, so that you get to see him and spend time with him without being burdened with any of that other stuff.'

'I'm not burdened,' she'd said quietly. 'And I want Danny with me. I'm sorry, Aidan, but no.'

He hadn't argued, not then.

'Of course, darling,' he'd murmured. 'We'll talk about it, we'll find a way. I just want us to be together.' And he'd run his hands down her back, leaving a trail of tingling thrills behind, and pulled her into the curve of his shoulder, where she fitted so perfectly that she knew they were made for each other.

Twenty-Two

Chloe was lying on her side, watching the lightning flash across the sky outside. Thunder had been rumbling off and on in the distance, as if trying to make up its mind. Another streak of brightness, followed by a reluctant growling sound. She held her breath to see if Aidan was stirring, but his breathing didn't change. He was right next to her, his elbow sliding up and down her back, a strange, disembodied stroking that made her belly churn ever so slightly. Her eyes flickered to the orange digits of her alarm clock: 11:23.

They always went to bed early. *We won't be like all those couples who get too busy to make love*, Aidan had once said. And Chloe, for whom everything was a novelty in those early days, could hardly wait for him to make his rounds downstairs, check the locks and turn off the lights before she pulled him up the stairs, laughing slightly self-consciously at her own daring. Two years on, with talk of a baby in the near future, their lovemaking had become more regular. Like clockwork, Chloe sometimes thought now, when Aidan turned off the lights at 9.20 and walked her up the stairs, his hand in the small of her back as if she might bolt if he didn't take care. Afterwards, he would shower, and fall asleep by 10.30. He'd go reluctantly, fighting it all the way, holding onto her as if couldn't bear to leave her behind, but sleep pulled on him, it always had, the one thing that claimed him completely and utterly. And then he slept, like a corpse in a tomb, scented and clean and perfectly straight, his hands folded across his body as if in prayer.

Chloe was the opposite. As if sleep used up its entire attention on her husband, it capriciously allowed her to drift off, lulling her into a sense of safety, only to abandon her and push her bolt upright in the middle of the night, heart hammering from some quickly fading nightmare she could never remember afterwards.

Cautiously she turned away from the clock, studied her husband's outline in the dark. Every now and then, a flash of lightning would dance over his face, abruptly illuminating his cheekbones, his brows, his jaw. Sometimes she relished this time to herself, the hours between 11.30 and 4, at which point Aidan often began to stir, his body waking for the day ahead, whispering in his sleep, reaching for her across the silk sheets before he was even fully conscious. But lately, it had simply become more time during which to worry about the strange nausea that had been dogging her, then the dawning realisation of what the cause of it might be, and now the fact that she didn't seem able to say it out loud.

She'd read a story in the papers once, about a kidnapped pregnant woman who'd gone three weeks past her due date only to give birth the moment she was freed, in the ambulance driving her away from her captors' house, as if she'd managed to hold off from bringing her baby into the world until it was safe to do so. Chloe rolled onto her back and stared up at the dark ceiling. Maybe it was like that with the baby secret she couldn't seem to talk about. Maybe the knowledge of it was clinging to her insides, refusing to emerge until it absolutely had to.

There hadn't been a good moment to mention it tonight, either. By the time she'd pulled into the garage, hidden her gear case behind their bicycles, then returned to the boot to retrieve the wheelchair, Aidan had heard her come in, was leaning in the doorway that led from the garage into the house. She'd had an explanation ready for him: errands running over, *went to see Danny on a whim, you know.* He'd nodded courteously, enquired after Danny's well-being, but she could tell that he didn't like it. His face had become very flat and quite still as he watched her talking too fast and gesturing too hectically.

No secrets, Chloe. He'd said it a million times. *Never any secrets between us.* She had always nodded. *Of course, darling.* And in the early days she used to love the brightness of it, the fact that there would be no doubt, no grey areas, just the two of them together in that clear way he had of approaching the world.

It had taken her a little while to realise that he didn't actually mean the two of them, Aidan and Chloe, moving through that world as equals, together but separate too. He'd meant Aidan, with Chloe in close orbit. It hadn't started until a while after they'd got married; in fact, Chloe sometimes thought of it like Danny's illness, the kind of thing that crept in almost imperceptibly, not apparent until you looked back, faintly surprised that it could possibly have got this far. Maybe, if there'd been a caesura that had divided the *before* from the *after*, she'd have been forced to take action. A pivotal moment, like the day her mum had left or the moment when her dad had sat her down and told her she needed to help with Danny from now on. The arrival of Danny's wheelchair. Running into Aidan at the wedding.

But there hadn't ever been anything clear or definite or pivotal; just a million and one tiny moments of Aidan's love wrapping itself around her and pulling her close. If anything, there had been *more* of his love with each day of their marriage. More overwhelming, more encompassing, closing around her so that she sometimes felt like she had to fight even for enough space to breathe. *Penny for your thoughts, Chloe darling.*

She never knew where it had come from, this overriding need of Aidan's to *know* her, to be right inside her head all the time. She'd never given him any reason to doubt her; she'd loved him, had been anxious to make it all work, this strange new world of a serious relationship, then a marriage, the inherent shibboleths and rules of which she was still working out two years later. It would be all right, though, she told herself. They were still finding their way; they just had to get to know each other a little better. Yes, Aidan had changed, had become more serious about their love, but hadn't she changed as well?

Her father had sometimes talked about a marriage taking work. That you couldn't go into it blinded by love; you had to be clear-eyed and understand what was needed from you, cryptic statements prompted by a neighbourhood divorce, which Chloe had puzzled over mostly because her dad talked about these things so rarely. But she was willing to do it, work at it and be clear-eyed. She would let Aidan know her completely, if that was the only way he could trust her properly. The more she let him in and the more she loved him back, the more secure he'd be in that love. And maybe then, the Aidan she'd run into at the wedding would come back, the man she'd fallen in love with three years ago.

But whatever she did, it never seemed quite enough. No matter how hard she tried to put his mind at rest over whatever doubts and anxieties he harboured, every word she said seemed to make him want to keep her closer than before. There was the day he discovered the emergency box, an old carton marked BICYCLE REPAIR KIT that held the Archers' most precious possessions. Two gold coins her father had inherited, a diamond ring her mother had forgotten to take with her when she left, some silver christening spoons, a couple of gold lumps that Danny always said had been discovered in California during the gold rush but which looked suspiciously like tooth fillings. The emergency box only came out when things were about to hit rock bottom, when something was absolutely essential and they just couldn't make it work any other way. Chloe had kept it exactly where her dad had always kept it, in the little space below the bottom drawer of the kitchen cabinet. Discovering it had unsettled Aidan deeply: the fact that she hadn't shown it to him, that she'd never mentioned it. What was she keeping it for? Why had she never told him about it? And from there it was just a short leap to more questions, a continuous loop of them, all the time. What were her plans? Where had she been? Who had she seen there and what had they talked about?

Even tonight, the way he had narrowed his eyes at her, had scanned down her body, taking in her dishevelled hair and the wheelchair, even tonight he was pulling on her. To reclaim her from whatever it was that he'd had to relinquish her to during the day. Sometimes she had the impression that this was how the world looked to Aidan these days, a collection of things that took Chloe away from him, and much of his time seemed to be spent anticipating what those things would be and heading them off at the pass. He tolerated the transitory acquaintances she made at the gym because he liked her looking toned, but when a friendship threatened to get meaningful, he'd bring up dinner plans or a film he'd been wanting to see with her. He dismissed her book club in a mock-laughing way as a group of faux-intellectuals, until she'd finally grown weary and stopped going altogether. He liked the snapshots she'd taken during the last few years, but *just as a hobby, Chloe, surely.*

Only Danny was different, and only because Chloe never even considered changing the way she'd always been with her brother. She was well aware that Aidan's early solicitousness for Danny's well-being had acquired a touch of impatience over the past couple of years; even, perhaps, a hint of jealousy. She'd learned to work around it. When Aidan took their then-only car on a day she'd planned on going to see Danny, she'd find the nearest bus stop. When Aidan insisted on her waiting until the weekend so he could accompany her, she promised to go again with him, but went on her own anyway. When Aidan talked about Danny's decline in the starkest terms to get her to *see the truth, darling*, she stood and waited politely for him to finish, then changed the subject because she knew what he didn't: that miracles did sometimes happen.

But now – she squirmed guiltily under the duvet – now Aidan really did have a reason to doubt her. She slowly curled herself into a ball, slid her hands between her knees and her belly, remembering the exact moment when she'd seen baby Danny for the first time, walking into the hospital room behind her father, who'd been anxious and unfamiliar-looking in his good suit. The baby had seemed so tiny to her, so precious, as if he'd break the moment you took your eyes off him. She hadn't wanted to touch him at first, convinced she'd harm him somehow.

'Don't be shy now,' her mother had said impatiently. 'You have to support his head, just so. Don't let him go, even if he wriggles. Don't let him fall, you hear me? Always keep a hand on him.'

Her mother had left soon after that, but Chloe remembered the words as if it had been yesterday. She'd done it at eight and eighteen, taking care of her brother and protecting him, and she was still doing it now, at twenty-eight. She turned her head slowly to look at her husband again, barely visible in the half-darkness of the bedroom. How could she possibly start all over again? How could she bring something as precious, as breakable as a soft little baby soul into a world that contained so many things it needed to be protected from?

All of a sudden, she couldn't stand it any more, couldn't bear another moment of lying here in the dark and imagining her baby coming into the world. Moving pretend-languidly, fake-fluidly, as if she was merely settling in her sleep, she slid out from under the duvet, immediately tucking it back so Aidan wouldn't be disturbed by the chill of her absence, and quietly padded down to the office to find her laptop.

Twenty-Three

Half an hour later, she sat back and raked her fingers through her hair. She must have taken hundreds of photos of Madeleine Hamilton, different poses, different angles, up high with the tripod and manually from all around. The light had hit the old woman's skin just right; her shoulders were set in a pose that might have made even Liz Tallis have to try hard to find something to grumble about. But the eyes didn't work at all. While Madeleine's body and face changed around them, her eyes were fixed on a point just next to the camera in a flat and unmoving gaze, distant and closed. Cursing when the old laptop – bequeathed to her ages ago by Liz when she'd upgraded her own – refused to move as fast as her fingers, Chloe clicked through to pick the three least disappointing pictures, then opened her editing programme and began fiddling with infinitesimal levels of brightness, hue and saturation, her eyes locked onto the images on the screen.

Just after 1 a.m., she sat back and rested her chin in her hands. She remembered the way the light had warmed Madeleine's eyes when she'd mentioned her husband, a good-looking man with untidy dark hair and a lovely smile she'd spied in a picture frame on the way out. And when she'd talked about Georgiana. Chloe pulled out the sketch, brought it into the light of the desk lamp. It was even more beautiful now than when she'd seen it the previous afternoon. The vivid flashes of colour, the confident jumble of lines that Madeleine's pencil had somehow managed to magically lift from the page to make these two beautiful girls come alive. That was what Chloe wanted for this photograph, and she'd be damned if she couldn't achieve something similar.

How old had Georgiana been that day? Twenty-one? There was something very grown-up in her eyes, at odds with Madeleine's sweetly innocent face. Georgiana seemed more restless, too, the way her body leaned forward, the suggestion of tightness in her shoulders. *She was the only mother I ever knew*, Madeleine had said. What would it have been like to be a mum to young Madeleine at ten, twelve, sixteen years old?

She remembered Danny at twelve. A gangly boy who'd filled out too quickly. Almost overnight, he wasn't her little boy to constantly patch up with plasters after mysterious bouts of 'wobbly knees', but an almost-youth on the cusp of a crippling, incurable illness. They hadn't talked about that last part much at all. At some point, between visits to the cardiologist and the neurologist, the speech therapist and physical therapy, the two of them had quietly decided that they weren't going to mention the fact that Danny was going to die, whether in two years from heart failure, or in twelve years from something else, or even in another twenty-four.

Instead, Chloe had thrown herself into making his life as normal as she possibly could. She spent so much time arm-wrestling with his school about adjustments for his impaired mobility that he was almost through with it by the time they'd finally established a schedule for classmates helping him up the stairs. She took him swimming and persuaded his physio to train with him at a boxing gym three times a week – a rough, loud place in a converted factory, where heavily muscled men pushed lorry tyres back and forth and did pull-ups on the old steel girders – just so that he didn't spend his whole life in hospitals and surgeries. Before too long, the combined might of Danny and Chloe Archer was legendary among Torquay social and medical services, and it was rumoured that certain social workers would run and hide when they heard Chloe's polite but steely tones at the front desk.

She encouraged Danny to be out and about with his mates as

if nothing was wrong; helped him there and back with his crutches, even if it wasn't convenient, even if it meant saying no to the boy who asked her out on Saturday, even if her girlfriends started forgetting to include her in outings altogether, knowing she'd cry off anyway. She was adamant that as little as possible should be different for Danny.

Her eyes went back to Georgiana. She rarely stood still, Madeleine had said. Had she been restless that summer, coming back from Europe to be with her sister? Had she wanted more, felt tied down? It didn't look like it, the way her hand was intertwined lovingly with the younger girl's. And yet . . .

Chloe had never once minded the obvious stuff of being a mum to Danny, the things that other people clearly thought an infringement on her freedom – or what Aidan insisted on calling 'a hard life' that he had swooped in and rescued her from like a knight in shining armour. Helping Danny, spending inordinate amounts of time at hospitals and clinics, organising carers, guys who were able to lift Danny and help him go to the loo after her dad had passed away. Words couldn't begin to describe how much her brother had hated his uselessness and neediness. He'd let her help him to the toilet exactly once, and never again.

'I won't let that happen to us, Chloe,' he'd said. 'I won't let you become *that*, and me become *that*. Changing my nappy and wiping my bum. Wheel me in front of the head of the NHS and I'll make it happen.'

But Chloe didn't mind. It had all become part of her without her ever thinking about it. Maybe because she never knew any different; maybe because Danny was so much part of her that taking care of him, loving him was as natural to her as breathing.

Georgiana looked back at her from the drawing, her chin lifted ever so slightly, as if she alone understood how Chloe felt. That she loved Danny, that Danny was her other half. It had always been the two of them, and she wouldn't have it any other way.

What she did mind, every now and then when no one could hear her thinking, was the heaviness of that love. What should have been ordinary sister–brother affection, with squabbles and fights and grudging apologies, had condensed over the years into a very different kind of thing. Responsibility and worry. The constant longing to be able to shoulder part of the other's burden. The raging at the futility of it all. The loneliness. Everyone else involved had someone to talk to, could shed their worries, go home at the end of the day and leave some of it behind. But the buck stopped with Chloe, who, until Aidan had come along, had had no one to talk to at all.

And deep down, where no one could ever see it, that heaviness had sometimes become so suffocating, so close that it was almost unbearable. You weren't supposed to think like that, not about someone you loved. And you could never say out loud, not to yourself nor to anyone else, that there were times when you wanted to run away as fast and as far as you could, because that seemed the only way to escape. But as Chloe locked eyes with Georgiana's one last time, she thought she saw just the faintest hint of exactly that in the other girl's gaze.

Twenty-Four

As fast as it had come, Chloe pushed the thought away, turning back to her laptop. Well, she'd just go back to Summerhill, like she'd promised Madeleine. She clearly couldn't hand any of these photos in to Matt Cooper, who sounded like he could potentially be a right pain.

She had barely finished the thought when an email notification popped up in the corner of her screen: *From: mattcooper@wonderlybooks.com*. She almost gasped out loud. Was one of bloody Matt Cooper's many accomplishments actually reading minds? Cautiously and very quietly, as if he might be able to see her sitting there in her study, she opened the email.

Dear Chloe MacAllister,
Just checking in to see how you got on yesterday. Brilliant, no doubt. Expect pictures soonest. Maybe a few thumbnails to tantalise the old taste buds? Later today?
Yours sincerely,
Matt Cooper

She ground her teeth, wishing she could reach right inside her inbox and give him a hard shake. It'd been less than eight hours; who did he think she was, Mario Testino?

Dear Matt Cooper,
Working on it. I'll be in touch. Soonest.
Yours cordially,
Chloe

She immediately regretted sending it, because if she was sitting here working in the dark, then so was he, and he would, no doubt, be encouraged to pepper her with more requests. Sure enough, within seconds, a reply came back: *Aha! Burning the midnight oil. I like your dedication. Tell me about the pictures. And about Mrs Hamilton.*

Chloe sent back a dignified response: *I can't until I've viewed all of them. Signing off now.*

Don't go. Call me. Or I'll call you?

Don't!

Predictably, less than three seconds later, her phone rang. The low buzzing bounced around the dark room and she snatched it up fast, heart hammering furiously as she stared at the shadowy rectangle of the door behind her.

'I said, don't call me,' she hissed into the phone. 'It's two in the morning, for heaven's sake, and I can't really talk.'

'It's only one forty-five,' came his amused drawl. 'And the day has twenty-four working hours, you know.'

'Your day maybe, not mine,' she whispered acidly.

'Tell me about yours, then,' he said reasonably. 'Come on, don't leave an old man hanging.'

'You don't sound particularly old,' she said suspiciously.

'Certainly not as young as you are.' He chuckled.

'All right.' She sighed. 'So . . .'

She recapped the meeting for him, leaving out her clumsy fumblings at the beginning, the way Madeleine had taken pity on her – though she had a distinct feeling that Matt Cooper would know about all that nonetheless – and, obviously, the fact that the pictures weren't really up to scratch yet. He let her talk, and didn't probe, only occasionally asking a question about the house and the way Madeleine lived, what she looked like, what they'd talked about. Oddly, it was quite nice to sit here in the dark, talking to this stranger about her day. She'd pulled the camera into her lap, and the weight of it was familiar and comforting; the night was cool and quiet, 4 a.m. was still a while off, and Matt Cooper, beneath the curt bluster and rude asides, was actually a rather good listener.

'Do you know anything about Georgiana Hamilton, by any chance?' she asked eventually.

'Madeleine's sister?' He paused, and Chloe imagined a tall man hunched over a desk in a study not unlike her own, pushing his hand through tousled hair. 'Not really,' he said eventually. 'She was co-author on the books, obviously, but Madeleine's always been our contact.'

'But did you ever actually meet her when she was still alive?'

'No, but then again I've never met Madeleine either. It's quite tricky to get in touch with her, as a matter of fact. She doesn't answer the phone, letters go unanswered, no agent to speak for her. You can't imagine how many times I had to approach her to get a photo taken. It was the sales team's idea, to have something new to tide people over until the book is finally here. I hope she wasn't too grumpy about it.'

'Well, she didn't seem particularly keen at first,' Chloe said cautiously. 'But then . . .' She thought about the odd sense of timelessness, the inexplicable connection between them in that vast, light-filled library, and a warm something flooded her insides. 'She was really nice, actually,' she said simply.

'Good news! She must really like you,' he said approvingly. 'Because even though she was perfectly polite to me, I somehow came away with a lot less information than I thought I had when I hung up. She's quite a clever conversation partner, let me tell you.'

Chloe smiled and high-fived the woman on the screen for possibly being the very first person who'd ever matched Matt Cooper in conversational acumen.

'You wouldn't believe how many people are breathing down my neck here. I'm quite terrified.'

Chloe snorted incredulously.

'I *am*. Did you find anything out, by the way?'

'No,' Chloe said firmly. 'And I didn't even try. I had enough on my hands—' Her heart suddenly jumped into her throat and her words died on her lips. She'd heard a noise, a door opening somewhere down the hall.

'Chloe?' Matt said into the phone, so loudly that Chloe was convinced the whole world could hear him.

She turned to the door, strained to listen, but all she could hear was a whooshing noise in her head and her own panicked breathing.

'I have to go. Please don't call me back, please, Matt,' she whispered. She ended the call without waiting for his answer and set the phone on the windowsill, then, with flying fingers, closed her laptop and slid it underneath the cupboard next to her.

By now, the sound of footsteps, very clear and decisive, could be heard outside, coming closer until they stopped in front of the door. She snatched up the closest thing, which happened to be the copy of *Foxy the Great*, which had been in with her photo stuff. She slid the sketch between the pages and, at the last moment, pushed the laptop cable to the back of the desk so it slithered out of sight.

When Aidan opened the door a few seconds later, she was bent over the battered book as if she'd never intended to do anything more than a spot of midnight reading.

'What on earth are you doing in here?' His voice was hoarse with sleep. 'I woke up and you were gone.'

'Oh, I couldn't sleep, darling,' she said brightly, forcing her shoulders away from her ears. 'You know me and my sleep.'

'Hmm,' he said, unconvinced. 'Reading a picture book at two in the morning?'

'Well, yes, I . . . that is to say . . .' She pushed her fingers in between the pages so Aidan couldn't see them trembling, but he plucked the book from her hands and studied it.

'This is that woman,' he said slowly. 'The photo that man

rang about.' He looked at Chloe over the top of the book, then scanned the rest of the room as if she might have hidden Matt Cooper somewhere. Chloe looked determinedly away from her phone, inwardly quailing as she imagined what would have happened if Aidan had walked in a few moments earlier.

'Why are you looking at this, Chloe?' he asked.

'No reason really, just a trip down memory lane.' Chloe was surprised how calm she sounded, even though her heart was pounding inside her chest. But then Aidan leafed through the first few pages and found the sketch of Georgiana and Madeleine. He might have been tired, but he was anything but slow, especially where Chloe was concerned, and it took him only a second to realise that the book and the sketch had been done by one and the same person. He raised his eyes to meet Chloe's.

'And where did you get this?'

She stared at him wordlessly, a flush creeping across her cheeks.

'Where, Chloe?' he repeated calmly. His voice never got agitated or rough; just like his face, it evened out, rid itself of any irregularities and edges, became flat and smooth. Only his fingers gave him away, tightening around the piece of paper, curling the edges upwards, then over. In a moment they would touch, would crease and flatten—

Chloe jumped up, so quickly that Aidan, who clearly hadn't expected her to move, took a step back in alarm, his hand involuntarily letting go of the sketch.

'I found it inside the book,' she said, picking up the piece of paper and putting it on the shelf behind her, smoothing it out in the process. 'It was my father's, all right? Look . . .' She took the book from him, opened it at the very front. *For Owen, 1956.* 'Now . . .' She yawned ostentatiously, closing the book and setting it on the shelf as well, covering the drawing. 'I'm very tired. Come on, darling, let's go back to bed.'

Twenty-Five

'Morning, sleepyhead,' a voice murmured right next to her. Chloe swam to the surface of a restless sleep, forcing open her eyes to see her husband sitting on the edge of the bed holding a cup of tea. He was fully dressed and the clock next to her showed 8:00.

'I have to go. And you've overslept,' he said. 'All that reading you're doing in the middle of the night.'

She dimly noticed a spiral of steam curling away from the mug as he put it on the bedside table next to her, but her stomach must have recognised the sweet, slightly artificial Earl Grey scent before she did, because it heaved ever so slightly.

He studied her. 'You don't look too good,' he said. 'Are you sure you're not coming down with something? I think you're spending too much time at that care home, picking up all sorts of bugs.'

'Just tired, sweetie,' she said hoarsely.

'You need to get yourself checked out,' he said. 'Why don't I call Dr Webb and make an—'

'Aidan, I'm fine.' She must have spoken too loudly, because Aidan raised his eyebrows.

'I really don't know what's got into you lately, Chloe,' he said slowly. 'You always seem to be on edge, and you're out and about at all hours.'

'Hardly. I'm always here. Where else would I go?' She hadn't meant to sound curt, but she needed space to wake up, to breathe away the nausea moving towards the top of her stomach. She looked down at the duvet, for a brief, ludicrous moment imagining the baby in there, that stupid secret that refused to be freed and that made her words sound uncharacteristically defiant. 'Darling,' she said quickly, reaching out to take his hand. 'I'm sorry . . .'

Aidan didn't say anything for a moment, intent on weaving his fingers through hers one by one. The angle was awkward and it hurt a little, the way her knuckles were overextended in his grip.

'You know, most women would give anything to have the life you lead,' he said in a conversational tone. 'A house, a home. Some people would kill for it.' His grip tightened the lattice of their intertwined fingers, bending hers the wrong way, and she gave a small gasp.

Aidan put his head to the side in curious bemusement.

'Don't you agree?'

'Yes, of course,' she said. But her answer had come a beat after it should have, and he squeezed her fingers again sharply before suddenly releasing them. He rose to let the blinds snap up with a loud clank that made her head pound, then stood by the window, his shoulders set tightly.

'Are you going to see Danny again today?' He didn't look round.

'Not sure,' she said cautiously. 'Maybe. I haven't—'

He didn't wait for her to finish. 'Oakwood are raising their fees, did you see?'

'No, really?' Chloe struggled into a sitting position. 'They're expensive as it is. How did you . . . I mean, was there a letter or . . .' She remembered what Dixie had said the previous afternoon. 'Did you go to Oakwood to talk to them about it?' She watched him, covertly rubbing her knuckles, not really knowing what to expect.

'Yes,' he said. 'The other day.'

'Ah,' she said. 'So you weren't . . .' She broke off. 'You didn't mention it, that's all,' she finished. 'We could have gone together.'

'It was on my way back from work. I put the paperwork on the dresser downstairs. It would be nice, occasionally, if you were fully aware of the whole picture at Oakwood.'

In her relief that there was a reasonably simple explanation for his visit, she glossed over the gross unfairness of that statement. 'Oh Aidan, I do appreciate everything you've done for him,' she said quickly. 'I could work, too, contribute to his upkeep, if you'd only—'

'Anything you could do isn't even on the same planet as those fees,' Aidan said dismissively. His beeper buzzed against his lapel. 'I have to run,' he said, squinting at it. 'I wish I'd never agreed to this whole surgery expansion, it's an endless loop of paperwork. But it'll all be worth it when I have more time, won't it?' His face creased in a smile. 'You do look very washed out, my love. Just stay in bed, rest today.' He took her hand in his, touched it briefly with his lips. 'And don't give Oakwood another thought. We'll sort it out. I'll always be there to help, you know that. We will talk about it tonight.'

Chloe had held out for as long as she could to keep Danny with her, working around Jerry's schedule and hounding the NHS for all the other bits they needed for at-home care. Eventually it was Danny himself who raised the matter, a few months after Chloe had met Aidan.

They'd been watching a film together, Jerry, Chloe and Danny, and Chloe had fallen asleep on the sofa, only waking when the final credits rolled.

'I'm sorry,' she'd said hoarsely. 'Bit tired today.'

Danny threw Jerry a quick look, and he got up to move the wheelchair so Danny was facing the sofa.

'Chloe,' Danny said gently. 'We have to talk. It's all getting to be too much – for us, and for you.'

She shook her head, tiredness making her slow in responding. 'I just fell asleep, that's all. I'm sorry—'

'No,' her brother cut in. 'Don't be sorry, not ever. You're the only reason I'm even still here, in this flat, with you. But . . .'

He threw a pleading look at Jerry, who said, 'Danny needs a care home. A proper one where they have everything on site. I'm full of admiration for this bulldog approach you have to life, Chloe darling, and far be it from me to stand in your way, but continuing this way isn't good for either of you.'

'No,' Chloe said. 'It's fine. *I'm* fine.'

'Danny needs more now,' Jerry said baldly. 'The way the illness is progressing – and trust me, I've seen my fair share—'

'Jerry, stop,' Danny cut in. 'Chloe, it's my decision. I want us to apply for a place in a care home.'

'But I don't *want* to,' she said vehemently. 'As long as—'

'It's time,' he said gently. 'I don't want this for you any more; I don't want this for *us*. I want you to be out there having a life. A good life. What I would love most in the world right now is for you to visit me and tell me all about your adventures.'

'Although not with that strapping doctor of yours,' Jerry threw in. 'We don't like him and—'

'Will you shut up, Jerry?' Danny said exasperatedly. 'The point is, Chloe, we'll still be together, you and I, we will still see each other all the time.'

'No,' Chloe said flatly.

It took a while for Chloe to be persuaded, but somehow, before she'd even extracted the emergency box from its space underneath the drawer to check what she could afford, it was already happening, and very fast. Aidan had a place in mind, a private facility not too far away from where they'd talked about moving in Plymouth. He'd called in a few favours – *I knew you'd come round, darling* – and without any ado at all, Danny was moved to Oakwood Home, which really was like a home, the way the sun came in through the chequered curtains, the generous common area that had been cleverly laid out like a living room, the nurse's cheerful smile as she wheeled Danny around to meet the other residents, without a hint of exasperation or condescension.

Danny pointed everything out to Chloe, marvelling at the heated pool and the exercise room and the physio's amazing tattoos. He seemed upbeat and optimistic and she almost had the impression that his speech seemed to be improving slightly, so much so that when the time came for her to leave, she felt marginally more capable of accepting the situation. And when she had mentioned payment, Aidan had brushed it off. *We're together now, you and I. It's my responsibility as much as yours.* So Chloe had pushed the emergency box back underneath the kitchen drawer and tried to stop feeling guilty that she'd left Danny at Oakwood with someone else paying for it.

It took time for that enormous weight of worry that had been clamped around Chloe for twenty years to shrink. It never went away entirely, but little by little, it lessened. To know that Danny was taken care of. To have Aidan to share it all with. To realise that things would be all right from now on. A few months into Danny's new life at Oakwood, she found herself driving away from one of their visits and realising to her surprise that she was happy. And, slightly guiltily, relieved. She looked across at her husband's profile and the strong, capable hands gripping the steering wheel as he navigated his way through Plymouth. And when he turned and smiled at her, he seemed to know exactly what she was thinking, and she'd felt so in love, so utterly lucky, that she didn't think it would ever change.

Chloe had come back up to the bedroom to fetch the teacup from her bedside table, but ended up sitting down heavily on the bed instead and staring out at the sky, where a mass of bluish-grey clouds was gathering above the treetops. They were moving and growing, little grey cloud rags pulling away, others banding together in a roiling mass.

Every time Aidan had talked about Oakwood's fees, and

many other times too, Chloe had suggested moving Danny somewhere more modest, or talked about starting to work again so she could help with the payments. She'd offered up the contents of the emergency box, which after its discovery had been moved to their safe. But Aidan didn't want her to help in any way. He just wanted to *talk* about it. *We will talk tonight.* That 'will' didn't command, it didn't threaten, not per se. It simply assumed, as a given, that Chloe would be there tonight, waiting to be talked to. But, thought Chloe as she emptied the cup of cold tea into Aidan's precious jade tree, that was hours away, and she had no intention of sitting around here, where the smell of Earl Grey conspired with the bonsai dirt to stir up trouble at the bottom of her stomach.

She marched along the landing to the study, where she retrieved her phone.

'Chloe! You had me worried.' Matt Cooper's growl was tempered by a distinct note of relief. 'I was going to ring right back, but you did say—'

'Thank you,' she said quickly, 'for that.'

'First time a woman's ever thanked me for not calling,' he chuckled. 'Everything all right?'

'Oh, of course,' she said quickly. 'It's just I'd woken up my husband and he really needs his sleep. He's been so busy lately,' she added, 'and it wasn't really . . .' She stopped, aware of how pathetic she must sound.

'A good time?' Matt suggested, all amusement gone from his voice. 'What did he say about Madeleine Hamilton? I know he wasn't particularly keen.'

'Oh, that.' Chloe gave a hasty, off-hand laugh as she picked up *Foxy the Great*, slid Madeleine's sketch inside and pushed the book all the way underneath the big cupboard holding the printer and assorted bits of paperwork. 'It's all fine. No problem. Couldn't be better, in fact.' She stepped back to check whether the book was visible from any angle.

'Chloe, I'm not sure what's going on, but I don't think I like it.' Matt sounded concerned now.

'It's not up to you to like it or not like it,' she shot back. 'Stop worrying, you *will* get your photo.'

'That's not really what I'm talking about,' he said in a low voice. 'You should tell him.'

He waited another beat, but how could Chloe possibly explain to him that Aidan and Summerhill didn't go together? How could she put into words the way the house belonged just to her, a secret parallel universe where everything else – her life here, Danny and Aidan – faded away altogether?

'Thank you,' she said instead.

'I didn't do anything,' he said gruffly, then added unexpectedly gently, 'I wish I *could*, you know, but . . .'

'For giving me the job, I mean.'

'I've questioned my own sanity on that matter more than once in the last few days. But,' he added brightly, 'I'm getting a good vibe from you. And I'm never wrong with vibes. Not wrong about much else either.'

'Of course not.' She rolled her eyes at the ceiling. 'Anyway, I should run . . .'

'Yes, you should,' he said approvingly. 'You have a lot of work to do.'

Twenty-Six

The clouds she'd seen from her bedroom that morning were gathering in earnest now, big puffy thunderheads that towered over the horizon as she drove away from Plymouth.

When she had come into the garage, she'd realised that, of course, Aidan had taken the Vauxhall this morning, leaving the Porsche sitting in the garage, covered by a cloth. Well, he'd never actually expressly told her not to take the Porsche, had he? It had always been understood that she would never in a million years have the guts to drive it. Well, then.

She had stalled the unfamiliar clutch twice before she'd finally managed to back the little red car out of the garage, and then again at the bottom of the road, where she let thirty-five cars pass before she stopped shaking enough to pull out. Now that she was on the A38, however, she was beginning to see the point of this whole driving thing, and the little car seemed eager to please, speeding up and slowing down at the slightest tap of the pedals, as she headed straight towards the thickest of the blue-black clouds ahead.

It had started to rain by the time she reached the Summerhill lane, and she slowed right down, because there was no amount of new-found courage in the world that would allow her to bring home the Porsche with even the slightest scratch. She winced when a branch swished across the door with the high-pitched squeak of a thorn on metal, and flinched when a loud boom of thunder suddenly sounded through the trees behind her. The foliage around her was so thick that the rain didn't penetrate the canopy, only occasionally flinging a small burst of droplets onto the windscreen.

The moment she emerged onto the courtyard, however, it was like driving into a sheet of water. Wind was whipping the treetops and surging through the gardens. The house was barely visible, and she was just squinting through the downpour, trying to figure out how to run in without getting her equipment ruined, when she spied movement by the tall windows.

She frowned, but it wasn't until a gust of wind blew the rain up and sideways that she recognised Madeleine Hamilton, hunched over and clinging one-handed to the window frame. The old lady had clearly been in the process of fastening the shutters, because one of them was closed, the little hasp pushed through the top, but the other was still free, slamming hard against the side of the house and then whipping back towards the window. Chloe shot out of the car, kicking the door shut behind her. The rain hit her like a handful of needles, the wind buffeting her as she battled her way to the front of the house, reaching Madeleine just as the enormous shutter collided with her shoulder.

'What on earth are you doing?' she shouted.

'They'll come clean through the window with this wind,' Madeleine shouted back. Her hair was plastered to her skull, her eyes blinking rapidly against the rain.

'Go inside, I'll fix it,' Chloe shouted, but Madeleine ignored her and reached for the blasted shutter again, which took the opportunity to whip backwards out of her one-handed grasp. Chloe scrabbled to grab the edge of it, and together they slammed it shut, shoving the clasp home.

'This one too.' Madeleine gestured at the window on the corner.

'It'll be fine,' Chloe yelled. 'The rain'll stop in a moment. You shouldn't—' The sound of the shutters slamming against the window drowned out the rest of her words.

Gesturing furiously for Madeleine to go inside, Chloe fastened the last two sets of shutters, then made a dash for the front door, where the old lady stood waiting to slam it behind her. The sudden absence of noise and water and wind was almost as loud as the impact of the elements had been, and Chloe swayed for a moment as she got her bearings.

'What on earth possessed you to go out there in this weather?'

'I asked the nurse to fasten them earlier.' Madeleine had taken off her cardigan and was shaking it out. 'She must not have put the hasp through, though. She was in a hurry to leave. Can't say I blame her: the weather hits quite suddenly on the coast. But I'm not *so* very sorry for her either. She's a bit of a harridan, always scolding me for things.'

She pinned back her hair more securely, then eyed Chloe.

'You look like a drowned kitten,' she said with a sudden flash of laughter in her eyes.

Chloe looked down at her shoes, which squelched with water; at her clothes, her dripping-wet hair. She rubbed her cheeks and felt droplets fly.

'So do you!' She giggled and pointed to Madeleine's feet, where a little puddle had collected on the tiled floor.

A clap of thunder made both of them jump. Madeleine picked up an old blanket from a bench nearby. 'You should get out of those wet clothes.'

'You go and change first.' Chloe peeled off her own cardigan. 'I'll sort myself out.'

Madeleine hesitated, then said, 'Go straight up, fourth door on the left. That's my old bedroom. I'm pretty sure there are still some shirts and things hanging in the wardrobe. It's all clean, I promise, I just haven't been in there in a while. I live mostly down here now. And then we'll have a cup of tea.'

It was warm and airless as Chloe walked up the stairs. She found a funny little loo squeezed between two bedrooms, where she dried her hair and washed her hands, then she stepped out into the corridor. Fourth door, Madeleine had said.

Opening the door and fumbling for the old-fashioned switch, she turned on the light. So this was Madeleine's old bedroom. A lovely room, too, with its silvery-blue faded wallpaper and light grey curtains, an ottoman and small armchair grouped around a low table, and an old sleigh bed, the bedspread matching the curtains. The air was so still that it was hard to imagine anyone moving through it recently; that there'd once been light flooding in and flowers on the bedside table, voices out on the landing, someone sitting at the mirrored table to pin up their hair or spritz themselves with scent from one of the dusty old glass bottles. And yet it didn't feel abandoned or desolate, but warm and quiet, so quiet you could hear the ticking of the little clock on the mantelpiece and the rustle of a small creature in the ceiling above. Homely sounds that mingled with the rain and wind outside, a melody from another world, faint and yet so utterly real that Chloe turned to the door, half expecting someone to come in at any moment, curls drawn back at the neck, holding a linen-bound sketchbook. *There you are, Chloe. Come down quick, Cookie has tea ready.*

She gave a self-conscious laugh, then advanced on the giant wooden wardrobe tucked into an alcove, a waft of mothballs and age-old dust billowing out as she opened the door. She breathed through her nose, taking in the blouses and cardigans draped on hangers. There was the odd pair of trousers here and there, but mostly there were dresses. Calf-length floaty dresses, and funny square ones with drooping waists. Bright polka-dot and rayon crêpe frocks with high waists, puffed sleeves and dainty collars. She stared at the contents of the wardrobe, shaking her head to dispel the strange illusion of timelessness. And that was when she saw it, stencilled on top of an old wooden box sitting in the bottom of the wardrobe, worn and scratched with use but still clearly legible: GEORGIANA ADA HAMILTON.

She picked up the box and gazed at it, confused. Why—

'You took the fourth on the right.' A low, even voice spoke from the door.

Chloe whirled around. Madeleine stood in the doorway, bracing herself against the frame with one hand, breathing hard from the exertion of walking up the stairs.

Chloe blushed fiercely at having been caught snooping. 'I'm so sorry,' she mumbled.

'Georgie's things will fit you much better anyway. You're the same shape, you know.' Flicking through the contents of the wardrobe, Madeleine quickly selected a pair of trousers and a blue blouse with an old-fashioned bow at the neck. 'A jacket too, maybe, just until the chill comes off.'

She held out the armful of clothes to Chloe, who realised to her mortification that she was still holding the box. Confused, she thrust it at Madeleine, who stepped back unsteadily. The box clattered to the ground with a deafening crash and the old lady lost her balance.

'Oh God, I'm so sorry.' Chloe lunged to catch her, and for a moment, they were caught in a tight embrace, so close that she could feel Madeleine trembling, small tremors that ran up and down her back, her fast, irregular heartbeat.

'Are you all right?' she said in alarm.

'I'm fine.' Madeleine pushed Chloe off her furiously, displaying a surprising amount of strength. 'I'll see you downstairs,' she said, her voice shaking but more controlled. Carefully, keeping one hand on the wall, she walked out through the door.

'Do you need help with the stairs?' Chloe called after her.

'No,' came back the decisive answer, followed by a polite but no less forbidding 'Thank you.'

Twenty-Seven

Madeleine had been right, Georgiana's clothes did fit Chloe, but it didn't quite explain her agitation and anger. She buried her chin in the collar of the jacket, warmth seeping back into her limbs as she looked down at the remnants of the box on the ground, putting off the moment when she had to go downstairs. She knelt quickly, touched the faded stencilling on the lid. Georgiana. Madeleine's *Georgie.* Who had lived here once, in this lovely silver-blue room. Who, if she'd still been alive, would be old now, in her late eighties, nineties even. Somehow Chloe couldn't reconcile the thought of a ninety-year-old woman with the Georgiana in the sketch, in the same way as she couldn't picture the young, long-limbed Madeleine turning into the slightly forbidding woman downstairs. For a moment, a powerful sense of unreality washed over her as features and faces oscillated in front of her eyes, young and old superimposed over one another with seventy decades in between. Bit by bit, though, she pulled forward the only image of Georgiana that she really knew: a young woman sitting at a kitchen table, her eyes looking out at the viewer, lovely and clever and restless, the tipped-up chin the faintest bit rebellious.

The box had broken clean open, its lid and bottom splayed wide. Chloe winced when she saw it. But then she realised that it was meant to do exactly that, to swing all the way open on its hinges to create a writing surface on the other side. Small cubbyholes held an assortment of writing implements, now strewn across the floor. Crouching, she started gathering paperclips and pencils, slotting them back into the compartments along with an old ink pen with a rusty nib, then reached for the papers scattered across the scratchy carpet. Postcards, once garishly colourful, now faded, covered with slanted loopy writing.

Maddy! Yours truly made it to Nantes. Cousin Xenia's place is wonderful. Bit stuffy, but so central to everything. I was naughty and dodged her company today, but she stops to chat at every corner and it took us half an hour just to cross the road yesterday! It was bliss poking about town on my own, although I wish you were here! Give Cookie and the others my love.

Foxy, you wouldn't believe the thunderstorm we had yesterday. Cousin Xenia spent the entire time shivering under the table with her dogs – she thought it was the safest place. I did my best to comfort her, but I wanted to be outside. I didn't tell her that you and I used to run around the courtyard in our swimming costumes amidst rain and thunder and lightning. She might have had a heart attack. She's now taken to her bed with ominous 'chills', and I'm sitting in a café eating the most delicious flaky pastry. Nothing beats Cookie's Victoria sponge, but this does come close. Miss you, lovely girl!

Chloe found herself laughing softly at the thought of the two girls running around in the rain and Georgiana sitting in a café in Nantes – sat, Chloe corrected herself, seventy years ago. The postcards had no stamp on them, and it looked as though Georgiana had decided not to send them; perhaps she would have returned home before they arrived. The third one didn't even have an address on it, just a short paragraph.

I've met someone, Maddy, someone wonderful. So different to you and me, but so right for me too, so utterly perfect. He understands everything I want to say before I can even put proper words to it, he seems to know what I think better than I do myself, and when I don't, he thinks it through with me until I feel light with relief at having sorted it out in my mind. It frightens me how easy it is to fall in love like this, and I wish, so much, that I could remember more about our parents' marriage, could talk to our mother about this strange construct, where you are asked to abandon yourself entirely, without any guarantee whatsoever. I'm learning more about it every day. His name is Victor and I hope you'll love him as much as I do. Well, maybe not quite as much, but you know what I mean.

Chloe swallowed slightly with the rush of emotions on the page and the unexpected intimacy, before shuffling together the rest of the papers, an oddly ragtag collection of notecards, a napkin, a newspaper cutting, brown with age. All of them, the napkin included, were covered with the same loopy writing, a lot of it crossed out and some so small as to be illegible, almost as if Georgiana had tried out her thoughts on paper.

I was dreaming about you last night. That day we went out on the bay in Papa's boat and you almost overturned it, do you remember? You'd been talking about being allowed to steer the boat for days, but you were only six, for heaven's sake, and I couldn't believe that Papa actually let you do it. One time you made it turn so sharply that the tiller threatened to rip right out of your hands, but you held on tight, shrugging at me as if to say, see, course I can do it, your foot braced on the bench, the bay before us, the house above, you driving that big boat like an old sailor.

I woke up and I realised I'd been crying, I don't know why. Maybe because I miss that girl. And maybe because sometimes I think it's my fault that you never found her again after the accident, because I didn't try harder to make you leave Summerhill, to face the ghosts of his death. That hard, furious, all-consuming love, like yours for Papa and for Summerhill – and for me, too – I'm beginning to see that that isn't always a good kind of love. It traps you, it never lets you go unless you find a way of being your own person again. I wish that for you, with all my heart, and I hope that when you do, it will be that gutsy, windblown, utterly brilliant girl with the tiller in her hand.

The letter ended so abruptly that Chloe looked up, almost startled to find herself alone, in her own time, and not in the company of this young woman whose voice had been leaping off the page. The decades slid across each other again, here in Georgiana's room, where her thoughts seemed to linger, where her clothes were still in the wardrobe and her jacket was belted around Chloe like a suit of armour.

Reluctantly Chloe dropped the letter back into the box, which she managed to close again, straightening one of the bent hinges. Lost in thought, she picked up her wet clothes and folded them: trousers first, a sharp-creased rectangle, then the shirt on top in precise edges, rolling up the socks into a perfect ball. That hard and furious love, when you'd given up too much of yourself and were trapped in it, had lost who you really were . . . She swallowed and forced herself to focus on the razor-sharp edges of her clothes pile. Suddenly, she snatched it up and picked it apart, bunching the jeans inside the shirt and stuffing the socks on top of the messy bundle. Yes, she knew that kind of love well.

She was about to leave the room when she spotted a stray piece of paper under the dressing table. Not a letter, but instructions: *Your gas mask – how to use it.* Old-fashioned drawings accompanied the various steps of handling the mask, presented by a well-dressed lady swinging a little boxy carrying case in her hand. Chloe eyed the recalcitrant writing box, now back in the wardrobe. Loath to do battle with it again, she shrugged, slid the paper into her pocket and stepped out onto the landing.

Twenty-Eight

When Chloe got back downstairs, Madeleine was sitting in her chair, her eyes closed.

Chloe waited, then said hesitantly, 'I'll be going then. I did bring my photo stuff, it's in the car, but by the time the sky clears up, it'll be too late.'

'They didn't work out, those other pictures?' Madeleine asked, her eyes still closed.

'They're all right,' Chloe said. 'But not great. Mr Cooper won't be pleased, at any rate,' she added with a grin.

'That man,' Madeleine said darkly.

'You know, I think he might not be half bad,' Chloe said, thinking of the relief in Matt's voice earlier. It had been a while since someone had been waiting anxiously for her to ring, had been concerned for her. Other than Aidan, obviously. 'And thank you for the clothes. I'll return them next time.'

Madeleine smiled and finally opened her eyes, saw Chloe standing there, her face framed by the collar of Georgiana's jacket, her copper hair tousled after the rain, eyes smudgy and tired.

'They look good on you,' she said after a moment, her expression unreadable. Then she shook her head and sighed. 'I'm sorry about snapping at you earlier. It's just that I find my sister's room . . . difficult. And I hate the way I am these days, sitting in this stupid chair all day. I used to be running up and down those stairs, barely stopping to take a breath. Now I'm merely a squatter here, unable to do the most basic things. The shutters, for example.' She gave Chloe a wry smile. 'Don't get old,' she said. 'It's not all it's cracked up to be.'

Chloe hesitated for a moment. 'Did you ever try to use a walker or something?' she asked. 'You could—'

'Not with this.' Madeleine nodded at her twisted wrist. 'A bout of arthritis has compounded it lately and . . . Well, I make do with my cane.'

Chloe digested this, then looked around. 'Is there anything I can help you with while I'm here? Make you supper. Do your laundry or—'

'No, no, gosh no,' Madeleine said quickly, and drew herself up a little, gathering her dignity back around her. 'I'm sorry, I was being silly there for a moment, fulfilling every stereotype in the book. I am perfectly all right, I can manage. It's nothing.'

'It's rarely nothing,' Chloe said, and they both smiled at the memory of their first meeting. She looked down at the hem of the jacket. *That love like yours for Summerhill.* 'Did you ever think about leaving here?' she asked. 'I would hate to if I were you, but surely things could be made a bit easier: a home, maybe, or assisted living . . .'

'I won't leave, ever,' Madeleine said in the same low, even voice she had used in Georgiana's room. 'They'll bury me here.'

'Who is "they"?' Chloe asked tentatively. 'Will you have any family to come and . . . Or your husband's family?'

'I have no family left really. We never had children, and my husband died ten years ago. I took my name back, you know, and ever since then, it's just been me. No, I mean the ubiquitous *they*, the government, the council and such, who come and clean things up when people die. God knows, I pay enough taxes, given the size of this place. They should bury me halfway decently.'

Chloe nodded. 'And the house? What'll happen to Summerhill? It's so . . . lovely.'

'I'm not dead and gone yet, girl,' the older woman said, a note of impatience in her voice that made Chloe breathe slightly easier. 'And with any luck I won't be for a while. Although there mightn't be much left of the place soon. But that's what the new book is supposed to do,' she added. 'To bring in more money to fix it, to pay the taxes and everything.'

'But that's a wonderful way of saving your home,' Chloe said eagerly. 'From words on the page to bricks and mortar. It could be a great publicity angle. Your book will be huge.'

'I hate publicity,' Madeleine said. 'And as for "huge", well, there's just the small matter of . . .' She paused, her eyes straying over to the sketchpad Chloe had seen when she'd first come in, the stash of pencils still wedged inside the elastic band. She looked back at Chloe in a speculative sort of way. 'Can you keep a secret?'

Unconsciously Chloe's hand touched her stomach for a moment, then she gave a wry grin. 'I'm fairly good at those.'

'I don't have it.'

For a moment, Chloe was confused. 'What do you mean, you don't have it?'

'There's no book. Wonderly paid me when I signed a new contract – probably ripped me off,' she added bitterly, 'just because I don't have one of those new-fangled agents. Still, it was enough to get the windows by the terrace repaired, the eastern wall supported.'

Chloe stared at her. 'But that's impossible,' she said in a low tone, as if Matt Cooper was lurking somewhere close by. 'You could draw the phone book and it would be completely and utterly wonderful.'

Madeleine looked at her for a long moment, her eyes glinting strangely.

'Has anyone ever told you that you're too kind for this world?' she finally said.

'Oh God no,' Chloe said, embarrassed but inordinately pleased, too. 'So how did the other books come about?'

Madeleine leaned back in her chair, rested her head against one of the wings and Chloe sat down on a little stool next to her.

'Foxy had lost his parents, see, and we brought him back to the house to be raised with the dogs. Oh, it was a hare-brained idea altogether; who ever heard of something like that, deep in the country, where people shoot them and a load of other animals besides. But Papa used to adore his dogs. He wouldn't get out his gun when one of them was sick; no, he'd fetch the vet in straight away. He'd already passed away by then, so it was just us. My Aunt Marjorie never really took to country living; she couldn't countenance Foxy anywhere close to the house, but Cookie let us keep him down by the kitchens. She spoiled us something dreadful. And he settled in well, until, that is, some of his . . . shall we say baser instincts came through. He started raiding the windowsill for pies and the chicken coop at night. He was terrible.'

She shook her head, smiling. 'Nothing the vet could have done about those hens, let me tell you that.'

'So you drew Foxy's escapades,' Chloe said.

'Yes.' Madeleine sighed, and in an instant, she was an old woman again with useless legs and a crooked arm. 'The only thing I knew how to do. My father loved my drawings. He was forever tinkering with stuff, watering systems and draining the sludge away on the upper fields, and a sort of automatic cow-feeding contraption. He would ask me to put down his structures on paper for him, so I got used to trailing behind him with my sketchbooks, which were full of Summerhill. Walking by the estuary, the flowers waking up in the early morning, the birds starting to sing. And in winter we would have to break the ice in the pails, and Summerhill would be different altogether, frozen and crisp and windblown, but no less lovely. And when he was gone, I just kept going. Did the same rounds, drew the same things . . .'

Her voice died away and she looked out of the window, where sunlight glinted off the puddles in the courtyard.

'And Georgiana?'

Madeleine pressed her lips together, and for a moment Chloe was afraid she'd stop talking. But then she nodded. 'It's good to hear you say her name. I don't get to talk about her to anyone any more really. Georgiana was the writer. Our governess, Miss Keane – she was such a bossy old boot, I sometimes think Mr Cooper must be channelling her – she loved Georgie, of course; the two of them were forever yammering away about writing and travelling the world. Miss Keane left early in 1939, signed up for the war effort. Georgie wrote the stories to match my drawings: nothing big at first, just little scraps, tales, funny incidents. We made them up sitting in the tree or lying in bed at night, laughing until Aunt Marjorie came in, full of wrath.'

Her voice was faraway, lost in memories, and for a brief moment, Chloe thought she could see the two girls in the darkness, whispering and giggling by torchlight. Her heart gave a sudden fierce tug when she remembered Danny talking at night. He'd always had so much to say. In spite of his body slowing down – or maybe precisely because of it – his mind continued at a million miles an hour. *Did you know that the Trans-Siberian Railway is 5,772 miles long? You can travel from Moscow all the way to the end of the continent. And if you catch a boat, you can go across to Alaska and all the way down to Canada – it's just a short distance. Wouldn't that be something, to go to sleep in Asia and wake up in America?* He'd talked on and on, and she'd lain there in the darkness in the tiny room they shared until she was thirteen, and his voice would slowly lull her to sleep, the knowledge that someone else was awake while she was sleeping so comforting. A little while after that, her father had moved Danny into his own room, and Chloe had never slept like that ever again.

With some force, she wrenched her mind back to Madeleine.

'. . . Georgiana came up with Whizzy after Papa passed away, to cheer us up. She made her fly – that American pilot, Amelia Earhart, had just been the first woman to fly alone across the

Atlantic. And sometimes I thought that she . . . well, that she made Whizzy fly because she was stuck here with me.'

She looked down at her hands, and Chloe had the impression that she hadn't ever said that to anyone.

'Pipper came from a game we used to play. He was perfect book material, very easy. They all helped. Foxy to get us through the years after the war, Whizzy with paying for the damage done by some terrible winter storms in the late fifties, and with more taxes over the years. Pipper with the roof repairs. But . . .'

A long silence fell.

'I can't seem to create that world again, or any world, really, without Georgiana.'

Chloe looked at her, a lump in her throat. She was about to speak when her gaze suddenly fell on the clock on the mantelpiece. She shot up from her stool.

'I'm so sorry,' she said, looking around frantically for her bundle of wet clothes. 'I have to go. Oh God, I didn't realise how late it was. This has been—' *the best time* she wanted to say if it hadn't sounded so odd. 'But I'll be thinking about all this. And I'll come back. How about tomorrow? Between the two of us, we can come up with a plan, I'm sure.'

'That would be lovely. But whatever you do,' Madeleine struggled up, 'don't tell that pushy Mr Cooper. He is perfectly capable of coming down here and bullying me, and I don't think I could stand that.'

'Leave Matt Cooper to me,' Chloe promised, 'but I really have to go. My husband wanted to talk to me tonight. Oh God, he's going to *kill* me.'

Twenty-Nine

Maddy

There was a rustle and an almost inaudible intake of breath when I opened the door to the boat shed half an hour later.

'It's just me.' I closed the door in Leica's outraged face to find William standing right behind it, one arm hanging awkwardly, the other hand up by his chest, clutching a lump of wood. 'Coleman's made it,' I added, breathless from my run down the hill. 'He's still in hospital, but he's better. You saved his life, you know. They think you're a hero!'

William stared at me incredulously, as if he couldn't quite take in the news.

'Oh, thank you,' he said hoarsely. 'Thank you, miss, I . . . I can't tell you how much . . .' He gave a long, shaky exhale, his chest deflating until he was slumped back against the wall and slid slowly down it. The piece of wood dropped away, but one end knocked against his arm and he gave a strangled yell.

'How is it?' I asked rather unnecessarily, setting the bag down and crouching next to him.

A sheen of sweat had broken out on his forehead, but he unclenched his teeth just long enough for a rather overoptimistic 'It'll be all right, I think,' before slumping back against the wall. 'Maybe we should just wrap it up,' he suggested hopefully. 'Sometimes splinters come out on their own, you know.'

'This one won't,' I said, my tone rather short now because that would obviously have been my preference too. When I drew his arm closer, I almost recoiled at the sight of the wound closing around the unnatural ridge, the black end of the splinter gleaming dully. I wiped the back of my hand across my face, trying to push away the memory of my father's splayed-open side on the rocks, his contorted body. I hadn't been able to do anything then; what on earth made me think I could do this? For one mad moment I wanted to run up to the house and fetch Georgiana, who would think coolly and who was never afraid. But Georgiana was organising lunch and drinks for her friends and there was no one else.

I took a deep breath, despite the stifling heat and the rank smell, and pulled at a loose board sticking out of the wall above me, working at it when it refused to give, cursing in a way that had William tsk-tsking censoriously.

'Miss?' he said. 'What are you—'

'Lie down.' I knew that if I started talking, I'd lose courage. Using a bandage, I bound his arm to the wooden board as tightly as I could, ignoring his hissed intake of breath, the sweat slick against my elbow as I touched his forehead. Then I tied the boarded-up arm angled across his chest, so that I could get at the gash. His eyes followed my hands as I uncorked one of the bottles I'd brought. Gin fumes filled the shed.

'Are you trying to get me drunk?' he asked hopefully.

'It was the only thing I could find in the way of alcohol. I need to clean the pliers, and maybe I should also . . .' I looked at the arm in a speculative sort of way, and he widened his eyes in alarm.

'Oh no.' He tried to twitch it away. 'Oh no, no, no . . .'

I glared at him, my knees digging into the gravelly floor of the shed.

'I'm sorry, miss,' he said, instantly contrite. 'I really appreciate—'

'Will you stop all the sorries and misses,' I cut in impatiently. 'It's Maddy.' I frowned. William was wiggling his fingers. 'What now?'

'Could I possibly have some of that before we start?' he asked timidly, jabbing his chin towards the gin bottle. 'I have a feeling I'm going to need it.'

A little while later, I had a feeling we were both going to need it. I'd put a piece of wood between William's lips – something I'd heard my father mention when he'd talked about a stint in the field hospital – and I could hear the crunch of his teeth as I poured gin across the wound in a slow, steady trickle. Air hissed in and out through his nose in quickening spurts, and he was doing the low keening groan again.

'Breathe deeply,' I instructed, wishing I had a piece of wood between my own teeth. 'Or you'll faint.'

He nodded, clearly thinking that fainting would be the better option just now.

'Ready?'

He made an indeterminate noise as I gripped the pliers tightly, pushing everything else away: the sound of the sea outside, the rank air, the steam engine noises coming from William's nose.

'Here goes,' I whispered, and pulled the wound apart.

It was probably a matter of minutes, but it seemed like for ever. The pliers gleaming in the shaft of light coming through the hole in the wall, the rubbery give of raw flesh as I started probing for the shard, the blood, the groaning from William, whose eyes were locked onto me as the waves rushed and receded, throwing an eerie greenish glow on the walls.

The dark grey metal edge was slick with blood and I couldn't quite grasp it with the pliers, which seemed too large for the wound. William had begun to tremble, his body fluttering under my hands, and his groaning had changed slightly, had become a monotone whine. I didn't dare pause or look at him. What if he went into shock? I had heard my father talk about it and knew that it could lead to death, if infection didn't get there first. The pliers slipped on the shard again, and when I tried to grip it harder, I only succeeded in pushing it further in. Sweat dripping into my eyes, I probed once more, a strange sort of fury pushing through me, trying not to notice that William had stopped making any noise altogether, until finally I had it. I pulled, slowly, then a bit faster, because it had to be finished soon . . .

'Done.'

The piece of metal was nearly two inches long, glistening with blood. I dropped it on the floor, and just about managed to reach for the iodine bottle and pour a liberal dose straight into the wound before I was on my feet and out of the door. Outside, I doubled over against a tree and unceremoniously threw up into the undergrowth. It didn't take long; I hadn't eaten since yesterday. I stood hunched over for a while, my eyes closed, my temple resting against the tree, before straightening up and walking across to an empty barrel next to the shed. I washed my hands in the rainwater that had pooled there, then straightened my skirt and bundled my hair into a damp knot.

When I went back in, William was lying on the ground, his eyes closed, the piece of wood on the floor next to him, teeth marks showing as deep gouges against the brown. The iodine hurt dreadfully, I knew that, but I couldn't really do anything about it. I squatted beside him and inspected the arm. It didn't look too bad, actually. The hard ridge from the splinter had gone and the skin had sunk back, the gash bloody and gaping. I applied a little more iodine, flicking a worried glance at William, but he didn't open his eyes.

I bandaged the arm and carefully lifted it into what I thought might be a comfortable position, if comfortable was the right word; then I tidied up the bits I'd used and opened the bag Georgiana had packed for our breakfast: a bottle of water, bread, cheese and – I smiled briefly – two of Cookie's rock cakes.

When he heard the clink of the bottle cap, William's eyes opened a fraction, and he gave me a watery smile. 'I'm not sure if I hadn't rather died than go through that. The iodine was much worse than I remembered,' he whispered hoarsely.

'Here.' I held out a cup of water, but his hands were trembling too much to hold it, and his lips were raw from biting on the wood, so I sat down on the ground next to him and tore off a small piece of bread, dipping it into the water. He chewed slowly and waited politely until I gave him another piece.

Time slowed inside the warm shed as I fed William bits of bread dipped in water, pieces of cheese and rock cake. His lips were soft on my fingers, his breath a warm, steady sweep across my arm, his eyes occasionally finding mine and holding them, his lashes throwing spiky shadows on his cheeks as he tried to smile. Bit by bit I felt the tension ease in his jaw, felt the tightness leave my own shoulders until he shook his head and I leaned back against the wall, still holding the small knife and a piece of bread.

'You know, I'm not sure that they aren't going about it all wrong; the War Office, I mean,' he said hoarsely. 'They should be sending women like you into war. You could show the Krauts how it's done.'

'I wouldn't be much use to anyone. All I know is how to draw and repair fences. I haven't ever left Summerhill, either. I'm not much of a prospect really.'

'You're a great prospect,' he said emphatically. 'No one else would have opened that door, not out here, all alone in the woods; no one else would have stayed to help. And certainly no one would have done *this* . . .' He swept his good hand around the shed, taking in the gin bottle, the pliers, then smiled at me, his sweet and cheerful smile, completely at ease, and it made my heart lurch slightly, to think that he trusted *me* of all people.

'I'll be back,' I said firmly, and he nodded, his eyes drooping with exhaustion.

'I know you will, Miss . . .' He opened his eyes one last time, flashed me another smile. 'I know you will, Maddy.'

Thirty

Maybe there was something like a delayed kind of shock, because even after I'd come back up to the house with Leica, I couldn't get the time in the shed out of my head. It followed me as I stole up to my room to change out of my dirty clothes and comb my tousled hair. It was there when I passed Aunt Marjorie, who had just read that the London Zoo would be killing off all poisonous snakes and spiders so they wouldn't escape if the zoo was bombed. It stayed with me as I walked down the narrow twisting path through the garden with Georgiana and her friends later in the afternoon, conversation flying back and forth above my head.

Is anyone haunting the maze, then, Gigi? I expect you to produce some self-respecting ghosts for me.

Come on, you'd run a mile if you ever met a ghost.

Not if he was handsome.

Could be a she . . .

The real question is, will there be something to drink? I'm positively parched.

It wasn't so much the gash in William's arm, or the blood or the raw flesh. It was the noise. The rushing waves, the sighing of the salt-water eddies as they receded, the guttural half-moan of pain that became part of the relentlessly churning melody until the water and the pain and William and another morning on a beach six years ago had all become one and the same, a restless hum of anxiety that made me want to burrow deep into the undergrowth, out of sight of the world. At the same time, I remembered the way William's lips had touched my fingers when I fed him, the way his eyes had found mine again and again, and that was when I wanted to turn round and run straight back down the hill.

I tried to laugh at the banter and marvel at Rana's purple dress, at the pretty buttons on Clementine's top, but the girls seemed out of place amidst the trees, their voices too loud. And when Georgiana threw her head back and laughed, opening her mouth to shout an answer back at Rana, I dropped my arm from hers and walked a little faster, catching up with Victor instead.

'Hey.' He smiled down at me. 'Had to go ahead for a bit of solitude. That lot,' he jabbed his head back, 'are completely oblivious to how beautiful it is down here.'

'Yes,' I sighed.

'Let's walk together.' He threaded my hand through his arm and we walked in companionable silence until the maze came into view.

The Summerhill maze had achieved a small degree of fame across the West Country because of its sheer size. In my father's day, the boxwood hedges had been kept trimmed with razor-sharp edges, but now, despite Frank's occasional determined attempts to get them back into shape, they had grown wild, branches and twigs shooting in all directions, covering the paths and obscuring the corners and giving the faint impression of a vast woolly animal crouching against the side of the hill. Georgiana had organised a simple picnic, consisting mainly of sandwiches, cake, fruit and champagne in two hampers, which she'd made the boys carry – a task they seemed bemused by but executed gamely. I crouched over the low stone benches to arrange the food, thinking of how William's eyes would light up at the big slices of Cookie's squishy sponge cake and the smoked ham laid out on bread. A small secret thrill went through me when I pictured his smile, and I gave a start when Georgiana materialised by my side.

'Honestly, Maddy.' She handed me a small stack of napkins to set out with the plates. 'I had just turned to ask you something about the party tomorrow, and the next thing I know, you're all the way ahead with Vic. And earlier, too, in the courtyard, you were gone all of a sudden. Where do you keep disappearing to?'

'Er . . .' I reddened. 'Nowhere really. Just the usual.' I stacked the napkins with exaggerated precision, because the last thing I wanted to do was talk about William here, with Laney and Clementine giggling and whispering and Gregory booming something about the picturesque wilderness of the English west.

'You two *are* awfully talky, aren't you?' she said suddenly.

'Talky?'

'You and Vic, silly,' she said, and gave another one of her slightly too loud laughs.

'We just walked together.' I shrugged. 'And you *did* tell us to get along.'

'Uh-huh.' She was still studying me, the contours of her face thrown into stark relief by the sun. We were so close, I could see that her eyes looked slightly swollen beneath the make-up, the bluish half-moon shadows underneath carefully covered with foundation and a layer of powder that had settled into the fine creases around her nose and mouth. She looked different, I now realised, and not just because of *Gigi*; there was something else, too, a strange sort of flush, a glint in her eye . . .

'You're not ill or anything, are you, Georgie? I heard you in the loo this morning.'

She flinched, spilling the bowl of plums she was just setting out on a tree stump next to the benches. She busied herself fishing for the plump purple shapes amidst the grass before straightening back up.

'I'm totally fine,' she said in a low voice. 'And please don't mention it to anyone, will you?'

'So there *is* something to mention?' I asked anxiously. 'If you're unwell, I want to know—'

'What's this, Gigi?' Victor said from behind us. 'You're not well?' We turned to see him raising his eyebrows questioningly, and Georgiana threw me an exasperated look.

'Just a little peaky this morning. Don't know what came over me, honestly.' She shook her head in mock-self-deprecation, motioning for Laney to join us. 'Can't hold my drink, apparently, although that's never been a problem for me before, has it, Laney?' She leaned into Victor and stretched up to give him a kiss, ignoring me.

'Yes, Gigi's notorious for putting away masses of liquor and still getting up the next morning to catch an exhibition at the portrait gallery looking like a vision,' Laney said. 'Must be all that bracing sea air. Are you as stout of constitution, Madeleine?'

She eyed my dress, a rather sober affair of grey cotton, which I'd hastily dug out of my wardrobe after spending too much time scrubbing William's blood from underneath my nails. I bit back a sudden hysterical laugh when I thought of Laney in the shed, sinking to the floor next to William in a cloud of silk. *Let me make you a turban. Brighten things up a bit.*

'Actually,' I took the bowl of plums from Georgiana, 'Georgie was always the pretty one.' I smiled at my sister because I couldn't bear the slightly hard look that had settled around her mouth as she hung off Victor's arm.

Above her head, Victor studied me. 'That she is,' he said. 'You are both beautiful. And don't think I've forgotten that you owe me that picture, Madeleine. My Summerhill memento.'

'Yes, well,' I said, putting the bowl on the tree stump. When I straightened, I caught Laney regarding me with an expression of sudden interest, and against the curve of Victor's shoulder, I thought I saw Georgiana's smile slip a fraction, her lips pressing together.

I was casting around for something to dispel the sudden awkwardness when Jonathan bounded up. 'Let's play a game, shall we?'

He had put his mind to the task with his usual enthusiasm, devising a rather complicated game of hide-and-seek crossed with a treasure hunt. It revolved mainly around him shedding some of his clothes – a favourite pastime of his, apparently – and hiding them in various places around the maze, requiring the rest to not only find the clothes but to hunt down Jonathan too and hand them over while – and this was most important – avoiding discovery by anyone else.

'Will we go in pairs?' Laney said, eyeing the profusion of boxwood hedges. 'It's all terribly au naturel in there, isn't it?'

'Yes,' Clementine said doubtfully. 'What if we get lost?'

'In that case, I want Madeleine,' Laney said quickly. 'Being a native and all.'

'Take Georgiana,' I retorted. 'She's the best at the maze.'

Georgiana was standing a little distance from me, silent except for the occasional comment on the rules, but at this, her eyes softened.

'Queens of the Maze,' she said. 'Remember?'

I did. That hot, endless summer of 1934, when all the world was surging to the beaches, when the river was full of pleasure boats and people splashing in the shallows, when my father had been dead less than a year and I couldn't bear the sound of water anywhere near me. Georgiana and I had spent that summer in the maze. Skinny and gangly like boys, Georgiana pulling me along by the hand, faster and faster, we'd played hide-and-seek, finding the shortest, the straightest, the longest, the cleverest ways to the centre. There were countless small alcoves and hidden pockets among the hedges, rumoured to have been used for smugglers' contraband. We'd found them all during those long summer days when our entire world had narrowed to the cool green shadows inside the leafy corridors until we emerged to walk home in the gathering darkness, making straight for the brightly lit kitchen, where Cookie would be waiting with our supper.

'Then *I* get Madeleine.' Clementine's grating voice broke into the memory of those sad, happy, sun-filled days, and I turned away from Georgiana's smile just in time to see Clementine's speculative look. Before I could say anything, Victor spoke.

'There aren't enough people to make pairs. We're all going alone.'

Thirty-One

A little later, the long branches of the boxwood hedges closed above my head as I ducked through the twisting channels, the last one to go after waiting the requisite three minutes.

Soft twigs caressed my bare arms, enveloping me in a cool embrace of green that obliterated all sound except for the swallows diving for flies in the last light of the sun. I walked on for a bit, then stopped in the middle of a path to get my bearings. Mazes were funny things: sound travelled oddly along the narrow paths, looping and turning in on itself, and something that seemed far away at one moment might suddenly pop up right next to you. Georgiana and I used to scare each other silly, waiting at certain bends to reach through the hedge and grab an unsuspecting arm or ankle.

There was a muffled exclamation nearby, and I paused, goosebumps running up and down my arms. Something rustled on my left – footsteps? – then disappeared again and all was still. The hedges swayed and sighed around me as I walked, the long branches hissing as they switched back into place behind me, as if I had never passed at all; as if I was a mere wisp, flitting by without substance. The notion took hold of my tired, overwrought mind and I stopped to listen for human voices, my eyes raking the dense foliage for a glimpse of one of the others. From somewhere, a stray snatch of laughter floated past. And then, so unexpected that I thought my heart would jump clean out of my chest, a hand grabbed me from behind.

'Found you!' a voice whispered.

'You scared me half to death!' I hissed back, and Victor laughed, not at all sorry.

'I'm lost.' He stretched in vain to try and peer above the swaying branches. 'I'm glad I ran into you. And look what I found . . .' He pointed to the hedge just behind him.

'Smuggler's Hatch.' I took a deep breath, my heart still hammering. 'Two hedges overlap for someone to hide. We once found the iron clasp of an old whisky barrel—'

'Shh!' Victor cocked his head. From the left came a muffled curse, then the sound of footsteps.

'Hello?' said an annoyed voice. 'Someone there?'

Without warning, Victor reached for my hand and pushed into the narrow space of Smuggler's Hatch, pulling me in behind him.

'What on earth are you doing?' I breathed.

'Hiding, what else?' He grinned, delighted with himself. 'It's a game, remember?'

When the hedges had been kept neatly trimmed, Smuggler's Hatch had been just about big enough for two people. But the moment I'd squeezed through the seam behind Victor, I'd realised that there was barely room for one now and that I was pressed up against him. Heat rushed up my chest and into my face, and my heart beat fast.

'No,' I said breathlessly. 'I'll just . . .' I tried to step backwards, to find the opening, when suddenly there was a voice next to us, loud and annoyed.

'Oh, this game is so silly. My shoes are positively ruined.'

I could see a flash of white through the hedge, hear the rustle of the leaves as Laney bent down, presumably to inspect the state of her shoes. Of all the options open to me right now, emerging from a secret hiding place with Victor, tousle-haired and flushed, to face Laney's cool-eyed curiosity was not one of the best. Blushing furiously, I shrank back into the hedge, made myself meet Victor's eyes, and slowly shook my head, careful not to disturb the branches further.

He smiled and nodded as if he'd known all along that this

was what I would do. And suddenly, unaccountably – this was Victor, *Victor*, my sister's beau, nice, courteous, lovely – I was afraid, a sharp needlepoint of fear that cut right through the awkwardness and the girlish blushing, making my heart beat hard and fast. My breath caught in my throat and I tried, in vain, to burrow into the springy boxwood branches, which refused to give an inch.

Laney was still muttering to herself on the other side of the hedge as I tried not to notice Victor's thigh lining up with mine, the way his arm was draped along the back of my waist because there was nowhere else for it to go.

'Almost over,' he mouthed, and I closed my eyes to block out his face, so close to mine, too close. It was wrong; all of this felt wrong. My body was tensed like a spring, and heat flushed my cheeks again when I felt Victor's fingers flutter against my own, the beat of his heart echoing mine. Every fibre of my being was telling me to run, Laney be damned, but when I opened my eyes, I found Victor looking at me.

It was a different look from any I'd seen before, strangely hard and narrow, and it pinned me into place so that I couldn't move. And then, it was almost as if it wasn't even happening, so slowly, so softly did those fingers slide up my body, feather-light and barely there, touching my jawbone, my neck, trailing across until they reached the round collar of my dress and the place where it fastened in the middle. Slowly they curved, hooked around the button – and pulled.

My face jerked forward and my mouth met his. His hand went to the back of my neck and held me there, his lips pressed hard against mine. He made a small noise, a groan or a smothered sigh, and at this, I finally came to, jerking away, making the small alcove rustle loudly just as the outside hedge moved and the feet in their high-heeled shoes started marching away.

I looked down at my dress, where the top button dangled from a thread, a flap of fabric falling sideways, then back up at

Victor, who unbelievably, horribly, was smiling the same warm smile he'd worn before.

'What have you done?' I pressed out, touching the button as if in a trance. 'Georgiana . . . and you . . .'

'But you wanted this to happen, didn't you?' he said softly, raising his hand as if to stroke my cheek again. I pushed him away.

'No!' I said in a low, shaking voice. 'No, I didn't. I was nice to you. I liked you. But you and Georgiana – I would never do something like this to my sister.'

'Why didn't you leave when Laney was there, then? You could easily have called out to her.' His eyes narrowed again, pinning me against the hedge, and then the fear was back, not a stab but a claustrophobic terror that made me back into the branches, resisting the urge to scream.

'I didn't want to alarm her,' I whispered, but even as I did, small things flashed at the edge of my mind: Red Lions and lemon roses, catching Victor's eyes across the terrace as he held my sister close. Walking through the fragrant woods down towards the maze together because everyone else was too loud, too shrill, and he'd seemed to understand without the need to explain.

He was watching me with a satisfied sort of expression, as if he could see them too, all those small things that together seemed to make something new and quite horrible.

'It wasn't like that,' I said hoarsely. 'You know that it was never like that at all. I didn't . . . *like* you.'

'But you just said you did.'

'Not like that, though! Stop twisting my words.'

'So what were you doing in here?'

'I'm . . .' But words failed me, because he was right, I shouldn't be in here. I knew Smuggler's Hatch. I should never have followed him in.

He smiled again and shifted, deliberately bringing his body close to mine.

'Get away from me,' I hissed. 'I don't know what you want from me, but stay away, do you hear me? I never want to speak to you again.'

And then I finally did what I should have done all along: I found the seam where the hedges joined and fell back out onto the path. Quick as a flash, Victor stepped through after me and held me back.

'Now, now,' he said very quietly, digging his fingers into my shoulder. 'We wouldn't want to do anything stupid, would we?'

But I'd been fixing fences and mending stone walls and carrying logs for years, and when I twisted, my shoulder slipped out of his grasp easily. And then I ran, like I had when Georgiana and I had been skinny and fleet-footed, racing each other to the middle of our father's maze.

Thirty-Two

Chloe

It was raining again when Chloe finally pulled up and saw, with a sinking heart, the Vauxhall sitting out on the driveway. The house was dark, though. Maybe Aidan had gone for a run? He sometimes did at the end of the day. If she drove the Porsche into the garage and covered it, then slipped back later to clean it off – the puddles in the rutted Summerhill lane had splashed muddy water as high as the fold-up roof – maybe he wouldn't notice that it had gone. She just needed to go quickly, tidy herself up, put away her stuff . . . Tiptoeing inside, Chloe pushed the case behind the laundry room door and carefully set the camera on a shelf in the linen cupboard, then bundled her wet clothes into the hamper. She stepped out and listened but the house seemed quiet and bland, washed out by the rain, only a sharp zing of ozone hinting at more thunder and lightning. She had barely finished the thought when a voice came from the kitchen.

'Do you have any idea how worried I've been?'

She stood rooted to the carpet, her toes digging deep into the fibres.

'Oh . . .' She flushed, then decided to brazen it out, and walked into the kitchen with a welcoming smile. 'You're home early, how lovely. I have a salad ready and some cold chicken. It's been so hot, I thought . . .'

Aidan didn't say anything; just looked at her. He hadn't turned on the lights, had simply stood waiting for her in the kitchen. In the early evening gloom, his face seemed particularly pale, his features almost two-dimensional, a white gash for a mouth, almond-shaped slits for eyes, fair hair disappearing into the whiteness of the room beyond.

'Do you have any clue how I feel when I come home early to check on my wife, thinking her poorly, and don't find her where I expect her to be?' He pushed himself off the worktop and came closer, so close that she smelled the medicinal tang of his hands. With a low rumble somewhere at the back of her oesophagus, the nausea, absent all day, started its lazy churning once more, the baby secret making itself heard. She twisted away from the sweetish smell, but he came closer still, leaning into her, his thighs hard against hers. 'And what on earth are you wearing?'

'I'm sorry to have worried you.' She breathed through her open mouth, but he was so close that the angle of her body was wrong, the way it arched back over the worktop with no space for any breath to go.

'I can explain . . .' She managed to half turn her body and slide along the worktop, gulped in a big lungful of air, and another one, reaching for a glass, the tap.

She drank deeply to flush away the acid taste at the back of her throat and to delay the fact that she really did have to explain now. Over her shoulder, she looked at her husband, who'd followed her to the sink, was right behind her once again, his eyes narrowed, the wool of his suit scratching the soft skin on the underside of her arm. She didn't want to do it, hand over the loveliness of Summerhill to him, share her time with Madeleine. He'd fill it with scathing words about old ladies and godforsaken places and the silliness of her job. He would make himself a part of it, closing in around it until he had taken over completely, until he owned it and it was no longer Chloe's at all.

But she gave herself a hard push. 'It's just . . . I ended up taking that job, Aidan. The one with the old lady. That's all.'

He moved back slightly in surprise, because whatever he'd been expecting, that certainly wasn't it. For a blessed moment, he widened the space between them and she breathed deeply before he was back again.

'You did what?'

'I got another call about it and it sounded like something I could do, something I wanted to do.' She resisted the urge to back away, knowing he would simply follow her until she was braced against the wall and had nowhere else to go.

'If I remember correctly, we said you weren't going to. That you had too much on here. Didn't need to earn the extra money.'

'I'm sorry I didn't tell you.' She filled the glass again, held it between them. 'I thought the money would come in handy, for Oakwood's fees. I thought you wouldn't mind.'

'Mind that you lied to me, Chloe?' He raked his hands through his hair and the smell of antiseptic was overpowering. 'Not that you can keep anything from me,' he added, and there was something close to triumph in his voice, almost as if he was glad that his long-standing doubts had finally been proven right. 'I knew there was something, I *knew* it.' He suddenly grabbed hold of her wrist, and water slopped over the rim of the glass and onto the sleeve of Georgiana's jacket. He snatched the glass out of her hand and dropped it into the sink where it shattered with a deafening sound. Chloe flinched. 'And this morning, too, God damn it, I *knew* it. What else is there? What else are you not telling me?' His fingernails dug into her skin, right between the little bones there.

'Aidan, let me go! Have you lost your mind?' Chloe tried to pull her hand back.

'You, apparently, have lost all sense of what a marriage is about. No secrets, Chloe, I told you. Is that where you went yesterday? When you said you'd been to see Danny?' The questions were gathering force, coming more loudly, until the sound of his voice was ringing in her ears.

'I did go to see Danny yesterday.' His proximity and the pressure on her wrist were making her stomach roil furiously. 'You saw the wheelchair. And you can ask Marie, I spoke to her—'

'The day has yet to come when I will humiliate myself by asking the stupid staff at a nursing home about my wife's movements,' he hissed. 'You. Will. Tell me. Without being asked.'

He pressed his lips together, his eyes brilliant against the flatness of his face, the smell overpowering, his grip on her wrist a sharp, blinding stab of pain. Any other time, Chloe might have softened and capitulated, smoothed things over with explanations and apologies, determined to make it work. But the day had started with her foot on the accelerator of Aidan's Porsche and it had ended with Georgiana's writing box and Madeleine confiding in her. That Summerhill feeling refused to let her back down, and so the two of them stood, locked in a furious, stiff embrace, eyes narrowed at each other, breathing hard, until suddenly there was the buzzing sound of a phone.

Chloe masked a quick exhale of relief, knowing Aidan would be claimed by a patient, might have time to calm down. But instead of moving away, he gave her a shove, digging his hip into hers until the small of her back was crushed painfully against the edge of the worktop again. Still holding on to her wrist, he dug roughly into her pocket – a horrible, intrusive burrowing – and then her phone was buzzing in his hand.

Her stomach dropped when she saw a familiar 0207 number flash up on the display.

'More secrets?' he said gently, almost lovingly, and he flicked the green button, hit the speaker.

'Chloe! Hoping you'd call to tell me how things went with the eminent Mrs Hamilton today.'

Matt's gravelly voice was improbably loud; magnified by the tinny speaker, it filled the kitchen until there was no doubt at all that he and Chloe were on easy telephone-speaking terms and that Matt had known about today's visit long before Aidan had.

'Are you there?' he said impatiently. 'I was wondering, actually, maybe I should go down to Summerhill myself. You could be my tour guide. It'd be nice if we actually got a chance to meet.'

It was so hideous and so much worse than anything Chloe could have imagined that her body simply gave up the struggle. Bent backwards over the counter, the pressure of Aidan's knee between her legs, his pelvis pinning hers, she waited for what was to come. Her mind was both overfull and empty of all rational considerations, but amidst the strange ringing inside her skull, one very distinct thought took shape. The baby. Immediately she stiffened, tried to move away from Aidan's knee. It was a small movement but enough to propel him into action.

'This is Aidan MacAllister,' he said coolly into the phone. 'I'm afraid you got the wrong end of the stick entirely. My wife isn't interested in pursuing this project.'

'What? No!' Chloe said, trying to twist her lower body away from him. 'Aidan, please don't do this . . .'

'Mr MacAllister, be reasonable,' Matt Cooper said very carefully. 'It's only a small project, over in a matter of days. Nothing to worry about.'

'You won't call her again.'

And before Matt could say anything else, Aidan had hung up.

'Aidan, no,' Chloe said in a choked voice.

'You'll stop this nonsense at once, Chloe,' he said in a low, even tone. 'I don't want to hear another word about it. And *I* will drop your phone off at the O2 shop tomorrow. To fix that patchy reception once and for all, don't you think?'

He held her wrist against the worktop and bent her hand backwards over the sharp edge, pushed hard. She wanted to scream with the horror of it all. Flashes of pain shot up her arm and through her hand, and his nails dug deep into her flesh until she knew he would pull apart her skin and stab his fingers right inside her.

He broke his hold so quickly that Chloe slumped against the worktop, wrist throbbing. Aidan had moved to the sink; she could see his stomach moving in and out as he breathed deeply. He believed in deliberate breathing, was always prescribing it to his headache patients. He reached for the pitcher in the cupboard, then glasses, controlled, efficient movements, while Chloe stayed where she was because somehow it was easier to watch parts of him than to straighten up and face him as a whole. His feet moving to the drinks tray, fingers unscrewing the bottle of gin, cutting two slices of lime, each the exact size of the other. The smell of the gin hit her nose, acrid and bitter, and it made her stomach heave again. She lifted her arm, saw the neat, leaf-shaped fan of finger marks bloom in vivid red around her wrist, capped by the precise indentations of his nails, because everything Aidan did was orderly and neat. She held her wrist against the cool granite and closed her eyes.

Thirty-Three

It was starting to get light out and Chloe hadn't slept much at all, drifting off in fits and starts and jerking awake whenever sleep was close, as if she couldn't allow herself to let go.

Aidan preferred to be woken by daylight – it helped his circadian rhythm, he said – but he had not yet stirred. Chloe moved her arm, brought it right up to her face. Slowly, as if it didn't belong to her, she watched the sleeve of her nightshirt ride up until she could see the ghostly shadow handprint on her wrist. Her skin was so fine it bruised easily, and the place where Aidan's long, tapered fingers had gripped her was clearly visible. Even in the bluish-grey light of dawn, it was a vivid purple, the edges lighter, bruises that would soon change, become yellow and green and then eventually fade away. In the same way that her body would repair itself, time would push what had happened into the past, and life would simply absorb it and go on.

Last night, after she'd picked herself off the worktop and cleaned up the broken glass from the sink, Aidan had grilled lamb steaks on the barbecue and they'd sat out on the terrace talking about their day, just like they always did. He hadn't mentioned the phone call or their exchange at all; he hadn't been overly solicitous to make up for it, or in any way particularly cool towards her to make her pay. He was exactly the way he always was.

Quietly, she reached over the side of the bed to where she'd hidden Georgiana's jacket the night before, pulled it underneath the duvet. The canvas was bulky next to her stomach, the metal buckle cold against her skin. She thought of the soft little baby soul inside her, its secret safe with her. Once it was out here, would the baby do what Chloe had done last night, go along with Aidan's pretence that nothing had happened? Would that be something it learned: that the human body had the ability to repair itself over and over again? Would it too become only ever a part of someone else's orbit, never separate, a person in its own right?

'Chloe, darling!'

Her hands froze around her stomach and she tried to make her back relax, look like she was sleeping. But Aidan was rarely fooled.

'I know you're awake,' he whispered, creeping a hand around her waist. The mattress creaked as he drew her closer, sliding her against him, pulling up her nightshirt.

'Surely it's not six already?' she murmured. 'Just a few more minutes, darling.'

He chuckled affectionately, ran his hands up her back. 'I'll miss you today, Chloe. I love you, my darling.' He turned her towards him and pulled her closer, fingers tracing the shape of her jaw, down her neck. 'And you?' he prompted when she didn't say anything, his eyes locked onto hers.

'Of course,' she said in a voice that didn't quite seem to belong to her. 'I'll miss you too.'

'Oh Chloe,' he breathed, and then he was on top of her. As if he knew that she had to be coaxed, he took a long time, and she held onto his shoulders, watching the bruises on her wrist move up and down in time with his body. He finished with a groan, then slid off her and held her close. When he eventually disappeared into the bathroom, she was left with a dull throb between her legs and the now persistent klaxon of oncoming nausea. And as a brand-new day broke and her husband started whistling in the shower, Chloe pressed her face into her pillow and cried.

*

Somehow she found the strength to get up and shower. She put Georgiana's thin long-sleeved blouse back on to cover her wrists, and Georgiana's jacket, too. The bulky material felt protective, like a shell. The weather had mercifully cooled after the thunderstorm last night, and wind was blowing hard through the treetops outside. She wasn't cold, precisely, but she seemed to be unable to stop the ghost of a shiver that ran up and down her back, and her heart was beating fast and irregular inside her heavy body, as if something fluttery and restless was trapped there. At the top of the stairs she leaned her head against the wall and watched Aidan reverse out of the drive. He'd taken the Porsche today, she saw, perhaps to get it washed and polished, to erase all traces of the secret she'd kept from him. He lifted his hand to wave at her as he always did, making some complicated gesture that presumably was telling her he'd be back soon, but she turned away from the window before he'd gone, and thrust her hands into the pockets of the jacket as she walked down the stairs.

In the kitchen, she stood looking aimlessly out of the window, trying not to think ahead to her empty day: putting a wash on, running a hoover over the carpet, going to visit Danny. Danny, who'd spot her wrist at once, who'd be tapping his fingers restlessly, his eyes anxious. Maybe she wouldn't go until tomorrow. She didn't want him to worry, and she wouldn't be able to pretend, not today.

Something rustled in the jacket pocket, and she pulled out the gas mask instructions from Georgiana's room. She smiled a little at the old-fashioned drawings of a woman sitting in bed, decently clad and in full make-up, sleep-tousled curls indicating the time of night, as she put on the bug-eyed mask while her husband stood by in striped pyjamas, already masked up. It wasn't really anything special, but she should return it nonetheless, along with the sketch. Not today, though. She didn't have the energy or the courage to keep her appointment with Madeleine. She'd call and cancel—

She stopped in mid thought. The reverse side of the instructions, the bit that had been hidden from view when the page was folded, was covered in loopy slanted handwriting.

I spent so much of my time away trying not to think about home. Not because I didn't miss you – I did, all the time – but because I wanted to feel that journey completely, with my whole heart. I wanted to be in the moment, every day, not stuck halfway back at Summerhill wondering what you were doing or whether Cookie's niece had had her baby. It was going to be a summer of firsts, of all the things I'd always read about but never done, and I wanted to feel all that away from Summerhill, away from everything I'd ever known.

But I found that I couldn't, not the way I wanted to. Travelling through Amsterdam and watching the barges made me think of the fishermen at Tremarron. At the fruit market in Paris, I thought of the orchards and whether the apples had started to ripen. And of you – all the colours you'd have adored. The vistas from the train, which would have taken your breath away. Wheat fields and pastures, oceans of tall grasses that moved in the wind like the water out on the bay on a calm day. See, there it is again, everything always came back to Summerhill – and to you. It made me realise that we've only ever felt things together. That we think together, you and I. That I write what you draw and you draw what I write. That's how our world has worked so far.

But at the same time, it was me, all by myself on the Continent. Because just as I thought of Summerhill and you with everything I saw, I also knew that you probably wouldn't ever see it. With everything I did, I was conscious that I was doing it alone, that this would be something you and I would never share. Just like I was resenting being reminded of home so much, it was equally unnerving to be separated from you like that. And since then, I cannot help but think that we shouldn't be like we've been, Maddy. I don't want it for you, my love, and I don't want it for myself. I could feel you pulling on me all the way across Europe. I want to continue to love you with all my heart, the way I always have, but I want it to be a free kind of love. Not dutiful or guilty or obligated because I've had to be your mum and you were my charge. And when I met Victor, and he made me talk about . . . everything, that's when

From here on, the letter started looking less neat, more hurried, with parts crossed out and corrected.

I used to think that I ~~was forced~~ had to be where you were, that it was the point of my life to be part of yours, ~~to help you and guide you~~. And I want to be with you, be close to you. But I need to be separate too, to become my own person, and, what's more important, I think you must too. ~~It's been too long~~ But I think we can be close even if we don't share every moment. Being part of someone's life but also separate is a good thing, Foxy, and I'm determined to make you see

Chloe flipped over the page, searching for the rest, but the beaming countenance of the gas mask lady and her stripy husband was all she saw. She pressed her fingers against her aching temples, then quickly shook the sleeve of Georgiana's blouse back over her wrist when the bruises bloomed again in front of her eyes. The jacket was making her warm and a bit woolly-headed, but she didn't want to take it off.

She smoothed out the piece of paper, traced the bold, hurried writing across it. The tone had changed from the pieces in the writing box, which had been more chatty, less soul-baring. Now, the writer had grown more confident of what she wanted to say, perhaps aided by the mysterious Victor, who'd helped her sort things through in her mind. Or maybe it was just that Chloe could feel it too, that need to breathe, the urge to figure out how to be together and yet separate, how to love someone without losing yourself. Loving Danny and loving Aidan was as different as night and day, and yet in some ways, they were two opposite sides of one and the same thing: a complicated kind of love that pulled on her every moment of every day, in both good ways and bad. And where would the baby fit in? Would Chloe love it the way she loved Danny, fiercely and unquestioningly, or the way she'd fallen for Aidan, with the wonderful promise of a new beginning, a delicious journey of first times and discoveries? Would she be able to teach it to recognise the right way to be with someone when she couldn't even figure that out herself?

What had happened when this letter had finally reached Madeleine, when Georgiana had started making her see? Feeling an odd surge of loyalty to the old woman, Chloe wanted to reach across the decades and tell Georgiana that Madeleine was fine. But was she? Somehow, Chloe didn't think Georgiana would be convinced by the sight of her sister now, sitting in that armchair most of the day, still obsessed with holding on to Summerhill, bound to it in the same way she'd clearly been for seventy years. She drew herself up, frowned at the clock. Well, there might be one thing she could do to help.

Thirty-Four

By the time Chloe finally got onto the A38, her sleepless night had caught up with her, and she had to stop and buy herself a coffee. The coffee made her even hotter, but it did perk her up, or at least it made her heart beat faster, so that when she got going again, she was both wired and exhausted, and on more than one occasion had to blink rapidly to bring the road into focus. The moment she emerged from the bumpy Summerhill lane and came to a stop, however, her heart seemed to slow and her breathing wasn't quite so shallow. She retrieved her camera from the back seat and went to open up the boot. It was only then that she noticed another car, a small mud-splashed Fiat with the words *Truro Cares* emblazoned on the side. This had to be the bad-tempered nurse Madeleine had mentioned the last time.

The front door was ajar, and as soon as she stepped into the hallway, she heard a babble of angry voices.

'Mrs Hamilton, for pity's sake, all I'm asking you is to hold up your arm, so I can do that sleeve back up.'

'Please stop treating me like a child. I can perfectly well do it myself.'

'Here, let me . . .'

'No!' Madeleine's voice had a horrible pleading note to it and Chloe crossed the last few yards to the library door quickly. 'I'm expecting a guest for tea, you were late, and now I'd really like you to leave.'

Chloe felt a quick, unexpected stab of pleasure at being the anticipated guest, followed by relief that she hadn't had to cancel, but then she stopped in her tracks when there was an exclamation of sorts, followed by a crash that sounded like a dinner service exploding.

'Now look what you've done!' shouted two voices in unison.

Chloe flung open the door and hurried towards the wrestling match by the purple armchair. A wiry nurse towered over the chair, a small metal dish with a syringe in her hand. Madeleine Hamilton was trying to twist out of the nurse's reach, both of them arguing at the top of their voices. It had indeed been china: a tea set, which now lay on the floor in a mess of brown liquid and shattered porcelain.

'Madeleine.' Stricken, Chloe looked from the broken tea set – two cups and a pretty pot, a plate of biscuits, most of which had disintegrated – to Madeleine's lovely silk blouse with a bow at the neck, and her carefully made-up face. The nurse picked up a cloth, clearly intending to dab at the offending stain on her charge's chest.

'Here,' she said quickly, plucking it out of her hand. 'I will help Mrs Hamilton.' She nodded in dismissal, feeling a little like the butler of the house. 'You have a schedule to keep and no doubt plenty of other important things to do.'

The sarcasm was mostly for Madeleine's benefit, but the nurse clearly took her at face value, because she pulled up her bony shoulders and sniffed loudly before making for the front hall. 'The office will be in touch,' she informed them.

'We're very much looking forward to it.' Chloe shut the door behind her with a bang, then turned back to Madeleine. 'I see what you mean about her: she's like an Enid Blyton novel. What an old boot. See, now she's making me do it, too. If I start talking about lashings of ginger beer, please throttle me.'

She didn't wait for an answer, but knelt and began to pick up the shards of china, using the nurse's cloth to mop up the worst of the spilled tea, chattering inconsequentially as she did so. She never looked at Madeleine directly, but she felt the old lady shift in the chair above her, heard the rustle of fabric, the clasp of her hairclip. Some of the biscuits had survived, and she carefully picked them out, blew on them to clean them and set them back in the box they'd come from.

'Custard creams are my favourite,' she said, sitting back on her heels and finally looking up to smile at the other woman.

'Mine too.' Madeleine didn't smile back, but her colour had died down to a faint flush high up on her cheekbones. She eyed the box and sighed. 'I was looking forward to them. Tea, too.'

Chloe handed her a custard cream, then took one for herself. For a moment, they chewed thoughtfully, watching each other carefully, then both of them started laughing.

'Look at me,' Madeleine finally said. 'Whenever you're here, I'm soaked.'

'You're a mess,' Chloe agreed. 'But go and find something to wear, because I have a surprise for you.'

Thirty-Five

When Madeleine saw the wheelchair parked outside the front door, she stopped so suddenly that she almost lost her balance. Clutching her cane, she stared at it, taking in the old stickers, the jaunty bow that Chloe had tied on the right-hand handlebar, her camera sitting on the worn seat.

'It was Danny's,' Chloe said quickly when a minute had passed and Madeleine still didn't say anything. 'It's a cross-country kind; he could do all sorts of tricks with it, when his arms still worked, that is. Jerry – his carer – retro-fitted it with a motor and joystick, although Danny only used that for a short time before he went to Oakwood. But I thought, even with your hand, you could learn how to use it. You did say you missed being out and about . . .'

Her voice trailed away, because Madeleine had shuffled forward and was circling the wheelchair, reaching to touch the handle, looking at the small cushion that Chloe had made to support Danny's back – she'd used his old Superman pillowcase from when he was a little boy, and even though it was so faded now that Superman had more or less gone, you could still make out the KA-POW!-type print above his fist.

'It's a little old,' she said to Madeleine's back. Maybe, just like Danny had when it had first become an issue, Madeleine hated the reminder that she was getting more and more immobile; maybe she couldn't stand the sight of it. 'I kept it at Oakwood, thinking . . . but, well, who am I kidding. Danny won't need it any more.'

There was a small sound, and when Madeleine turned round, Chloe saw that tears were running down her cheeks.

'It's fabulous,' she said, choking back a sob. 'I can just imagine him sitting in it and racing down the street.'

Chloe's eyes, too, were suddenly swimming in tears, but she smiled. 'For someone so ill, he was amazingly reckless,' she said. 'Do you . . . do you want to give it a try?'

'Of course I do!' Madeleine laugh-sobbed.

Chloe put the camera on the ground, and Madeleine lowered herself into the seat.

'It's very comfortable,' she pronounced. 'And I love that little cushion.'

Chloe crouched in front of her, adjusting the height of the side rails. She stood up too quickly and had to shake her head to get rid of a wave of dizziness, keeping her hands on the wheels to steady herself.

'Chloe?'

'I'm fine,' she said quickly. 'I didn't sleep much last night, so I feel a bit . . . peculiar. Nothing that a little jaunt won't cure.'

But Madeleine wasn't looking at her face. Instead, her eyes were fixed on Chloe's arm, where the sleeve of her thin blouse had bunched up to reveal the reddened fan of fingers curling around the white underside of her wrist.

'You said your husband was waiting for you yesterday. Was he . . . I mean, were you late?' Madeleine frowned.

'Oh, it was fine.' Chloe hurriedly flicked the sleeve back over her wrist before she picked up the camera and stepped behind the chair.

It took a lot of muscle, most of which Chloe appeared to have lost since pushing Danny in the chair all those years ago, and they seemed to be going uphill for a lot of the way. By the time they had reached their destination, she was blinking to keep the path in focus and gripping the wheelchair hard to stop her hands from shaking, but Madeleine's eyes were sparkling and she looked around her, smiling and exclaiming at familiar landmarks.

'Here we are.'

They stopped at the foot of an enormous oak tree. The trunk was bigger than two people reaching their arms around, Chloe thought, and the crown was enormous, extending far above the little knots of trees and hedges surrounding them, a widespread tangle of thick limbs that practically invited you to start climbing up into the sky.

'It's so beautiful,' she said, awed. She showed Madeleine how to put the wheelchair in park and how best to lift herself out of it, folding out the little footpads and pushing off with her good hand to settle on the old wooden bench below the tree. Then she circled the tree with her camera, walking a little further up to where the house was just visible in the distance.

'God, how did they even manage to build it?' she called back. 'It's like someone's taken a toy house and stuck it on the steepest part of the hill.'

'They were more enterprising back then,' Madeleine said. 'It used to be a smuggler's den; being inaccessible was part of the charm.'

She was looking up into the tree, her head resting on the back of the bench, one hand still on the handlebar of the wheelchair.

'Tell me about Danny,' she said when Chloe had come back and sat down next to her, cradling her camera in her lap.

Chloe sighed, her smile fading. 'He has a horrible disease where the muscles in your body slowly give up. Your mind and vital organs are the last to go. He's . . .' To her great embarrassment, her voice broke and her eyes filled with tears. 'I keep hoping he'll get better. I know it's a foolish hope. Everyone says so. I'm not stupid, I know they're right. It's just hard when he was so very alive, before all of this. I . . . I miss him. All the more so because he's still actually there. And not there.' She picked up her camera again, curled her fingers around the lens, relieved by the weight of it in her fingers, the way it fitted into her hands, the leathery surface of the sides. 'You know how there are some people who just seem more alive than others? They take up more room. Not like me: I was more of a shadow.'

Madeleine nodded. 'Me too. No need for everyone to be in the thick of things.'

'Danny was littering the neighbourhood with broken hearts even as a little boy. So good at making friends. Not many of them have stuck around, sadly.' Chloe fell silent.

'Georgiana was a bit like your Danny when we were growing up.' Madeleine shifted on the bench, stretching her arm along the backrest. 'She always felt everything a little bit more than the rest of us. She made things happen because she was too impatient to wait for them to sort themselves out on their own.' She smiled, and in the half-shade of the tree, her eyes were clear and bright and lit with warmth.

'She hated our bath, the way you had to wait for so long for the boiler to heat the water, or else boil it on the range and bring it all the way upstairs. Hobson would have done it for her – he adored her – but one February, she became obsessed with fixing the hot water properly. She ploughed through one of Papa's books, and Frank let her use his tool kit, and by the time April came around, we had hot water every morning. Of course, it was warmer then anyway, and she'd singed one of her eyebrows on the gas flame so she had to walk around looking lopsided all summer. But she had her warm baths and she was happy. As was Susan, who didn't have to carry pails up and down the stairs any more.'

'And you?' Chloe asked.

'I was happy when Georgiana was happy,' Madeleine said simply. 'I was quite a strange child, found it difficult to be with people after my father died, preferring my own company.' She smiled wryly and swept her hand around the deserted gardens. 'Not much has changed, eh? But Georgiana liked other people, loved a good party or going to a point-to-point. We only kept one horse at Summerhill, Star he was called, and when he died we never got another. But it was enough to turn her into a fierce rider. Goodness, how my father scolded her when she took Star out jumping one morning. Not so much because she almost broke her neck but because she almost lamed him, and was about to mow me down in the process. I was sitting on a stile with my sketchbook, and she wanted me to draw her the exact moment she was airborne. I guess I was like you with your camera, just with a pencil.'

She fell silent and they sat listening to the breeze in the trees, with Georgiana's ghost and thoughts of Danny around them.

'It feels good to remember,' Chloe said, looking up into the tree. 'I've not wanted to do that, until I came here. Rediscovered Foxy. Started talking to you.'

Madeleine nodded. 'It's a funny thing, that. Georgiana and I didn't talk about our parents nearly enough. There were a lot of things I just wanted to forget, but it must have been hard for her. That's why Victor was so good for her. He drew her out of herself, talked to her the way I should have talked to her, listened like he was genuinely interested. There were so many things I never listened to. Though he didn't turn out to be quite so good for her in the end . . .' She broke off, her eyes far away.

'Victor was her husband?' Chloe asked cautiously.

'Her beau.' Madeleine said the last word mockingly. 'He wasn't . . . a good man.' She met Chloe's eyes with her golden ones. 'Kind of like your husband, I suppose.'

The words came so unexpectedly and the tone in which they were delivered was so matter-of-fact that Chloe felt herself flinching in an automatic recoil of denial.

'No,' she said quickly, 'Aidan is fine. It's not what you think.'

'It's not?' Madeleine said quietly, her eyes flicking down to Chloe's wrist. Chloe flushed a bright red.

'It's not like that,' she repeated furiously. She pulled the sleeve of her blouse down again, but the movement was so jerky that the old fabric tore at the cuff. 'Oh no,' she said, and when she heard the sound of her own voice, pitched high and desperate amidst the fragrant Summerhill afternoon, she was suddenly filled with a horrible, helpless hatred for the way Aidan had managed to come here after all, to this secret place where he didn't belong. She hated the way Madeleine's eyes and her voice and her stupid assumptions made her feel naked and exposed. She hated the shame flooding her face and pushing tears into her eyes because of who she'd become, this malleable, weak shadow person who'd clung to a stupid hope of change, but who, during the million and one small moments of working at her marriage, had somehow forgotten what she should actually be fighting for.

'Chloe, I'm sorry,' Madeleine said, stricken. 'It's all right, let's—'

'No,' Chloe said hoarsely. 'It's not all right. Oh God.' She buried her face in her hands. 'I'm going to have Aidan's baby. And I don't want it, but I'm going to have to. And I haven't told anyone because I keep thinking that something, I mean . . .'

She pressed her lips together and dug her knuckles into her eyes, filled with such a surge of self-loathing that for a moment she was convinced she would suffocate with the shame of it all. She felt dizzy, nausea washing over her, and abruptly she stood up.

'I've got to go,' she said in a low voice. 'I don't want to be late.'

In silence, she helped Madeleine into the wheelchair and pushed her back to the house. Once she had parked the wheelchair next to the hall table and handed the old lady her cane, she turned to go.

Madeleine held her back. 'You can do it, Chloe, and you know it already,' she said quietly. She smoothed down the frayed cuff of Chloe's blouse and buttoned it back up over her wrist. 'You don't think you're strong now, but when the time comes, you will be.'

Thirty-Six

Maddy

My feet found their way among the hedges of their own accord, past the centre, where I caught a flash of Rana's purple dress, past the turn-off leading to the exit, shooting straight out of the entrance and across the deserted clearing. I would have kept on running, too, if I hadn't collided with a thin, wispy-haired figure engaged in packing up the remains of the picnic by the light of a lantern.

'Careful now!' Susan exclaimed.

I recoiled from her too; was about to turn and run the other way when she reached out and managed to grab my hand.

'Maddy, miss! It's only me.'

I'd known Susan most of my life. We'd grown up together since the day she'd arrived, a shy girl refusing to be parted from Cookie, who'd brought her to Summerhill when her cousin had too many children to cope with. And when I finally forced myself to stop this stupid raspy breathing, I realised that there wasn't anyone I'd rather see right now. Only Georgiana, maybe, but . . . I felt my face flush anew, hot with the kind of shame I'd never known before. It all came back to me again, the way I'd laughed and danced and talked, which must have been, I knew that now, so obvious, so . . . inviting.

'Here.' Susan pushed me down onto a tree stump right next to the lantern, retrieved a bottle from the basket and poured out a beaker of water. 'What's happened?' She crouched in front of me, eyeing my smudgy cheeks and wild hair, her eyes travelling over my red face and down to the button dangling from the top of my dress. It was darker now, and from behind us came sounds of laughter and shouting, indicating that people would soon be joining us. Any moment now, Georgiana would be here. Was Victor right? Had they all seen it, the way I'd behaved? Had they been watching me and Victor, talking in low voices among themselves about Gigi's peculiar sister, who didn't seem to know that if you laughed with a man, it was never innocent? And Georgiana? I remembered the tight set of her lips earlier, the offhand shrug as she turned away from me. My beautiful sister, who'd been chirpy and bright-eyed with happiness: what was she thinking, what *would* she be thinking if she knew what I'd done?

I felt fingertips at my throat and jerked back in revulsion as my body remembered other fingertips just moments before.

'Hush now,' Susan whispered. 'Let's fix you up a bit before the others come.'

With some effort, I relaxed into her hands as she pulled the button back through the fabric on the dangling thread and expertly knotted two bits together to secure it. She hesitated for a second, then quickly ran her hands over my hair, smoothing it down, tucking in a few loose ends, pushing it firmly back behind my ears and finding a stray pin to fasten it there. She took the cup from me, dipped the end of her apron into the water, cleaned up my face. Her small hands were warm and gentle and she smelled of yeast and plum juice and wood smoke.

'I didn't mean for it to happen. I didn't think I was doing anything. But they'll all think it was my fault,' I said in a hollow voice, even though she couldn't possibly know what I meant.

'Mr Deverill.' It wasn't a question but a statement, and that fact horrified me more than anything else.

'So you too, you think . . .' I said, my voice choked with horror.

'No,' Susan said firmly. 'I don't think anything. You were just . . . yourself. You don't know about any of this.' She swept her hand across the clearing. 'But ever since what he said in the kitchen yesterday, I've been watching him, and he was too . . . well, I thought to myself that he was being too friendly with you. I don't think any of them noticed, though – don't forget that they're all used to that kind of stuff, not to mention drunk half the time.'

'But Georgiana, she isn't used to it,' I said miserably.

'What actually happened?' Susan cut in quickly, looking over her shoulder to where rustling hedges indicated that people were moving in our direction.

'He touched me. Here and here. And here.' I tapped my lips and neck and the top button of my dress. 'He kissed me.' I made a gagging sound at the memory of his tight lips, his teeth, the cigarette breath.

Susan exhaled in evident relief. 'So nothing happened really.' She raised her eyebrows.

I shivered, swallowed. 'Not like that, no, I suppose not.'

She was right, it wasn't really anything. Things like that probably happened all the time. But Susan hadn't been there, she hadn't seen the hard expression in Victor's eyes, paired with the incongruous casualness of his touch, which hadn't hesitated, had expected no resistance. And he had got none, either. I'd just stood there and let him do it. I dug my fingertips into the skin above my collar and tried to rub away the sensation of his touch, which made me feel dirty and exposed. And ashamed, so hot and itchy with shame that I felt it seep from my very pores. And beneath it all, the slow drumbeat of fear because if Georgiana ever found out, I couldn't bear it.

'Then forget it, Miss Maddy. Forget it and move on,' Susan said quietly.

'I don't understand why he would even do it,' I whispered. 'He's in love with my sister. What could he possibly want with me?'

'What do men ever want?' she muttered darkly and shook her

head. 'Stay out of his way until the weekend's over; it's only another day or two. And then war is coming, and everything will change. God willing, it'll take him away from us altogether, him and all the others, too.'

It was that magical time when the day teetered on the edge of dusk, when tendrils of darkness muted the bright jewel colours of the flowering trees around the clearing in readiness for the night. Birds were rising and dipping for flies from the nearby pond and the heat was like syrup, warm and heavy, although a hint of coolness in the sun's absence signalled the end of the day and, beneath it all, the slow turning of late summer into early autumn. And autumn would become winter, when the windows were icy with frost and the treetops white with fog, followed by spring, when Summerhill would come back to life and another summer just like this. Except it wouldn't contain Victor or any of these other people. They would tire of our country ways and Victor would go to war and Georgiana would remain here with me and I could put tonight outside my Summerhill heart, and it would stay there. That was what I would do. Susan was right. It was nothing that would still matter when all this had passed.

'I'm going back to the house, I think.' I got up slowly from the tree trunk. 'Just tell Georgie that I was tired, will you?'

Over by the maze, Victor was asking Georgiana a question that made her double over with laughter. He laughed and cupped her face in his hands, bent down for a kiss.

I dug my finger into the skin at the top of my throat again. It was nothing.

'I will,' Susan said. She put the bottle of water back into the basket and fastened the top. 'I'll clean up the rest here, fetch the picnic blankets. But promise me that you won't think on it too much. Things will look better in the morning. They always do, trust me.' Her back was in shadow, but a shaft of lanternlight caught the tip of her nose and her eyelashes, picked out her delicate fair eyebrows in brilliant gold. She smiled back at me, a sweet, kind smile that reminded me of something. And someone.

'Tell Georgie not to disturb me when they come back in,' I said quickly. 'That I will see her in the morning. And I'll take that basket back for you.'

The bottles inside clinked softly as I picked it up, and with a small wave, I turned and disappeared into the gathering darkness of the Summerhill grounds.

Thirty-Seven

Down in the bay, the tide was coming in. I could hear the impatient rushing of the water, the waves rolling restlessly against the edges of the river mouth. My father used to say that if you were very still, you could *feel* the tide inside you. The pull as the atmosphere became dense and expectant, the slow tug of withdrawal when it receded, leaving behind a yearning, an emptiness that was refilled and emptied again, a push-pull that never ceased.

It was eerie walking down here in the dark, the familiar shapes of trees and saplings shivering in the breeze, throwing shadows on the clearing in a faint echo of the water out there, restless and moody. But oddly, I was glad that my familiar Summerhill was so strange tonight. An unknown world that obliterated all that had happened, narrowing the universe down to just me and the person waiting for me in the shed at the edge of the woods, making it easy to leave everything else behind.

It took my eyes a moment to adjust to the darkness, and I groped my way along the rough wooden wall only to discover, with a sharp pang of disappointment, that the shed was empty. Where had he gone?

There was a rustling, then the sound of a disembodied voice from the other side of the wall.

'Miss,' it whispered. 'Maddy. Out here.'

He was sitting on the warm flagstones next to the shed, his back against the wall. One long leg was stretched out in front of him; the other was bent, carefully supporting his arm, which lay there, bandaged and lumpy.

'I thought you had left,' I said, gruff with relief.

'It was so hot in there,' he said, squinting up at me with a contented smile. 'And it's so beautiful out here – no one could possibly stay inside on a night like this. Come, sit.'

For a moment, I stood rooted to the ground by the corner of the shed, clutching Susan's basket. I'd been walking so fast that I'd almost forgotten about the proximity of the water. I slid down the wall, the bottles in the basket clanking as my legs folded and deposited me in a rather ungainly manner next to him.

'Oh,' he said fervently when he saw the contents of the basket. 'Thank you!'

He picked up the water and drank deeply before holding the bottle out to me. I took a sip, then pushed my hands between my thighs to stop them shaking.

'How are you feeling?' I squinted at his arm.

'I try not to think about it,' he said pragmatically. 'I find that helps.'

'With most things,' I agreed as the water lapped at the slipway a little distance from my feet. Covertly I studied him in the moonlight, red welts and cuts all over his skin. He'd rolled up his trousers, showing more bruises on the bare part of his thighs. But already the marks seemed lighter than they had that morning; had settled in on themselves. The human body really was astonishing, I thought, fragile flesh and bone defying something as momentous, as horrific as a plane crash. Involuntarily I reached to touch the biggest bruise, just above his knee, felt the firm flesh, the skin stretching smoothly over the swelling. He started a little at the touch of my fingertips, but then he smiled and traced the outline of the bruise in the wake of my own fingers.

When our hands collided, I came to with a start and quickly snatched mine back, hot with shame again. What would William think if he knew about the maze?

He hadn't noticed anything, though. 'Yep, it's a corker, as my dad would say,' he remarked matter-of-factly, tapping the bruise. 'I feel like a lorry's driven over me, to be honest.'

I pushed thoughts of Victor back up the hill, behind the silver-starred curtain of the night. Surely touching William's bruise was no odder than tending to his arm, feeling his lips on my hand when I fed him earlier. Nothing was odd about this, actually: just two human beings sitting by a shed in the middle of the night.

'Did anyone ask where you were going?' William's voice broke into my thoughts.

'Yes, but I didn't tell them anything.' I smiled. 'And thankfully, the grounds are big enough to hide a herd of elephants without anyone noticing.'

I expected him to laugh, but he didn't.

'The *grounds*, huh?' His voice sounded a little funny, and I turned to look at him, surprised.

'Well that's what they are, aren't they?'

'And what would your sister say if she saw us sitting here together? The lady of the manor with the lowly schoolmaster's son?'

'Oh, I don't think anyone would be bothered.' I shrugged and smiled at him. 'Summerhill isn't really like that, you know. We all live here together, and no one cares about Cookie being down in the kitchen and me up in the library. It's always worked fine for us.'

He frowned. 'It doesn't quite work like that in the real world.'

I thought it over for a moment, then said, blushing slightly, 'Well, it's up to us, isn't it? What to think?'

He looked down at his hands, but I thought I could see him smiling. 'If you say so, my lady.'

'Oh, stop. No one in their right mind could ever call Summerhill a manor, and I am certainly not a lady.'

He put a hand on my arm. 'I'm teasing. I just think . . .' He broke off, then shook his head. 'Never mind. Here, look across the bay, Maddy. If you half close your eyes, it's like you could walk all the way over to the other side.'

The breeze carried scents of salt and wetness and sent goose-bumps up my back, hardening in a tight band around my neck. But William's arm was warm next to mine and I felt the fine hairs stroking my skin, tiny electric tingles that travelled up my arm and down my spine, a faint something echoing somewhere deep in my belly. And finally, I looked up.

Never had I wished for my sketchbook more than in this moment. A canopy of inky blue stretched into infinity, a careless scatter of stars flung across both sky and water. All around me was deep blue and bright white and shiny silver, the midnight sky reflected in the water below, and if you looked hard enough and long enough you couldn't tell the two apart, as if William and I were floating in a sea of blue and silver.

'Isn't it pretty?' he said delightedly when he realised I was finally looking.

I nodded wordlessly, because 'pretty' wasn't enough for this strange, unearthly beauty. My fingers were twitching on my thigh, curling around an invisible pencil to capture the way the wind moved in tiny gusts across the water, making it whisper and shiver. Waves rose and fell, little whitecaps dancing joyfully in the moonlight; more tiny wavelets ran up the slipway, chattering excitedly, before falling back disappointed when we wouldn't come and play.

'The water is wonderfully cool, actually,' he said thoughtfully.

'Cookie says it's cold. She does sea swimming on her day off. Has a group and everything.'

'It wasn't all that cold yesterday,' he said. 'The summer's warmed it up, I think. And I *am* quite disgracefully dirty . . .'

He was studying the slipway just below us with a speculative expression.

'You're cut all over, and your arm's got to heal.' I shook my head. 'You'll just have to be hot. I could get some water, sponge you down.'

'Sponge me down?' he said disgustedly. 'Do you think I'm some kind of nancy boy? There will definitely not be any sponging whatsoever. And salt water would be good for me, don't you think?'

He moved one of his long legs and stretched out his toes towards a little wave whooshing up.

He sighed in rapture. 'Oh, it's like being dipped in a cloud.'

'Quite the poet, aren't you.' I frowned.

'Come on,' he said, and unbelievably, he started to get to his feet, steadying himself on the shed wall. 'I'll hold it above me,' he decided, grimacing at his arm.

'What on earth do you mean by "come on"?' I said incredulously. 'I am certainly not going in there.' I shrank back against the wall. Was it my imagination, or had the wind picked up, making the water rush more loudly across the flagstones, filling the small crevices and pools between the big rocks further out, waves lapping at us, coming closer, the tide reaching . . .

With a groan, William crouched down in front of me again, holding out his hand.

'Come with me,' he said. 'I'll be right there. I'll look after you.'

'I can't.'

'Course you can. And someone's got to make sure my arm doesn't get wet.'

'That'd be your own fault completely,' I said, finally opening my eyes. 'And someone might see you.'

His lashes were dipped in white, the long, straight nose a bright slash between broad cheekbones. He looked ghost-like, but his eyes were turned up at the edges and his smile was reassuringly real.

'It's the middle of the night and we're at the ends of the earth,' he said. 'There's no boats out there, and if we stay in this little cove, no one will be able to see us at all. Please, Maddy,' he said. 'Come.'

So I did. After six years, I, Madeleine Hamilton, went into the water around the headland from Hangman's Bluff because a hideaway airman asked me to.

Keeping my eyes carefully averted from William, I took off my dress and followed him towards the slipway in my petticoat, hoping the moon would hide my undergarments. At the water, I hesitated, but William had no such compunction. In three strides, he was down the ramp and in the sea, arm held carefully above his head, an expression of pure bliss on his ghostly face.

'Come,' floated back to me again, and with a last internal wrench, I pushed off the slipway and stepped into the water. And gasped. Not from the cold, but from the unexpectedness. It was like wading into cool gossamer silk. The stones were slick with algae and I had to dig my toes in for a moment, my petticoat billowing around me as the waves rushed up to greet me again. A breath caught in my throat, but when the water pulled away, I wanted it back, that silkiness against my legs, and obligingly, it returned, pooling once again around my feet, taking away the heat and misery of the evening, unclenching my jaw muscles and loosening my shoulders. It flushed across my skin, every wave washing me clean, making me forget the maze altogether, leaving nothing but coolness. I laughed out loud.

'That's the ticket,' William said approvingly, coming towards me in a rush of water.

'Don't you dare splash me,' I warned. 'Your arm . . .'

But he had already scooped up an armful of water and released it in my direction, leaving me gasping and spluttering.

'You'll pay for that,' I said threateningly, wading in further, pushing down the wet wads of my petticoat and feeling the water slide above my shoulders.

He laughed and hopped away, slipped a little, and suddenly disappeared beneath the surface.

'William!' I smothered a shriek and flung myself headlong after him.

He emerged, groaning and rasping and pushing wet hair away from his eyes, his face a grimace of pain as the salt water hit the wound. 'Oh, that hurts, that hurts, that bloody well *hurts* like a son of a . . .' He broke off and clenched his teeth, smothering further obscenities in a stream of huffing and puffing.

'Are you all right?' I asked anxiously.

He nodded, his eyes still screwed up, his arm bobbing up and down in the water as he breathed hard against the pain. For a moment, we both bobbed with that arm, until he finally opened his eyes and regarded me darkly.

'That was your fault,' he said. 'You made me lose my balance.'

He splashed a small handful of water my way, then pushed off the bottom edge of the slipway and started swimming.

'Hey!' I called after him. 'Your arm . . . we should get out.'

'Under no circumstances,' came back clearly. 'It's already wet anyway and it stings like the blazes; might as well make the best of it. I want to see what sea swimming is all about.'

I hovered for a little while, keeping my eyes trained on his head as he ploughed through the water with an awkward one-sided stroke, criss-crossing the water with plenty of groaning and huffing as the salt water connected with more of his wounds, but eventually I had no choice but to follow him. I barely had time to wonder whether I could even still swim, but my insides – my wonderful, treacherous, complicated insides – remembered everything my father had taught me when I was a little girl. My arms pulled me through the silky-cool waves, my feet paddled to propel me forward. And now I did feel it, what my father had always talked about. The pull of the tide, its rhythmic yearning, the constant contracting and releasing. Day in, day out, year in, year out, the water had been reaching for Summerhill, and now it was taking me in.

I was breathing hard when I drew level with the dark shape bobbing in the water, a white flash of teeth showing me his grin.

'You can swim,' he said approvingly.

'And you're in heaps of trouble,' I said, my teeth chattering with cold and delayed panic, my legs feeling like jelly. I wished I could shed my petticoat, which was billowing and dragging on me. 'What if we both drown?'

'We won't,' he said reassuringly. 'Look, we're so close to the shore. And there's no one here at all. But I'll hold your arm if you want me to.'

'You just want to splash me again,' I retorted darkly, and kicked myself backwards.

'You're too smart for your own good.' I could hear his gurgling laughter behind me.

'You won't catch me.' I swam faster. 'Race you to the jetty.'

Thirty-Eight

The moon had wandered a good way around the edge of the headland before we finally clambered up the slipway again and collapsed onto the flagstones.

They were still warm from the day's heat, and I stretched out along them so that every inch of my back touched the ground. Next to me, I felt William do the same, his legs extending beyond mine, his good arm folded behind his head. Little by little, our breathing calmed and our bodies settled as we lay under the stars, the taste of salt water on our lips.

'Why are you so afraid of it?' he said. 'The bay, I mean.'

Automatically my mind braced itself, pushing all thoughts of my father towards the blank space outside Summerhill. But that space had been filled, with water and silver waves and the luxury, the sheer and utter bliss of muscles melting against warm stone after cold water. And in an odd way, my father's story seemed to belong here, in this strange place that seemed only to exist for William and me.

'I just thought, living in this beautiful place and all, you'd be out on the water all the time,' he said, gesturing across the sky.

'I used to. My sister and I both did; we practically lived on the river when I was a child. But my father died in an accident when I was ten. Right where your plane went down, actually.' I swallowed. 'He fell down the side of those cliffs and I went after him. To help, you see. But I got cut off by the water when the tide came in.'

By the time I might have been persuaded to leave my father and go for help, the sand had all but disappeared and waves were lapping against the rocks below us and up the steps on the far side of the cove. There would have been no way for me to make it across and back up the cliffs. My father knew that. He also knew that before long, the tide would find the space above the rocks where he was lying. I saw it in his eyes as I crouched down trying to find a flat rock to make his head more comfortable. He screamed with pain when I touched him, and then he told me again to go, to try and climb up the rock face, the steep place behind us where we had never been allowed to climb before, but which would now be all right, *quite all right, Maddy love. You go on up, you're ever such a good climber. I'll watch you.* It was an enormous effort for him, I could tell, because his face was screwed up and his teeth clenched, but he continued to coax me, and then, when I didn't heed him, he shouted. That he would be fine. That I needed to be strong now and go. Be safe.

But how on earth could I have gone? How could I possibly have left my father lying there, splayed across those sharp-edged boulders, grimy with bits of half-dried seaweed that would before long be floating in seawater once more. He screamed again when I tried to drag him up towards the bigger boulders, a scream like I'd never heard before, but I pulled him as far up as I possibly could, trying to block out the raw, red insides of his flesh and his splayed, bent-backwards leg, the tears running down his cheeks and the low, guttural sounds that came from his throat when he finally stopped telling me to climb back up the cliff. At some point – I didn't know when – the sounds stopped altogether, and his eyes were closed, and I sat next to him and held his hand and watched the water's slow advance.

A gust of wind swept across my damp petticoat, sending a shiver over my skin, and for a long moment, the sound of wind and water was overwhelmingly loud in my ears. Then a hand touched mine and I froze.

'Shh,' William whispered, leaving his fingers lightly on mine. 'It's just me. No need to be afraid.'

And actually, there wasn't. This was my night world, mine and William's, and so I let my body relax and closed my eyes, feeling his fingers slowly interlace with mine, one by one, so gently that it felt like they'd always been there.

'I would say I'm sorry,' he said softly. 'But that seems hardly adequate. I *am*, though, very sorry. That's a terrible thing for a child. What happened then?'

'A boat came,' I said. 'A fishing boat had seen us, I think. It took them ages to get close enough to us, and one of them . . .' I swallowed hard, 'one of the men swam out to us with a piece of rope.'

'He swam?' William twitched his head sideways to look at me. 'With the surf, that's nigh on impossible.'

I tried to close my eyes more tightly, focus on William's hand again, because of the many things I didn't want to remember about that night, this was the hardest. Watching the men confer on the boat, shouting to me and gesturing wildly, holding up the rope. How one of them – James Morley had been his name; I'd never forgotten it – had started pulling off his boots, thrown one leg over, then the other, clinging to the side of the wildly tipping boat for a few moments to gauge the swell of the water, then jumped right into the churning waves.

My grip on William's hand tightened, and red-hot spots seemed to dance in front of my eyes. He pulled my arm underneath his so he could inch closer, until our shoulders touched and his side lay all the way along mine. His warmth and the sound of his breath eased my throat until finally I looked up at the sky and felt a strange sort of peace stealing over me.

Thirty-Nine

'It hardly seems real, does it?' William broke the silence. 'So much space. When I was a little boy, I wondered what it would be like to be up there. Until I first set foot in a plane, that is. Then I never wondered again.'

I sneaked a quick look sideways and saw that he was frowning to himself.

'Why did you join up, then?'

My question broke the magic. He moved, his fingers slipping out of mine, sat up. With a small internal sigh of regret, I sat up too, more slowly, blushing a little when I suddenly remembered that we were both in a state of semi-undress, and that my petticoat clearly showed the outlines of my body through the damp material. Turning away and crouching low, I put on my dress and buttoned it all the way up, but when I came to sit next to him, I realised that he hadn't noticed anything amiss. He was holding a small pouch, fumbling one-handed with the clasp. It was a kind of waxed canvas and had been wrapped so tightly that its contents had, miraculously, survived the plane crash and the swim around the headlands. There were a few papers, some banknotes. And inserted into the middle fold, a photo, old and a little fuzzy, showing a man and a woman.

'My parents.' He nodded at it. 'My da just before he went off to war in 1916. He was twenty years old.'

I studied the photo. The man was a bit older than William was now, but the sweep of his mouth and his high forehead were the same. He was looking straight into the camera. His mouth was unsmiling – perhaps they'd been told to be serious – but everything else about him radiated excitement and movement. He looked rather dashing, in fact, all sharp cheekbones and smooth skin, clear eyes blinking with suppressed merriment, and my heart gave a sharp and very strange squeeze when I thought of William looking like that in just a few years. His features hardening, his body filling out, his expression confident and rakish, like this man's. I swallowed down the odd feeling in my stomach and suddenly I wanted to touch the smooth, hard surface of William's arm again.

'Now *he* could fly,' William said, oblivious to the way I pushed my hands between my thighs. 'My mam always said there'd been a terrible mistake the day he was born, and that somewhere up there, a birdie was whizzing around who'd swapped places with my da.'

'That sounds . . . exciting,' I said, wary of William's use of the past tense.

'She didn't like him going away to fight, of course, no wife does, and she was ever so glad when he came back, even though . . . Well, he got a medal, too; it's been sitting on the shelf for ever. He was on reconnaissance first, then later, in 1917 and '18, he was right in the thick of it. He went down, though, planes not being what they are now. He survived but lost his leg. They did their best, but they couldn't save it; amputated it above the knee. The amputation was terrible: they didn't have enough morphine to go round, just had to get on with it.' He swallowed, lifted the arm with the jagged wound. 'He wouldn't have carried on like I did with this thing,' he said darkly.

'I always knew I was going to go into the air force. There's an airfield close to where we live. As far back as I can remember, my da took me to watch the planes there, taught me the different models, told me about his time in the air. He made it sound so beautiful, Maddy, so light and weightless, really and truly like a bird. The day I left for training, he was almost as excited as if he had been going himself. And I was, too. I couldn't wait, you know.' He turned the photo in his hand. 'And then, later, I climbed into a plane for the first time, and I was utterly terrified. My mind simply shut off, and it was all I could do not to run, right then and there. When I came back down to the ground, I swore to myself, never again. But I did go again. And again.'

He drew in a deep breath and his grip tightened around the photo.

'He would be waiting for me when I came home on my days off. He'd ask about it, how it was up in the air. He was so proud, too, told everyone about me. I suppose, for him, the next best thing after flying himself was having *me* fly.'

'Did you ever try to talk to him about it? Surely he'd have understood?'

He settled back against the wall, flinching when he involuntarily twitched his injured arm.

'I tried to. Many times. But I just couldn't. It sounded so weak, so cowardly when he'd lost his leg fighting the Red Baron and was dying to do it all over again. How on earth could I possibly tell him that I was afraid? Just afraid, nothing else. There'd be a good moment to do it and I'd let it pass, and then another opportunity and I still couldn't find the words. All the ground classes, the fiddling with the planes, I loved that part, I was really good at it. But they shortened the training – they're desperate for pilots – so the flying came around awfully quickly, and it was . . . agony.

'The flying and then the not telling and then having to go back and do it all over again . . . it became a nightmare I was trapped in. And each time he opened the door, put his crutches aside to embrace me, insisted on me having the biggest helping at dinner, endlessly talking about flying, it got worse and worse, until all I could think about was running away. I was waiting for an opportunity, but I couldn't quite make myself do it. I couldn't bear them thinking me a coward, stealing away in the dead of night.'

He looked down into his lap, running his fingers gently across the picture. 'And yesterday, I stopped thinking altogether. But if I go back, it'll just start all over again.'

A small pause fell as I tried to put words to all the things that were wrong with this.

'William,' I edged closer and put my hand on his arm, 'you can't stay here. You have to let them know you're all right.'

'I know,' he said, without looking at me. 'I *know* everything you're going to say, Maddy. I've been over it a hundred times in my mind. And I will think about it again, tomorrow. But just for tonight, could I sit here and watch the stars with you? I mean, if you want to.'

He shifted again, and now I could see his eyes and his mouth, turned up in a smile.

I opened my own mouth and closed it again. 'Yes,' I whispered. 'Yes, of course.'

And when we stretched out on the warm stones again, any urge to talk faded altogether, because he was right, nothing else belonged down here, in this tiny space at the edge of the world, where William was holding my hand and watching me as I drifted into sleep.

We woke as the dark-blue sky started to lighten, slowly, as if the night, too, knew that everything would change the moment it disappeared, that it would take with it our midnight bubble and make both of us face the real world again.

William walked me through the trees to where the little track to the orchards began.

'Will you . . .' But I didn't finish my question, because I didn't actually want to know.

It was still dark under the trees, and he lifted his good hand and felt his way up my arm and shoulder, cupping the nape of my neck and curling his fingers around to draw me close.

'Yes, I will,' he said, resting his forehead against mine. 'I'll be here.'

Forty

I came downstairs just after eleven that morning. I could hear distant noises of activity, footsteps, a shout, and from the direction of Aunt Marjorie's nook, the sound of the wireless. It occurred to me that I hadn't seen much of Aunt Marjorie the previous day, and on an impulse, I walked down to the little room, put my head around the corner.

'Good morning, Aunt,' I said. 'Any news?'

She sat with her back to me, her hands twisted around a piece of paper, a letter from Aunt Hilly, I thought, recognising the handwriting. I expected her to launch into her usual effusive hatred of Herr Hitler, but she didn't even look at me; just sat, her shoulders slumped in a defeated sort of way.

'Aunt?' I said, and stepped around to face her. To my great surprise, her cheeks were wet with tears.

'What is wrong? Are we . . .' I swallowed hard.

'It's a matter of hours,' she said. 'Hitler's in Poland; unimaginable what he'll do to the people there.'

She bowed her head and looked down at her hands gripping the letter, seeming not even to notice the tears falling across her ample bosom and disappearing into her shawl.

'How have we let it come to this, Madeleine? How do we do this again and again?'

'It will be fine, Aunt, you'll see,' I said desperately. 'They say it'll be over by Christmas.'

'That's what they all said last time. But when has a war ever been fine, or over in four months?' She jabbed her thumb at the map of Europe behind her. She'd been sticking little pins into it, connecting them with threads to show Hitler's movements across the Continent.

'We'll be safe here, though.' I knelt and looked up at her. 'You don't have to worry.'

She looked up slowly, regarding me with red-rimmed eyes. 'What is safe any more?' she said quietly. 'And look around you, Madeleine. It's not like we even need war; we do a fairly good job of dying ourselves. My sister, your papa. That poor airman. And half the world about to go at it all over again. God, I hate this place.'

I stared at her wordlessly, but she didn't say anything else, didn't even look at me, just smoothed out her letter and turned up the wireless, and eventually I left to find Georgiana. The breakfast room was empty, though, only a few crumbs indicating that people had recently left, and I stood at the bottom of the stairs for a moment, unsure of what to do now.

Maybe, if I tried really hard, I could pretend that everything was still exactly as it had always been. That Georgie and I were starting another day of talking and working on our stories. That we would hunker down here until the trouble in the outside world had passed. I closed my eyes, listened to the creaking of the wood panelling along the stairs as it expanded and contracted in the sun, a sound as familiar to me as breathing. A fly buzzed against the glass, the house martins chirped outside the drawing room window, where they'd built a nest for their little ones. They were late leaving this year; should already have started heading south, the way they did every year.

When the clock wheezed and chimed the hour, I started, waited for it to settle back down and for my body to settle with it, join the old rhythms of the house, become part of it again. But the truth was, I wasn't the same Maddy any more. I'd patched up an airman and swum in the bay at midnight, I'd talked about my father's death for the first time ever, and—

A sound cut into my thoughts and my eyes snapped open. The hall was quiet, but then I heard it again, from the library.

'Yes, I can see why you think this would be a good idea. I'll speak to Father when I get back, he might well be interested.' A voice came from inside as I pushed open the door with a little more force than necessary.

The long room at the front of the house, with its big windows overlooking the courtyard, had been my father's space and the hub of the estate. This was where Georgiana talked to Mr Pritchard when he came to discuss Summerhill's *Situation*, as he always ominously referred to it, and where Aunt Marjorie occasionally received visitors. Over the years, however, the library had become mostly mine. Little by little, I'd brought my drawing things here. I had commandeered one of the low sideboards to lay out my pencils, and moved the sketching stand that my father had built especially for me – with a top that could be adjusted – into the alcove by the window, where the afternoon light was the best.

Now, Victor stood leafing through two ledgers and talking to Jonathan, who was studying the enormous map of Summerhill that hung next to the desk. We'd compiled that map together, my father and I, just after he'd had the land surveyed about a year before he died. We'd walked the estate to sketch out the grounds, then I'd filled in the details meticulously, adding paths and bridleways, lanes and roads, houses, cottages, tenancies, trees and fields. Forge Fields, the Bottoms, Clover Meadow, Milking Banks, Fairings Corner, Pixie's Wood. Even the ancient oak was there, down to tiny branches feathery with foliage.

'Excuse me,' I said loudly. I suddenly realised that this was the first time I'd seen Victor since Smuggler's Hatch, and I cringed at the memory, but then I caught myself and took another step forward, because that moment, too, belonged to the old Maddy. 'What are you doing in here?' I demanded.

Jonathan turned quickly and his mouth closed without

elaborating on the *good idea* he'd be talking to his father about. For a moment he seemed at a loss as to what to say. He rallied quickly, though, and by the time he'd straightened from his elaborate bow, a big smile was fixed on his face.

'Madeleine, what a pleasant surprise. Have you caught up on your beauty sleep? Not that you need it,' he added gallantly. 'Exquisite as ever, my dear.'

Since no one in their right mind would ever call me and my wardrobe 'exquisite', I ignored him.

'What are you doing in here, Victor?' I asked him directly.

'Gigi asked me to look through some of the accounts,' Victor said, not rising to my tone. He took his time to light a cigarette, take a long, even drag. 'Your financial situation—'

'Is none of your business whatsoever,' I cut in more coolly than I felt. I walked over to the desk, ran my hands over the ledgers. How on earth could Georgiana have asked him to do that? These were ours, our family's affairs. But, I realised with a pang, if she had roped him in to help, I had only myself to blame. I had never wanted to listen when she'd talked about Summerhill, had never stuck around for her meetings with stuffy Mr Pritchard. What exactly *had* I done, with all my talk of keeping the estate the way my father had wanted it? Walking around in Frank's footsteps with a shovel to fix the bloody walls? I lifted my head to look Victor in the eye.

'Neither of yours, actually,' I said. 'Now, if you'll excuse me.' I turned towards the door in clear dismissal, and Jonathan gave me another polite bow as he obediently took his leave, walking out into the hall, where Clementine's high-pitched chatter could be heard in the distance.

Victor, however, remained where he was, even, I saw with mounting anger, perching himself on the edge of my father's desk, *my* desk, as he smoked his cigarette. He was holding something in his other hand, and my heart skipped a painful beat when I realised that it was my sketchbook. He smiled a little when he saw that I'd noticed, and drew his thumb lightly across the green linen, a slow, loving caress that made me want to gag.

'Give it back to me,' I said furiously. 'You have no right to snoop through my things.'

'I found it on the hallway table,' he said pleasantly. 'I didn't want it to get lost. I know how precious it is to you.' He kept his eyes on mine, moving his thumb back and forth across the front, and I felt a surge of revulsion at the thought of him looking through my drawings, looking at *my* Summerhill and somehow making it his. Moving fast, I snatched it out of his hand and clamped it under my elbow. I couldn't believe that only yesterday, I had found Victor warm and lovely, when now – the way he carried himself, his smug smile, his cigarette breath – he seemed simply repulsive.

'Lovely stuff,' he observed admiringly. 'That drawing you did of, who is it, your cook? Is that a swimming costume? And is that your gardener sleeping in the chair so attractively? You certainly are all very cosy in here, upstairs, downstairs, all one big happy family. Very modern.'

'You should leave now,' I said in a low voice.

'Well, I'm glad to have run into you, actually,' he said. Without warning, he grabbed my elbow. 'Where do you keep going, by the way?'

I tried to wrench my arm away. 'None of your—'

'Oh, I know,' Victor said pleasantly. 'You're a very discreet person, aren't you?'

'What?'

'It's refreshing when girls don't feel constantly compelled to go blabbering every little thing out into the world.' I gave another pull on my arm. 'That's why I like you. You're clearly very good at keeping secrets.'

He put a small emphasis on 'secrets', so small it wouldn't have been noticeable to anyone but me, but which angered me so much that I blurted out, 'If you're referring to what happened in the maze, I haven't said anything because there is nothing to say, nothing at all. It's not a secret. I'm just ignoring it, I'm ignoring *you*, and hoping it'll go away somehow, that you will go away . . .'

'Madeleine.' He straightened up and brought his face very close to mine so that there could be no mistaking his words. 'I won't. I will never go away. Never.'

It was such a strange, unexpected thing to say that for a moment I ceased to struggle against his grip.

'There you are! Everyone, they're in here, we can go.'

Clementine and Laney came clattering into the room in a rush of high heels and clouds of perfume, Rana following more slowly behind. Victor quickly dropped his hand and moved back, picking up his lighter just as Georgiana appeared, looking slightly harassed and distinctly annoyed.

'Victor, I thought you said you were going to bring the car round,' she said impatiently. 'Never mind, I've got ours now, we're ready to go. Maddy, where on earth have you been?'

'Sleeping,' I said, willing the angry flush on my face to subside.

'And then she wanted to show me her artwork.' Victor said apologetically. 'I'm really sorry, Gi, we got sidetracked.'

'Did she now?' Laney flicked a glance at Rana, whose expression didn't change as she regarded my flushed face.

'No, I didn't,' I said furiously as he gestured for me to walk ahead of him. 'Georgie . . .'

'Oh, let's just go.' Without another word, Georgiana stalked out through the front door.

'We're going to the village.' Clementine sidled up to me.

'Why?' I shook her off and followed Georgiana, narrowing my eyes against the sudden brightness outside. Leica appeared round the corner of the house to wind around my legs, whining softly.

'They wanted to see it. And Hobson's asked me to pick up a

few things for tonight.' Georgiana wrenched open the car door. 'You don't have to come if you don't want to,' she added coolly.

I hated the tone in her voice, the set expression on her face. I opened my mouth to say something, anything, to make her smile, but Victor got there first.

'If Maddy doesn't want to go, then I'll stay, too. I don't really like villages.' He came to stand next to me with his usual easy smile, half raising his hand as if we were already waving the others off together.

'Fine,' Georgiana said angrily. 'Suit yourselves, both of you.'

'Who doesn't like villages?' Laney's eyes were round. 'They're perfectly sweet.'

'And it's got shops,' Clementine added.

'One shop.' I rolled my eyes. 'It sells food and stamps. And I'm coming with you.'

Georgiana, already half inside the car, stopped and turned. 'You are?'

'Of course.' I climbed into the front seat.

'You don't have to,' she said, now anxious, all annoyance forgotten. 'It's fine, Maddy, I was just being cranky. I didn't mean for you to . . . I know you don't like leaving here much.'

'I want to,' I said firmly. 'It'll be fun.'

She laughed at the blatancy of my lie. 'No excuse now, Victor,' she called over her shoulder as she slid behind the wheel and he climbed into the back seat.

I scooted close and leaned into Georgiana's shoulder under the pretext of making room for Laney, who was fastidiously arranging her skirt on my other side, but really to watch Victor in the mirror. He was staring out of the window, smoking in deep, long drags.

'Open the window, will you?' I said pleasantly.

'So people are coming around eight tonight,' Georgiana chattered next to me. 'It's not anything special, but Becky – you know, across at Landis Place – she rang me, incensed that she hadn't been invited to the party. It's not a party, I told her, just a small gathering. With drinks and music and a bit of dancing.'

'I think you call that a party.' I smiled and patted her arm, but my thoughts weren't on whatever entertainment she'd cooked up for her restless friends. Much as I didn't want to, I would have to talk to her about Victor.

I will never go away. Never. It didn't make sense. Nothing made sense about the way he had changed so suddenly. The maze. The library. An entire perfectly pleasant conversation that seemed to have been so full of strange needling and deliberate baiting and triumph and anger that I could still feel myself trembling slightly. I frowned, running my fingers distractedly across the green linen of my sketchbook, but even when we reached the outskirts of the village, I still had no idea what was wrong with Victor Deverill.

Forty-One

Chloe

Chloe stood at the sink washing potatoes. Aidan had come home with another big bunch of flowers, which now stood in a vase on the table behind her. Their cloying scent mingled with the muddy potatoes and made her stomach slop slowly back and forth. He was chatting away next to her and she was listening just enough so she could throw in the odd 'is that so?' and 'how exciting' when he drew breath.

She felt strangely hot, and her eyes were so heavy she had to close them for a moment, and yet her insides were heaving and roiling, her mind circling endlessly over Madeleine's parting words. It all came down to the baby now. She had wished for a pivotal point in her marriage and . . . well, it couldn't get more pivotal than creating a family together. She had to make a decision.

She tunnelled her knife into a potato to dig out a black spot. But what was it to be? Surely you couldn't run at the first sign of trouble. For better or worse actually meant exactly that. The potato oscillated a little in front of her eyes and she blinked, trying to push back the headache and the queasiness at the same time. God, was this what pregnancy was like, feeling like you were going to keel over at any moment? Maybe Aidan had been right, maybe it had been stupid to take that job. She hadn't been able to do it anyway, as he had predicted, and she'd come away with a whole lot of other things she hadn't remotely bargained for.

She looked over at the bottle of sparkling grape juice, which she'd nestled in between the water bottles in the fridge earlier.

'Penny for your thoughts, darling.'

She hadn't noticed that a small silence had fallen, and now that she came to think of it, she hadn't contributed anything in the way of *Is that so*'s for a while.

'I'm having a very one-sided conversation here.' He frowned and tapped his fingers on the worktop. 'Chloe?'

She looked down at the knife. Even her hands felt hot, the skin stretching thin and dry around her fingers. She fixed a smile onto her face, forced herself to put the potato down, then moved around him and opened the oven to check on the roasted sprouts that were his favourite. A surge of hot sprout-scented moisture billowed out of the oven and she slammed the door shut before it could dislodge the tsunami of nausea pushing up from her stomach.

'So, I've been thinking . . .' Aidan's arm touched her side, and his hip bumped against hers. Revulsion rose, thick and felty, against the back of her throat and she swallowed, dragged a hand across her hot cheeks. Once the news was out there, she'd feel better. Lighter. Things would start to change; they had to, soon.

'. . . about Danny. Are you listening, Chloe?'

'Er, what?' Chloe blinked several times.

'About Oakwood's new fees,' Aidan said. 'They really are quite outrageous.'

'Yes,' she said, swallowing. 'I'm sure there must be cheaper options.'

'Oh yes,' he said thoughtfully. 'Although there is the upheaval of moving him, too.'

'Aidan,' Chloe said tiredly, 'if you feel Oakwood's too expensive, then I'll find him a cheaper alternative and Danny will be absolutely fine with that.'

'There's no need to take that tone,' Aidan said, and frowned at her. 'I'm just saying . . .'

'Well, don't,' Chloe said before she could stop herself. She knew she should be trying to smooth things over right now, but she was getting very tired of having Oakwood's fees held over her. She was very tired generally, and hot, too.

'Anyway, it's not only a question of the expense.' He waited until she looked up. 'It's also about how long he'll still need a home at all.' He smiled now, glad to have her full attention. 'A move might not be worth it in the end.' He took a long sip of his drink, regarding her steadily over the rim of his glass.

'Aidan, stop,' she said in a low voice. 'Just stop.'

'Darling, don't be naive.' He held up his hands. 'We need to think ahead is all I'm saying. Ataxia cases at this stage, they progress quickly. Danny's body is starting to shut down.'

'He's still got movement in his fingers, his head.' She was only dimly aware of raising her hands in front of her, overlarge and almost comical in their oven mitts.

'But for how long? How long until he'll be fed through a machine or breathing with an oxygen tank? At some point soon, he'll just be a shell, nothing more. Need a hand with those sprouts, darling?'

He plucked the mitts off her hands and bent to open the oven door. 'This looks delicious.'

The stench of sprouts washing over her as he lifted the tray out of the oven and the sight of him wearing her oven mitts and smiling at her, innocently and almost sweetly, finally dislodged everything she'd been holding in. She turned and ran to the loo.

Once she'd started, she found she couldn't stop. On and on it went, her body bucking under the strain, as if her stomach was trying to turn itself inside out to rid itself of all the secret things she hadn't allowed herself to think about, along with the sprout-scented kitchen, Aidan's smile and Danny's shell waiting for his death.

Eventually, Aidan prised her away from the loo and carried her, vomit stains and all, to their big en suite bathroom. There she sat, shivering, watching him through a haze of tears as he filled the bath, testing the temperature several times. He guided her in, then lowered himself onto the side of the tub, sliding his hand back and forth through the water, creating a gentle swooshing sound.

'It's all making sense now,' he said wonderingly. 'The tiredness, the weight gain, being generally off.' And then he was kneeling next to her on the bath mat, his face level with hers, and she saw to her utter astonishment that his eyes were full of tears. He reached out to grasp her hands, which were ice cold despite the warm water.

'You've made me the happiest man today,' he said softly. 'And I'm sorry about last night. I hated the thought of something taking you away from me, but now I see I didn't need to worry at all, because we'll be closer than ever. You and me and the baby. This is it. Us. Together for ever.'

'For ever.' She closed her eyes.

When she woke a little later, her head hurt so badly she didn't even want to open her eyes. She felt hot all over, but cold, too, spasms contracting her limbs every so often. She lay very still to keep her head from pounding, the soft ticking of the clock magnified tenfold. She rolled carefully onto her side to look at it, her whole body aching with the movement. 11:15 p.m.

It hadn't taken Aidan long to establish that not only was Chloe pregnant, she also had a flu bug with a fever, which explained a lot of the hazy, floaty feeling that had dogged her all day. He had been kind and attentive, carefully drying her off, finding thin, soft clothes and putting her to bed with just a sheet covering her. He gave her paracetamol and cooled her face with a wet cloth, then drifted around the room, checking her temperature off and on, putting things away, getting ready for the night. When he finally crawled into bed, he didn't touch her; instead, he talked about the baby, wondered what it would look like, exclaimed over their good fortune, made plans for the future. The sound of his voice followed her as she drifted off to sleep, his words reaching for her through the fog in her brain. *Just think, Chloe, our own little family.* And then, his favourite phrase: *For ever. For ever. For ever.*

The orange digits of the clock swam in front of her eyes, which were swollen and sore, her throat raw. She hadn't realised there were so many bones in a human body and that every one of them could have a pain of its own. The nausea, strangely, wasn't quite so insistent any more, just a faint background thrumming to the achiness. It would start to change about now, the leaflet from the surgery had said. A sign that your body was moving on to the second trimester, when the baby would finally become a certainty.

She closed her eyes. Part of her wished that she had been the one to tell him, that she could have stood tall, chosen the time and the place and perhaps the direction her life might have taken, instead of letting him prise the secret from her the way he had. But another part of her was simply relieved. The decision had been made for her, it was out in broad daylight, and now, she was surprised to discover, she was just . . . empty, as if she'd simply deflated around the place inside her where the secret had been.

Aidan was cross with her because he was convinced she'd picked up the bug at Oakwood. All those old-people germs weren't good for the baby.

'No more visits to Danny for the time being, do you hear me?' he said firmly when he came out of the shower early the next morning. 'Having the flu when you're pregnant is serious. I'm going to take a couple of days off and take care of you. I don't want you to worry about a thing. I'll call Dr Webb and sort out your appointments, get you more vitamins and feed you up.'

She tried to protest, but her lips were dry and cracked, her bones felt like rubber and her entire body was so achy that she closed her eyes.

The days slid away from her. Dr Webb agreed with Aidan, prescribing bed rest until the flu had passed, and Aidan fed her chicken soup along with big, bulky vitamin pills that hurt as they went down her throat. The only sign of time passing was the light changing around the edges of the blinds as she floated on a feverish haze, only dimly noting that Aidan had welcomed the pregnancy with the enthusiasm she'd known he would.

'The heart forms first,' he said, pushing a pillow beneath her knees and settling down next to her with a pregnancy book. 'It beats faster than the mother's heart, and the rate changes throughout pregnancy, did you know that, Chloe?'

'Hmm,' she heard herself answer, eyes closed against the afternoon half-light. But as time ebbed and flowed around her, the notion of her baby's heart beating so very fast beneath hers grew and expanded in her mind, taking over her thoughts. Surreptitiously she felt her stomach under the sheet, trying to imagine life growing and taking shape inside it. A second later, Aidan's hand closed around hers, mirroring her movement, a fond smile on his face.

'Surely you can't feel anything yet?' He shifted closer, looked at her face eagerly. 'It's too early. But maybe if you concentrate really hard?'

She shook her head, winced at the pounding inside her skull. 'Soon, probably,' she said tiredly.

She drifted off again, but Aidan didn't take his hand away, as if he wanted to make sure he was the first one to feel the baby move, trying to reach for it through the thin layer of Chloe's stomach wall.

Forty-Two

Eventually Aidan's patients were clamouring for his return and he reluctantly left the house to tend to them, ordering Chloe to stay in bed and rest. She did so gladly, surrendering to the pleasantly blank fog of post-illness lassitude, half waking, half sleeping, thinking of nothing in particular. Her first day on her own passed uneventfully, but on the morning of the second day, a package arrived.

She had dragged herself out of bed and was standing at the kitchen counter, staring at the kettle and waiting for it to boil. Aidan had left her a box of herbal tea and she was trying to work her way through it, too tired to argue with him when he pointed out that she really needed to be thinking of Baby with every single thing she put into her mouth. That was how he was talking about it now, *Baby*, no article, as if the only baby that mattered in the world was this capital-B MacAllister *Baby*.

The thud of the post dropping on the doormat made her look up. A letter from Derriford Hospital, addressed to both of them; a few bills. And a padded envelope with her name on the front: Chloe MacAllister, Photographer, Queen's Park Road, Plymouth. She blinked at the envelope, weighed it in her hand. There was no return address; instead, a small stick figure was waving a tiny bunch of flowers in the top left-hand corner. Inside, well wrapped in brown paper, was a rectangular object, and tucked into the package a piece of thick, textured sketchbook paper.

Dear Chloe,

I tried to ring you a couple of times but your husband said you were ill. I got in touch with Mr Cooper in the end to get your address as I'm anxious for you and hope this finds you on the mend. I am so very sorry that our lovely afternoon ended the way it did and I wanted to send you something that I hope will make you smile as you recover. I had put Foxy behind me, along with too many memories, but you brought him back to me and for that I'm grateful. So here he is, ready to cheer you up. It's a loan, mind, so make sure you come back soon to return it.

Madeleine

Chloe dropped the letter and carefully unwrapped the brown paper to reveal Madeleine's green linen-bound notebook. It fell open at the centrefold. 'The Big House at the End of the Lane' said a doodled signpost in the corner of what looked like a map of Summerhill, and tiny footsteps walked across the top and on for several pages until they finally arrived at a bigger drawing of a door, through which flowerpots and a cat sunning itself beneath an apple tree were visible.

'Oh,' Chloe said into the still kitchen, a strangely hoarse sound that made her realise she hadn't actually spoken in a while. After days of feeling nothing, of revelling in the absence of sensation, the brightness of the sketchbook was almost overpowering, the colours so intense that they hurt her eyes. And as morning turned into midday and Chloe sat on the kitchen floor, Madeleine's home took shape on the pages before her. It was dogs jostling for attention as two girls walked through woods and pastures. It was sitting at a scrubbed kitchen table to be fed bread and jam. It was the sun rising and setting each day behind a squat, sturdy house on a hill. It was the colour of trees and the smell of an early-morning breeze; it was apples and watering cans and Foxy's face peeping from between the bushes.

Yearning was building in Chloe's body, rising in her stomach and spreading through her chest, a surge of longing for this lost world of Madeleine's, but also a more basic and immediate need for her own mother, who'd left behind nothing but three postcards; for her father, who'd simply given up at some point. For Danny. For Georgiana, who'd been torn between loving her sister and wanting to be free. And now, the baby. Chloe slid her hands across her stomach. That feeling of home, of closeness and freedom, being separate and whole, together. That was what she wanted for her child. If it could be like that, then it would be easy to be a mum again; then it would be . . . lovely.

Bit by bit, she felt herself coming back to life, that pale ghost from the past few days taking on colour again as she absorbed the spirit of Madeleine's drawings, the optimism and grit emanating from the pages, until she finally surfaced, looking around her kitchen in a slightly baffled way, wondering who on earth could possibly live in this empty white house.

Call Madeleine, that was what she wanted to do. She pulled herself to her feet, then had to clutch the granite work surface for several seconds until the dizziness had abated and her vision had stopped swimming. But when she finally went in search of her phone, she made a rather startling discovery.

Her mobile sat on the hall table where they kept the phones charging during the night, but she seemed to be unable to actually make a call. Further investigation revealed that the SIM card had been removed from the small flap in the back, so she could dial the emergency services but no one else, while the landline, which they rarely used any more because Aidan was obsessed with all the new mobile technology, had disappeared altogether, along with the entire charging base.

After the exuberant fizziness of the sketchbook, her brain had slowed to a crawl, moving sluggishly through the possibilities without getting anywhere at all. Holding onto the hall table, her hands trembling from post-flu exhaustion, she leaned back to inspect the place where her handbag usually sat. Empty. Suddenly something swam up to the surface of her woolly brain.

Your husband said you were ill, Madeleine's letter had said. So they'd talked, presumably when her phone still had its SIM card. And presumably the ensuing conversation – she flushed a little when she pictured it: Aidan's haughty, dismissive tone, Madeleine trying to hang onto her temper for Chloe's sake – had culminated in the extraction of that card. And if they'd talked, then Aidan would know that she'd gone back for more pictures even after he'd expressly asked her not to. And that would mean . . .

Chloe froze. 'God, please,' she whispered and started to run, awkward on her jelly legs, down the corridor to the laundry room.

The space behind the door was empty. Her camera . . . he'd have put it in the office, she thought, darting back out, pausing once to steady herself against the door frame. It always sat on the bottom bookshelf next to the desk. He must have been tidying, putting things back in their rightful places, as he always did. He knew how much her camera meant to her, he *knew*. But that was exactly what was making her feel faint with fear, because Aidan knowing how much something meant to you was not always a good thing.

When she stepped into the long, narrow office, she saw immediately that her camera wasn't there. The room was tidy and clean. Books stood orderly and free of dust, the rug was perfectly straight in the middle of the wooden floor and the chair was pushed firmly against the desk as if to make it clear that Chloe would not be working here in the foreseeable future. She dropped painfully to her knees, reached under the cupboard. Thank God he hadn't found *Foxy the Great*. But – she ran her hand once more across the empty bottom shelf, pulled open drawers, rifled through the cupboard top to bottom – both her laptop and her Nikon were nowhere to be found.

She sat on the floor, staring numbly around her. She remembered buying the Nikon like it was yesterday. It had taken her months of saving, and even that wasn't quite enough. So when Liz had agreed to take her on, Chloe had thrown caution to the wind and sold one of the pieces of jewellery from the emergency box. Worry and guilt about using the emergency box when it wasn't, technically, a life-or-death situation had made her haggle so hard that the pawnbroker, who'd been smiling in delighted anticipation of an easy sale from the pale young woman in his shop, ended up bowing her out, slightly puzzled at having parted with a lot more than what he'd been prepared to give.

For years, she hadn't gone anywhere without her camera, more worried about it being stolen than she was encumbered by the weight of it over her shoulder. *You and that camera*, Aidan used to say, bemusement tinged with a hint of jealousy, when she checked on the Nikon at night, much like you'd tuck a child into bed. She tried to think back to when that had stopped, the nightly ritual, but she couldn't remember. As time went by, she had taken fewer and fewer pictures of herself and Aidan, and eventually the need to check every night had faded because the Nikon so rarely left its spot on the shelf to begin with.

Chloe thought of Aidan's hand on her stomach. She understood now his amiable mood, his cheerfulness in the face of her flu-induced listlessness, his kindness and attention. She'd attributed it to the baby, had even felt vaguely guilty in her fever haze that she'd ever doubted his devotion. But more frantic searching through the house revealed that while her keys, too, had disappeared, the rest of the house was stocked to last a siege. He'd gone shopping for every conceivable food whim; he'd bought books and magazines; there was wool to knit with and small pots for therapeutic gardening. He'd ordered maternity clothes for her, too, heaps of packages that sat opened and ready for her to inspect them. Bras and pants and tops. Soft, stretchy trousers, floaty tunics. No jeans, no jumpers. House clothes.

She backed away from a box from Lilly's Baby Boutique and walked quickly to check the garage, where the Vauxhall stood, immovable and useless without car keys, which were nowhere to be found either. She went through room after room, picking up things at random, tossing them back down, still trying to reason with herself, to quell the sense of unreality. He was only taking care of her, wasn't he? She'd been sick, he was worried. Of course he was. Maybe he thought he was making things easier for her, helping her with the clothes and things.

But then she pushed open the last door, the spare room where he'd kept his exercise gear, his punching ball and weights, and clapped her hand to her mouth in horror. Nursery furniture, all in white, dazzlingly, blindingly bright; a feeding chair, a changing table. White gauze curtains billowed gently in the draught from the sudden opening of the door; newly fitted white blinds nestled in the window frame. A Moses basket sat inside a cot, nappies and wipes were piled up against the back of the changing table, and a mobile had been hung above it, little white sheep dangling jauntily.

Oddly enough, it was the sight of those sheep that cut right through the woolly feeling in Chloe's brain. He'd made her a prisoner in her own house, with no means to leave, no way to get back in if she did and no money to go anywhere. While she'd given in to the blank floating, Aidan had taken away everything that had made her *her*, pointing her firmly to a future in which her sole purpose was to carry his baby and deliver it into his waiting hands, tying her to him for ever. *You just stay and rest. You need to take care of Baby now.*

You know it already, Madeleine had said. Yes, she'd known. Of course she had. She'd known when Dr Webb had confirmed the news, when she'd read Georgiana's letters and when she'd talked to Madeleine. She'd thought the baby wasn't right for her world, but in fact it was her world that wasn't right for the baby. Well, it was time for a change.

She went through the house once more, slowly gathering everything that belonged to her, pathetically little though it was. Madeleine's sketchbook and letter, *Foxy the Great,* the drawing of Georgiana and Madeleine at the table. From her boxes in the attic, two photo albums, three postcards, a piece of china with the words 'make lemonade' on it, and her old photography portfolio. Then she selected a few items of clothing and packed everything into an old rucksack, which, seeing as it had evaded Aidan's thorough search once, she flattened and pushed underneath the cupboard in the study.

On the way back to the bedroom, she passed the spare room. She thought of the white furniture behind it and the jaunty sheep, and her hands clamped tight around her stomach. Yes, she might have made it easy for Aidan to take her life away from her, had given in to him, naive and blinded and afraid. But this baby was not yet his. She eased her grip and gave it a gentle pat.

'Don't you worry, little one,' she whispered. 'I'm going to take care of you. I promise.'

Forty-Three

Maddy

We parked at the edge of the village and walked the short distance to the square. Georgiana had recovered her good mood, although she still seemed a bit edgy as she assured Gregory that his car would be fine and deflected Laney's complaints about the state of the road and its detrimental effect on her shoes.

Victor really didn't seem to like villages. He was walking with his shoulders hunched over and his hands in his pockets, keeping his eyes on the ground so that I had no difficulty in pulling Georgiana away from him.

'Georgie, I was just wondering – how did you actually meet Victor?' I said in a low voice. 'I don't think you ever told me.'

'We met in London,' she smiled dreamily at the memory, 'when I first got to Cousin Claire's. Her Louisa . . . she's eighteen now and quite nice, although she lives in a different world altogether. They have such a lovely house, Belgravia, you know—'

'So Claire knows him,' I interrupted her, throwing a quick look back over my shoulder. But Victor was busy talking to Jonathan and hadn't noticed us walking ahead.

'Yes. She threw a party for me and Vic was invited. Louisa and Laney know each other, from school or somewhere, so they sort of all move in the same circles, and Louisa was quite smitten with Victor. To tell you the truth, I'm not sure Claire was all too pleased. She's such a snob, you wouldn't believe it, Maddy, constantly going on about Lady This and Lord That and who's who; thinks anyone who works must be selling eels' heads at Billingsgate. But thankfully none of that matters remotely to me, and Vic and I got talking. He introduced me to the others and . . . well, the rest is history. When he heard I was going to Europe via Amsterdam, it turned out he had business in Holland and he offered himself up as a tour guide. And then we travelled into France together. Cousin Xenia was too busy burying the family silver in the back garden to really pay attention, and before too long, of course, everyone started leaving in droves and—'

'So Victor lives in London, does he? Have you met his family?'

'They're scattered all over apparently. Vic said he'd take me to meet them sometime. He's lived with an uncle in London since he was fourteen. Laney says they all think him quite a marvel at Wilson's. It's a very elegant set-up; they do business all over the world.' She smiled proudly.

'So how long have they all known each other? Like Jonathan and Victor, for example.'

'Why all the questions all of a sudden?' Georgiana frowned.

'Just curious.' I resisted looking back over my shoulder again.

'Hmm. Well, Vic's known Jonathan for ages and Jonathan's known Laney for ages, they're engaged obviously, and Laney and Clem are best friends. And Rana's just always been there, too, and Gregory . . . not sure how he fits in exactly, he's just sort of tagging along for the English experience, I guess. According to Claire, Laney and Jonathan are both very proper, and she didn't mind me spending time with them. It was really nice, actually, to get to know them right at the beginning of my trip. We all just fit so well together and—'

'So really you've only known them six months?' I said.

She narrowed her eyes at me. 'Madeleine, kindly tell me what you're aiming for and I'll do my best to accommodate you.'

'Well, that's just it, I don't really know.' I faltered at the expression on her face.

'I can tell you don't like them.' She scowled at me. 'Don't think I haven't noticed.'

'Sorry, darling, I got distracted.' Victor had drawn level with us and held out his arm to my sister, who was still glowering at me. His gaze slid across my flushed face and I looked away quickly. Just yesterday, I had told my sister that I thought her boyfriend was really nice, that I liked him. How on earth could I possibly tell her now that he was inappropriate and strange and made me afraid? I quailed inwardly when I remembered her hard expression after Victor's compliments and the knowing looks Rana and Laney had exchanged in the hallway earlier. Somehow I didn't think any of them would believe that I hadn't been in some way responsible for what had happened in Smuggler's Hatch, nor that Victor, their long-time friend and Georgiana's handsome boyfriend, was behaving in a way he shouldn't.

The conversation ebbed and flowed around me as the first scattered houses and front gardens turned into the little warren of streets around the village green. And bit by bit I stopped thinking about Victor and Georgiana altogether, because the village – sleepily cheerful in my memory, the sound of church bells drifting across on the breeze on Sundays – was so different to how I remembered it from sporadic visits in recent years. A sense of anxious expectancy hung in the air, and people's faces were tight with worry as they passed each other in the streets, exchanging sombre greetings and the latest news. Who'd been called up for military training and who had volunteered; what news had come in from London, Germany, the world.

Posters in windows urgently reminded passers-by about the black-out and funny little upturned shelters had sprung up in some of the back gardens. Windows were criss-crossed with brown tape, presumably to prevent breakage but making it look as if children were setting up targets for bow-and-arrow shooting. The shiny weathervane on the church tower had been taken down to avoid attracting attention from the air, and there were stakes around the village green – where Georgiana and I had occasionally played ball with the village children when we were little – to mark areas for possible vegetable planting. I knew this because Hobson, who was a devoted cricketer, had sat in the Summerhill kitchen and argued with Frank at length about the atrocity of potentially having to give up the cricket field. Frank had come down firmly on the side of edible vegetation. *You'll not want to play cricket when you've been eating cardboard bread and beans floating in water for weeks*, he'd said.

But I hadn't given it nearly enough thought, I now realised with a lurch of shame, the same kind of shame I'd felt when I came across Victor looking at the ledger earlier. I'd been sticking my head in the sand, stupidly thinking it would all eventually pass, when I should have started paying attention long ago. It was one thing to sit comfortably in the kitchen and laugh at a village squabble about cricket. It was another thing entirely to pass a small house where a kitbag sat next to the door, a cap on top, and know that a young man – my heart squeezed when I thought of William's face, the sweep of his lashes feathering my cheek when we'd said goodbye last night – would be leaving at any minute, ready to board the bus just pulling into the square ahead.

'Goodness, it is all rather quaint, isn't it?' Clementine remarked, and even the bus's engine splutter couldn't drown out her grating voice. I blushed when I caught the eye of a woman holding the hand of a little girl and watching the bus with a troubled expression.

'Yes,' said Jonathan, 'and where for heaven's sake is the pub?'

At this, the woman turned with a frown and pulled her daughter away from us down the side of the square.

'What was I thinking, putting on these shoes? They'll be ruined,' Laney complained, and Clementine laughed and opened her mouth, no doubt to make another scintillating remark, but I had suddenly had enough.

'Will you just shut up, all of you?' I said fiercely. 'You' – I glared at Laney – 'just wear *normal* clothes, like anyone else, and *you*, the pub's down that way. And you . . .' I turned to Gregory, who took cover behind Jonathan, peering over his shoulder in mock-fright. 'Oh, just go away, you big fat oaf!'

'Madeleine Louise Hamilton!' Georgiana said in outrage. 'Whatever has come over you?'

'How can you not see that they're beyond stupid, Georgiana?' I hissed. 'Good God, look at them. Just *look* at them.' I jabbed my hand at Laney, who had crossed her arms in a sullen sort of way and was regarding me haughtily, standing with Clementine and Rana, whose outfits were almost unbearably garish next to those of the women walking by in sensible cotton dresses.

'You could at least be civil,' she snapped back. I gripped her elbow hard and turned her to face Jonathan and Gregory, who'd lit cigarettes and were throwing a rolled-up newspaper back and forth, Chamberlain's crumpled moustache sailing past us. But she wrenched her arm away and slipped it ostentatiously through Victor's, and I regretted my outburst almost instantly, because I didn't want to be shouting at Georgiana; I wanted to be the one standing close to her to watch the village boys leaving for war.

There were voices and the occasional shout, someone calling goodbye. Birds chattered in the trees, a car backfired, the purr of a plane engine could be heard in the distance. But there was an odd hush, too, a subdued disquiet as small knots of people gradually filled the square. Three more housewives stopped to watch, one of them holding a lumpy brown package; two young women with a shopping net joined them. Children were chasing each other until they were caught by their mothers. A couple of older men leaned against a wall, one of them smoking a pipe.

The bus was revving its engine, a sign that it was time to leave. Through its windows I could see villagers' faces interspersed with those of the young men, some sprawling casually in their seats, chatting with the person next to them, others quiet, looking back at whomever they'd left behind. Georgiana's expression was set, only her eyes moved, tracking the progress of each person boarding the bus. Next to her, Victor's face was serious too, but I could tell that his mind was elsewhere because his eyes were roving round and round, taking in faces and figures from beneath half-closed eyelids.

'That'll be you before long,' I heard her say with a half-sob, but the rest was unintelligible as she nestled into his neck, her shoulders shaking. I turned to say something, only to find that Victor was leading her away, down a small lane off the square and out of sight.

Georgiana's friends had started to wander, too, peering into windows and gardens, and so I stood alone. I didn't want to. I didn't want to be there at all. I wanted to take the path through the woods back to Summerhill and slip down to the boat shed, where William would be waiting for me, his eyes bright and laughing in our little secret world. I might even have turned to go, but at that moment I noticed a woman standing a few paces away from me, almost unnaturally silent amidst the low murmur of noise and the horrid revving of the engine. She was staring right past me and when I followed her gaze, I saw her looking at the last man boarding the bus. He stopped for a moment and waved, but the woman turned her head and looked away, pressing her lips together so hard they were white. Over the noise of the bus finally pulling away, I could hear her making little sounds with each breath, small sobs that made me hold both hands over my mouth, my eyes filling with tears. I imagined her walking back to their house, now empty and silent, crawling into bed and pulling the covers over her head, looking ahead to weeks and months of worrying and imagining.

Without thinking, I reached to touch her arm. 'Let me walk you home. Where do you live?'

Her gaze never moved from where the last puff of dust from

the bus had settled back, leaving no trace of the men other than a track in the ground.

'Her name's Lucy Flynn and she lives behind the church,' someone next to me said.

'Mrs Claxton.' I heaved a small sigh of relief at the familiar form of Cookie's sister.

'What times we live in, Miss Maddy,' she said, shaking her head woefully. 'Come now, Lucy, it'll be all right, love.'

Forty-Four

We stopped in front of a small whitewashed cottage.

'Do you have anyone to sit with you?' Mrs Claxton asked kindly. 'I would, only I have to get back to the post office. Peak time for letters, you know.' She made a reasonably good attempt at a chuckle.

'I'll go in with her,' I said.

'Oh no, Miss Maddy, I'm sure that's not necessary.' Mrs Claxton shook her head doubtfully. 'I'll just pop round to the neighbour, shall I, and then you can go back to your friends. You'll need to get ready for the party tonight.'

I blushed a little and avoided looking at Lucy Flynn, because who on earth could possibly throw a party when all of *this* was happening?

'They're not my friends and I'll be fine,' I said grimly, and taking Lucy's arm, I half pushed her across the threshold and manoeuvred her into a small sitting room to the left of the stairs.

'I'll make tea,' I said when I spied the kitchenette. 'That'll warm your cockles right and good,' I added, because that was what Cookie always said to Frank in the mornings and it seemed appropriate here, although Lucy Flynn blinked a little in astonishment.

Making tea took ages. At Summerhill, the old range never went out, but the stovetop here seemed reluctant to come to life at all. I busied myself measuring tea into a chipped teapot, finding cups and a strainer, a little jug of milk, hoping the stove would magically light itself then advancing on it one more time with matches in hand.

Behind me, Lucy Flynn chuckled, a low, almost masculine sound, then got up from the chair and took the matches from me.

'It's like a child,' she said, smiling slightly. 'You have to treat it just right.'

We stood awkwardly by the stove, watching the kettle and casting around for something to say.

'I might not have minded so much,' she said eventually, 'if he'd been called up and didn't have a choice. But he was so keen for it, couldn't wait to enlist. I said to him, they'll be taking the younger men first and others for training, see. Just wait until it's your turn. But he went anyway.'

The kettle sputtered with little humid puffs that made the already warm room even warmer.

'We've been rowing about it for days now.' She brushed her hair away from her face, her eyes intent on the kettle, as if she could make it boil just by staring at it. 'This morning, too. You know when you can't help yourself, when you listen to yourself saying things you shouldn't, and you just can't stop. I almost made him miss the bus. And now that'll be his last memory of me.'

The kettle erupted in a shrieking hiss and she snatched it up with a practised flick of her wrist, poured the water into the pot. We watched it steam out of the spout for a moment.

I nodded to the bag lying next to the chair, little brown packages spilling out of the top. 'Did you mean to send that with him?'

She looked down at the teapot. 'Sandwiches. But I was so cross I didn't even say goodbye properly, and then I forgot I had them. How childish and stupid.' She dragged a sleeve across her eyes and held it there for a moment, her shoulders shaking.

'You could send them,' I said. 'Send them over today.'

She shook her head. 'It's too far. I couldn't pay for it, and anyway, they'd surely spoil.' She sighed shakily and pulled down her sleeves. 'We might as well eat them now. Come and sit down, miss . . . I'm sorry, I don't even know your name.'

'Maddy,' I said. 'And I would love a sandwich.'

They were quite dry, the cheese warm and a little fetid-smelling, the pickles big chunks of vinegary onion, but we tore pieces off the dark bread, chewed determinedly, washing them down with dark brown tea so strong it made the insides of my mouth pucker. Without asking, I took a second one and so did she, although our enthusiasm had waned considerably by then and I was almost glad when there was a small clanging noise from the garden gate.

'That'll be our lodger.' Lucy rose from the chair, taking a last gulp of tea to wash down the bread. 'He needs a bit of help with the stairs, poor man.'

'I should probably go anyway.' I got up too, but she held me back.

'I'd been dreading that moment in the square for days.' She took a deep breath. 'And I was dreading returning to an empty house almost as much. So thank you for coming in with me.'

'Of course,' I said awkwardly when I remembered that I'd been about to run away altogether, stealing down to the boat shed. 'Maybe I could visit you again,' I suggested, flushing slightly.

'If you have time, I'd like that.' She gave me a smile over her shoulder as she went to open the door.

'You're back already,' I heard her say. 'I suppose that means there's—'

'No news.' A man appeared on the threshold, gave a polite nod and touched his hat. When he started walking towards the stairs, I was struck by the absurd idea that he was drunk, because he was lurching from side to side. But when he got closer, I saw that his right leg was missing from above the knee. I stopped halfway through shrugging on my cardigan, because something was tugging on my memory, and a moment later, I realised what it was.

The slight stoop over the cane couldn't disguise the breadth of his shoulders, and although dark shadows below his eyes and around his jaw made him look tired and old, my mind immediately filled in the blanks, imagined a rakish expression, brown eyes alight with secret amusement and barely suppressed excitement.

'Mr Davies!' I said before I could stop myself.

He stopped and turned, searching until he found me standing behind Lucy, my cardigan dangling from my arm. 'Do we know each other, miss?'

'Madeleine Hamilton.' I flushed. 'No. But . . . that is, I heard . . . I didn't know you were here.'

He frowned, clearly not quite sure what to make of me.

'Mr Davies has just arrived in the village,' Lucy said quickly. 'He's lodging with me until . . . I mean, he's . . .'

'Waiting,' Mr Davies said evenly. 'I'm waiting for news.'

An awkward silence fell across the narrow front hall. I couldn't get the colour to drain from my face, was radiating so much heat I thought the other two would surely notice any moment. How could I, who knew so well what it meant to lose a loved one, not have spared more than a fleeting thought for this person standing in front of me? *Could I sit here and watch the stars with you?* William had asked, and, stupidly, thoughtlessly, I had let him.

'I live at Summerhill,' I stammered. 'Where Will . . . I mean, where he was last seen.'

'You've met William before?' Mr Davies looked confused. 'You knew each other?'

'No, of course not.' I stumbled over the words. 'It's just . . . it's close to the cliffs.'

'But the way you said his name . . .' He shook himself. 'Never mind. I'm sorry, miss, I should go.'

'Yes, have a little rest,' Lucy said encouragingly. 'I'll make some more tea. Goodbye, miss. I hope I'll see you again some time.' She disappeared into the kitchen.

How easily I had given in to our midnight magic, I thought as I hovered by the front door. How much I had wanted to sit under the stars with William, had wanted to hide him away, this wonderful secret waiting for me at the bottom of the garden that kept the real world at bay. And all along, of course, the world had continued to turn, and this poor man—

'Mr Davies, wait,' I said desperately.

He turned awkwardly on the stairs, balancing on one leg.

'It'll be all right,' I said. 'I promise you. I know. It will be all right.'

Mr Davies frowned. 'If you know anything I don't, I beg you . . .'

'I promise.' And before he could ask me any more, I turned and hurried away.

When I got back to the square, Mrs Claxton came rushing out of the post office.

'There you are, lovey. Your sister's in a right state. I did tell her you'd be back in a jiffy.' She hustled me towards where Georgiana's friends were clustering around Laney, who looked distinctly droopy, apparently only managing to stay upright by clinging to Jonathan's arm.

Georgiana bore down on me murderously, 'Honestly, Madeleine, if it wasn't so hot and horrid, I'd leave you behind and never come back. Mrs Claxton said you went off to have tea with someone. What on earth? Who do you even know here, stuck at the house all day the way you are?'

'Don't be cross, Miss Georgie,' Mrs Claxton said soothingly. 'It's a different sort of day for everyone, it is.'

'It certainly is for some people.' Georgiana flashed me a furious look.

'I'm just coming now, Georgiana,' I kept my voice even. 'Thank you, Mrs Claxton, I'll see you later.'

'Goodbye, Mrs Claxton,' Georgiana said, grappling belatedly

at a semblance of dignity, then turned on her heel and marched away, the others trailing behind her.

I was just about to leave when Mrs Claxton held me back.

'Miss Maddy, might I ask – who is the young man with Miss Georgie, the tall, blond one?'

'You mean Victor?' I sighed. 'He's my sister's new, er, friend. From London. They're all from London,' I added apologetically. 'They're not really used to how things are down here. I'm sorry.'

But Mrs Claxton wasn't listening. She was looking after Georgiana and Victor as they rounded the corner towards the cars.

'Why?' I stepped out of the way of two women with shopping baskets.

'I don't know,' she said. 'It's just . . . he looks awfully familiar.'

'Familiar?' I said, astonished. 'Have you ever been to London?' I reddened, thinking that must have sounded rude, but she hadn't noticed.

'I'm so good with faces usually – you have to be, as postmistress, you know – but I can't quite place him. Though I could have sworn . . .'

'What, Mrs Claxton?' I pressed her.

She paused, then shook her head, and I suddenly had the impression that she didn't want to meet my eyes.

'Maybe it'll come to me,' she said evasively.

'When it does, will you let me know?'

She lifted her hand in farewell. 'Of course, Miss Maddy. I'll be seeing you later, then.'

Forty-Five

By the time we got back, tables had been moved and chairs brought in. Everywhere was a flurry of activity, and food smells floated up from downstairs. Upon arrival, the group dispersed quickly to their rooms, and when Hobson commandeered Georgiana's attention, she was still so cross that she followed him into the drawing room without a backwards glance at me. I lingered in the front hall, but when I looked across to the drawing room doors, I saw that Victor, too, was waiting, pacing around the ladder set up to fix the blackout, drawing so hard on his cigarette that I could see the red glow bristle and sputter.

I pretended to tidy my hair in the hallway mirror so I could watch him, realising that for the past three days, there hadn't been a single moment when Victor *hadn't* been there. I remembered catching his eye through the kitchen door. He hadn't called attention to himself, had simply stood and observed Georgiana and me sitting together. He'd been there on the terrace. The courtyard. The walk to the maze. Smuggler's Hatch. The library. The village. Always there, talking and listening. Watching. Suddenly I couldn't stand it any longer. I turned on my heel and pushed open the front door, leaving Victor to wait for my sister.

I didn't have to go as far as the boat shed this time. When I let myself out through the gate at the bottom of the garden, William was lying in the long grass opposite the pump, fast asleep. There was a bucket next to him, and a little bowl; it looked like he had been trying to work the temperamental pump one-handed, before giving up.

I drew water into the bucket, then settled cross-legged on the ground next to him, my sketchbook in my lap. William's face was relaxed, dark smudges under his eyes, lashes fluttering in rhythm with his even breathing. I started drawing him, not sleeping, but the way I remembered him from the night before, his eyes alive and amused when he looked at me, his hand pushed into his hair to make it stand up in untidy spikes.

It was oddly intimate, the way I ran my pencil around the nape of his neck and up his cheek, a secret, hidden caress along the smooth skin of his shoulder, tracing the length of his spine, the soft down on his forearms. I froze when he moved in his sleep, then sketched a smile into those eyes, a secret smile just for me . . .

'You look very serious when you draw.' His voice was slow and sleepy with heat, and I started guiltily, closed my sketchbook and slipped it underneath the cardigan next to me.

'Secrets?' he said hoarsely, eyeing the cardigan with interest.

'Not for you.' I dunked the bowl into the bucket and offered it to him.

'Always you bring me water,' he said, smiling. 'You're like one of those old-fashioned Roman water carriers. I think they might have been goddesses, actually. Beautiful they were.'

I swallowed and focused on the bowl, almost spilling most of the water when his fingertip touched mine and sent a tingling shock right up my hand and then into my mouth, which smiled treacherously back at him, the same kind of smile I was horribly sure I'd just tried to hide in my sketchbook.

'I wasn't sure if you'd come back.' He gazed at me over the bowl.

'I can't stay long,' I stammered, slightly unnerved by the way he was looking at me.

'You're here now, that's all that matters.' Unhurriedly, he reached out and tugged on a stray curl, and I flinched at the touch of his fingers on my cheeks.

'How . . . I mean, how is your arm?'

'I tried to wash.' He sighed, then flashed me a quick, mischievous smile. 'I was expecting company, you see.'

I pumped more water as William took off his shirt. I averted my eyes, feeling silly and awkward in equal measure, because just last night, we'd been swimming together in our underwear. But the way the light gleamed on the ropes of muscles on his shoulders and the neat grid of his ribcage echoed my drawing in a disconcerting way that made me flush as I glanced at him covertly. He was practically submerged in the trough now, only his arm sticking out, and I knew that if I hadn't been there, he'd have shed the rest of his clothes. The thought made me flush even more, pushing at the handle with all my might until finally he gave a gurgling laugh and took a step back.

'Done,' he said. Holding his arm carefully aloft, he shook himself, flinging water droplets everywhere, then wiped his chest and shoulders with his good hand. He was about to pick up his shirt when I heard a familiar sound: Frank whistling as he pushed a wheelbarrow down the hill.

Hastily I pulled William down to a low crouch behind the blackberry hedge that grew against the old wall at the bottom of the garden.

'Who is that?' he breathed.

I frowned and put my finger to my lips, straining to listen as Frank passed by, beating out the rhythm with the secateurs on the metal edge of the wheelbarrow. He was probably out gathering flowers for the evening festivities.

'Au revoir but not goodbye, soldier boy. Hmm, hmm . . . deep blue sea. Tu-dum.'

The cheerful song faded, but snatches of it kept floating down to where we were crouching, and I shifted my weight to my heels, feeling the sun beat down on the crown of my head. Heat had collected against the hillside, and I could almost taste it in my mouth, dusty and dry. William nodded to the shadowy space against the stone wall, where the bushes had created a canopy. 'In there,' he breathed.

I hesitated, but only for a moment, then crawled in after him.

It was much cooler among the bushes, and pleasantly green. William struggled for a moment with his shirt until I took it from him and slid the fabric over his bad arm, working slowly and carefully, pulling it across his shoulders and around his neck. When he leaned towards me to let me button it up, the edge of his jaw nestled against my hand and I held my breath, fumbling with each button, feeling his skin cool and smooth beneath the fabric. When I looked up, I realised that he was looking right back at me, unsmiling and serious. I swallowed and dropped my hands away from his chest.

'What were you drawing?' he whispered. 'In your book.'

'Just . . . you,' I said, looking down. 'I wanted to be able to remember. You. And last night. For ever.'

'I wouldn't let you forget.' He hesitated, then lifted his hand, slowly as if he wanted to give me plenty of time to protest should I want to.

I didn't want to.

Slowly, unhurriedly, he tugged at the pins that held back my curls, finding one after the other until my hair fell down around my shoulders. It was odd, this feeling, both exciting and new, and for a moment I thought back to Smuggler's Hatch and a very different moment that had left me feeling wrong and itchy with shame. I wasn't ashamed now, though, not when it was the most natural thing in the world to catch William's hand against the side of my head, thread my fingers through his.

'I think I was dreaming of you earlier,' he murmured. 'Just little snatches of you. The way you laugh. Your eyes. They're the most lovely colour. And the water. So cool and dark, and you were there with me, swimming under the stars.'

He pulled me closer, sliding his fingers deeper into my hair and then down the nape of my neck, slowly travelling down my back, electricity zinging up and down my spine. I wasn't sure whether he pulled me or I moved myself, whether he kissed me or I kissed him; all I knew was that the kiss happened, and even when we broke apart, breathless and flushed, he didn't let me go far, but put his cheek against mine, his lips soft on the side of my jaw, tracing light circles that made my breath catch painfully in my throat.

'I wish we could stay right here, always,' he whispered, and I smiled against his softness, breathing in the clean scent of skin baking in the sun, the earthy smell from the ground, the floral bitterness of the blackberry bushes. In that moment, I wanted nothing more than to be back where we'd been the night before, our secret place, with no future and no past. Instead, I pulled away. His hand slid out of my hair, the air was cool on my cheek as I pushed him gently back to look into his face.

'William, it's time.'

His expression didn't change immediately; his smile was still warm, his eyes holding mine.

'You should go,' I tried again.

He gave a tight nod of the head. 'So you don't think it would work, then.' He pressed his lips together. 'Not even with your unusual Summerhill ways.'

'Work?'

'You and me. Out there in the real world.' He didn't smile now, just regarded me steadily.

I bent forward and took his hand. 'Of course it would work.'

'But?' His hand hung heavy in mine and he put his head to the side.

'But you can't stay here.' I took a deep breath. 'Your father is in the village. I saw him.'

For a moment, everything went still; even the birds seemed to be drawing breath. 'He's here?' he said at last, stumbling slightly over the words. 'Did you . . .'

'I talked to him.' I held up my hand when he opened his mouth. 'I didn't say anything about you, but I wanted to, William. My heart was breaking for him. You should have seen his face – and he looks so much like you, too, you know. How could we have let him go through that, left him just to *wait*?' I hung my head. 'I was so ashamed. It was all I could do not to tell him right then and there.'

'You have nothing to be ashamed about,' he said abruptly, his cheeks flushing a deep red. 'It's my doing, my choice.'

'But I went along with it and it was wrong. It's not too late, though. I can get Hobson to take you into the village, or Georgiana will drive you.'

'Who is Hobson?'

'Our butler,' I said impatiently. 'He could—'

'Your butler.' He jerked his hand out of mine. 'And what would you tell your butler? Or your sister?'

'Well, that I came upon you, and you were . . . confused. Not yourself. That you'd changed your mind about hiding.' My voice was high and awkward, and even to me, it sounded weak. 'Or whatever you wanted me to say,' I stammered, trying hard not to look at his red face, his narrowed eyes.

'No, thank you,' William said evenly. 'I don't need your butler or your gardener or your sister to help me. I can sort out my own problems.'

'You weren't so cocky when you let me fix your bloody arm,' I said furiously.

'Don't swear.' William straightened and pushed through the bushes out onto the path. 'It's unbecoming for a lady.'

I took a deep breath and resisted the urge to say something very rude. 'William, why are we fighting?' I climbed out after him, ignoring the thorns digging into my arm and neck. 'Your father is mourning you as if you're dead, just because you—'

'Can't bear it that he might think me a coward,' he finished bitterly, turning around to face me on the narrow path.

'You're not a coward,' I said hotly. 'If you don't want to fly, then don't. Be an engineer, maybe, an outfitter on the ground.'

'And have all of them jeer at me?' he said in a choked sort of voice. 'Mock me and belittle me.'

'No one would mock you,' I said. 'They all think you're a hero.'

'A hero who ran away.' He shook his head. 'I don't know what I was thinking. It was so lovely here. Waiting for you. Talking to you. I thought you understood.'

When he looked up, the flush had receded from his cheeks, leaving him pale. He fixed a polite smile on his face.

'Thank you for all you've done,' he said evenly. 'I'll get out of your hair now.'

'William, you're not in my hair,' I said desperately. 'You really aren't.'

But he was already walking, and before I knew what had happened, he was at the edge of the clearing and had disappeared into the woods.

Forty-Six

Walking up the stairs to my room, I thought I could actually feel the worry over William's disappearance weighing me down, pulling me back to the woods to keep searching until I'd found him. And now I was back in the house, there was even more to worry about. Georgiana. Victor.

'Have you seen my sister?' I asked Susan as she passed me on the stairs.

'Saw her go to her room earlier.' She shook her head when she took in my dusty skirt and torn cardigan. 'Need help with your dress for tonight?'

'Goodness, no, when have I ever needed help getting dressed?'

The sound of her laughter followed me as I walked along the corridor, where small lamps threw shadows across walls and ceiling, making the old portraits look strangely alive in the half-light. I was about to push into Georgie's room without knocking when I remembered that the last time I'd been about to do that, Victor had been in her bed. I'd just lifted my hand to knock when his voice suddenly floated from the room.

'Gigi, she clearly has no idea how bad it is.'

My hand froze.

'You asked me for my opinion and I'm giving it. I honestly don't think you can go on like this for much longer. You have to talk to her.'

Looking up and down the corridor, I gingerly pressed my ear against the wood.

'I'm well aware of that, darling. It's just . . . with everyone around, and the plane crash . . . then every time I turn around, she's gone.' She sighed. 'Truth is, I don't want to do it. I hate everything about it. And maybe we can plod along for just a little while longer. Sit out the war here, try to get back on our feet afterwards. Don't you think?'

'I can't see how.' Victor's voice was clearer; he had to be standing closer to the door. 'Looking at the accounts, you're already struggling; it'll be nigh-on impossible when the war begins in earnest. Shortages, no men around to help you, no petrol to get anywhere . . . You might have a solution now, right in front of you. Jonathan sounded keen enough. Why not take it further?'

I frowned at the door, because it sounded almost like he was saying . . .

'I know, believe me, I *know*, Victor.' Georgiana spoke impatiently, and outside the door, I shrank back a little, 'But surely you must see how difficult it would be to tell Maddy that Summerhill might have to go?'

Downstairs, Hobson was pushing open the doors to the drawing room. There were chinking sounds as tables were set up with glasses and bottles. Somewhere someone was laughing, and, perhaps to set the mood, the gramophone was playing 'Mad About the Boy'. But the sound of Noël Coward was muffled through the roaring in my ears, as if he too belonged to another world, a world where Summerhill would continue to be here. For Susan, who'd come here as a little girl and knew no other home. For Frank, who claimed that Summerhill mornings were the only thing worth living for. For Hobson, who'd found peace here in the last twenty years and who'd been helping to put Summerhill back together as quickly as it was falling down. For my father, who'd entrusted this place to us, whose memory was still in every corner of it. For me and Georgiana, who were going to live here with our stories for all the years to come.

'Well, that's my two cents anyhow. I'll leave you to it. I'm dying for a drink.' Victor's voice got louder, and I knew that any second now he would appear at the door. If there was one thing I was good at, it was running away, and without a moment's hesitation, I turned on my heel and disappeared into my room.

'Maddy, are you ready?' There was a knock, then the door opened. 'You're not even dressed! Come on, darling, what is the *matter* with you?'

I was sitting on my bed, holding my sketchbook tightly and looking out of the window.

'And you're sitting on your dress, too. Oh, grow up just a little, Maddy, will you?'

A flash of bright red appeared at the edge of my vision as Georgiana bent down to tug at something beneath my thighs. I didn't move, though, just turned to look at her. Her eyes were carefully made up and flowers were pinned artistically into her hair. She smelled of violets and looked shiny and perfect, but close up, I could see the layers of foundation and powder, giving her a mask-like expression.

'Maddy!' She gave the dress another impatient tug.

'Is it true?' I said woodenly. 'That's what you meant when you said we needed a plan, that first day in the kitchen? You want us to sell Summerhill?'

She froze halfway through pulling at the dress, then sat down abruptly on the bed.

'No. Yes. Oh, I don't know what to do.' She looked down at her hands. I could see her jaw moving slightly as she bit the inside of her cheek. 'It's all coming undone. No money. The war. Frank leaving soon, Aunt Marjorie desperate to go and live with Aunt Hilly.' She twisted her hands in her lap and I put my hand over them.

'Georgie. This is our home, all of ours. Susan and Cookie, Frank, Hobson, you and me. We can't sell it.'

Georgiana reached for a strand of hair that was falling across my face, gently tucked it behind my ear, cupping my cheek. 'Do you want Hobson and Cookie to be left destitute in their old age when we can't pay them anything? What kind of a future is there here for Susan? And for you, my love? You need to start making a new life for yourself, away from all the memories. Maybe,' she kept her hand on my cheek for a moment, 'this is your chance.'

'Just give us till the end of the war,' I said urgently. 'I'll find a way to get us back on our feet, I promise you. Now that you're home, we can work together. We'll finish our book, I'll find a job . . .'

'Doing what exactly, Maddy?' Georgiana shook her head, dropping her hand. 'Growing cabbages? Drawing pictures? And, well, the thing is . . .' She broke off, laced her fingers together, picked at her nail.

I looked at the hands twisting in her lap again, and suddenly I felt a pang of yearning so sharp that it took my breath away. The days when you couldn't tell where one of us ended and the other began, when we seemed like one and the same person, so close that nothing else existed, those days seemed impossibly far away. Too many things were sitting between us, secrets and misunderstandings and frustrations. If I wanted to hold onto her, then it was time to get everything out into the open, Victor and William and Summerhill, then maybe we could get back to what we had been.

'. . . I'm pregnant.'

Forty-Seven

She didn't sound apologetic, nor did she seem either sad or overjoyed. Slightly stunned, in fact, as if she couldn't quite get her head around it, was trying out the words on me to fully understand their implication herself.

'Victor?' I said disbelievingly.

'Of course!' She frowned at me. 'Who else? Good God, Maddy. As if I'm in the habit of taking random lovers.'

'Yes,' I said, shaking my head to get rid of the strange woolly feeling. 'No.'

A baby. With Victor. My mind couldn't quite process the information, not because it wasn't trying hard to but because I refused to let it acknowledge the fact that Georgiana, my Georgiana—

'Yes, no – what exactly are you saying?' she snapped. 'And you don't need to sound quite so dismayed, either.' She picked at a red sequin on her dress and I noticed for the first time that her nails were so short, not a sliver of white was left. 'We were careful, of course, but it happens to the best of us.' She added the last bit in an attempt to lighten the mood, but she didn't meet my eyes and we both knew that this wasn't remotely what was supposed to happen.

'I only just realised it,' she continued, as if that was the part that was so very shocking. 'I thought I'd had too much to drink at first, but . . .' She gave me a wry smile. 'Things have been tasting a bit off, too, which must be part of it.'

She shrugged, a mix of self-consciousness and defiance, and it was then that I suddenly realised that Victor, far from leaving, really would be in our lives for ever. No matter what happened from now on, whether he spurned Georgiana or took her away from here, Victor Deverill would be part of Summerhill, part of our family, of me.

I swallowed. 'What does Victor . . . I mean . . .'

'I haven't told him, not yet.'

She fell silent, and a small dart of hope skimmed through my rush of panic.

'Are you worried?' I strove to keep my tone casual. 'That maybe he won't—'

'No!' she cut in. 'He will. I know he will.' She took a deep breath. 'It's just, I don't really want to—'

'Then don't do it, don't stay with him.' I sat forward, grasped her hands, relief almost making me dizzy, because here, finally, was the answer to everything. 'Georgie, you don't need him. Just have the baby here at Summerhill. We'll look after it, we can raise it together, the way you and I used to be.'

'—have a baby, was what I was going to say.' She eyed me with a frown. 'You know I can't possibly have this baby by myself, not here or anywhere. I need to get married, and soon.'

'But you don't have to,' I said desperately. 'You've never cared about all that proper stuff. And Victor, he's not right for you—'

'Madeleine, where on earth is this coming from?' she cut in. 'You've been so strange these past couple of days. I don't understand you at all.'

'I just want you to be happy,' I said desperately.

'Well, I *am* happy,' she replied defiantly. 'And I wouldn't be marrying Victor because I *have* to. I adore him. I would *love* to marry him. It's just . . . it's *a baby*, you know.'

She was chewing on her cheek again. She used to do it all the time when we were growing up, worry away at the inside of her mouth until it was raw and red and I got her cold chamomile tea to swill it out with.

'You'll be a wonderful mother, if that's what you're worried about,' I said quickly. 'Nobody knows that better than me.'

I expected her to smile, but she just looked at me for a long moment.

'But that's just it. I don't think I'm ready for that, not again, not so soon. I've been talking to Victor a lot about it, how it was back then, I mean, and it has opened my eyes about what we went through. What *I* went through after Mum's death, and then again after Papa's accident. I will never presume to know your pain, Maddy, and I wish I could have taken some of it away for you. But I had to be a mother when I was just a girl myself. That's what you do when you love someone, but it doesn't mean . . .' She paused. 'It doesn't mean that it's not a heavy burden to bear. It's relentless, that kind of responsibility, looking after someone when you desperately need some looking after yourself. Victor says . . .'

She broke off and blinked, as if she'd suddenly remembered that I was there and who I was.

'Victor says I was a burden?' I said evenly. '*You* think I was a burden?'

'No, my love, of course not.' She reached to touch my cheek again, but I twisted away. 'That came out all wrong. But being away, it made me realise that I want something different for my life. I want to *do* something, out there and not here. And I don't have to be ashamed of it either,' she added, almost angrily. 'We're different people, Maddy, we don't *have* to want the same thing.'

I stared at her. 'It's Victor,' I finally said in a hoarse voice. 'This is all him.'

'Victor has nothing to do with it.' She shook her head. 'Mr Pritchard's been talking about the *Situation* for ages, and Aunt Marjorie's been on at me about bloody Yorkshire and the Germans. But yes, I did ask Victor's advice. Anyone can see that we can't go on like this for ever; someone's got to be sensible, and it sure as hell isn't you, is it?'

'Sensibly suggesting that you sell our family home?' I hissed. 'Telling you I've been a *burden*?'

'He's not . . . I'm . . . Oh, stop twisting my words.' She jumped up from the bed. 'All these years I've taken care of you, have loved you with all my heart. No one, not a single person, least of all you, can blame me for wanting more.' Her hands were shaking now, and patches of blotchy red showed through the layer of powder on her face. 'Don't you see that this place is full of sadness and death? I don't want that any more, I want to be – free from it. And no, I don't want to be a mother. There, I've said it. I missed Mother so much, Maddy, all the time, and then Father gone too. And there you were, this little thing, following me around, expecting the world of me, thinking the world of me. It was me, always, who had to decide and console and reassure and hold your hand and tell you it would be all right.' She pressed her own hand in front of her mouth. 'I was fifteen, for heaven's sake. I don't know that there was anyone, ever, who held *my* hand, who told *me* that it would be all right.'

She looked at me and I could see that her eyes were bright with tears. Her mouth trembled, then she blinked and the tears spilled over, running over her knuckles and down the curve of her jaw, and I suddenly remembered her the day before Papa's funeral.

She had disappeared and I'd been looking everywhere for her. I couldn't be without her for long, I clearly remembered that. It was like I needed her so that I could breathe, needed her to walk ahead of me so I could copy her and put one foot in front of the other. I'd run up and down the garden and through the house looking for her, down in the kitchen, tear-stained and sodden and desperate, until I finally came across her in our mother's dressing room. It still held her dresses, most of them carefully wrapped in large cloths, but Georgiana had unfastened one of them and crawled right into the bottom of the wardrobe so that only her legs protruded. She was clutching big fistfuls of fabric in her hands, her face pressed into the folds of red brocade. Her shoulders were twitching convulsively, her whole body was shaking, making the dresses rattle softly on their hangers, and when I crouched down by her feet, touching her leg hesitantly, she didn't respond. I crawled in next to her, finding her arm and putting it around my shoulders so my whole body was pressed against her, and still she cried, a hard, relentless, painful sobbing, which was swallowed by our mother's dress before it could make itself heard to the outside world.

It was a long time before she moved and even longer before she let go of the dress, which was wrinkled and splotchy with her tears.

'I didn't know where you were,' I said, by way of an explanation for my presence, and she nodded, tried to smile, then got to her feet, holding out her hand.

'I'm just trying to find something to wear for the funeral,' she said.

She selected two dresses from our mother's wardrobe and, enlisting Cookie's help, we sat up most of the night with the kitchen scissors, needle and thread. By dawn the next day, she'd fashioned two dark dresses. She brushed my hair back behind a black band, and like two pale shadows we followed Aunt Marjorie to the chapel, where the county had come to pay their respects. Afterwards, we stood at the edge of the Summerhill lawn and watched people eating the food set out by Cookie. It was a windy day, and the breeze played with coat tails and dark sashes and parasols, taking the snatches of murmured conversation and bearing them away until my father was finally, completely gone.

Yes, Georgiana was right. I'd clung to her, I'd followed her everywhere, had taken all my worries to her, had claimed her and subsumed her utterly and completely without a single thought about who *she* could turn to. I still did it today, was automatically looking for her, waiting for her wherever she went. And all that time, I'd thought that was just what you did when it was the two of you against the world.

Georgiana was still now, watching me.

'I did it all without question, because I *love* you, Maddy,' she said quietly. 'And I will never stop loving you, but that doesn't change the fact that we have to become two people now rather than two halves of one and the same person.'

Her face was almost serene, as if she was relieved to have it out there, to have cleared the air, and that frightened me more than anything else so that I did exactly the thing she was asking me not to: I wrapped my hands around hers and pulled at her – too close, I knew that now, but I couldn't help it because my heart simply refused to accept the fact that she was leaving me.

'Gigi!' A voice drifted up from downstairs. 'They're here.'

Georgiana disentangled herself, gently enough but with a devastating finality, the red sequins shimmering as she straightened her dress.

'We'll talk later, all right, Maddy?'

It was odd, this moment, as if we were saying goodbye, as if she was shutting the door, not loudly or in my face, but just as final. I wanted to get up and follow her, to the ends of the earth, the way I'd done when I was ten. The way I would always do. Because to me, Georgiana would always be there, just ahead of me, half turning and laughing, holding out her hand to me. Instead, I sat on the bed and watched her go.

Forty-Eight

Chloe

Chloe was back in bed when Aidan came home, the blinds still down, the rest of the house put back the way he'd left it. She pretended to wake from dozing when he entered, and he smiled happily when she said she didn't feel up to being up and about quite yet.

'You just stay and rest,' he said, touching her forehead and scanning the rest of her body with medical dispassion, lingering briefly on her stomach. 'Can I bring you anything?'

She resisted the urge to jerk back from his touch, and closed her eyes again as if she was too tired to talk. 'I'm fine, darling. I had something to eat earlier.'

She listened to him move around the room and eventually go downstairs. As soon as she heard the glass door to the kitchen open, she was up, tiptoeing noiselessly to the top of the stairs. She'd been making a mental list as she'd waited for him. She needed her driving licence. Her birth certificate. Danny's birth certificate. The contract with Oakwood. Her laptop. Her camera. The emergency box. Her handbag. But first, she needed access to the safe. It was a fancy built-in one and Aidan, paranoid as he was, always kept the key with him, along with a whole bunch of useless keys to confuse potential thieves.

She heard him humming to himself, liquid being poured, the fridge closing. His phone beeped and she shrank back, watching his legs walk past the bottom of the stairs to retrieve it.

'Dr Webb? Thank you so much for phoning back.' The rest of the words were muffled, and then the living room door closed.

His briefcase sat right next to the hall table. Chloe eyed it thoughtfully, calculating how long it would take her to run down, check through it for the key, and get back up here. Her knees buckled, half in exhaustion, half in fear. Heart hammering, she crept closer to the banister, then twitched back when she heard the door open. Aidan's hands came into view, stuffing a couple of papers back into the briefcase, then he carefully locked it and slid the keys into the inside pocket of his jacket. He straightened the jacket so it was hanging properly, then turned to the stairs. Chloe didn't wait a moment longer. She dashed back to bed, pulled the covers up to her neck and willed her breathing to be even and calm.

Exactly seven hours later, she was downstairs in the dark hallway, her hands inside the perfectly arranged folds of her husband's jacket. She'd spent most of those hours talking herself into what she was going to do, but even at the last moment her courage had almost deserted her.

Now she snatched up the briefcase and, muffling the clink of the keys in her nightshirt, slipped into the downstairs loo.

Patient files were stacked on one side of the case, a newspaper, a few pieces of correspondence. Some cables rolled up in a perfect circle and secured with a clip. And – and this seemed almost too easy – in one of the little pockets, a small bunch of keys. She extracted the safe key, then carefully nestled the bunch back into the pocket, trying to make sure it looked identical to the way it had before. Clutching the key tightly in her fist, she was just about to close the briefcase when her eyes caught the label on one of the folders. BABY MACALLISTER, it said in Aidan's neat handwriting.

Inside, a letter from his old boarding school, of which Aidan was insanely proud, informed him that they were *pleased to confirm receipt of your early application for a spot on our waiting list. As you know, our intake is highly competitive and we ask that you explore other options alongside ours . . .*

Over my dead body, she told her unborn child. *Over my lifeless corpse will you go to that bully-producing hotbed of cruelty.*

Her curiosity piqued, she leafed through the rest of the papers, saw that he'd taken out a life insurance policy, and was apparently setting up a trust fund for the baby as well. And then her eye suddenly caught her own name.

Dear Mrs MacAllister,

Further to your request to speak with Dr Lindow regarding a medically necessary Caesarean section, please call the office to make an appointment as soon as possible.

There was a contact number and forms as well, which Aidan had already filled out, stuff about pelvic structure and potential obstruction and so on. Chloe stared at it for a moment, putting an involuntary hand on her stomach. Why on earth would Aidan want her to have a Caesarean? Hadn't he always said that mother and child needed the bond of a natural birth? Although, she frowned, maybe that was exactly it, that bond. She had a sudden, terrifying vision of disappearing into a haze of anaesthetic, the surgeon cutting her open, retrieving her baby and handing it straight to Aidan, who'd be right there, reaching for it eagerly . . .

Her fingers were trembling. *Just until tomorrow*, she told the baby, *and then* . . .

But the truth was, she wasn't completely sure what exactly she was going to do. Wherever she went, Aidan would follow. She had to hide, just for a while, and she had to keep Danny safe while she was gone, because Aidan would use him as leverage, that much was— She froze, frowned at another folder beneath the Baby MacAllister one.

DANIEL ARCHER.

Inside was a whole sheaf of forms and information leaflets and printouts. *How to fill in the form. Where to submit. Who to talk to. FAQs.* Her eyes roamed the page, catching the same combination of words again and again. *Lasting power of attorney.*

So Dixie had been right. Aidan, always jealous of the closeness between the Archer siblings, had looked into assuming a degree of legal control over Danny's future. Danny would have to sign the forms, witnesses would be required, so Aidan hadn't got further than gathering information – yet.

Chloe shivered, remembering the early days when he'd been so interested, so involved, so solicitous: how easily she might have decided to get Danny to put them both down on the form, anxious to make sure he would be provided for in case something happened to her. She bundled the papers back together, roughly at first, then more carefully, despite the fact that she wanted to take them away with her right now, every last scrap of them. She couldn't risk arousing Aidan's suspicion in any way before she had gone.

She spent some time tidying the briefcase, making it look exactly the way it had been, which wasn't hard given Aidan's propensity for symmetry, until there was only a single sheet of white paper and a pen left on the bathroom floor.

Aidan, she wrote grimly in large letters.

The last few days have given me a lot of time to think and I know the moment has come for us to face up to the reality of our marriage. We can't go on like this. I'm not happy, haven't been happy for a long time, and the baby has made me see that it's time to make a change.

She left a little space and then wrote, on its own line and bigger than the rest of the text, so there was no way for him not to see it: *I am leaving.*

She paused, waited for something. Sadness, maybe. Regret. Fear. Uncertainty. All of those came immediately, a whole gamut of emotions crowding into the small bathroom with her, but mostly, there was relief. Not only about the actual leaving part, the thought of which filled her with terror as much as anything else, or about the future, which she didn't really know how to tackle, but about the simple fact that it had been her who'd made the decision. That she was acting on it, in control. Already, the last two years were starting to take on a strange, dream-like quality, as if it hadn't been Chloe at all, but a small, pale shadow of her, floating through this big, empty house in Aidan's wake.

She shook her head slightly and focused on the paper in front of her, because there was a good long way to go before the dream was over and Chloe Archer would return.

> I have a safe place to go to. I will make sure everything is done right for the baby. And I'm going to take care of Danny, so he will no longer be a burden for you. I'll be in touch again soon to discuss arrangements. Please don't try to find me in the interim. I need time to figure out what to do from here.
>
> Chloe

She underlined 'don't' twice, then read the note through again; thought about tweaking a word here or there but decided to leave it. There was no good way of saying what she had to say, and Aidan wouldn't believe it anyway.

It was just gone one in the morning when she stole out of the loo, set the briefcase back in its customary spot, stashed the torch in the drawer where it was kept for emergencies, slipped the key back into Aidan's jacket and stole upstairs, the letter rustling faintly in the pocket of her dressing gown.

Forty-Nine

Chloe wondered if something in her biochemistry had changed, whether her new resolve gave off pheromones or some other imperceptible signal, because, as if he knew, Aidan seemed particularly reluctant to leave this morning. He brought her toast and a boiled egg with freshly squeezed orange juice, and lingered, watching her eat to make sure it all went down.

'I've left a small pie in the fridge for you,' he said, taking the plate from her. 'You just need to heat it up in the microwave. And a salad. Make sure you eat the salad, and maybe an apple. And then just—'

'Rest, I know.' She made her smile weary-looking. 'I'm sorry I'm so useless, Aidan. Whatever this flu is, it's really got me down. I'll be better soon. But maybe I should start doing some of the washing and—'

'No!' He shook his head emphatically. 'I've done what I can, and my shirts are at the launderette.'

'All right,' she said as pleasantly as she could, settling back into the pillows, keeping her eyes on his face from underneath her lashes. Her feet were twitching beneath the duvet, and she forced them to stay still as he puttered around the room indecisively, only leaving when his mobile rang downstairs.

'I have appointments all morning,' he said before he went. 'And surgery in the afternoon as well. But I'll be back as soon as I can. I hate leaving you, I really do. You know that.'

'Darling, please don't worry about me.' She yawned to emphasise her point. 'I'll be glad to just lie here and be lazy. Such a luxury.'

That seemed to reassure him, because he gave her a last smile before he ran downstairs. Every fibre in her body was ready to go, but she forced herself to wait for the garage door to open and the sound of the car starting up, the rumbling turning into a faraway purr as he drove down the street and around the corner.

She dressed quickly, then fetched the backpack from beneath the cupboard, adding her toothbrush, vitamins and a few last bits and pieces. And then it was time for the safe. Carefully she lifted down the photograph of her and Aidan on their wedding day. *Please*, she prayed. *Let it all be here.*

Aidan must have been confident that she wouldn't be able to open the safe, because it really was all there. Her driving licence, birth certificate and passport; her laptop and – her breath caught in her throat – the Nikon in her father's old bag. Fingers shaking, she lifted it out, the familiar shape of the bag settling against her side, and in an almost Pavlovian response, the caught breath moved smoothly into her lungs and her throat opened up. Her gear case was nowhere to be seen, but there was a spare charger in her camera bag and she'd just have to find a way to buy anything else she required.

Which brought her to the last item she needed from the safe. Her hand touched something soft, and for a moment, she paused. A blue velvet cloth held the jewellery Aidan had bought for her over the last few years. Necklaces with diamonds sparkling in the middle, solid gold bracelets, a ring with a ruby as wide as her middle finger. Matching earrings, intricately designed and sparkly with gems, were neatly inserted into clear pockets. The novelty of their weight at her earlobes and throat had worn off quickly, because despite Aidan's insistence on her showing off his thoughtful gifts, they'd never quite felt like her.

She hesitated, just for a moment. They were hers, after all, weren't they? It would be so easy. Couldn't she . . . A chain with a diamond pendant had escaped its pouch, sparkling in the light from the overhead spots. She nudged it back, making up her mind then and there. She bundled the cloth back together with some force and shoved it deep into the safe, fumbling instead for what really was hers: the flat cardboard box marked BICYCLE REPAIR KIT.

I don't know why you still worry, Chloe. I'll take care of you, you know that. She shook her head and gave a wry smile. For so long, Aidan had talked about how hard her life had been, how tough for a girl, a young woman, until she'd almost believed it herself. But it had never been about her, had it? It had always been about Aidan and his supposedly indispensable role in her life. A rescuer, a hero. Chloe touched the two gold coins in their yellowing plastic bubble wrap, lifted a small, tarnished silver bracelet and dangled it over her palm for a moment. Her life might not always have been easy. But it had been hers.

It was 9.30 when she left the house. She had put the letter on the dresser, right in the middle where he couldn't miss it. On the threshold, she paused one last time, but she didn't turn, didn't even breathe. She simply reached behind her and closed the door with a soft click.

As luck would have it, Marie was manning the front desk at Oakwood, rather than Stella, who would have sold Chloe down the river and thrown in an extra oar to boot.

'We missed you last week,' she said. 'Your husband called to say you were ill. Nothing serious, I hope?'

'Just a bug. I'm much better now. I was wondering, could I have a quick word?' Chloe hesitated. 'In private?'

'Of course.' Marie's thin, friendly face was creased in concern. She waved Chloe into the little room behind the reception desk. 'What's up?' she said, taking in her pale cheeks, the slight tremor in her hands. 'Are you all right? You don't look all that well.'

'Oh, I'm fine.' Chloe remembered Oakwood's strict policy on contagion and followed her words up with a big, carefree smile.

She opened her backpack and pulled out an envelope. 'Listen, it's about the increase in fees. I wanted to take the opportunity to make some changes I've been thinking about, and was wondering if you could check for me how far ahead Danny's bills here have been paid?'

Marie frowned in surprise. 'It's a standing order,' she said. 'The money gets taken from your account and there's a small budget for incidentals. It's all been set up by your husband; you don't need to worry about that.'

'I know.' Chloe chose her next words carefully. 'It's just that I'd like to swap the standing order over from one account to another.'

Marie hesitated. 'But your husband . . . I mean, it's an ongoing arrangement; there's no reason to change it, is there?'

'I'm not changing Danny's plan or anything, simply where the money is coming from.' Chloe forced herself not to sound impatient. 'I have a cheque here to cover next month's bill, just in case there's a lag between swapping over the information.'

'Right.' Marie sounded doubtful. 'Why don't I give your husband a quick call?'

'There's absolutely no need for that,' Chloe said brightly, more brightly than she felt, because the cheque had eaten up a lot of the emergency box, and she'd have to be very creative, very quickly, to fill the new account she'd just opened at the bank around the corner. She hadn't taken her bank cards from the safe, because she was done taking anything from Aidan anymore. From now on she was on her own. 'Marie, I've been coming to Oakwood a minimum of three times a week for two years. That's at the very least three hundred and twelve times. You *know* me. I'm Danny's next of kin; there is no nexter of kin than me. All I want is to make sure that I'm in control of how my brother's treatment is being paid for, whatever . . . well, whatever might happen.'

'Oh, Marie, for heaven's sake, don't be such a ninny.'

There was a loud clattering noise, and both Chloe and Marie turned towards the door. Dixie was tugging on her trolley, a newspaper tucked under her arm.

'The girl's handing you money. Just take it. As for the rest, I'll vouch for her. If for some reason she leaves here and gets run over by a car, then you know where to find me.' She glowered at her oxygen tank and gave it an impatient shove. 'Since I'm not leaving here any time soon.'

'Dixie, this is a private conversation,' Marie said impatiently. 'And for heaven's sake, stop manhandling that thing. You'll break it again.'

'Then I'll buy a new one. I have a lot of money, you know,' Dixie said serenely.

Chloe smiled and took the newspaper from underneath Dixie's arm, then patted the oxygen tank.

'I'll be extra careful crossing any roads,' she promised.

'Death is ever watchful,' Dixie pronounced, but there was a small smile lurking around her mouth as Chloe turned back to Marie and handed over the cheque and a little piece of paper with her new account information.

Dixie was waiting outside the reception desk, watching two window cleaners attack the sliding doors to the courtyard, when Chloe emerged, having filled in the requisite forms.

'Thank you,' Chloe said fervently.

'Don't mention it.' Dixie waved her away. They made their way down the corridor together, followed by the soft squeak of the oxygen trolley.

'Keep an eye on Danny, shall I?' Dixie enquired as they rounded the corner.

'Yes please.' Chloe nudged the machine forward. 'I'm going to sort out a new place for him, but I don't know how quickly I'll find something and I don't want anyone to take him away in the meantime.'

'Anyone, eh?' Dixie's eyes were sharp under her white eyebrows. 'Good on you, Chloe. Always knew you deserved better.'

'I suspect you're the only one here who thinks that.' Chloe sighed as one of the carers passed with a cheerful 'Good morning, Mrs MacAllister!'

'They're young,' Dixie said dismissively. 'Everyone wants to marry a doctor when they're young.'

Chloe laughed. 'I'll see you soon, all right?'

'Sure, angel,' Dixie said. 'And you take good care of yourself now, you hear me?'

Fifty

Danny's face lit up when she tracked him down in the common room, and fell just as quickly when he saw how pale she was.

'You look t'rrible.' He shook his head.

'I'm fine,' she said quickly. 'But . . . well, there is something. Something quite lovely, actually.'

They found an empty corner, but Danny didn't stop looking worriedly across at Chloe until she produced a can of Tango from her bag.

'Chloe,' he said in a shocked whisper. 'I don't think I'm allowed.'

'One celebratory swig won't kill you.' She stuck a straw into the can and held it out. He drained a third of it with his one swig, and an expression of pure bliss spread across his face.

'What're we celebrating?' he said.

She took the can from him and set it down between them, then took a deep breath, resisting the urge to look over her shoulder.

'I'm leaving Aidan,' she said in a low voice. 'I've left, that is. I'm not going back.'

Danny looked at the backpack bulging with her things, the camera, the portfolio, then back at her.

'Oh, Chloe,' he said in a hoarse voice. 'Oh, thank God, thank God.' He drew in a laboured breath. 'So worried about you,' he finally managed. 'Didn't know how to tell you without sounding . . .'

She looked down at her hands. 'I kept hoping it would change. I don't think I knew nearly enough about relationships and love to figure out where it had gone wrong.'

'Not your fault,' Danny told her sharply. 'He's—'

She held up her hand, shook her head. 'It's not my fault that it went wrong, maybe, but to stick it out for so long . . . It's a bit like us.' She stroked the side of the Tango can, not looking at him. 'You know, in the early days, how we always refused to go along with your illness, convinced ourselves that you *would* get better. That it would be different for you. I was always hoping it would get better with Aidan, too.' Tears sprang into her eyes, but she forced them back, because it was important to say this out loud.

'But neither of those things will change. And I'm going to have to stop pretending nothing is happening to you, that you'll get better just because I find it unbearable to think that one day I'll be without you. I don't know how I will go on when that happens, I really don't, Danny. But I'm going to have to make a start, because it *will* happen.'

She clenched her teeth hard and finally looked up at him. His eyes were closed, and for one mad, desperate moment she thought that something had happened to him.

But then he spoke, very slowly and carefully, so he could get all the words out.

'Talk to me properly, then, instead of avoiding all the things that aren't good and that you don't want me to know. Remember us. And when the time comes' – he finally opened his eyes, and she could see that they were very bright, but dry, and that improbably, he was smiling – 'you'll do it, Chlo. Like you always have. Strongest person I know. And now . . .' he paused for a moment, 'I can stop worrying about you. Concentrate on the rest of our time together.'

He stopped abruptly, his face drooping, his breath coming fast with the exertion of saying so much, and Chloe couldn't speak either, because her throat seemed to have closed up altogether now. She tried, with some effort, not to think about that time coming, then shook her head, because she couldn't do that any more, not think and hope for the best.

'I'm pregnant,' she said instead. He frowned for a moment, clearly thinking he hadn't heard right, but when she said it again, a little louder this time – 'A baby, Danny, I'm going to have a baby' – he got it.

'A baby?' he said uncertainly. 'Aidan's?'

'Mine,' she said.

He gave a sudden, choked laugh and shook his head. 'Don't do things by halves, do you? An uncle.' He put his head back and looked up at the ceiling. 'Wow.'

They both knew that Danny wouldn't be around to be an uncle for very long, but he was here now, smiling his Danny smile, and that was all that mattered.

'You'll be the best uncle ever,' she said, and patted his hand.

'Not difficult. I'll be the only one.' He chuckled. 'An uncle. That's really something.'

Aidan's schedule was unpredictable, and this would be the first place he'd come looking for her, yet Chloe made no move to leave. They sat close, the Archer siblings, their backs to the rest of the room, heads down, and everyone else kept away as they clearly had important business to discuss. But they didn't, not really. They didn't talk about Danny's future or Chloe's marriage or how she would have to fight Aidan for custody for the next eighteen years. Instead, they reminisced about Jerry and the amazing curry down the road from their old flat; they talked about what'd been on the telly, and baby names, and established that under no circumstances was Chloe allowed to raise the baby as anything other than a devoted Arsenal fan.

Eventually, though, the sounds of lunch being served drifted through from the dining room, and Chloe knew she couldn't put it off any longer. She sat up reluctantly and reached for her bag, picked up the can of Tango.

'Take me,' Danny suddenly said next to her. All the laughter had disappeared from his face. 'With you. Please, Chlo. I'll go anywhere. Don't need any of this fancy stuff, just . . .'

She bent down and hugged him hard, cables and edges digging into her ribcage.

'Of course I will,' she said fiercely into his ear. She stood back a little so he could see her face. 'Don't do anything, don't sign a single thing or believe anything unless you hear it directly from me or from Dixie. And I've made sure that your fees are paid up until I can get you, so nothing can happen to you. *Nothing.*'

'Emergency box?' he said resignedly.

'It was all I could come up with at short notice. But you're not to worry. I'll start working again next week, whatever I can manage, and the NHS will have some brilliant schemes set up for you. An invalid and a single mum: I mean, can we be any more eligible for government help?'

She smiled down at him, and he smiled back, and despite the drooping corners of his mouth and the lopsided angle, his smile was the same as ever, warm and happy and full of life, and Chloe didn't see the big wheelchair or the immobile form inside; just the little boy she'd raised and loved and would never let fall.

Fifty-One

Maddy

I listened to Georgiana's footsteps fade along the landing and felt as though my heart was breaking into a thousand pieces. I imagined her going to tell Victor, the relief in her voice at the release from the memories and the house, from me, and I couldn't bear it, not for her to feel like that and not for her to tell Victor, who would nod sympathetically, take her in his arms and pull her even further away from me than he already had.

I balled my fists when I thought of him. He'd been setting her against me, had rewritten her history, *our* history, into something that didn't include me any more. And there was nothing I could do about it. Nothing I could say about what had happened in the maze would sway her now, because she'd think I was trying to sour things between her and Victor. And even if I could somehow make her see the truth about him, she'd still be leaving Summerhill, because he'd encouraged her to discover how much it was holding her back. The worst thing was, it was partly my own fault. I'd always deferred to someone else, relieved not to be in charge, not even willing to listen. If I was losing my sister and my home, then I was to blame as much as Victor, because I'd willingly surrendered any power to change things a long time ago.

'What a stupid mess,' I said out loud. I pulled the crumpled dress from underneath my thighs and frowned at it. It was a hideously juvenile confection of pink tulle netting and cotton, which I'd worn when Georgiana had made me go to Alicia

Draycott's coming-out dance. I threw it into a corner, then picked it up again. I couldn't fall to pieces now. I had to think of something.

There was a soft knock at the door and Susan entered, wearing a starched white apron and a little cap perched on the back of her head.

'Well, I thought we needed to look our best,' she said with a self-conscious shrug when she saw me staring at her.

'Yes,' I managed, 'of course.' I tried very hard not to think about the moment I'd have to tell her about Summerhill. Maybe she could come with me, wherever I was going. Not with Victor and Georgiana, that much was sure.

'You do know that Miss Georgie's guests are arriving as we speak?' She surveyed me, my bristling hair, the balled-up dress. 'She asked me to come and help you. I think she wanted to make sure you were actually going to show up.'

'Oh, she did, did she?' I said savagely. 'I can take care of myself, you know.'

Susan raised her eyebrows and took the pink tulle from me, smoothing out the worst of the creases.

'No,' I said flatly. 'I'm not going down to join bloody *Gigi* and Victor and the others looking like a birthday cake. I refuse.'

We both studied the dress for a moment, then she said, 'I think I have something else. Wait here. And for goodness' sake, Miss Maddy, do get moving and at least wash your face, or we'll both be in trouble.'

When she returned a few minutes later, Susan was holding a very different dress. Long and cut straight, with panels of gauze high across the neckline, and sleeves of the same gauze coming down to the elbows, it was a beautiful silk, the dark green of Summerhill pine trees at the bottom of the garden, shot through with the blue of the river.

'It's from your mother's dressing room,' Susan said hesitantly. 'I hope that's all right?'

'It's beautiful.' I fingered the fabric wonderingly.

She lifted it over my head and let it drop, and I felt it slither down over me until it settled on my shoulders. I tugged at the sleeves and tweaked the layers into place, then fastened the high neck before turning slowly to look. I almost didn't recognise my reflection, this grown-up, sombre person in the mirror. But then I moved and the dress shimmered and sparkled in the lamplight, and despite everything, I smiled. I was thinner than my mother had been, and must have been taller too, because the dress hit me at the knee rather than just below it, but the cut was forgiving and timeless. I turned from side to side to make it move, and imagined the way William's eyes would light up if he could see me now, looking like a water-carrying goddess. A sharp pang shot through me when I realised that he too was gone. I swallowed.

'Maybe it's a bit . . . much?' I looked at my bare face and tousled hair.

'It's perfect,' Susan said, and shook her head in wonder. 'But quick, your hair still needs a tidy. Here, sit.'

She pushed me down into the chair, started arranging my curls with quick, efficient movements. 'There's no time for much, but your skin's lovely as it is . . . There, done.' She pushed the last pin behind my ear, squinting to admire her handiwork. She'd been working fast, but now she seemed to hesitate, tweaking my hair again even though she must have a million other things to do. I watched her in the mirror for a moment.

'Something the matter?' I asked.

'I'm not sure.' She hesitated, looked back at the door. 'I know I shouldn't be prying,' her face was red now, 'but I was returning some shoes to Mr Elton's room just now—'

'Mr Elton? Oh, you mean Jonathan?'

Susan nodded. 'Yes, well, he's ever so messy, clearly used to someone doing for him all the time. I thought I might have a very quick tidy, and that's when I saw this. It was spread across the bed and I wasn't sure . . . and, well, I took it. I'll return it,' she hastened to add, 'but I thought I'd show it to you first.'

It was a map of Summerhill. Not as big and detailed as the one in the library; more of a basic layout of the estate, the fields and cottages. There was writing all over it, fields crossed out with a date next to them or annotated with a question mark. I felt a lump in my throat when I realised just how much Summerhill had shrunk over the last six years, heart-shaped no longer but a ragged oval pressed against the river.

'He was in the library, too, earlier today, with Mr Deverill,' Susan said. 'They'd got out some of your papa's ledgers and were going through them when I came in to fetch something.'

'Georgiana asked Victor to look at some accounts.' I frowned at the map as I tried to think it through. Had Victor put this together to show my sister how much we were struggling? But the map didn't look like it had been written up at one sitting in the library. The paper looked as though it had become soft over many years, ripped at the creases from being handled and folded, and in some places the writing had worn away entirely.

'Well, that's all right, then,' Susan said quickly. 'I didn't mean to be telling tales, you know, it's just . . . not quite what house guests would do, is all. And the way Mr Deverill was with you in the maze.' She gave me a level look. 'I know I was the one who said to forget it, but when you really think about it, that's not what a house guest would do either, is it, not when he's with your sister. It doesn't make sense.'

'I know. None of it does.'

You might have a solution now, right in front of you. Jonathan sounded keen enough. That was what Victor had told Georgiana. And hadn't Jonathan said, earlier in the library, something about talking to his father about it? Was Victor encouraging Jonathan to look into buying Summerhill in the same way he'd encouraged my sister to be free of her old life? Whichever way you looked at it, it all kept coming back to Victor.

The ancient gramophone gave a sharp shriek from downstairs and Susan started, held out her hand for the map. 'You should go,' she said. 'I'll just nip back to his room.'

'No,' I said defiantly. 'We're going to keep this. And I'm going to have a look in Victor's room, now that they're all having a grand old time downstairs.'

My mother's dress whispered encouragingly round my legs as I walked to the door and opened it.

'We shouldn't, really,' Susan started, but I stood back and held the door for her. 'All right, then. We'll pretend we're turning down the bed or something.'

We both made the same sound, a slightly hysterical giggle, at the thought of Victor coming upon the two of us turning his bed down on the eve of a party, then Susan stepped out into the corridor and I followed, closing the door quietly behind me.

Fifty-Two

Victor had been given the blue room at the far west corner. If Aunt Marjorie had been trying to make a point by putting him as far away from Georgiana as possible, it clearly hadn't had the intended effect, but it worked in my favour now, because there was less chance someone would walk past and accidentally discover us. The blackout had been pinned tightly into place, and the lingering smell of cigarette smoke mingled with the thick air as I switched on the little lamp on the table. From far away, laughter could be heard, and another indignant shriek from the gramophone.

'He certainly is very tidy,' Susan said approvingly.

'I think that's because he hardly has any stuff.' I pointed at the wardrobe. 'Look.'

Victor's clothes were neatly arranged, but that didn't disguise the fact that there didn't seem to be nearly enough for someone expecting a proper country house weekend. A couple of dressy shirts. A pair of trousers, a jacket, a lightweight jumper. A pair of shoes below. A small vanity kit and a hairbrush sat on one of the wardrobe shelves.

'Goodness. Mr Elton brought about five times as much,' Susan said incredulously. 'And six pairs of shoes. How strange, with Mr Deverill being a gentleman and everything.'

'Well, not a gentleman perhaps, but certainly a wealthy businessman,' I said, realising not for the first time how little I actually knew about Victor.

Susan made a small moue of unease. 'Better be quick.'

She turned to watch the door as I ran my hands over his jacket, felt in pockets, then moved on to the desk. There was a letter rack on top of it, with old-fashioned stationery that was yellowing and collecting dust at the edges from disuse; a lone pen in a leather cup. The only sign of life here was a vase of flowers, although it must have been put there a few days ago, because the flowers were already drooping. A stack of papers on the desk proved to be business documents and letters bearing the Wilson's letterhead.

'He knows how to make the bed,' Susan said, pointing to the sharp hospital corners.

Giving myself a little push, I felt under his pillow and down beneath the blanket. My feet hit something hard under the bed.

'Your dress!' Susan hissed reproachfully as I dropped to my knees and pulled out a suitcase.

The leather was polished and buffed to look a lot more opulent than the inside, which proved to be faded and scuffed. I felt into all corners carefully, and then, suddenly, a quick, sharp pain. I jerked back my hand. Closer inspection showed that the lining had been cut and pinned back together with a safety pin, the tip of which had come loose and burrowed into my nail bed. Blood welled, and with great presence of mind, Susan stuffed my hand into a fold of the dark-brown bedspread before any of it could drip on the lining of the case. Then she slid her own hand inside, and when she pulled it back out, she was holding an old folder. The black leather was shabby and cracked in places. The clasp must have come off at some point, because it had been carefully stitched back together with newer thread, but the metal had rusted and discoloured and it was difficult to undo.

'Hurry, Miss Maddy,' Susan breathed. 'It really, *really* wouldn't be the thing to be found in here.' But then she fell silent and we both found ourselves staring at a drawing taped to the inside of the folder. Two figures sitting on a kitchen bench, heart-shaped faces, a flash of auburn next to chestnut.

'I can't believe it,' I said angrily. 'He took it.'

Victor had sliced my drawing out of the sketchbook so carefully that I hadn't even noticed it was missing. The thought of him sitting here, on this sharp-cornered bed, looking at this picture of me and my sister made me feel slightly queasy. Resolutely, I slid my thumb under the tape.

'What are you doing?' Susan whispered.

'Taking it back, of course.' I tried prising the picture away from the leather, but it resisted, and when I pulled harder, the folder suddenly slipped out of my hand, scattering its contents on the bed.

'Oh dear God.' Susan rarely swore, but when I bent over the pieces of paper, I felt like doing the same.

The chapel at Summerhill estate was crowded last week when family, friends and neighbours of Alexander Hamilton gathered to pay their last respects.

Mrs Marjorie Lancaster, Miss Madeleine Hamilton and Miss Georgiana Hamilton desire to express their thanks for the kind expressions of sympathy shown them in their recent sad bereavement.

The eighteenth birthday of Georgiana Hamilton, daughter of the late Alexander Hamilton, was celebrated at the family home.

There were other newspaper cuttings too, some yellow and grimy with age, others newer. Georgiana at a masked ball at the Penberthys', Georgiana and Cookie manning the jam stall at the village summer fair. And among them, records of fields sold, plots of lands changing hands.

Messrs Rowe and Knowles will sell at Auction Lot 7: TWO FIELDS situated at Tremarron, comprising about 6 acres, now in the possession of the estate of A. Hamilton, Ordnance Nos . . .

Wordlessly, Susan handed me the map and watched me run my finger across it until I came to the fields sold as Lot 7, two crossed-out parcels of land up in the north-western corner of Summerhill. Dropping it onto the bed, I rifled through the rest of the stack. Among the cuttings and typed-up notes was a piece of paper covered with names. They were connected with arrows and lines, some of them looping and doubling back on each other. I traced the lines between my mother and her sisters, Hilly and Marjorie, followed cousins and aunts on my father's side, further and further down until I suddenly stopped. Cousin Claire was circled in red and an arrow went straight down to Louisa and then on to Georgiana.

Louisa was quite smitten with him.

'He's been *following* Georgiana.' I found my voice. 'He must have engineered a meeting with her. It looks like he was actually waiting for her at Cousin Claire's.'

'But why?' Susan's hands were trembling as she folded up the map again. 'Why on earth would he do that?'

'I don't know. All I know is that I have to talk to Georgiana now.'

I shuffled the articles back together and slid them into the folder, and was just about to fasten it when Susan grabbed my hand.

'Miss Maddy, look!'

I looked, and then I looked again, the two of us bending so close over the cracked leather that Susan's hair tickled my cheek. For a moment I focused on the shell-like ovals of her fingernails curved around the edge of the folder, because surely it wasn't real, it couldn't possibly be?

There, in letters that had once been stamped into the leather, now faded, the grooves only barely discernible, was the name JAMES MORLEY.

'But . . .' I pushed out the words with some effort, 'James Morley is dead, remember?'

James Morley had saved my life, that was what people said. He had jumped off the boat and into the water, managed to reach the rocks where I was. The rest was a blur of water, noise and movement. People told me about it later and I probably nodded in answer, but all that had remained in my mind was a blank space around which small memories congregated: the limpness of my father's hand in mine, the sound of water hitting the rocks, rushing and pounding relentlessly, the salty smells, the brief shock of the cold seawater, the rough feel of the jute rope cutting into my arms. The heave as I threw my leg over the side of the boat. The shouting as James Morley disappeared into the water.

Over the years, the fact that I couldn't remember James Morley had me panicked, because I knew that I owed it to him, this one single memory of how he died. I tried to recall his wet hair, the look on his face as he held out his hand to me, the rope wrapped around his body. But my mind refused to ever bring him into clear focus, and in the end, I'd just held onto his name. And once a year, I stole across the fields to the village cemetery and put something on his grave. Flowers. A little wreath of pine cones, a ring of small, smooth, perfect stones I'd gathered specially.

As I touched the name stamped into the leather, I suddenly wanted to take off my grown-up dress and put on my old brown trousers, whistle for the dogs and go back to my life a week ago, when all that had been important was to sit with my sketchbook and wait for Georgiana's return.

'Maddy? Are you all right?' Susan whispered. The sound of music from downstairs, now smooth and lovely, cut through the fuzziness in my mind, and I took a deep breath.

'So Victor knew James Morley,' I said haltingly. 'Or is it just a coincidence?'

'If it is, then it's a very strange one,' Susan said slowly. 'And what about the other things, the newspaper bits, the map?'

'And Georgiana is pregnant,' I said bleakly, because we might as well have all the facts in the open.

Susan clapped a hand over her mouth, her eyes round above her small nose. 'What do you think he'll do? Oh goodness, Miss Maddy, what if he won't marry her?'

'And what if he will?'

We looked at each other for a long moment, then Susan kicked the suitcase back beneath the bed, and I clamped the folder under my arm and wrenched open the door. Faint sounds of conversation and laughter drifted up, the smell of cigarette smoke and perfume. I had just ushered her out ahead of me and turned to close the door when I suddenly heard her gasp. There at the end of the corridor was the red glow of a cigarette.

We stood frozen for a moment in the musty, blackout-smothered silence. Then Victor moved and we drew close together, bracing ourselves. But he didn't come towards us; instead, he turned on his heel and disappeared around the corner.

'He's going to find Georgiana,' I said, my voice choked with terror.

'You'd better be quick, then.' Susan gave me a little shove, and I started running.

Fifty-Three

Chloe

It was late afternoon when Chloe finally turned into the lane that led to Summerhill. She felt like she'd been running all day. Adrenaline and exhilaration had kept her moving forward, but by the time she'd got to Truro bus station, it was fear more than anything else that drove her. Looking over her shoulder constantly, she was convinced that every red car contained her husband, who had come home early and was now driving around looking for her. She'd taken the little country bus to Tremarron, then pulled out the piece of paper on which she'd drawn a rough map to Summerhill and started walking. Leaden tiredness was making her legs drag, her shoulders ache under the weight of the backpack, the sharp edge of her portfolio digging into her armpit.

Almost there now, she told the baby as she stumbled along the green tunnel of trees. *At the very end of the lane, where the world is done, remember?* She'd taken to talking to it ever since she left Oakwood, a constant inaudible crooning that kept her going and gave her hope.

When she finally reached the courtyard, she stopped in the shadow of the treeline. It was after five. Aidan would have read her note by now and would be considering his options. Chloe had gone through those herself endlessly in the middle of the night, had tried to anticipate what he would do. Call the police maybe, although with a note to indicate that she'd gone willingly, they wouldn't be of much help. Get in touch with the few people she knew, who in turn would know nothing. Arrive at Oakwood to bully Marie. She smiled grimly when she thought of the cheque, and Dixie. That wouldn't do him much good. And lastly, he might come to Summerhill.

Chloe nestled into the rhododendrons, squinted across the hot, deserted courtyard towards the house. It wasn't all that easy to put Summerhill and Madeleine together, however, unless you knew exactly what you were looking for. Chloe had searched for information on the internet before she'd first come here, but Madeleine had kept so successfully out of the public eye that there was little to be found, except for the occasional walking guide or Ordnance Survey map. And Chloe had never mentioned the name of the place in Aidan's presence, not that she could recall.

Leaving the shelter of the rhododendrons, she made her way to the front door and knocked softly.

'Madeleine?' she said in a low voice, then, startled by the sound in the quiet afternoon, she opened the door and stepped inside. 'It's me. Chloe.'

There was movement from the library, and then voices. Two voices. Chloe froze, put her hand back on the door handle, saw the outline of a man disentangle itself from a chair. She didn't wait for him to turn, but pulled open the door again and threw herself outside, started running across the courtyard, towards the trees.

'Wait!' called a voice, and then there were footsteps crunching across the gravel behind her, coming closer. She was too slow, her backpack hitting her painfully in the lower back, getting heavier with each step, slowing her down.

I don't think we can do this after all, she might have whispered to the baby. And then her legs disappeared and the ground came up to meet her. At the very last moment, she managed to half turn her body, curling over the place where the baby was, and when she felt her shoulder hitting gravel, she closed her eyes.

'Oh bloody hell, I'm too old for this!'

The sound came from far away, but it didn't quite sound like her husband. She wanted to lift her head, look around, but her body refused to move another inch. The footsteps came closer, and then she found herself scooped up and off the ground.

'Don't,' she said thickly, her head lolling against an arm.

'Chloe!' This, now, was a voice she knew well. 'Here, put her on the sofa. There's some water through there, quick. Chloe, can you hear me? Chloe!'

Chloe forced her eyes to open.

'Is he . . . here?' Her tongue felt so heavy, she had to work hard to get the words out.

'Your husband?' Madeleine said. 'No, of course not. Why . . . Oh, you mean . . . no, that's just Mr Cooper.'

'Oh. Really?' Chloe struggled to sit up as a man approached, a jug of water and a glass in his hand.

'Just lie still for a moment, child. Are you sure I shouldn't call the doctor?' Madeleine put a hand on her shoulder, her face anxious.

'No, please don't.' With some effort, Chloe pulled herself upright, feeling her hands slip a little on the velvet back of the narrow sofa. 'I'm sorry. The heat and the long walk, I must have . . .'

'Oh, hush, don't be silly. I'll go and fetch a cold cloth for your head; it is awfully warm today. And maybe something sugary to eat.'

Madeleine's face disappeared from Chloe's circle of vision, to be replaced by a large glass of water. She looked up, blinking rapidly to clear her head.

'I can't believe you made me carry you across that courtyard, Chloe MacAllister.' Matt Cooper shook his head. 'I'm much too old for hero shenanigans, you know.'

He didn't look as if the shenanigans had done him much damage. And he didn't look all that old, either. Tall and thin, the way Chloe had pictured him, although not in a suit but in jeans and a button-down shirt that were soft with age and clearly much loved. Late forties, early fifties, Chloe thought, as he folded himself into a chair opposite her. With his craggy face and dishevelled hair, he looked exactly the way he sounded on the phone, as if he didn't care what anyone thought but was fully prepared to put them in their place regardless.

'I'm sorry, I thought . . . I didn't expect you here,' she said hoarsely.

'Mrs Hamilton was worried about you, rang me at the office. I almost fell over in shock when I picked up the phone,' he added in an undertone. 'She must be really quite fond of you to overcome her aversion to the outside world. Anyway,' he said more loudly, just as Madeleine came back into the room with a packet of biscuits and a small towel, 'I agreed that it all seemed a bit off, especially after your husband so rudely barked into the phone at me the other day. So I decided to come down and check on things, finally meet Mrs Hamilton in person. Talk about the book. Make sure all was well.'

Unexpectedly, Chloe felt a gurgle of laughter at the back of her throat. 'Although you're certainly no stranger to barking at people either,' she pointed out.

'Well, I never heard back from you,' he said in an accusatory tone. 'Phone making funny noises again, didn't answer your door. How's a man not to worry?' He reached to relieve Madeleine of the biscuits, held one out to Chloe.

'You came to my house?' She frowned but all she could remember was the swirly white fog in her brain. 'I had the flu. And then this morning, I left.'

There was a pause, then Matt said quietly, 'The flu, hmm?'

His eyes stayed on hers for a moment, as if he was trying to put together all the things she hadn't said out loud. For some reason, it didn't feel probing or intrusive, however, but reassuring, and Chloe thought to herself that she wouldn't mind so much telling this man about Aidan and Danny at some point.

'Well, I'm glad you left the, er, flu behind, anyhow,' he said briskly. 'Get those biscuits down you, and I'll see what I can rustle up for dinner. Kitchen's downstairs?'

'You really don't have to,' Madeleine and Chloe began at the same time, but he was already disappearing through the door.

'Prepare yourselves for the meal of a lifetime,' they heard him call back. 'Cheese on toast. My speciality. Eat your biscuits.'

'Better not to argue with him,' Madeleine said resignedly as she sat down on the sofa next to Chloe and handed her the damp towel.

The biscuits were a little stale, but Chloe forced herself to eat two, chewing slowly. Then she closed her eyes and gave in to the sheer relief of finally sitting down somewhere quiet, the cloth cool against her hot skin, the biscuits settling her restless stomach. Sounds of clanking and a curse or two floated up from downstairs. She could feel the house all around her, in the curtains and the books, the mirrors and the mantelpieces, the old clock that needed to be wound, the paintings turning dark with age. It was warm and friendly and safe, the way she remembered her father's checked shirt, Cuppy's worn ears beneath her fingers, and for the first time that day, she felt her shoulders drop away from her ears and her ribcage relax.

'I can't believe you're here,' Madeleine said suddenly, as if she'd read her thoughts. Chloe opened her eyes. The old woman was looking down at her hands, twisting her fingers. 'I felt awful after the other day, and then I talked to your husband on the phone. He was perfectly pleasant, you know, but nonetheless, I was . . . afraid for you.' She drew in a deep, shaky breath. 'I was even contemplating making my peace with Truro Homecare if I could have got the harridan to come out and drive me over to Plymouth.' She threw Chloe a wry half-smile. 'On balance, Matt Cooper seemed the better option, though.'

'I didn't have anywhere else to go.' Chloe fiddled with the towel. 'I hope . . . I mean, I hope it's all right with you. It would just be for a couple of days, until I figure out what to do.'

'Hush, child, of course it's all right. I'm glad you're here.' Madeleine took the towel from her and set it aside. 'I will help you to sort this out in any way I can.'

'Sort what out?' Matt was balancing a large tray, hampered slightly by the kitchen roll tucked under one arm. 'If it's anything to do with a certain book and a photo, I'm going to—'

But they would never hear what exactly Matt Cooper would be doing, because just then, there was the sound of tyres on gravel, the smooth purr of a motor as a car came to a stop in front of the house.

Chloe felt the colour draining from her face. 'It's him,' she whispered. 'Oh God, he's here. How can he possibly have found me already?'

A car door slammed, then footsteps, absurdly steady and brisk, were marching towards the front door. Without even realising it, Chloe was up and backing around the sofa, holding on to the armrest when she felt herself go woozy again. She had to be strong now, for the baby. She'd hide in the grounds, just for a little while . . .

'Chloe, you need to talk to him.' Matt Cooper's voice was gentle, and he held out a hand to her. 'I'll be right here, and Madeleine as well; we'll help you.'

'No,' Madeleine said, struggling to her feet. 'Absolutely not. Chloe, out through the glass doors at the back, that way is safest.'

'Madeleine, be reasonable. She can't keep running away.' Matt shook his head. 'This isn't some TV crime drama.'

A sharp rap sounded on the door, followed by two more, perfectly timed and precise. 'Hello?' a voice enquired pleasantly. 'Anyone home?'

'He won't go away.' Chloe looked up into Matt's craggy face. Even as she said it, the truth of it sank down into her belly, shifted and settled there like a lead weight, and she wondered how she had ever thought she could leave with Aidan's baby and get away with it. 'He never will, not when there's a chance that I'm here.'

She looked at Madeleine, who gestured urgently to the drawing room.

'The terrace,' she said in a low voice. 'There's a small path that runs right around the house. Wait by the corner, we'll get him to come inside and then you can disappear through the orchards. I'll turn on the lamp in the drawing room when it's safe to come back.'

'Good God, it really is a crime drama' Matt said incredulously.

Chloe didn't wait for Aidan to knock again. She darted into the drawing room, ran past Madeleine's bed, past the half-open wardrobe to the stretch of floor-to-ceiling windows that opened onto the terrace. There she paused, listened. She heard the front door opening, an exclamation of sorts, and voices. She pressed herself hard against the wall, trying to still her breathing, which felt so loud, she was sure Aidan could hear it all the way from the hall.

'Chloe!' she suddenly heard Madeleine call.

That wasn't part of the plan, and it sounded urgent, but Chloe didn't know why. She turned, then turned again, changed her mind. She had to get away, run into the grounds, hide somewhere.

'Wait!' she thought she heard, but she was already at the glass doors, reaching for the handle.

The door opened easily; in fact, she didn't even have to turn the handle, because out on the terrace, stepping aside courteously to let her pass, fair hair glinting in the sun, stood Aidan.

Fifty-Four

Maddy

I barely noticed how different the drawing room looked as I came downstairs and hurried towards the babble of voices and music, scanning the crowd for a sign of my sister. Free of clutter, chairs grouped haphazardly together at the edges, it was more spacious than usual, and yet the blackout curtains closed it in too, muffling conversation and music and cigarette smoke, sapping what little air there was in the warm night so that guests crowded around the long table for water and other drinks.

Georgiana's quiet invitation had grown exponentially, as if people were eager for this one last chance to pretend that their lives weren't going to be irrevocably changed with the expiry of Chamberlain's ultimatum to the Germans tomorrow morning. Cars had felt their way along the roads and country lanes by torchlight, and occasionally the forbidden beam of a headlight, quickly smothered during the drive through the villages in case an overzealous ARP warden jumped out and presented them with a fine. Anxiety over the inevitability of what was to come was overlaid with a strange sort of giddiness and too-bright laughter.

I moved through the knots of people quickly, my head snapping left and right, absent-mindedly greeting people I hadn't seen in years. I passed Aunt Marjorie in conversation with an older woman; skirted Laney and Clementine, who were smoking by the drinks table and surveying the country set with raised eyebrows, smugly complacent in their own sophisticated elegance. When someone stopped me to ask for a dance, a young man I vaguely recognised but who clearly had no idea who I was, I shook my head, because a thought had suddenly come to me.

The blackout was firmly in place in front of the glass doors leading out to the terrace, presumably to discourage people from going out, but Hobson and Frank had created a few air locks that allowed air to come into the ballroom without letting light out. I sidled behind one of the panels and felt my way along the glass until I came to the open door.

Outside, not a chink of light from inside the drawing room could be seen, but German bombers wouldn't have had any difficulty finding us, because the moon, like the night before, was flooding the terrace with a cold, eerie wash, picking out the contours of the ornate balustrade, the vases and urns and stone benches, throwing sharp-edged shadows across the flagstones. The breeze stirred the trees and bushes at the garden end of the terrace, bringing the scents of honeysuckle and night air and salt. Two people were standing in the far corner, and I could make out the shimmer of silk and a short, sleek bob glossy with moonlight.

'Georgiana,' I said breathlessly, and walked quickly towards her. 'I've been looking all over for you.'

'Maddy.' Something in her voice made me stop just in front of her. Victor raised his eyebrows and smiled politely, but I pointedly ignored him. 'Georgie, there's something I have to tell you.'

'I already know.' The moonlight made her eyes strangely opaque.

'You *told* her?' Stunned, I turned to Victor, only dimly hearing Georgiana exhale, a cross between a sigh and a sob.

'She deserved to know the truth,' Victor said.

'The truth?' I repeated slowly, but when I looked at Georgiana, it dawned on me that, quite possibly, we weren't talking about the same thing at all. Her strange moonshine eyes seemed to be looking straight through me, and her voice was hard.

'You know, Maddy, I didn't believe it. I didn't want to . . .'

'Neither did I,' I broke in, relieved.

'. . . but then it all made sense. The way you were so distracted, so flustered all the time. And whenever I saw you, there was Victor.' Unexpectedly, she laughed, a horrible, bitter sound. 'You were so changed, too, yesterday after the maze; even the others remarked on it. Well, I suppose trying to kiss your sister's boyfriend and being spurned could do that to you.'

'*Me?*' I spluttered, horrified. 'That's not at all what happened. He trapped me in Smuggler's Hatch and I couldn't leave. And then—'

'Madeleine, it's all right, you don't need to feel awkward,' Victor said gently. 'I could tell you had feelings for me. It's perfectly normal and I do really like you, but not like that. It's been weighing on my mind and I knew we had to get it all out in the open. Who knows how quickly things will be moving now. I wanted to be honest with Georgiana.' Unbelievably, he reached to touch my arm as if to draw me in, but I yanked it out of his reach.

'I don't know what strange, twisted game you're playing,' I hissed. 'He's lying, Georgiana. I found papers in his room and—'

'You went through his things?' she said incredulously. 'In his room? Good God, Maddy, what is *wrong* with you? This isn't you, snooping around and throwing yourself at men, even this dress . . .' she gestured at me. 'I don't feel like I recognise you any more.'

'It's not me, it's *him*.' I spat the word in Victor's direction. 'He is always there, pushing between us.'

'So that's what this is about,' she said incredulously. 'Me having someone else in my life, someone else who is important to me.'

'Someone who told you I was a burden, who's been poisoning things between us,' I said furiously.

'You kissed Victor because he was poisoning things? Or did you actually like him? Either way, it's not a particularly sisterly thing to do, from where I stand. Never, Maddy, *never* in my life would I have thought that you'd betray me like this.'

'I didn't,' I shouted. 'He touched me, kissed me, and I hated it.'

'Then why didn't you *tell* me?' Georgiana demanded. 'Just now, in your room. Victor wasn't there; why didn't you tell me then?'

'Because you were so busy talking about the baby,' I said furiously. 'The thought of which you hated because you didn't want to be tied down. Because of me.'

'The baby?'

Georgiana twitched angrily, but it was too late. Victor had turned to her, a strange grimace of pain and longing on his face. Instinctively I moved to step in front of her, but he reached her first and pulled her into his arms.

'It's true?' he said roughly, his eyes searching hers. 'You're having a *baby*?'

'Yes,' Georgiana bit the inside of her cheek as she looked up into Victor's face. 'I'm sorry, Victor. I was about to tell you. I know the timing is awful and we haven't known each other very long, but—'

'A baby,' he repeated slowly. His voice had a strange cadence to it, broadening into a softer West Country lilt, and I couldn't help but wonder whether this was the first true thing he'd said all week. 'Why didn't you tell me?' he said. 'Our baby – we must get married immediately.'

He disentangled himself from her. She tilted her head and I could see tears running down her face, the look of relief and joy strangely flattened by the eerie brightness, her mouth trembling.

'Yes,' she said shakily, 'please. Oh, Victor, I love you, darling—'

'Georgiana,' I said very loudly, pushing in between the two of them, 'please listen to me.'

Georgiana withdrew with great reluctance, keeping a hand on Victor's arm.

'Madeleine, if you don't mind, I'd really like to enjoy this moment. And my *engagement*! Oh, Victor!' She leaned into him again. 'I was so worried about telling you—'

'There's nothing to worry about,' he interrupted, and again his voice broadened into that incongruous West Country homeliness. 'It's a baby. A little family, just the three of us.'

He looked straight at me as he said the last bit. There was a strange glint in his eyes and it took me a moment to realise that it looked oddly like triumph. Triumph not over Georgiana, but over me. And suddenly it all became clear.

'It was never about Georgiana at all, was it?' I said in horror. 'It was about *me*. Me and James Morley.'

'I don't know what you're talking about,' Victor said smoothly, but there was an edge to his voice now. 'Georgiana, maybe we should leave your sister to compose herself, go back to your guests, announce the happy news.'

But I barred his way.

'James Morley,' I said, struggling to think it through. 'The accident. I have so little memory of that moment on the rocks. If you knew him, if he is the reason you're doing all this, then please, help me understand.'

'Maddy!' Georgiana said, annoyed. 'What on earth are you on about?'

I held up the folder to reveal the faded letters stamped into the leather. 'This was in his suitcase,' I said, keeping my eyes on Victor. He was staring at the folder and I could see his throat move as he swallowed. 'It belonged to the man who drowned after Papa had fallen on the cliffs. Please, Victor, I want to help. How did you know James—'

'Don't!' Victor said suddenly, and his tone was so sharp that Georgiana flinched. 'Don't you dare say his name again.' He took a deep breath, then another one. 'Georgiana, this is silly.' He tried for an off-hand laugh. 'Come on, darling, let's go back inside.'

'No, I want to hear about James Morley,' she said, frowning.

'Don't,' Victor snapped. His hair fell across his forehead as he snatched the folder from me. He shoved it into the inside pocket of his suit jacket and pushed his hands through his hair. 'I told you not to say his name,' he said in a hard, controlled voice. 'Either of you. Do you hear me?'

'We won't,' I said breathlessly. 'We won't say his name again if you tell us why.'

'Why?' Victor said. 'Why? Are you mocking me? You . . .' His voice cracked on the last word. His face was working and he was breathing hard, a silver sheen of sweat glittering across his forehead. 'You killed him, Madeleine.'

'It was an accident. I . . .' I broke off as he gripped my shoulders and dug his fingers into the flesh around my collarbone.

'He was my brother. And no, it wasn't an accident. You killed him.' He shook me so hard that my teeth made a loud clacking sound.

'Victor!' Georgiana shouted, horrified. She pushed between us, tried to prise his hands off me. 'Stop! You're hurting her!'

But he didn't pay any attention to her.

'I'm going to make you pay for his death, by God I will, if it's the last thing I do. All these years I've waited for this. Yes, I followed you, of course I did. Oh, I know everything about your family; I was watching and waiting for the moment when I could see the great Hamiltons of Summerhill go down in flames. You will pay for what was done to my family, for what *you* did, Madeleine.'

With a sudden, hard shove, he let me go and I stumbled backwards until I felt the sharp edge of the balustrade scrape along the backs of my legs. As he towered over me, Georgiana trying to hold him back, a voice suddenly came from behind him.

'Leave her alone.'

Fifty-Five

Chloe

'Here, let me help you.' Aidan reached for Chloe's hand even before she had consciously acknowledged his presence on the terrace. Automatically she flinched, tried to pull away. He would be so angry, she knew, she could feel it coming.

'Look, let's sit over there on that balustrade for a moment.' He guided her across the terrace. 'Some fresh air will do you good, darling.'

'Aidan, wait.' She tried to stop her mind from spinning. Dimly she heard voices, and the heady-sweet breeze rustling through the leaves of a gnarly old wisteria that grew on the hill-side below them, bright little gusts that made it hard to properly absorb the fact that Aidan was actually here, at Summerhill.

'You don't need to say a thing, darling.' He gathered her close to him and, very gently, set her hand on his chest, covering it with his own. She could feel his breath against her hair and the thrum of his heart beneath her palm, and his voice was very light when it whispered in her ear, 'I've been so worried about you, sweetheart. You know that I love you above everything, and all that matters is that you're safe. I've been imagining you in a ditch somewhere, in a dead faint at the supermarket. Oh Chloe, it's such a weight off my mind that you're all right.'

'I left you a note,' she mumbled. 'I told you I was leaving.'

Her hand vibrated with his laughter. 'Of course you did, darling,' he said fondly, caressing the back of her hand with his thumb, his nail making a faint scratching sound on her skin.

'But you didn't say where you were going and when you'd be back. Thankfully Mr Cooper mentioned this place when I first talked to him. It took me a while to locate it, but I made it in the end . . . Ah, here they are now.'

Madeleine had appeared through the glass door just as Matt Cooper hurried around the corner of the house. Aidan held out his free hand in a friendly greeting, but Madeleine only looked at Chloe, anxiously searching her face for confirmation that she was all right. Chloe couldn't quite process what Aidan was doing. Shaking her head hard, she tried to focus on his face, smooth and golden in the evening sun, to make out his eyes properly above his wide smile.

'Mrs Hamilton.' His eyes flickered over Madeleine's misshapen right wrist and he gave her a courteous nod instead of a handshake. 'I'm sorry to barge in like this – I saw the path and I thought maybe you were all out on the terrace and hadn't heard me knock. I'm so very grateful to you for taking care of my wife. She's been ill, you know.'

'She's doing fine here,' Madeleine said evenly. 'You don't need to worry about her.'

Aidan held out his hand towards Matt. 'Aidan MacAllister. And you are . . . ?'

'Matt Cooper.' Matt's eyes went from Chloe's face to her hand, still in Aidan's.

'Ah, yes,' Aidan said quickly. 'Please, before anything else is said, let me apologise for our last phone conversation. I was unspeakably rude and I'm sorry. Caught off guard, end of a long day. And I do get a little overprotective of Chloe sometimes, you know.' He gave Matt a wry half-smile, followed by a self-deprecating shrug. 'But who can blame a man. The world's not always a safe place, is it?'

Matt nodded cautiously, and when Aidan pulled her even closer, his smile so rueful and disarming, his voice filled with such real, honest concern for her well-being, Chloe found herself leaning into his arm. Almost of their own accord, the twisted little knots of questioning and worry and fear about what she had done and what she would do from here started unspooling in her mind until a straight, clear path of action lay ahead, the way it did with everything that Aidan touched. Of course. The world was difficult. Maybe it really would be better for her to go home.

'You must be very proud of your wife,' she heard Matt say. 'She's a talented photographer. I personally cannot wait to see Mrs Hamilton's portraits.'

'I'm always proud of her.' Aidan's voice was pleasant. 'But it's getting late. We should call it a day, pick things back up tomorrow.'

Tomorrow, Chloe thought numbly. Aidan was still holding her hand, and his other hand slid down to the small of her back and stayed there, fingers splayed, pressed slightly into her flesh. *As if she might bolt*, a small voice suddenly said in her head, and involuntarily, she twitched. His grip on her hand tightened, his fingers thrust uncomfortably through hers, and a small zing of pain shot up her hand. It cut straight through the woolly feeling in her mind, that zing, bringing with it unwelcome memories. *You don't have to work, do you? You have me and the house.* And *No secrets.* And *I'm your family now. You and I belong together. For ever.*

And just like that, the fog in her mind stopped swirling.

Fifty-Six

Maddy

'Leave her alone, I said.'

Victor turned in surprise and I stumbled sideways, holding onto the edge of the balustrade. A figure was walking towards us, cradling his right arm awkwardly.

'Who are you?' Victor snapped. But then he frowned and looked more closely, gave an incredulous laugh. 'You're the missing airman. I don't believe it. Where've you had *him* stashed away then, Madeleine?'

'Maddy?' Georgiana said, sounding almost helpless now. 'What is going on?'

'William Davies, ma'am.' William spoke pleasantly enough, but he kept his eyes on Victor, well aware that he was at a decided disadvantage in this scenario. 'Leave her alone,' he told Victor again. 'Both of them.'

'It's no business of yours.' Victor laughed unpleasantly.

'Yes, it is.' William kept his eyes on Victor as he gave me a quick smile. 'You look beautiful. Just like I imagined. And I'm sorry about earlier.'

'Victor!' Georgiana said loudly, her face red. She had clearly decided to leave the issue of William appearing out of nowhere for the moment. 'I don't understand any of this. I'm so sorry about your brother, but why are you taking it out on Maddy? She was just a little girl when it happened.'

He looked at her for a long moment in silence. 'She refused to get into the boat, did you know that?' he said eventually. 'He was already dead, your father, right there on the rocks. She was still alive, though, and Jimmy, well, he just had to go and rescue her.' His voice was a low, faraway trickle, as if he wasn't here with us on the Summerhill terrace, but on a boat tilting and moving with the surf, watching his brother rescue a small girl off the cliffside.

'But she wouldn't let go of him; she had that man's hand gripped so hard that Jimmy couldn't prise her away, spent precious moments trying to persuade her. She'd rather have died too. And I wish she had,' he said, still in that horrible soft voice. 'I wish he'd left her there. But he finally got her off the rock and had her on his back, and then she was in the boat, but she was carrying on something fierce, the stupid girl, crying and hollering and kicking. And that's when it all went wrong. The tide had come up further, the surf was too strong; Jimmy was thrown against the rocks. He was fighting it until the very last moment. I could see him struggling to get back to the boat. I tried to help him, held out my hand for him; we threw him another rope. But it was no good. He hit his head, and right there, with my own eyes, I saw him disappear.'

He turned, looked straight into my face.

'If it wasn't for you, my brother would still be alive. My father would have been able to keep going, my mam would still be around. I wouldn't have left home at fourteen because I couldn't bear to be here any more. I went to live with my uncle, took his name and tried to move on. But I couldn't ever forget it. You destroyed my family that day, Madeleine, just because you wouldn't let go of a dead man's hand.'

'I . . .' In my mind, wind was roaring in my ears, salty and wet, the water rushing and breaking just below my feet. Dimly I felt William put his hand in mine, squeeze it, and the heat of his touch, the connection of my cold fingers with his warm ones, made me suddenly remember. The boat in the distance. I had shouted for them until my throat was sore and my voice broke and the boat had blurred in front of my eyes. But most of all, I remembered that hand reaching for me, pulling at me. And yes, it was the truth, I had fought against it the moment I realised that he wouldn't take both of us. I'd hit him and screamed when he took me off the cliffside, and again when he pushed me into the boat. And then, suddenly, he had slid backwards again, and into the water.

My skin tightened into a hard band around my throat and I struggled for breath as I remembered the way he'd fought the water, reaching out for something to hold onto, missing the rope over and over again. And then, the knowledge of what was to come dawning on his face . . .

I clapped my hand over my mouth, anything to stop the horror, the feeling of dread, of abject fear. 'Oh God, Victor,' I pushed out. 'I don't know what to say, except that I'm sorry, so very sorry . . .'

He put his head to one side, studied me, his face dispassionate in the moonlight. Then he smiled. 'You don't matter to me any more. I've thought about you for so long but now I've finished with you. I'm going to marry your sister. She wasn't part of the plan to begin with; it was you I wanted. Always you. But when I realised how close you were, how much you depended on her, how much she loved you . . .'

When he turned to Georgiana, his expression was so calm it looked almost deranged. She stared at him, her face ashen.

'How can I possibly marry you, Victor?' she said hoarsely. 'Maddy, I'm so sorry . . .'

'Be reasonable, darling.' Victor smiled. 'You have no money, your house is falling apart. Oh, I've done my research; what do you think I've been doing for the last six years? Jonathan is waiting in the wings. He's just in raptures over the place. And now you're having a baby, *my* baby. A life for a life, how's that for justice?'

'Victor, listen to me,' I said desperately. 'I'm sorry for your brother's death, sorrier than I can ever say, but if you have any feelings for Georgiana at all, then leave her alone. James—'

'I told you not to say his name.' He hissed the words through clenched teeth. 'You stupid little girl, I would rather die myself than give up now. I'm taking her away, and you'll be alone, homeless, forever alone . . .'

Then, suddenly, incoherent with rage, he came for me. The terrace was razor-edged and sharp in the moonlight, angles and corners jumping out at me as I stumbled backwards and found myself trapped against the balustrade, right where Laney and Jonathan had danced together just a couple of days ago. I shook my head, momentarily distracted by the memory, so that, when Victor's body connected with mine, I lost my balance.

I half turned, buckling at the knees, and he flew past me, straight across the balustrade. At the last moment, his hand shot out. Scrabbling at the air, it found my right arm and closed around my wrist.

Fifty-Seven

Chloe

'Aidan, I'm not coming home with you,' Chloe said in a low, hoarse voice. She tried to pull her hand free.

'Darling, of course you are.' Aidan shook his head as if she'd said something profoundly silly.

'Let go of her,' Madeleine said. 'She's staying here.'

'Here?' Aidan laughed. On the surface, the sound was still pleasant, but his eyes had flattened a little. 'Don't be absurd, you can't possibly have a pregnant woman living down here. What if something happens, darling?' His grip tightened around Chloe's fingers and she gave a strangled cry of pain.

'Enough!' Matt reached for Chloe's arm. 'You need to leave, Mr MacAllister.'

'And afterwards, where will you live with the baby?' Aidan continued as if Matt hadn't spoken. 'It needs a proper home, two parents. You have to have money to raise a child. You have none of those things, Chloe.'

Aidan half turned away from Matt, who was hovering next to them, clearly unsure of what to do. Her husband's face seemed relaxed, his voice was soft, gentle almost, but his teeth were set so hard that little ridges were visible on the smooth skin along his jaw, and the strange glint in his eyes sent a shiver down Chloe's back.

'Aidan,' she said, very quietly so as not to disturb whatever she could see in those eyes, 'I will make it work, I promise you. The baby will have everything it needs. It's us that doesn't work.

I'm sorry that you could never trust me. I wish I could have made you see how much I loved you. With all my heart. But I can't carry on like this, and I won't have our baby go through it.'

'And suppose the baby is like Danny?' Aidan dropped his voice further, so it was barely a whisper between them. 'What if it's ill and suffering? If it's born only to die, just like Danny will.'

Involuntarily, a breath caught in Chloe's throat. Aidan heard it, and a small, triumphant smile flashed across his face. 'See? So let's just put all this nonsense behind us and go home.'

'No.' Chloe clenched her teeth and moved back as far as his grip on her hand allowed. 'The baby will be fine. But if it is sick, then I will manage. I managed before I met you, and I was good at it, too. I'm leaving you, Aidan. I'm going to file for divorce, and if you try to stop me I will fight you with everything I have, so help me God.'

She didn't think she'd shouted the last bit, but she must have, because Aidan's mask of composed amiability finally slipped.

'Stop being stupid,' he hissed. 'We're going.'

He jerked her towards the glass door and managed to drag her a few paces across the flagstones before she dug her heels in. 'I'm not coming,' she insisted.

Her hand was turning white in his vice-like grip but she ignored the pain shooting up into her arm and pushed her whole weight backwards, pulling him with her.

'Please, Aidan, give it up,' she begged. 'If you take me now, I'll run again, and I will do it over and over again. Just let me go.' She bucked against his hand, trying to use her body weight to free herself, but he was still holding onto her when suddenly—

'STOP!'

Sometimes, when Chloe thought about this moment afterwards, she was convinced it was she herself who'd shouted the word, because through the pain and the effort of trying to move backwards, be free, all that stood out in her mind was how to make it stop. Make the pain stop and Aidan stop and her life in the empty white house stop. But actually, it was Madeleine, whose face had suddenly appeared at the periphery of Chloe's vision, her hand pointing at something behind her, and when Chloe turned, she saw, just a few feet behind her, a large gap in the balustrade.

'Aidan!' she screamed.

And Aidan finally let go of her hand.

Chloe fell backwards, groping uselessly at the empty air, desperate to find anything that would break her momentum. But her balance was off and her feet couldn't get any traction on the gritty flagstones as she slid towards the edge of the terrace. The moment splintered into fragments. The jagged, crumbling edges of the broken balustrade. The sound of footsteps and endless, horrible screaming. Madeleine's face distorted in wordless horror as she fumbled in vain for Chloe's hand. And then there was a strangled cry and Aidan's body came out of nowhere, diving at her. Driving his shoulder hard into her armpit, he pushed her sideways, away from the gap. As she hit the ground, she was dimly aware of Aidan tumbling over her, and then a sickening thump as his head connected with the stone.

Fifty-Eight

Maddy

Victor's hand gripped my wrist so hard I was lifted off the ground, and for the briefest of seconds, we were both airborne. But even as I registered it, gravity reached for us. He was still holding onto my wrist, clinging to it with the kind of desperation that came with mortal terror as he hung above the steep drop of the hill. I heard a scream, and then there was a crack that reverberated through my body as my bones snapped under the pressure, and still he held on, because there was nothing else for him to do. Pain shot up my arm like I hadn't ever felt before. It flooded my entire being and I felt myself give in to it, knew I had to follow that pain, and I started sliding across the balustrade after Victor.

I knew this place so well, knew the steepness of the fall, that my mind immediately realised what was going to happen and tried to stop it, flailing and kicking to keep me from slipping. The screaming continued, and I wasn't sure who was making it, this horrible, shrill sound, but suddenly someone was on top of me, pinning me against the low wall. The scent of violets filled my nostrils, soft skin on the nape of my neck, a cheek against mine.

Below me, Victor's face twisted in relief and he tried to pull himself up on my wrist in order to reach the top of the wall with his other hand. I screamed again, the pain so searing I thought I would break in half. Startled, he fell back, and then his hand started sliding along my wrist, his grasp slowly, inevitably opening wider as it reached my palm, which was slick and slippery with sweat.

Suddenly, another hand came into view, reached down. A mighty pull, another scream, and then William's good hand found Victor's, and my arm was lighter than air.

Victor clawed his way up the outside of the balustrade, scrabbling for a hold, half losing his grip, and William leaned over to help, although he was awkward with his injured arm. And then, I think what happened was that William lost his balance. Or maybe Victor's grip on the balustrade was too desperate and he pulled too hard. Forever after, I was never sure what actually happened. All I knew was that William gave another mighty tug on Victor's arm. Georgiana, still on top of me, held out her hand to him. And then, suddenly, there was the sound of crumbling stone and a small shout – not a loud one, more of a gasp of astonishment – as a whole section of the balustrade gave way.

It's not safe . . .

The very last thing I saw was my sister's face between the pieces of broken wall, her mouth open in surprise. I wanted to remember it, I wanted to recall it for ever. But it blurred at the edges and went hazy, and then I was pulled back and connected with the flagstones of the terrace and everything went black.

Fifty-Nine

Chloe

'Oh God, oh God, oh God . . .'

Blood roared in Chloe's ears and black spots danced at the edge of her vision, which had narrowed down to a dark tunnel, at the end of which lay her husband, crumpled and still on the ground next to the balustrade. She was shaking too much to actually make it to her feet, so she scrambled away from the gap on all fours, her face sticky with blood where she'd skinned her cheek and neck.

'Aidan . . .' She formed the words with some difficulty. Matt Cooper, his craggy face ashen under his stubble, was crouching next to him, holding his wrist.

'He crashed into the wall head first,' he said hoarsely. 'He pushed you away from that gap, but it all happened so fast, I couldn't even . . .' His voice trailed away.

'You're bleeding, child, you're hurt.' Madeleine was bending down to Chloe, touching her face with trembling hands.

'I'm fine, it's just a graze.' Chloe winced as she leaned over her husband. 'Aidan, can you hear me? Aidan!'

Aidan twitched and groaned, moved, groaned louder, went still. His eyelids flickered.

'Don't move any more,' Matt said urgently, fumbling for his phone. 'You've hurt your head, your back possibly. Yes, hello? We need an ambulance . . . yes, immediately . . . Here, Madeleine, tell them how best to get here.'

Madeleine's voice was tremulous at first as she gave directions, but when she came to the last bit, she spoke more confidently and quite loudly. 'And we need a police officer here, too. As soon as possible.'

At this, Aidan's eyes opened. He looked up at Madeleine, then at Matt, who raised his eyebrows. Finally his gaze came to rest on Chloe's face.

'You're all right?' His voice was faint and a bit breathless. He frowned as he flicked his eyes across her body, her stomach, taking in the grazes on her face.

'Yes, I think so,' she said. 'The ambulance is on its way.'

He started to nod, then thought better of it. 'The hospital,' he said instead. 'You'll come?'

'Yes, of course,' she said automatically, but when she saw the tiniest hint of a smile push his mouth up, she bent forward, suppressing a groan at the pain in her ribs, where Aidan's shoulder had pushed her out of the way, and looked him straight in the eye. 'I will come to the hospital. I will make sure that you're all right. I will help you as much as I can. But as for the rest – nothing has changed between us. Nothing *will* change. I want you to understand that. Whatever happens.'

The smile, if it had been there at all, faded and he looked at her for a long time before closing his eyes.

The hours that followed were a blur of hospital corridors and tests. The doctor tending to Chloe picked gravel and sand out of her grazes, lingering on the bright splotches on the back of her hand and the matching finger-shaped bruises on her wrist, those a much fainter yellowish green. He probed her ribs, pronounced them possibly bruised but not broken, and then insisted on keeping her under observation for the night, something she wanted to resist at first but then gave in to gratefully, because she didn't think she could possibly ever move again, and because listening to her baby's heartbeat on the monitor as she lay on the narrow bed was the most comforting, soothing thing she'd done in a while.

Aidan was concussed and had broken his shoulder in three places. It wasn't clear yet how long he'd have to stay in hospital, and even less clear what would happen then. There had already been questions. From doctors. A hospital social worker called Mandy. A policewoman with a weather-beaten face who looked as though she'd be more at home out on the water than crouching opposite Chloe as they watched the paramedics bend over her husband on the terrace. What had happened? What *exactly* had happened? How long had she been married? Why had she been at Summerhill? Why had *he* come to Summerhill? What was her relationship to Mrs Hamilton? To Mr Cooper?

Chloe had hedged, partly because she couldn't face thinking about it, partly because it was one of those things that, once out, could never be taken back, and had finally asked the policewoman if she could talk to her properly in the morning. But now, watching her baby's heartbeat zigzag across the green paper of the monitor, there was nothing to do but think. Over and over again she felt her body arch backwards, straining against Aidan's grip, which was going to pull her away from Summerhill and back into his life. Madeleine's shout. The sudden release. And then the impact of his body on hers. He'd saved her life, a life that wouldn't ever have needed saving if it hadn't been for him holding on to her, the way he always had, so close. Too close . . .

She drifted into sleep, jerking awake occasionally, a spike of adrenaline leaving her breathless with panic, then fading back into unconsciousness.

She woke to bright light filtering through orange curtains, and a soft scratching noise. When she turned her head, she saw Madeleine Hamilton sitting in Danny's wheelchair next to the bed. She was holding a sketchpad, braced awkwardly across the armrest of the chair, and her pencil was moving slowly across the page.

'You're drawing again,' Chloe said hoarsely.

Madeleine looked up quickly. 'Oh, just some scribbles. I had forgotten how soothing it is. How are you feeling?'

'Like I've been raked across hot coals.' Chloe pulled herself upright with a groan and looked around for her clothes. 'How are you? Surely you haven't been here all night?'

'Just a little while. The nurse looked in on you. She took the monitor away, said the doctor would be round eventually and then you'd be free to go. You slept through all that, and through some child kicking up a racket down the hall. Matt is around somewhere, too, trying to track down a decent cup of tea. Chloe, child, are you sure you should be getting up? Just wait for the doctor . . .'

'I have to find Aidan, talk to him if I can.' Chloe gingerly pulled on her T-shirt, wincing as it slid over grazed and bruised patches of skin. 'And then to the police again, if I have to,' she added in an undertone. At the thought, her legs suddenly felt rubbery and her stomach churned, and she decided to sit back down and breathe deeply.

'You should press charges,' Madeleine said quietly. 'If only for the sake of starting a record, for the future. Because he won't ever leave you in peace, not you, not the baby.'

Chloe rubbed her face and stared ahead, fixing on a snail-like whorl in the linoleum to quiet the roiling in her stomach. 'Yes,' she said tiredly. 'I know.'

'You should ask for copies of your medical notes, too, before you leave. And I brought this.' Madeleine reached around the back of the wheelchair and unhooked Chloe's backpack. When she opened it, there, on the top, was Chloe's camera. 'I thought I could . . . you know . . . help you take pictures. Of your injuries. Your wrist and hand.'

Chloe stared at her. 'Good God, Madeleine,' she finally said.

She had cried hardly at all during the last few hours, but now, looking at her Nikon in Madeleine's hands, she suddenly felt a sting of tears. That a marriage and a pregnancy, with all their promises of joy and love, could boil down to this, to taking close-ups of bruises in a shabby hospital room: it filled her not with rage or fear but with a sense of desolation so profound that for a moment she couldn't breathe.

'Chloe.' The older woman's voice was gentle. 'If you're not ready, then . . .'

Chloe pulled up the sleeves of her T-shirt and held out her hands.

'I have to be, don't I?' she said bleakly. 'That button there will take the picture.'

Sixty

When Matt came in, a little while later, he found the two women sitting in silence. Chloe's eyes were very red and she was clutching her camera in her lap as Madeleine patted her leg. He looked from one to the other and gingerly lowered himself down next to the backpack on Chloe's bed, handing her a cup of tea.

'God, hospitals give me the creeps,' he said, clearing his throat. 'But I've been busy, you'll be pleased to hear. Checked on your husband – lovely nurse at the desk sent me away at first, told me I wasn't related, but I got her to part with a few important details in the end.'

Madeleine raised her eyes to the ceiling. 'Must be your excellent social skills,' she said.

'Well, there's definitely going to be more surgery on his shoulder – he managed to break or rip something really complicated in several places. Sounded ghastly, I really did feel for him, poor man. Months of rehab coming up, I'm sure. And they were running some more tests on his head. His mother is arriving later today. The nurse didn't seem to be looking forward to *that* event: something about her bringing her own sheets and the doctor having to be available the instant she arrived. Oh, and the police left a message asking you to call. I can drive you to the station if you like.'

Chloe wiped her eyes and he studied her.

'You'll be all right,' he said finally. 'Take a while, but you'll get there.'

'Yes.' She fiddled with the buttons on her Nikon.

He nodded at the camera. 'Impressive work ethic, by the way. The light's lovely in here.' He nudged her leg and she smiled obediently but didn't look up, just drank her tea in small, methodical sips.

'They were back at Summerhill this morning,' Matt suddenly said. 'The police. We left them looking around on the terrace. I wonder why they're so interested. I mean, your husband might have wanted to do many things yesterday, insane man that he is . . .' He raised his eyebrows at Chloe. 'But it's not like he was going to murder you or anything.'

Chloe flinched and slopped tea down her front.

'Mr *Cooper*!' Madeleine said sharply. 'That is more than enough. You're banned from speaking for at least thirty minutes. Honestly! And that's not why they're still there,' she added, more quietly now. 'It's because . . . well, someone else died in that very same spot, seventy years ago. No wonder they're a bit suspicious.'

Chloe stared at her. 'What do you mean?' she said faintly.

'Remember Victor, my sister's beau?' She said the word in the same mocking way she had under the oak tree. 'He'd come to Summerhill with one purpose only, and that was to destroy us. He'd sought out Georgiana during her travels, engineered a meeting, courted her. Very successfully, too. He pushed between me and Georgie, set us against each other. Because what he really wanted was to hurt me. He held me responsible for the death of his brother.'

'And were you?' Chloe asked cautiously.

Madeleine didn't answer for a long time.

'Yes, I was,' she said at last. 'His brother did an immeasurably kind thing. He rescued a little girl and he paid the highest price for it. I can never make that right. And so Victor did the only thing he could: he tried to take Georgiana from me. A life for a life, that's what he said. And he succeeded, because it wasn't him who ended up dying on that terrace . . .'

She fell silent, and for a moment Chloe wasn't sure if she was going to speak again.

'It was Georgiana.'

Chloe gasped. For a moment, she felt a sharp, burrowing pain as the connection between herself and Georgiana was severed, and her eyes filled with tears again. She'd known Georgiana had been dead all along, she reminded herself, blinking hard. Matt had told her so. But the vividness of her features in Madeleine's drawing, the immediacy of her words on the page, which seemed to be talking to Chloe and Chloe alone: part of her had always pictured Georgiana exactly like that.

'Her name was on the books,' she said, stricken. 'I just imagined she'd died not too long ago.' She wasn't sure how she could put into words the kinship she'd felt with Georgiana, the inexplicable connection, but when she caught Madeleine's eye, she thought that maybe the older woman knew. 'She was so young,' Chloe finished, fumbling for a tissue. 'What happened?'

'We argued, he pushed me and the balustrade broke.' She swallowed. 'He fell across, hung on for dear life, right above the drop. And when Georgiana and William tried to get him back across the wall, a huge piece broke off. She fell through the gap.'

Madeleine looked down at her hands, the healthy one stroking the twisted one gently. 'It really was a life for a life in the end. My sister for his brother.'

'Oh, Madeleine,' Chloe whispered. She leaned forward and looked into the older woman's face. 'I'm so sorry.' She flicked her eyes across to Matt Cooper, whose head was tilted to the side a little, his face very sad.

'It happened a long time ago,' Madeleine said quietly. 'But I've never stopped thinking about Georgiana, not for one single day. We'd parted in anger, you see.' She took a deep, shaky breath, her good hand fiddling with the edge of Danny's little Superman pillow.

'Tell me,' Chloe said.

Sixty-One

Maddy

William's face was the first thing I saw when I opened my eyes. For just a moment, I felt warm stone underneath my shoulders and could smell the night air all around us, and I might even have smiled at him; in fact I must have, because I was so very glad to see him, so sure everything would be all right now. William would speak to his father and I would finally introduce him to Georgiana and . . . But then I moved, and his face fell, and I knew that Georgiana was gone.

My right arm was nothing but screaming pain and I could see bones pushing through the skin. I struggled upright, still in my stupid green-blue dress, crying and gasping for breath all at the same time, and William stayed close as I braced myself against the terrace wall. My mind was slipping and sliding all over the place, desperate to push the unspeakable horror away from me, outside my Summerhill heart, which was meant to keep me and my sister safe. But the pain kept me right there, standing by the wall and looking down at my sister's body as I listened to Victor pacing the terrace behind me, shouting accusations and lies about how I had meant to kill him, had killed his baby, had killed my own sister, until Frank got hold of him and eventually he was silent. His silence distracted me, and I looked over my shoulder to see Cookie running towards me, Hobson in her wake, and Susan, too, her face ashen. I breathed through the pain and my mind stopped sliding for a moment because I could see the truth in their faces, their shock and grief, as down below, people bent to pick up Georgiana's body, covering her with a blanket and carrying her up the hill.

I kept looking for her everywhere, my eyes automatically tracking the moving shapes around me for my tall, beautiful sister, who would surely soon be here to talk to the constable and the doctor; who would get Aunt Marjorie to stop making that hideous noise and lie down; who'd smile at William and promise to come and talk to him properly once she'd sorted out the mayhem. For the briefest moment I would hold my breath as hope surged through me, because at any moment she would have to appear. But with the exhale, the hope faded and died, until the next breath came and brought another flicker. It was a constant ebb and flow of hope and despair, and it didn't stop, even when I woke up in hospital the following morning, fuzzy with pain and medication, and immediately looked around for Georgiana. Instead, it was Susan's face I saw. And then William, both perched awkwardly on stools next to my bed.

'Oh, Miss Maddy.' Susan bit her lip and twisted her hands in her lap. 'You . . . How is your wrist?'

I studied it indifferently, noticed that it thrummed with pain, then shrugged because it didn't really feel as if it belonged to me at all.

'Hobson and Frank are taking care of everything at the house, and Cookie is coming any minute now with your things,' Susan said breathlessly. 'Your aunt is lying down. Mrs Claxton is staying with her.' She broke off and looked down at her hands.

'And Mr Deverill is . . . Well, he'll be gone by the time you get home,' William said quietly. 'He's been distraught. Obviously. As we all are. I'm so sorry, Maddy, so very sorry.'

In a detached sort of way I watched Susan's eyes well up with tears and heard William clear his throat repeatedly. Home. To Summerhill. That felt even less real than being here, where the sun bounced sharply off the white sheets and gave the silver bed frames a hard, steely glint, and where a nurse could be seen at the far end of the ward sorting through a shallow bowl of instruments.

'Did you talk to your father?' I asked William, noting that my voice didn't really seem to be mine either; it was a cracked rasp pushed out through a throat that was raw and sandpapery, as if it had been screaming all night.

'Yes,' he said slowly. 'It took me a good while of walking around in your woods. But eventually I realised that you were right. I should have known all along. I'm sorry I shouted at you; I don't know what came over me.'

I nodded.

'I walked across the fields to the village and found him. Told him everything. It was quite awful, actually,' he said and looked down at his hand. 'He was so upset and disappointed. Not because of the flying so much,' he added with a grimace, 'but because I'd left my mam thinking I was dead. Said prison was too good for me.' He gave me a half-smile. 'But eventually he agreed to help me, with telling Hughes and whatever else will happen to me now.'

'I'm sure it'll be fine,' I said in the same remote voice. 'I'm glad you're reunited.'

He exchanged a glance with Susan, but I looked away from them, feeling strange and floaty, as if my body was barely touching the sheets. My arm was pounding fiercely now, and I felt a sheen of sweat break out on my forehead. 'It hurts,' I said faintly, when I couldn't ignore it any longer.

'Here's the nurse now,' Susan said, and William politely excused himself. Obediently I moved limbs and opened my mouth for inspection and answered questions, noting the sharp creases of the nurse's cap and the way the sun shone in Susan's wispy halo of hair. Dimly I heard voices talking, then a shout and the sound of footsteps hurrying back to us.

'Mr Davies,' the nurse's voice was crisp, 'I must ask you to wait outside. Please!'

I lifted my head and saw William standing at the foot of the bed, his face white, smudgy black circles under his eyes.

'Really, Mr Davies, I insist!' she hissed. But William ignored her.

'The prime minister's addressing the nation,' he said. 'On the wireless, just now.'

The nurse stopped what she was doing, and Susan jumped up from her chair, clapping her hand over her mouth in horror.

When William spoke again, his voice was choked. 'We are at war.'

Sixty-Two

Chloe

'At that very moment, when Neville Chamberlain declared war on Germany, at eleven o'clock on a beautiful Sunday morning in September, that's when I stopped looking around for Georgiana.' Madeleine gave Chloe a pained grimace. 'That's when life without my sister began. Three days, that's all it took to change everything . . .'

Chloe and Matt listened to Madeleine's account of those fateful three days in silence.

'Afterwards, Aunt Marjorie stayed at Summerhill until I was nineteen, although it was Susan and Hobson and Cookie who were truly there for me. They'd always been our real family, ever since our father had died, and weeks went by when I couldn't bear to be anywhere but in the kitchen with Cookie and Susan, or in the grounds with Frank. He and William patched up the terrace, but I never went back out there, in all the years. Well, you saw the state of it. Yesterday, when I saw the balustrade . . .'

She swallowed, then gave Chloe a determined smile. 'You know, you would have liked William, I think. He took it all in his stride, people talking about the way he had suddenly risen from the dead, and why he'd been hiding, and then the whole rigmarole of sorting out his situation. He'd been right, thank heavens, that they didn't execute deserters any more, but if he hadn't saved that other man's life, they would have court-martialled him, and then, who knows. After prolonged negotiations, he transferred into the army. He came back to Summerhill whenever he could, and at some point, although neither of us could actually remember when it had been decided – not properly, on one knee or anything – we got married.'

She opened her bag, rummaged for her purse. 'Here, that's us.'

Matt and Chloe both leaned in to look at the small black-and-white photo; saw a young Madeleine smiling up at the soberly uniformed but indecently happy man holding her hand.

'He's lovely.' Chloe smiled and touched the cap perched at a cheeky angle on his hair. 'I'm glad.'

'It wasn't much of a wedding, but then again, we were in the middle of a war. Frank had left and we didn't know if he was even still alive. But Hobson had dusted down his good suit, and Susan was a witness, and Cookie had somehow conjured up a wonderful wedding feast, despite the rationing. It was heavy on the cabbage, perhaps, but then so was all our food back then. After the war, none of us could stand even the smell of it.' She chuckled wryly, her eyes lingering on the picture. 'We opened Summerhill for convalescing soldiers towards the end of the war. Frank would have approved – about both the cabbage and the soldiers. He never did come back, Frank. But Lucy's husband did. And William as well, and I'll be forever grateful that I was granted that at least, half a lifetime with a man I loved.'

For a moment, the three of them sat in silence. The hospital had woken up around them, footsteps and voices and the clanking of what smelled like the food trolley.

'What happened to Victor?' Matt finally broke the silence.

Maddy sighed and carefully tucked the picture back into her purse. 'The rest of Georgie's friends went back to London. Unsurprisingly, Jonathan had lost interest in Summerhill. But Victor, I don't know, he just couldn't keep away. He tried to sue me – God knows for what; it was *my* sister who'd died – and he kept stirring up trouble in one way or another, even though by then the war started in earnest and no one had much time for a young woman who'd died in a tragic accident. Eventually he was called up. We later heard that he fell in France, but that he'd acquitted himself well, was decorated for bravery in battle. I wasn't surprised. He had a lot of rage. I was afraid of him and I sometimes still have nightmares about that moment on the terrace. But I also knew, probably better than anyone else, what grief can do to you.'

She paused. 'I decided to publish the stories in both our names. It seemed only right, because they were half Georgiana's after all. That was the other thing that kept me going, her writing. Her stubbornness and quirky sense of humour, her passion. The stories reminded me of her, of the way she'd been before Victor had got hold of her. And I've never stopped wishing, not for a single day, that I could have talked to her one last time. About our parents. About the two of us and what could have been different.'

Chloe turned to look at her backpack. She set down her camera carefully, then fumbled for her copy of *Foxy the Great* and opened it.

'Maybe you've already seen this. It was in her room that day I went looking for clothes.' She bit her lip and blushed. 'I know I shouldn't have taken it, I'm sorry. I would have returned it, I promise.'

Madeleine picked up the drawing of herself and Georgiana, then the folded gas-mask instructions, smiling slightly at the illustrations.

'Look on the other side,' Chloe said. 'She's trying to work out what to say. About the two of you, and perhaps about Summerhill.'

Silence fell again as Madeleine unfolded the paper and started reading. She took a long time, lingering over sentences, then rereading when she'd come to the end.

'I wish I had known,' she said finally, and her eyes were bright with tears, 'how much she worried about me. It's my own fault, though. I never listened.' She looked up at Chloe. 'All those years, I've seen her walking out of my room before the party started and I've heard her saying goodbye.' She looked down at the letter, wiped away tears before they could fall onto the loopy scrawl. 'Thank you,' she finally managed.

'There were more papers in that writing box.' Chloe took a deep breath. 'They helped me, too, made me see so many things I probably should have realised years ago, about Aidan and Danny and myself.'

Madeleine gave her hand a squeeze, then dabbed at her eyes with an ancient handkerchief.

'We're a fine pair, the two of us, you know,' she said in a choked voice.

'Do you think you'll be able to do another book, without her?' Chloe asked tentatively.

Matt cleared his throat, and the two women gave him a startled look, because he'd been so uncharacteristically quiet, they'd almost forgotten he was there.

'Frog in my throat,' he said, coughing slightly. 'All this sadness getting to me. Now, a book, on the other hand . . .'

'Oh, stop it,' Chloe said exasperatedly.

'Maybe I could.' Madeleine looked down at the drawing of two girls sitting at a kitchen table on a sunny afternoon seventy years ago. 'If you stuck around for a little while and helped me.'

Epilogue

It was a day straight out of *The Grand Adventures of Foxy the Great.* As Chloe got out of the car, the sky was the deep azure of the bluebells at Fairings Corner in springtime and the warm air smelled of apples ripening in the orchard.

'I brought more paper,' she called as she pushed open the front door. 'And some custard creams.'

Madeleine looked up from the desk and smiled. Pencils and pieces of paper were strewn across the old pocked surface and along the top of the sideboard next to it.

'How is Danny?' She stretched and flexed her hand, the small bones crackling as she straightened her fingers.

'Oh, fine. He's settled in so well at the new care home. It's not Oakwood, of course, but it's lovely and small, and a nice-sounding man has moved into the room next to him. And there's a view of the harbour. Masses going on all day down there. He loved the pages, by the way, and would like to see J, K and X tomorrow if possible. No pressure, eh?' Chloe grinned and deposited the shopping bag on the ground next to Madeleine's desk, then threw herself into the armchair and wiped her face. 'God, it's still so hot, isn't it? How're you getting on?'

Madeleine had decided to put together an ABC book featuring new drawings of all her old characters. It wasn't going to set the world on fire, but she was hoping that inspiration for a new book might strike at some point in the process.

'Here.' She held up a rough sketch of Foxy tugging on a sausage, while a small dog was stubbornly holding onto the other end. 'I thought it could be "eXcited".'

Chloe laughed. 'That's called cheating,' she said reprovingly.

She sighed and reached into the bag for the biscuits. 'I think I deserve one of these right now. Aidan's solicitor cancelled the meeting we had scheduled for tomorrow. I swear that baby will be finishing uni before we've agreed on even the basics. Still, one step at a time, I suppose. Baby steps in Aidan's case, ha!'

'That man,' Madeleine said, which was what she always said when Aidan's name came up. She frowned at her drawing.

'Madeleine, it looks fab.' Chloe got up from the chair. 'All of them are gorgeous. Even *he* won't have anything to complain about.'

Matt Cooper's long frame came striding past the window, swinging a toolbox. He had taken to dropping in over the past few weeks, ostensibly to check on the two of them, but really, Madeleine said, to breathe down her neck until she was so terrified she would do anything to make it stop.

'Are you ready?' He came into the library with a jaunty swing in his step.

'Matt, it'll be ready when it's ready, honestly,' Chloe said.

'You've been saying that for days now,' Matt said. 'But for a change, I don't mean that infernal book. The boat's waiting, ladies. How about we take her out for a spin?'

He had started repairing the old boat in the garage and, as Chloe had muttered to Madeleine, proved surprisingly nifty for someone so amazingly impatient. He'd cleaned and oiled the motor, patched up a leak in the side and generally tinkered until the boat was seaworthy. He'd acquired a rugged tan in the process, and the weekends off seemed to do him good, because his bark had softened gradually into something approaching a normal human voice.

'I'm going to pass,' Madeleine said quickly.

'You'll be fine. Meet those demons head-on, I'd say.' He beamed at her.

'I've been ruing the day I ever told you about my demons,'

she said darkly. But when he practically bounced on the spot with excitement, she sighed. 'Oh, all right, then.'

Matt manhandled the wheelchair through the orchard with so much enthusiasm that he almost sent Madeleine spilling down the hill, while Chloe trailed behind carrying the picnic and her camera. He then expertly manoeuvred Madeleine into the boat from the little jetty at the bottom of the garden, ignoring her empty threat that she would go right back up to the house if he didn't stop treating her like a piece of baggage. Finally he held out a hand to Chloe.

'Come, my dear lady, let's go to sea.'

The motor cooperated, bar an occasional disgruntled sputtering, which ceased almost immediately under Matt's quelling frown, and they chugged out into the middle of the river before turning in a long, lazy arc and heading towards the bay, where the warm inland air turned sharper and the breeze picked up.

Madeleine had fallen silent. Her good hand gripped the railing so tightly that her knuckles stood out, but her face was calm. Chloe didn't speak either, just sat watching the seagulls squawking indignantly as the wind blew them across the sky, the sound of the water growing louder and more restless the further out into the bay they got. Keeping a safe distance from the shoreline, Matt steered them around Hangman's Bluff, where they could see waves crashing across a small sandy cove in the distance.

'It looks smaller,' Madeleine said wonderingly. 'So much smaller from out here.'

Matt was wrestling with the boat, cursing softly when the tiller got stuck. He barked a command back at Chloe, so she was distracted and only caught the movement out of the corner of her eye as Madeleine extracted a piece of paper from her pocket. Keeping her hands in her lap, the old lady quietly smoothed it out and looked at it for a long moment before extending her hand above the water and letting go. The wind blew it forward, playing with it for a few seconds before it bore the paper away, but it was just long enough for Chloe to see two figures, sitting close and smiling, their hands intertwined.

Author's Note

When I started thinking about *Summer of Secrets*, I wanted to write a novel about love. Not a love story, but rather a novel about the many things love can turn out to be: the wonderful promise of romance, the newness of discovery, the deep attachment of caring for someone. And its dark side: emotional dependence fuelled by fear. Possession and control. Cruelty. Violence.

The three women in my story are all driven by love, but, as in real life, it is never simple: Georgiana, coping with the loss of her parents, has to become a mother to her sister at fifteen years old. The trauma of witnessing her father's death has made Maddy emotionally dependent on her beloved sister. But it is Chloe's story that was the most painful and at the same time the most important for me to explore: that fluid borderland when a relationship turns into a prison, when emotional attachment becomes abuse cloaked in love, when joy becomes fear. Chloe cannot bring herself to accept or even to fully recognise what her marriage has become. She is determined to work at it, to take the good with the bad, and has already changed herself to match the change in the person she thought she had married. And poignantly, through it all, she still clings on to hope, that wonderfully redemptive power in us all that enables us not only to change but to endlessly endure.

The Office for National Statistics in the UK estimates that one in four women is subject to domestic violence in her lifetime and that each year well over one million women experience incidents of domestic abuse. Horrifying as these statistics may seem, official numbers will never even come close to truly representing the extent of the situation. Too much of it happens behind closed doors, is hidden and suffered alone, in a spiral of self-blame, shame and silence from which it seems impossible to break free.

Many women, especially those who experience emotional or psychological hurt rather than actual violence, might never truly recognise the reality of their everyday life as abuse, even though it can be every bit as devastating as its physical counterpart. Being isolated from friends and family, kept from working and from having any kind of financial control. Being told what to wear and how to act, who to see and where to go. Being threatened and intimidated, bullied and manipulated until you are convinced of your own worthlessness. All that is an emotional hell of its own, but it wasn't until 2013 that the government broadened existing definitions of domestic abuse as one act or incident of violence to include patterns of controlling behaviour. And it wasn't until the Serious Crime Act 2015 that 'controlling or coercive behaviours in intimate or familial relationships' were finally labelled an actual criminal offence, punishable by law.

Within my fictional universe, I had the option to set Chloe on a path of self-awareness and to follow her as she gains strength and finally escapes from her controlling, destructive marriage. But too many women are unable to turn their hope for a better future into the difficult decision to end the spiral of self-loathing and fear. And all too few then go on to report it, to start the painful process of coming out into the open and breaking, what is still for many, an unspoken taboo. More education at a younger age is needed about the reality of domestic abuse, more professional training for those involved in dealing with victims, a clearer look at ways to help, and less judgement when a woman finally comes out of the darkness to ask for it.

While many of the issues in the story are real, some devastatingly so, all of the characters that live through them are purely a product of my imagination. Similarly, while an effort has been made to respect geography-at-large, the setting has been adapted to the needs of the plot. Summerhill does not exist and neither does the cove, Hangman's Bluff, or the coastline around them. What does exist, however, is a corner of the world that is one of the most beautiful and magical places I know. Cornwall's coastline is stunning almost everywhere, but if Summerhill did exist, then it would most likely be found in the lovely stretch between Helston and Plymouth. Here, towering cliffs and sandy coves alternate with the lush, verdant landscape of tidal rivers and creeks; a beautiful, often mysterious and always changing landscape where it sometimes really does feel as if you've come to the very ends of the earth.

If first novels are hard to write, then second books are even harder, and I couldn't have done it without the amazing help, guidance and all-round brilliance of the team at Headline and my wonderful agency Hardman & Swainson. As ever, thanks also to my family and friends for providing such a rich canvas of stories, encouragement and laughter; and finally, to my husband and boys, who are a daily inspiration and, always, a joy.

Don't miss Nikola Scott's unforgettable first novel, *My Mother's Shadow*.

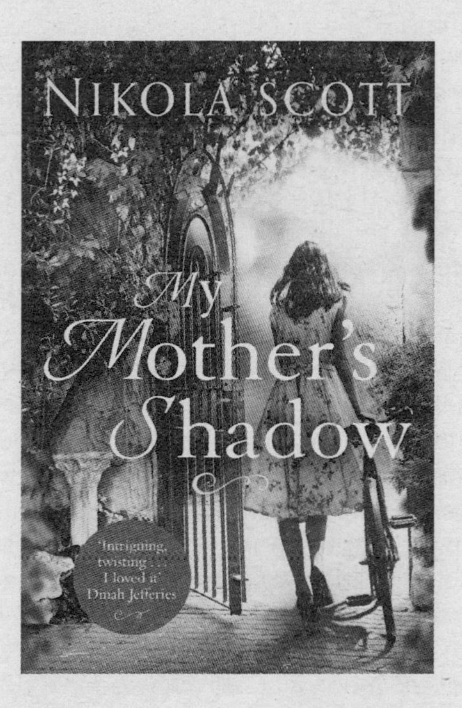

A perfect summer. A young woman in love. And a shocking secret kept for decades.

Turn the page to read the opening chapters . . .

1958

There are many things this house has seen and many secrets it has heard, whispered things in the night that drift on the breeze and curl around chimneys and slate-covered gables, mullioned windows and white pebbled paths, wind their way through roses and rhododendrons and the trees of the old Hartland orchard. Loves found and lost, the pain of unexpected death and the deliciousness of forbidden trysts. Midnight tears and laughter in summer nights, all the dreams to be dreamed and all the worlds to be found. The house has kept them, without question, without judgement, preserving them in the shadows of its walls.

And these days, life at Hartland is rife with memories. The war, and the death it brought, is still fresh in everyone's minds. It's not been so very long, after all, since England came out of the bleak years of rationing, bombed-out houses and Nissen huts, blinking against the unexpected onslaught of new luxuries and sweets in the sweet shop and jangly new music everywhere. But the future is bright now, and so it's little wonder that they grasp at life with both hands, these young people of 1958, that this country house summer has made them all a little giddy with the promise of having it all.

Or maybe it's the moon that has made people giddy tonight, the way it hangs in the sky as if pinned there, low above the stables and bursting full with a strange orange light. You only need to look at it, you only need to taste the champagne prickling against the roof of your mouth and smell the heady scent from the rose garden, and you'll feel a pull at the bottom of your stomach, a reckless moon-madness that speaks of endless possibilities, of making the world your own. Lanterns are strung up all around, waving and twinkling in the evening breeze like so many coloured fireflies, and 'Magic Moments' is crooning around the couples swaying and laughing and smoking, perched on the low walls of the terrace with gimlets and lemonade to cool flushed cheeks. One of the girls hired to help for the evening stops to watch as she tops up the lemonade pitchers and punchbowls, sets out a new platter with puff pastry squares, marvelling at these golden young men and women who seem to have no care in the world other than to celebrate a seventeenth birthday, to cheer on a young girl's entrance into adulthood.

Two people are missing, though, two have slipped away from the terrace, made their way past a croquet mallet lying forgotten among the rhododendrons, down garden paths and through the trees, hands across mouths to hold back laughter and the occasional gasp as a stray branch hits the backs of bare legs. One is the birthday girl, seventeen today, who has in her short life already known too much heartbreak and for whom much worse is still to come. But tonight the girl has shed all her worries and fears, and she knows, deep down, that life can never ever be as deliciously forbidden, as wonderfully new as this summer night. So yes, she, too, is grasping at life with both hands, and who can blame her, holding on to the hand of a man who's been smiling at her for days, lazy, bemused smiles with drops of sea-water clinging to his lashes, wide innocent grins when others were watching, and secret, promising eyes when they had a brief moment alone in the Hartland rose garden. She can't see the smile in his eyes tonight, only moonlight and firefly lanterns, but she can feel him close to her, so close that his skin is warm against her arm and the smell of him mingles with that of freshly mown grass and the darker, more mysterious night smells of a garden unwilling to be disturbed, even for a first love as urgent as this one. Here, among the trees in the orchard, the air is cooler and involuntarily the girl shivers, and that's when he slips his arms around her and gathers her close, tips her face up with his other hand, and in this one single moment, life is perfect.

But already, and the house knows this, trouble is in the air, and the golden facade of this perfect summer, the glow of the heady, fragrant night, is about to be tainted. The house has always been a faithful keeper of all its secrets, and so it won't now give away what lies ahead. Instead, it takes the fleeting memories of a girl's first love, to keep them safe forever.

Chapter One

Death is a funny thing. Not *funny* funny, obviously, and really not funny at all, but strange. By rights, it should come with a bang, announcing its cataclysmic blow with machine gun harbingers of doom; instead it sneaks up like a thief, waiting for a too-eager foot stepping out into a traffic light or that single rebellious cell in our bodies that suddenly decides to start its devastating multiplication. Death always watches, biding its time until it strikes, and when it does, nothing will ever be the same.

Given the disproportionate awfulness of death, I don't remember much at all about the day my mother was hit by a lorry. Disjointed little bits, maybe, like the absurd amount of glass the lorry had showered across Gower Street and my father's pinched face as we waited for the taxi that would take us to her body; my sister Venetia arguing with the policewoman who, surely, had made a mistake, and was no one doing their jobs properly anymore?

The one thing I do remember, very clearly, was the moment I was told about it, because it was in this moment – I was standing in front of the dairy fridge holding sixty-five eggs for the day's meringues – that all the tears I might have cried vanished, and my eyes suddenly and inexplicably dried up. And dry they remained, through weeks filled with coroner's statements and my mother's favourite Countess roses on her coffin and making sure my father got up each morning over at the big, now-empty house on Rose Hill Road; all throughout, I never once shed a tear.

Some people simply don't cry very much, so this in itself was perhaps not a true measure of one's grieving abilities, but I had never been one of those people. On the contrary, I used to be particularly good at crying, in fact, it was one of the things I excelled at. When I was little, I cried so often and so readily that my mother claimed my body had to be made up of two-thirds salt water. My very own vale of tears, she said. I cried over molars accidentally flushed down the sink and white spots at the back of my throat, I worried about what lurked in my wardrobe and under my bed and at the bottom of the swimming pool. I followed stray cats and collected baby birds that had fallen out of their nests and wrestled with their fates for days.

For heaven's sake, Addie, my mother would say and push a handkerchief my way, twitching impatiently when my eyes got big and shiny and my throat was working to swallow back those sobs that were so weak and futile when one should be strong, square one's shoulders, get on with things. *Buck up, darling. Look at Venetia, four years younger and you don't see* her *cry.* I must have been an immensely exasperating child, because so many things about me brought forth that twitch on my mother's face, a sort of lifting of one cheek and compressing of her lips into small, white folds, that I'd started hiding when I saw it coming, mostly in the downstairs loo, which was always warm and smelled of Mrs Baxter's lavender cleaner and was rarely visited by anyone. Years later, after I'd moved out and bought my own apartment, one of the things I loved most about it was the absence of a downstairs loo.

And now, when my old nemesis, my private vale of tears, actually had a chance to shine, in a perverse twist of fate, it had gone and the most I was able to procure was a choked sobbing, swallowing convulsively to dislodge a strange lump that seemed to have got itself permanently stuck, like a fat little troll, at the bottom of my throat. It wasn't that I didn't miss her. Of course, I did. Who in this sad world doesn't miss their mother when she's gone? But the more Venetia mourned, as a golden child does, by losing weight and turning wan and shadowy, the more mutinously dry my own insides became. This worried me a great deal, until it occurred to me that maybe I was actually doing exactly what my mother had always wanted me to, being strong and squaring my shoulders. Were my eyes staying heroically dry from some deeply ingrained impulse to ward off the white-lip mouth-twitch, nurtured through forty fractious years with my mother? Was somewhere deep inside me a little girl smiling, because all the way into the grave, her mother would finally be pleased?

* * *

Venetia, who expected me to pay appropriate homage to our mother, was inevitably disappointed by what I produced instead. Newly pregnant and dangerously volatile, she swanned in and out of Rose Hill Road with homeopathic remedies, shop-bought chicken soup and lots of unnecessary advice. I tried to stay out of her way as much as I could, because while she held centre stage with her pregnancy and her bereavement counsellor, my father had gone very quiet in the side wing.

The one time he broke down, about two weeks after the funeral, was completely unspectacular in that he simply didn't get out of bed. Finally, on day four, when his bedroom door was still closed at five in the afternoon, my brother Jas and I took him to the doctor and then the hospital, from where he emerged a week later almost eerily calm. With some relief, my siblings went back to their own grief and respective careers and impending families, but I lingered, unnerved by the look in my dad's eyes. It was hard to believe that this was the same person who'd taught me chess when I was ten, who'd re-enacted the Allied landing with a stapler, two pencils and a hole punch when I needed help with my history homework and who was always game to get a flashlight and study those white spots at the back of my throat. *It's not a tumour, Adele, I'm sure of it. It's germs fighting a battle with your body and, open wider, just a bit wider, yes, I think your antibodies are currently in the lead. Here, maybe a Polo mint will help.*

Now, more often than not, we exchanged polite news of our week over tea or stared out silently at my mother's garden wilting in the back, and the chessboard hadn't seen the light of day for ages. Sometimes, I had to resist the urge to pinch him, very hard, just to make sure that he hadn't also died and left his body behind to get up and go to work and return for cups of tea, the cold dregs of which he left all around the house to be collected by Mrs Baxter, who came in four mornings a week to keep an eye on things. Still, I was hoping that maybe one day soon he'd be waiting for me, holding two cups of tea, throat-scaldingly hot, the way we both liked it, his face creased in a smile. *Addie! There you are. How about a game of chess with your old father?* So I continued coming to see him, making my way across North London after work, at first through too-bright summer dusks and then autumn evenings and eventually sharp and wintry nights that turned once more into a beautiful London spring, ticking off the twelve months after my mother's death by the way the bark changed on the trees on Hampstead Heath and the shadows of the little supermarket outside the Tube station had lengthened when I rounded the corner towards my parents' house.

Long before Venetia had started throwing about ideas for how to mark The Day of her Death, I'd started to dread it. But the calendar that hung in the patisserie kitchen had a big red splat on the corner of 15 May, raspberry sauce I think, which seemed to grow in size whenever I looked up from decorating Mrs Saunders' birthday cake with seventy-five pale pink fondant roses, forcing down the swallows that rose up my oesophagus like sluggish bubbles on a pond.

Venetia had wanted to get some of the family together – Jas and Mrs Baxter, my father's brother Fred, and a variety of other family flotsam who lived in the vicinity, to 'draw solace from each other's company', and 'let this day go by amongst close family', which, according to her bereavement counsellor, would be an important step towards Stage Five in the grieving process. Rather over-optimistic, in my opinion, because my father had barely progressed past 'Denial' yet and even though I generally tended to go along with things, especially where Venetia was concerned, this time I did try to argue. Being in our big, bright kitchen where my mother was so conspicuously absent was not remotely the way I wanted to spend the day, and I was fairly certain my father didn't either. Venetia overrode all objections, however, made me swap shifts, ordered an indecently large box of pastries from the patisserie and made sure I left on time to deliver it to Rose Hill Road.

And now I was here. The door gave its usual soft groan as I stepped into the front hall and involuntarily I held my breath. But it was very quiet, the grandfather clock ticking in the corner as it always did, and it smelled the way it always had, like books and dust and Mrs Baxter's lavender cleaner, even though this time last year my mother had died. To my right, jackets hung on the ancient coat stand in the corner and several umbrellas dripped onto the stone floor tiles, indicating that the family had come together only a short while ago.

Silently, I crept across the front hall, eyeing the light that spilled through the door to the downstairs kitchen. A subdued mumble floated up, then a laugh, quickly stifled into a discreet cough. Uncle Fred, I thought, my father's brother, who lived in Cambridge with his three dogs and a collection of rusty cars he was forever fixing up. I strained my ears hopefully for answering sounds from my dad, but his deep, slightly hoarse voice couldn't be made out amidst the low thrum of conversation. He'd been working more than ever lately, and from what I could tell, his heartburn had got a lot worse. I hoped he'd gone to the doctor yesterday like he was supposed to. There was another mumbled question. Jas, probably, who must have come straight from the hospital in his rush to do Venetia's bidding.

I dug my toes into the sisal matting at the thought of them all draped around the big kitchen table. Venetia's bereavement counsellor had said to leave our mother's chair empty, as a sign of respect. I hated the bereavement counsellor, who was a cadaverous-looking man called Hamish McGree, and I hated the thought of that resolutely empty chair, with its curved armrests and straight back and the jauntily chequered wedge that my mother had stuck under the lining to help her bad back. I tried to remember when I last saw her sitting there, looking at her garden, her expression faraway in contemplation of the day's to-dos or frowning as she scanned the newspaper headlines. But I couldn't. Her face remained blurry and unfocussed, and all I could see were little bits of her: her hands, long-fingered and slightly tapered like mine, or the strands of her hair falling forward as she bent to blow on her coffee, which she had liked tepid, almost white with milk. It'd been like this all through the year. As people around me recalled funny moments and entire conversations and whole afternoons spent in her company, I was still working on simply remembering her face, the way she'd put on her lipstick in the morning, the twitch of her mouth when she was impatient and the tight set of her shoulders at night when she was cold and looking around for her scarf. It was a shrapnel rain of memory fragments that my mind seemed to be expecting me to put together when my ability to remember her was stuck in the same barren place that my tears had disappeared to, a dried-up riverbed of disabled grief, where memories were barrelling along like tumbleweed, never connecting, never whole and, somehow, rarely good.

More subdued laughter, turned discreetly into a cough, and, just like that, I realised that there was no way I was going to walk down those stairs, to that empty chair and the blurry echo of my mother's face. Backing away from the kitchen stairs, I dumped the cake box onto the hall table with a squishy thud and shot, sodden jacket, bag and all, through a door on the right where I sagged against the wall and, for a long moment, simply stood, savouring the cool darkness against my pupils after a long day staring at the raspberry splotch on 15 May. The ticking of the grandfather clock was louder here, because its back was against the wall, but it thudded in a comforting sort of way, like a heartbeat, and finally I exhaled and opened my eyes, pushing down a twinge of fear at my own daring. Venetia would be livid.

My mother's study. I hadn't been in here for a long time, not since Venetia and I had come and gingerly poked through the desk for her address book to do the death announcement cards, practically exiting at a run. Every now and then, Mrs Baxter would suggest having a clear-out, but every time Venetia dismissed the idea out of hand, so the room had remained exactly the same as the morning my mother had left to teach her popular seminar on 'Emerging Creative Outlets for Women Writers' for the last time. Books and folders and papers were lined up neatly along the shelves, post-its daring only occasionally to stick up here and there, pens stood ramrod straight in an old mug that was too good to throw away, as if they were waiting for my mother, who liked her pencils straight and sharp and ready to go. There was her telephone, the old mustard-coloured kind that still used a rotary dial, and her roll-top desk hulking against the wall, with drawers and cubby-holes and gadgets we'd made her for Christmases and birthdays because we knew that she liked things orderly and put away.

She'd been in here every evening, a sliver of her visible through the half-open door as she worked on lecture notes, student essays or manuscripts or, more mundanely, read the newspaper. She read that paper with an almost religious fervour, every single night, whether we were asleep or awake, in bed with chickenpox or out on the town. Sometimes, watching her unfold it to cover the entire desk, I wished that she'd look at me, or at the very least at the burglar in my wardrobe, with half the focussed attention she gave the small advertisements in the back and the obituaries and the robber held at a police station in Leeds. But things between my mother and me had been difficult. It was mainly my fault, really, because I was too soft, always had been. I didn't put myself into life's driver's seat, I didn't square my shoulders enough. My mother wasn't soft and she wasn't weak, she was like a hard, shiny gem, and however much we both tried, my soft, desperate-to-please self and her brilliant one could not but rub each other the wrong way, all the time, relentlessly, like stroking a cat against the grain, like golden vanilla custard splitting into a curdled mess. That's how things had been, between my mother and me.

I'm not sure how long I stood there, on the threshold of her space, breathing in the faint echo of books and determination that had been the very essence of my mother, waiting for tears and wishing for at least one small good memory of her, because today, of all days, I should remember her face, I should remember *her*, properly and whole.

Obviously, something had to happen, and something did.

The phone rang.